Praise for the Books of Maggie Giles

The Art of Murder

"Maggie Giles masterfully peels back the layers of small-town perfection in The Art of Murder, delivering a suspenseful, twisty ride through loyalty, deception, and the dangerous line between right and wrong. With tension that tightens like a noose and characters so real they'll haunt you, this thriller is impossible to put down. Giles proves once again she's a standout voice in the genre." —Jen Craven, author of *The Skiers* and *The Baby Left Behind*

"Provocative and Thrilling. *The Art of Murder* by Maggie Giles teems with secrets and delves into different manifestations of evil. Set in a once serene Canadian town, the murders start piling up early. Both friendship and family are tested as tension builds, past stories unravel, and the future becomes ever more dangerous. Two best friends think they know everything about each other and commit to hiding the other's mistakes, but as the bodies pile up so do their doubts and fears. Don't miss this sensational new thriller." —Kathy Dodson, Author of *Tequila Midnight*

"Wow! Gripping, propulsive, and action packed. Giles has woven an intricate plot of murder, lies, and secrets. I devoured every dark and twisted word!" —Marie Still, author of *My Darlings, We're All Lying,* and *Bad Things Happened in This Roon*

Twisted

"Twisted is the perfect word to describe the way you'll feel as this thriller reaches that OMG moment when you finally figure out what's going on. It'll keep you guessing until the very last page." —Lyn Liao Butler, Amazon Bestselling author of *Someone Else's Life*.

"With an intricate, inventive plot, TWISTED by Maggie Giles is a fascinating suspense that had me theorizing every which way while enthralled with the clever clues. As a detective trying to solve a jewelry theft stumbles on a high-class escort service, nothing is as it seems. This wild, gritty thrill ride will knock you for a loop and blow your mind." —Samantha M. Bailey, international bestselling author of *Woman on the Edge* and *Watch Out for Her*

Wicked

"Immersive and hard to put down, *WICKED* is a thrilling ride into the underbelly of a pharmaceutical gone wrong where the balance between right and wrong isn't just blurry; it's wicked."—Tanya E Williams, Historical, Women's Fiction Author

"Edgy, haunting, and unputdownable, *Wicked* confirms that Maggie Giles is a master at crafting intricate webs of twists and lies. An intoxicating thriller, *Wicked* picks up the threads from *Twisted* as Detective Ryan Boone and a forensic specialist, Cora Porter, investigate a slew of murders connected to a rogue pharmaceutical company. Giles's novel holds readers hostage as each new layer of complexity is revealed. A gripping read."—Kristin Kisska, Agatha Award-nominated author of *The Hint of Light*

The Things We Lost

Distinguished Favourite in the 2023 Independent Press Awards

"The many plot twists and turns will keep readers flipping through the pages at lightning speed. This novel has it all: love, laughter, murder, and hope." —Booklist starred review

"This intriguing Sliding Doors-style story makes the reader think about how a single decision can change our entire future. Both suspenseful and emotional, THE THINGS WE LOST will keep you turning pages right until the end." —Kathleen Barber Author of *Are You Sleeping*

"In THE THINGS WE LOST, debut author, Maggie Giles has crafted a page-turning contemporary allegory about the domino effect of our choices and our desires. Book clubs are sure to devour this one, as Maddie Butler's "Then" and "Now" intertwine and interrupt with unexpected twists and reveals that will have readers contemplating the "What If?" in their own lives as well!" —Amy Impellizzeri Author of Award-winning Author of *Lemongrass Hope*

THE ART of MURDER

MAGGIE GILES

This book is a work of fiction. Any references to historical events, real people, or real places are used fictitiously. Other names, characters, places, and events are products of the author's imagination, and any resemblance to actual events, places, names, or persons, is entirely coincidental.

Cover Illustration © Nat Mack
Distributed by Simon & Schuster

ISBN: 978-1-998076-48-2
Ebook: 978-1-998076-49-9

FIC031010 FICTION / Thrillers / Crime
FIC031080 FICTION / Thrillers / Psychological
FIC030000 FICTION / Thrillers / Suspense

#TheArtofMurder

Follow Rising Action on our socials!
Twitter: @RAPubCollective
Instagram: @risingactionpublishingco
Tiktok: @risingactionpublishingco

For Katie and Lindsey.

I'm so lucky I get to call you my big sisters.

THE ART of MURDER

1

Alexa Huston

Saturday, July 8

Blood crawled across the hardwood floor, oozing from the gaping wound in the dead woman's head. The pounding in my ears couldn't silence Dean's heavy breathing. He muttered to himself, pacing his bedroom as he came down from the high. Paranoid, frightened, panicked. What had we done?

The sickly-sweet stench of metal filled my nostrils. Vanessa's perfectly styled hair was now matted with the dark crimson liquid and whatever else came out of a person's head. Remnants of cocaine covered Dean's dresser, and a small baggy of white powder still rested on top. We'd indulged only moments before the accident happened.

Poor Vanessa.

If she knew today would be her last, maybe she would have chosen something less revealing to wear other than the miniskirt clinging too tightly to her narrow hips.

Touch it, something whispered. Feeling like I was in a trance, I reached for the blood, moving my fingers around the pooling liquid. A feeling all too familiar. Like a long-forgotten memory. No, not a memory, a lie. A trauma response. *It wasn't real. It wasn't real.* But this time it was.

I traced her porcelain skin, sliding my fingers down her neck and dipping between her perky breasts. A definite loss. She'd been a pretty little thing, a fun toy for me and Dean. Only a bit of roughing up and she ended like this. Just a fragile little creature with a petite frame. Dean would have been too much for her. Guilt swirled around me. I should have picked another woman.

It wouldn't have mattered, a soft voice whispered.

"Alexa." Dean's cold hands grabbed my bare shoulder, jerking me out of my trance. He was scared; I could hear it in the way he said my name. He'd been my boyfriend for only six months, but I could read him better than anyone. "What the fuck happened?"

A stupid question. We'd played this game more than once: bring home a strange girl with the promise of a good after-party. Wild, consensual sex, and the next morning we drop her off never to see her again. It made our relationship exciting, unique.

Now deadly.

My skin prickled, remembering the feel of Vanessa's cool fingertips as they caressed my breasts. Her touch was so soft, her breath sweet with red wine. Dean watched from the bed, his eyes tracing our every move. Would it have been different if she hadn't been as lonely, if she hadn't been as drunk? Would she still be alive?

Whoever this girl was didn't matter anymore. She was gone forever, thanks to us.

I remembered her soft lips pressing against mine, inhaling her warm scent: a mix of sweat from the dance club and alcohol. From beneath it came the sweetness of her perfume. The softness turned to lust the moment Dean grabbed the back of her neck and turned her towards him, crashing his lips against hers.

I watched him devour her as I moved to the waiting bed. When he was ready, Dean flung her towards me, his usual move to assert his dominance. She flailed, landed wrong, her head colliding with the corner of the bedside table. She tumbled to the floor. Blood pooled. She was dead.

"Alexa." He shook me this time.

"It was an accident," I said, shaking my fuzzy head clear of the memories replaying themselves. A drug-induced accident. Manslaughter, not murder.

"What?" His grip on my shoulder tightened. His voice fell into its familiar threatening tone. "Her body can't be found here. Do you realize what will happen to me? To us?"

The air was heavy, polluted with the smell of warm blood, making my head swim, daring me to replay the death again. Was this what people described as shock? Maybe, though it felt different than the time they told me my mother had died and the nightmares that had haunted me.

I squeezed my eyes shut and ignored Dean. He was only worried about himself. I tried to silence the guilt; nothing could be done about it now. It was a weird sensation, knowing we'd committed this horrible act, yet something inside me enjoyed it.

"You didn't do it on purpose."

"Do you really think the police will care?" His fingers dug into my shoulder. "Do you think my father will care? He'll have me locked away. And you with me. Or worse."

I pushed his hand from my shoulder at the mention of his tycoon father. Despite being thirty, Dean still acted like a sixteen-year-old around his parents.

Still, he was right. We couldn't plead accident to this. This was a dead tourist in a small town in Northern Ontario.

"Alexa."

"Relax, I'm thinking." Slowly, I lifted myself off the floor and from beside Vanessa's body. "No one knows she's here. We have time." I tried to ignore my racing heart and the strange feeling inside me as I thought back to every crime show I'd ever seen. We'd have to clean the mess and find a way to dispose of her body.

Dean resumed his anxious pacing, his eyes darting from the pool of blood to the door and back. The mess must be killing him. Part of me was surprised he hadn't dashed for the cleaner the moment her blood began to spill.

I wiped my blood-smudged hands on my shirt. "Can you stop?" His movements made my head pound. How long had it been since we had a drink? Or a bump? I glanced to the desk, where the rest of the cocaine lay, and went for it, knowing it would help me see things more clearly. I formed a line and quickly snorted; after a couple of minutes, a feeling of focus and euphoria washed over me. I motioned him to join me.

Dean glanced at Vanessa's lifeless body once more before stepping around her and coming to my side. He dipped his sandy-blond head and snorted what I had left for him. His usually well-styled low fade had been mussed from the foreplay, but his worried gaze slipped, and his blue eyes lit up as that dumb grin fell in place.

"Better?"

He nodded. "Always."

I turned back to the problem at hand. "We have to get rid of the body. Drop it in a field, anywhere." Luckily, there were a few of those surrounding this town. "We need to clean the body, make sure there's no trace of us anywhere." At least sex hadn't happened yet, and I didn't have to worry about Dean's DNA being inside of her.

"I'll grab my camping tarp. That'll be good enough to wrap her in to get her into the back of your car. You get her to the bathroom and clean her up. Everything off her, clothes, jewelry. We have to get rid of it all." The coke seemed to level him out, and now the frightened tone in his voice had vanished. He ran from the room.

I bent down next to her pretty face and touched her soft cheek. A real shame. She'd been one of the prettier ones to join in our escapades and to know I'd never get beyond her soft kisses made me wonder about what I'd missed. For a moment, I gazed into her lifeless eyes, remembering the way they'd took me in with uncertainly when I invited her home. The way they'd sized up my body then glowed with interest. She was one of the few who seemed more interested in me than Dean, a rare treat I'd lost in a moment.

Turning her head offered a good look at the gash in her scalp. A weird feeling of déjà vu washed over me, and the urge to touch the blood came back. Shuddering, I pushed it away and lifted Vanessa's small body off the floor. Her weight fought against me, she being heavier than she looked, until I managed a firm hold for the short trip to the bathroom, where I deposited her in the tub, then stripped her remaining clothes. I hesitated when I removed her jewelry. *Take it*, the voice whispered. Most of it I tossed into the pile of clothes but couldn't resist keeping one piece. I clutched the silver star stud earring from her left second piercing between my fingers. It shone like new and reflected the dull bathroom light. The feeling inside hummed with approval as I glanced behind me before slipping it into the pocket of my jeans. Dean wanted everything gone. *This was mine to take*, the voice said.

The creak of the floorboards told me Dean entered the room. He didn't speak, and when I glanced at him, his eyes were fixed on Vanessa's nude body. A plaything he'd never get to touch.

"She's dead," I reminded him.

"I know." His retort was dry, as his eyes shifted to my own, and he offered a box of latex gloves. "Need these?"

I reached for them. "I don't want to know why you have these."

"Cleaning." He shrugged and left the bathroom. He'd always been an over-the-top neat freak. His home often smelled of disinfectant, and he screeched anytime I stepped past the welcome mat with my shoes on.

After slipping on the gloves, I reached for the tap and started my work, cleaning every inch of her body free of our trace. My neck prickled as I lifted each limp limb and scrubbed at it like I was giving a sponge bath to an invalid. I tried to keep all the guilty thoughts from my mind, focusing only on the task at hand. If I could dissociate from the crime, maybe it wouldn't affect me. Inside me something cackled at my inner turmoil. When I finished, I discarded the damp gloves and returned to Dean's bedroom. I found him on his hands and knees, scrubbing the floor. The stench of bleach made my eyes water and my nostrils burn.

"I need your help with her body."

He didn't look at me. "Almost done."

"Sure." I reached for her discarded shirt, to add with her other clothes. All of which would be best to burn. That would make them less traceable—or so *Criminal Minds* implied.

As I tossed the silk fabric piece into the pile, I was graced with the image of a lively Vanessa pressing up against me, allowing my hands to travel beneath the garment and gently lift it over her head, freeing the perky, petite breasts beneath. How I longed to have another chance with her. To do this dirty game right. She'd been so playful.

I pushed the nausea and guilt that rose up aside.

I shook my head. Like with most of my dreams, there was no reason to dwell. It would never come to fruition.

Dean joined me in the bathroom only a few moments later. Blood continued to drip from Vanessa's wound and began to pool in the bottom of the tub. It dripped to the floor when we lifted her body to the waiting tarp. The way her head flopped against me like an old ragdoll gave me pause.

She'd been a vibrant woman once, and because of us she was gone. The feeling left me riddled with guilt, knowing how death could destroy a person. Weirdly, through the unease of the crime, there swirled a feeling of joy at what we had done. I couldn't explain the conflicting emotions fighting against one another in my head. She'd been an innocent. But her death fascinated me. She was so young. And yet the idea she was here then gone by one simple act was invigorating. We were killers. Dean and I had control over her life, and it was snuffed out in a moment. Goosebumps rose on my arms. Again, I felt sick.

"Let's get her out of here." Dean wrapped the body then flung it over his shoulder in a firefighter's carry like she was nothing more than a bag of wood. He cast one last glance at me. "Bring her clothes and anything covered in blood." His eyes dipped down to my chest. "Including your shirt."

I followed Dean down the stairs and out to my car. The street was empty, as it always was in this dead-end town past midnight. Life stopped after 1:00 a.m. here, unless you opted to travel fifteen minutes to the

Cape, a resort with countless restaurants and clubs. Even at this hour, the Cape would be quiet.

That was where we picked up Vanessa two hours ago as her night wound down, with the promise of cocaine and a good time. Drunk tourists were easy. Love them, then leave them. Or in this case, kill them. A voice cackled inside me, and I stiffened at the strangeness.

He tossed her body into the car, followed by a shovel from the garage. Then Dean took the driver's seat, a move he often did and one I never questioned. It may be my car, but Dean treated it as his own.

I remained silent as he sped out of town, listening to the gravel from one of the many dirt roads bounce against the car.

"Where are we going?" I asked, my mind going to a dark place. Would Dean see me as a liability? Could I be next? I reached for my cellphone in the console between us. *Do it first*, the voice urged.

"I don't know, Alexa, I just turned, okay?" His voice became frantic again. The cocaine high was wearing off.

I squinted out the window, trying to make out the surrounding fields in the darkness. How far would be far enough?

"What about here?" I asked.

"A little farther." Dean kept his eyes fixed on the road.

"And then?"

"We'll get rid of everything else." Dean's grip on the wheel tightened. He puffed out a long breath. "What the fuck happened tonight?"

"Seriously?" We'd been high, he got aggressive. What did he think happened?

"She freaked out." He shot me a cold glare before his eyes found the road again. "You said she was game."

"And she was." I'd told her the deal. Free drugs and rough, wild sex. She was into it. They always were.

"Except now we're dealing with a dead girl."

I didn't answer him, knowing I couldn't offer an ease to his panic. I'd found her wasted in the corner of the bar slumped on a stool, glossy-eyed and ready for home. Just another drunk girl alone at the bar. The guilt made me nauseous again, and I forced myself to look out the window at the darkened fields around us.

"Who saw her with us?" Dean asked.

I shook my head. "No one."

"Cameras?"

I hadn't thought about that. Most of the clubs in the Cape had some sort of surveillance. "I don't think so."

Dean gritted his teeth and punched the accelerator. "That's not good enough."

I didn't know what else to tell him. Our hands, our drugs, killed her. It may have been an accident, but if we didn't want to face the consequences, we needed to get rid of her before anyone realized she was missing. Her connection to us didn't go beyond the Cape bar scene. Nothing tied her to us. We couldn't be safer. As long as we could live with the guilt and weren't caught red-handed with her body.

The car screeched around a corner, and Dean slammed on the brakes. The headlights shone through the darkness down the empty gravel road.

"You stay here." He dropped the keys into the centre console between us, then reached up and flicked the headlights off. "I'll only be a minute."

The sky was clear and the moon nearly full. It lit the area with a bluish glow suited for the eeriness of the disposal. *Leave*, the voice whispered. And I considered it. I could drive away right now, leave Dean digging a grave in the dark soil with a dead girl beside him. Let him get caught. Another feeling of guilt coursed through me.

I didn't leave, fighting off the voice, unwilling to leave him hanging. I didn't abandon people. I wasn't like my parents. Instead, I climbed out of the car and watched as Dean grunted under Vanessa's weight as he tried to balance the shovel under his arm. I took it from him without a word to ease his unsteadiness and followed as he disappeared into the lush green stalks of the cornfield.

Somewhere in the middle he dropped her body and took the shovel from me, quickly pressing it into the damp ground and digging a shallow, makeshift grave. His overpriced designer shirt was stained with sweat and dirt. A sight to be seen. So unlike him.

When Dean deemed the hole large enough, he thrust the shovel in my direction and began unwrapping the tarp. He rolled Vanessa's body into the shallow grave, her pale skin looking sickly in the bright moonlight. Her dead eyes stared at me until Dean took the shovel and covered her face with dirt. Soon, she was buried, left in the ground to rot.

We returned to the car in silence. Dean tossed the tarp and shovel into the back before climbing into the driver's seat, and we set off without a word.

I got lost in my own thoughts of the night's events. I couldn't properly describe my feelings. The strange déjà vu. The awful guilt. The conflicting feelings. I was curious, frightened, mesmerized, remorseful.

Dean pulled into his parents' empty driveway.

"What are we doing here?" I asked.

"Only place I can think of with a fireplace big enough to get rid of the evidence."

My stomach turned. "This seems like a bad idea."

"Do you have any others?" Dean growled.

I didn't.

He climbed out of the car. "Didn't think so."

I followed, glancing around the street. Doing so made me realize it wasn't as bad of an idea as I'd initially thought. His parents' street was dark, free of streetlights, and populated with several overgrown trees. Many of the surrounding mansions were shuttered with empty driveways; rich people had better places to be in the summer months. Dean's parents had been at their lake house three hours east for nearly a month.

The inside of the house put me on edge. I hated this place, as much as Dean's parents hated me. It represented everything I wasn't. My family was more likely to work for the Millers than date one. Maybe that was why Dean asked me out.

"Take a seat." Dean gestured to the large leather couch across from the unlit hearth. "This might take a while." He busied himself with preparing a fire. His shirt strained against his muscular back as he set up a tower of kindling in the fireplace and struck a match. When he had a fire roaring, he turned to me. "Give me your shirt."

I did as he said but now was stuck in his parents' house wearing only my bra. "What am I supposed to do when we leave?"

"You should have thought about it before you started playing with blood." He sneered. Annoyance boiled up inside me. Guilt told me to let it go. At least it wasn't my body he buried tonight.

I didn't answer as he tossed my once-favourite, pick-up tank top into the flames followed by the rest of Vanessa's things. I did nothing but sit and watch. The rising flames made me think of the fire that damaged our house back in Toronto. It had been the final straw for my mother, the thing that forced the move to Cedar Plains. I'd been thirteen at the time and desperate to get back to the city. Fifteen years later, I still hadn't left.

I shivered in the warming room as the climbing flames reminded me of the way they'd licked at my bedroom wall and engulfed the room in a cloud of choking smoke. I'd narrowly escaped.

With each item, the evidence of our crime burned away and something else ignited within me. A new feeling. Something urging me to do it again. The scent of Vanessa's fresh death lingered in my nostrils, and although Dean destroyed almost every bit of evidence, I held on to the experience within me. The guilt and the excitement created a turmoil inside me I couldn't grasp.

I placed my hand over my pocket, feeling a pointed shape beneath my palm. Everything was gone, except the earring pressing into my thigh. That was my trophy.

Cherish it, the voice whispered. *And do it again.*

2

Courtney Faith

Sunday, July 9

I drummed my fingers on the café table, my patience wearing thin. Savannah sat beside me in her wheelchair, sipping her iced coffee. She alternated between fiddling with the end of her long, dark ponytail and adjusting the oval glasses that were perched on her nose.

"She's late," I said, unable to stop myself.

Savannah turned towards me. "Are you surprised?"

I pursed my lips, trying to keep from directing my annoyance at her. I simply glanced towards the large front window overlooking the street outside. Alexa was always late.

"Court," Savannah said, drawing my attention back to her as she tapped her manicured fingers against the arm rest of her chair. "Why don't we start without her? We've already gone over most of it anyway."

The meeting had been more of a formality, an attempt to get Alexa more involved. This was getting ridiculous. Alexa had texted twenty minutes ago saying she'd be arriving soon. Apparently soon wasn't for another half hour.

I sighed and flipped the folder open to start going over the details with Savannah. At least she was a reliable bridesmaid. Loyal to the core. Maybe

I should have picked her as my maid of honour over Alexa. Savannah had been there for me whenever I needed her.

"Ladies, a refill?" The young server walked by our table carrying a coffee pot. I was used to seeing her, as I used this quaint café for all my meetings. Its square wood tables and cozy lounge seating were perfect for quiet, one-on-one chats. I'd frequented this place since high school. Alexa and I first became friends right here.

With a quick smile, I pushed my empty mug towards her. "Thanks."

The door chimed as Alexa finally made her way through. Her blond hair looked knotted, and heavy blue bags rested beneath her tired eyes. The grey tank top she wore was stained and wrinkled. Probably Dean's fault. The creep.

"Sorry," Alexa muttered as she slid into the seat across from me, barely glancing at me or Savannah.

"Everything alright?"

Alexa risked a glance. Her eyes were bloodshot, making the green in them brighter. "Yeah, I'm sorry, really. Just got held up."

I shared a look with Savannah and hoped the criticism wasn't evident in my tone. "With Dean?"

Alexa offered me an apologetic smile. "Yeah, last night got a little bit wild. I overslept."

I pursed my lips but said nothing. I'd long outgrown the type of party nights Alexa and Dean had together

"And what did you guys get up to last night?" Savannah asked, though I wished she hadn't. Alexa had always been short with Savannah no matter how she tried to engage with her. I wished they'd get along.

"Can you not?" Alexa lowered her voice as she dumped two packets of sugar into her dark roast coffee, followed by two creamers.

Savannah and I shared a look. I simply shook my head as an attempt to apologize for Alexa's bluntness.

"And are these shenanigans going to be a part of my wedding?" I asked. "I mean, from here it looks like you were up all night coked out of your mind."

"I was," she said. "Is that what you want to hear?"

Savannah dropped her eyes to her lap.

"Of course not, Lex." I shook my head. "I can't stand watching you do this to yourself. I'm worried about you."

I could already imagine what my friends and relatives might think about Alexa and her boyfriend's habits. I quickly shook the thought from my head. Alexa and I had been best friends for so long, and I knew her struggles better than anyone. Still, she never failed to show up for me and, come my wedding, this little hitch in our plan would be completely forgotten.

"Please don't worry about me. I'll make sure your wedding is perfect." She stirred her coffee, meeting my eyes with a soft smile. "I made him promise to leave the drugs at home. Trust me, okay?"

My jaw ached from the stress Dean and Alexa caused. I missed how she used to be. Before Dean, she cared about our friendship, our secrets, but for the past six months, I had to fight to get her attention, fight to get her to remember *us*.

I glanced sideways at Savannah who had picked up her phone and started busying herself to avoid the conversation. We'd been friends only five years, and I'd spent most of that time trying to convince Alexa to be nice to her.

"I thought we were meeting alone," Alexa said, after a moment, glancing at Savannah with a cold stare.

"No, I told you last night Savannah was joining us." I shook my head.

"Please don't talk about me like I'm not here," Savannah said, placing her hands on the arms of her wheelchair and straightening her back to sit higher. "Besides, someone needs to be there for Court during this whole process."

Alexa rolled her eyes. "Yeah, right, like she needs her charity case tailing along and saying yes to all her plans."

"Alexa!" I nearly shouted. "That's enough."

"What? I still don't get why Wheels here tags along on everything you do." Alexa smirked.

I stared at my friend with wide eyes. She knew why Savannah was always around. She knew what I owed her. What I'd done.

I was pulled from my fear when Savannah placed a light hand on my wrist. "Court, I'm going to go."

"No, it's okay." I tried to placate her.

Savannah shook her head.

"Don't stress," she said, wheeling herself away from the table. "I think you need a few minutes to deal with *this*." She glanced pointedly at Alexa. "I'll see you tomorrow at the boutique." With a nod goodbye she wheeled herself out of the café.

I turned on Alexa. "Wheels? Are you serious?"

Alexa laughed. "It was a joke. Lighten up."

"Sometimes I can't believe how different you can be with other people." I reached for the wedding folder I had in front of me and flipped it open.

"You're my person," Alexa said simply. "I don't owe anyone else anything." Then she forced a smile. "Besides, I can see how the guilt ways on you. Do you even like Savannah or is it just a pity friendship?"

"Of course, I like her." At least I'd convinced myself it was true. Savannah had been a good friend with a sunny personality while Alexa sank deeper and deeper into the darkness of her life. I missed the girl who'd been so hopeful at nineteen. The one who had dreams, before her father had dashed them all.

"If you say so." Alexa shrugged. "Just be thankful I'm here to make sure this wedding isn't a totally pretentious event." She grinned with a warmth in her eyes. Sometimes I got whiplash from how her old self could pop out as easily as it could disappear.

She didn't give me a chance to speak before she continued, "Are you excited for our little bachelorette romp? Less than two weeks away now! It's going to be killer."

"So you keep telling me. Too bad you aren't being very forthcoming with the details." Letting her oversee my bachelorette might have been a mistake. The last time I partied was over a year ago, before Brett and I got engaged. I'd ended the night wrapped around the toilet and puking up my dinner. I'd taken it easy ever since. Alexa was in a whole different bracket.

"Details, Schmetails!" Alexa waved off my concern, tucking her messy hair behind her ears. "Just know it will be epic."

I had to smile. This was the Alexa I knew and loved.

"That's cute," I said, changing the subject as I noted the new star-shaped earring in her second piercing. It was silver with a tiny diamond in the centre.

Alexa flushed and shifted her hair, letting it cover her ears again. "A gift from Dean. Something about me being his moon and stars."

I raised my eyebrows, trying to stop my amused grin. "That sounds like some terrible *Game of Thrones* knock off."

"You know Dean and his love of fantasy." Alexa waved off the question. Not that either of us could argue with him. We'd been diehard *Lord of the Rings* fans since our fifteenth birthdays. It had been a coping method for Alexa after she lost her mom to the accident.

"Mhmm," I hummed, instinctively running my hand over my left forearm where the words *not all those who wander are lost* was tattooed in messy cursive. I looked back to the wedding binder I'd brought. Going over everything with Alexa seemed pointless now. Savannah had been dutiful with her support, and her feedback had been great. Especially since she owned the only wedding dress boutique in town and was married last year. She always thought of things that completely slipped my mind.

"Everything okay?" Alexa asked. She reached up and fiddled with her matted hair, a nervous habit she'd had since we'd met, which was when I noticed the purple bruises on her forearm.

"What happened there?"

Alexa quickly dropped her arm below the table and out of sight. "Nothing. Banged it. You know how clumsy I am behind the bar." She forced a laugh. "Remember when you were still working at Big Shot with me? I used to walk into everything."

"Oh, I remember." Alexa easily walked away with several bruises after a late-night shift at the dive bar. I was glad I didn't have to work those shifts anymore.

"Lou still asks about you." Alexa winked.

"Of course, he does." I tried to keep the disgust from my voice as I thought about the regular patron who got handsy one too many times with me. Once, when I was in university, Brett clocked him in the face after he'd touched me while I was dropping off their drinks. Brett was banned for a year following the incident. I didn't work there much longer after that. With university graduation, came a real job in commercial real estate.

"He always loved you."

I rolled my eyes. "Don't remind me."

"At least he tips well." Alexa sipped her coffee again. "Most of those dirtbags are terrible tippers. I can put up with a bit of creep as long as they pay me for it."

"Most of those dirtbags are your dad's drinking buddies." The words came out before I could stop them. Talking about Danny Huston was supposed to be off limits.

Alexa's expression pinched with disapproval. "Yeah, well, it's a good thing he doesn't show his face there when I'm working the bar."

"He's smarter than that." At least I hoped Alexa's dad knew better than to cross his daughter. Back in high school, my crappy home life brought us together. While our other classmates worried about which boy liked them, I was sleeping over at Alexa's to avoid the brawls at home. Then, when her mother died and my father went to prison, we found an uneasy comfort in my mother's safety and her dad's devoted new girlfriend, Phoebe. That peace only lasted for a time, then Phoebe left, Alexa's dad fell deep, Mark got out on parole, and once again neither of us really had a safe place to call home.

Despite the hard times as we grew up, Cedar Plains had always been my hometown. It was an outdoor playground, away from the bustle of Toronto. I'd always planned to live here and to raise my kids here. It was safe. Nothing bad ever happened in Cedar Plains.

"Who's walking you down the aisle?" Alexa changed the topic, poking at the gaping wound that was the complicated relationship I had with my parents. I was sure it was payback for insinuating her father had a conscience.

"Miles."

"What a good brother," Alexa said.

"He is." I was thankful Miles would make the four-hour trip back to Cedar Plains to be a part of my wedding despite his issues with our parents.

Alexa reached for her coffee again, but it was empty. She waved the server over with a casual *excuse me*. "So, what about your mom?"

"What about her?" The topic was one I wanted to avoid.

"Is she coming?"

"Not unless I invite Mark." I spat the name out like the poison he was.

Alexa chuckled. "Ouch. First name basis. Whatever happened to 'Dad?'"

"You know he stopped being Dad the first time he hit me." I looked down at the table between us.

"Well, here's to our shit dads." Alexa raised her coffee cup in mock cheers, a playful smile on her face.

"Why is this so amusing to you?"

She shrugged. "Because it's not like it can be helped. We're both stuck with families we didn't choose. This is why we have each other."

"And why I choose not to think about it." I rifled through the binder in front of me and pulled out two pieces of paper: my proposed table numbers and programs for the day. I slid them across the table towards her, looking for an opinion. Okay, looking for an approval. I didn't want or expect her to make a change.

"They look good." She slid them back to me. The table number was a white square with a cursive number in bold black. The card was outlined by connected loops, giving the piece a classic feel. The programs were more detailed with a silver outline and script font in black. It welcomed guests to the wedding of Courtney Faith and Brett Knight, and laid out the straightforward events of the day, starting with the outdoor ceremony and concluding with a reception at one of the local ski clubs, a six-course meal, and an open bar.

"Nothing else to add?"

"Of course not," Alexa said, reaching across the table to cover my hand with her own. "I know you better than that. They're perfect. Just relax. You've got this."

"Thanks."

My phone buzzed on the table, drawing our attention. My mom's number flashed across the screen, accompanied by a picture I'd picked out over a year ago when I got the phone. My favourite picture of her, in which she looked genuinely happy. A rarity these days.

"Get it," Alexa said. "I'm going to step out for a smoke." She was up and gone before I had the chance to criticize her. Weeks ago, she said she was quitting.

I looked back at my phone and considered ignoring the call. At the last moment I grabbed it.

"Hi, Mom."

"Courtney." Her voice shook. Her words were soft, barely a whisper. "Courtney, I need help."

My heart hammered against my ribcage as I started to move, grabbing my purse and leaving a twenty on the table. "What's wrong?"

She choked on a sob, sniffing before speaking again. "He's bad, Court. I can hear him downstairs. I need you to come get me."

"What did he do?" I kept my voice low, careful not to draw attention to myself. In a town this small, the slightest bit of distress could cause gossip.

"Just please come."

"I'm coming." I motioned to Alexa when I saw her outside. Her brow crinkled with confusion and waved a hesitant goodbye as I turned for where I parked my car. "Stay on the line, okay? Did he hurt you?"

"He's upset." Another sniff. "I shouldn't have upset him."

"Mom, call the cops. Please."

"No, Courtney. No police," she pleaded. Her voice was fragile, ready to break. I could picture where she sat, in the upstairs closet, door locked, cowering against the back wall seated on a pile of dirty sweaters and surrounded by hanging, unworn summer dresses like they'd met the executioner the moment my mother decided to let my dad back into her life.

"I'm coming." I turned the car down the street, listening to my mom's ragged breathing and worrying about the mess I would walk in on this time.

3

Alexa Huston

Sunday, July 9

My cigarette bounced across the asphalt, sparking each time it hit the ground. From where I stood, I could still see Courtney with a worried expression on her porcelain face, cellphone pushed tightly to her ear, practically hidden by her flaming red hair. She climbed into her car and sped down the street without another glance in my direction. I could guess what was causing her distress: her parents. If only Mark had died in prison like he was supposed to, then all her problems would have disappeared.

Still, I found myself unable to focus on her trials today. I couldn't get Vanessa's lifeless eyes out of my mind. I'd barely slept the night before, too coked up and wired from the deadly events, and when I'd managed a bit of shut eye, my dreams were plagued with Vanessa's gentle touch and the image of her blood creeping across the floor. I reached up, running my finger across the new silver star stud earring in my second piercing. Something inside me preened with pleasure, catching me off guard and forcing my hand to drop to my side. Last night when I first put the earring in, a feeling of content had overtaken me. Was it this voice that blossomed inside?

I grabbed my phone, shooting Courtney a quick text to make sure everything was okay. I didn't expect an answer, so when my phone buzzed, I was pleasantly surprised. That was until I read Dean's name and the short words accompanying it.

Be at my place by 8. We have to talk.

Irritation welled up inside me before I processed his words. A strange feeling that put me on edge. I shook my head, as if freeing the demons from my mind and focused on the message. Did someone find the body? Or was Dean slowly becoming more unhinged? Was I? I couldn't shake the strangeness inside me I'd felt since last night. As if seeing her death had given life to something long dormant in me. Again, I shook away the thought, willing myself to silence the crazy. Reminding myself of what my former therapist had said all those years ago. *It wasn't real. It wasn't real.*

If Vanessa's rotting corpse had been found, I would have heard about it. Either from Courtney—her cop fiancé was a terrible gossip—or the local news. There hadn't been a word.

"Alexa?"

I glanced up at the sound of her familiar voice as Savannah wheeled down the sidewalk towards me. A swell of anger welled inside me, and I quickly pushed it away, ignored Dean's message, and shoved the phone in my pocket.

"Yeah?" I tried to keep the disdain from my tone. I'd long grown tired of Savannah's company. The accident that paralyzed her had garnered sympathy from the entire town and had been in the headlines for weeks. They never caught the culprit. They never would.

She pulled up beside me and looked up at me with narrowed eyes. "You need to clean up. Courtney is counting on you."

I rolled my eyes and turned away from her. "You don't need to worry about me and Courtney."

"I'm not worried about you," Savannah said, wheeling to catch up with me. "I'm worried about *her.*"

Her. I didn't think of Courtney. I thought of Vanessa. The woman I couldn't get out of my mind. Her blood, the way her dead eyes stared at me as if they saw right through me. The way her fair skin looked paler as the blood flowed from her head wound. I thought of the metal stench, warm and sticky on my fingers, and the way I wanted to caress her lifeless face. The strange sensation—so foreign but so right.

"Alexa?" Savannah said, eyeing me with scrutiny.

I shook my head free of the images. "I said I don't need you to worry about me and Courtney. I've got this."

I turned on my heel and walked away from her, my pace quick, hopeful she would take the hint and leave me alone.

"You're going to lose her if you're not careful," Savannah called after me.

I didn't turn around. Years ago, Courtney promised to never leave me, to never be one of the people that just disappeared from my life. And despite trying to push her away, she never wavered on that promise. She never would. Then, it was out of loyalty. Now, I knew too much.

I turned down the path to my dad's, following the ravine that led the way to the harbour and the bay. Watching the flowing water, I was immediately transported back to Toronto after my tenth birthday. The first time I'd ever seen a dead body.

I'd been standing at my bedroom window, listening to my parents scream at each other one floor below. I scurried upstairs the moment

Dad returned home, and Mom threw the glass she was holding at him. I never knew why they fought, only that sometimes they did.

It was a hot summer afternoon, and the wailing sirens drew my attention, distracting me from the shitstorm brewing in my own home.

The uniformed officers piled out of their cars, descending into the wide ravine that ran behind our house. When the body was pulled from its watery grave, I wasn't even certain it was human. The ashen skin of the grotesque, bloated corpse looked more like a monster from my nightmares than a once-living person. Even at ten I'd been fascinated by the story, curious about the circumstances and the way the corpse decomposed with the elements around it.

Now, my feet kicking up the gravel on the path made me think of the road Dean and I took last night, and I wondered how Vanessa's corpse was faring buried in the shallow grave. Had her thin limbs begun to stiffen? Had maggots burrowed their way into her open wound? I tried not to imagine her once-beautiful face gnarled and frozen from the rigor mortis that had no doubt set in. Beautiful, the voice murmured, and for the first time since it had spoken to me, I found myself agreeing, listening.

Vanessa was only inches from me when she met her end. Her body had still been warm as I scrubbed it clean of any evidence. When would Vanessa be found lost in the cornfield? Whenever she'd start to smell strong enough for someone to investigate. Or maybe the coyotes would find her first.

Would someone eventually realize she was gone and notify the police? Did she have family or friends? I knew nothing about her life. Not even her last name. The idea frightened and fascinated me at the same time. I couldn't reconcile the feeling inside me. The tragic loss of an innocent person, and yet, the darkness inside me was pleased every time I thought of Vanessa.

A siren sounded, making me jump from my thoughts. I was on edge, though who could blame me? Too many drugs, not enough sleep, voices in my head, and a dead woman haunting me. The lone police cruiser whipped down the street at breakneck speed, and I watched it until it disappeared, heading in the direction of the fields. Did they find Vanessa already? I shuddered at the thought.

My phone buzzed again. Another text from Dean. Only question marks. My hands shook as I tucked it away again without responding. I should answer him if only to try and get another bump to shake off this awful withdrawal. Even as I thought it, the voice told me it wouldn't be enough. That it would never be enough again. I wanted something else now.

A light summer wind rustled my loose hair, and I reached up to tame it. Courtney had looked at me like I was a complete drug addict. If only she knew the truth. I supposed it would have put us back on even ground. She owed me a life-changing secret, after all.

The third text from Dean I answered, telling him I was still with Courtney, and I'd get back to him when I could. After that, he didn't message me. This time he got to ignore me. Dean was awfully petty sometimes.

I reached my condo after a forty-minute walk and hesitated before entering. My dad had been out cold on the couch when I'd left and dealing with him was the last thing I wanted. I'd grown tired of supporting his habits. The disability barely covered the rent. My income supplemented our lives. I'd been his sole provider for too long. But I'd never leave him.

I'd considered moving out years ago, giving up on him and finding my own life away from the trauma we'd both seen. He was the only family I had left. Even with all the bad, I wasn't ready to cut ties with the only person who'd ever loved me without condition. Even if he was far from that man now.

The stench of stale booze and musky air invaded my senses as I pushed the door open. Strong enough to make me stop and gasp for air. There, sitting in the main room, was my dad. While upright, he looked haggard with his unshaven face, messy hair, and bloodshot eyes. He lifted his head to acknowledge me, then shifted his gaze back to the TV. The sounds of muffled voices accompanied his loneliness. The newscasters—his only friends. *Sad. Pathetic*, the voice whispered, telling me his weakness was a part of me, that I wasn't far from being him.

"You look like shit." I kicked off my shoes.

"Be nice, Lex," Dad said, his voice raspy. He didn't look my way again.

"It's not like you'll remember it anyway." I stomped across the room and swiped his cigarette pack from the table, stealing a dart and lighting up. He reached out as I discarded the remaining ones, taking one and doing the same. Then he patted the couch beside him. I didn't take the seat.

"Where have you been?"

"Out." I blew out a long puff of smoke as I turned away from him.

"Not with the delinquent again, I hope." Dad's preferred nickname for Dean.

"Don't pretend you care."

"You know I care."

I ignored him as I turned for the stairs.

"Where are you going?" he called after me.

I didn't look back. So many years of anger and betrayal were kept bottled up inside me when it came to my dad. First Mom died suddenly, then he tried to start a new life with Phoebe—my pseudo-stepmom and her best friend—but after his accident and her sudden departure, Dad had been a drunk and broken man.

I used to think about Phoebe often, scrolling her Instagram and keeping tabs on her best-selling novels. A successful indie romance author, like she knew anything about romance after running out on my dad. Years ago, I'd reached out more than once, though all my messages went unanswered. I hated her for abandoning us and never explaining why, simply leaving in the middle of the day for me to come home and pick up the pieces. Perhaps by then I should have been used to it. Everyone left me in one way or another. To death. To drink. To marriage. Alone, the feeling said. They always left me alone.

Still, I hated my dad for the simple fact I wasn't good enough for him to try and live for after all he lost. I was nothing. And yet I continued to carry his burden. To foot his bills. To stay.

In my room, I flopped onto my bed, tucking my hands behind my head and staring at the blank, white ceiling. Vanessa's face appeared in my mind again. And, once again, a pleasure filled me. I'd pleased the voice in my head. She was still alive, vibrant, beautiful. In my mind, I could see my hands wrapping around her throat, cutting off the air from reaching her lungs. She didn't struggle. She let me control her. My palms began to itch. The feeling urged me to do more. To feel it again. I removed my hands from behind my head and stretched my fingers before me, curling them again. What a weird sensation, this desire to kill. I wanted to understand it more.

My phone rang, pulling me from my murderous thoughts. "Hello?"

"Lexa, you busy?"

I closed my eyes for a moment, silencing the desire in my mind and allowing the fuzziness to fade so I could place the voice. It was Kaylee. Another bartender at Big Shot. "What's up?"

"My shift starts in an hour, but I could use a bump. Have you talked to Dean today?" Her awkward tone made me imagine the way she fidgeted when she was nervous. Dean provided coke for a few people I knew. I never asked questions; I didn't want to know. "He's not answering my messages."

"Briefly. I think he's gone to Barrie."

Her silence was only disrupted by the way she ground her teeth. "Can you try calling him? Maybe he's screening. I really need it today."

"Sure." I sat up in bed. "I'll give you a shout after."

"Thanks, Lexa."

I hung up without saying goodbye, then stared at my phone for a few minutes trying to decide if I wanted to call him. The buzzing in my head returned, willing me to feed the desires. I considered ditching my phone, when it pinged with a message before I got a chance. Kaylee, asking if I'd reached him.

With an annoyed sigh, I dialed his number. It rang twice before he answered.

"Done with the ginger, finally?" Dean sneered. No hello, no affection. He and Courtney had always had a strained relationship. Though given that he was Brett's best friend, if it wasn't for Courtney, I'd have never met Dean. You'd think he'd at least be grateful for that.

I disregarded his question. "Kaylee won't leave me alone. She said you were ignoring her."

"Like fuck," Dean groaned. "I hadn't got around to it yet. I've been a bit preoccupied," his voice lowered, "making sure my bases are covered. You're one of those, in case you forgot about last night."

That irritation rose up inside me again, and I quickly pushed it aside. "I haven't." How could I?

"And you've kept your mouth shut," Dean hissed. "You know how Courtney likes to talk. A bit of gossip is all this stupid town needs."

I rolled my eyes at his comment. Courtney was the only one I could really trust with a secret.

"I won't say anything." I bit down on my lip hard. "I'm in this, too."

"Damn right you are." Dean lowered his voice. "Don't forget I could ruin your life with a single story. Crazy, white trash with an alcoholic father kills a tourist out of spite. The media would eat that story up. They'd never look twice at me."

The voice cursed him, wishing he wasn't a part of our little secret. I clenched my jaw. His cruel words weren't wrong. Dean was a wealthy local. Came from a family of means, ones who had donated to and helped grow this town into what it was. If he wanted to blame this all on me, he probably could find a way. I closed my eyes for a moment and reminded myself why I'd started dating Dean months ago. He'd offered me an escape from the life I knew. He stayed when he could have left me multiple times. We weren't perfect but being with him was better than being alone.

"Now you sound paranoid," I shot back. "Can you call her, please?"

"Fine."

"Thank you."

"I'm out of town tonight," he said in a clipped tone. "I'll be back tomorrow, so come by."

"Where are you going?" I asked.

"I'm getting your car detailed like the great boyfriend I am," he jeered.

For a moment that surprised me. Then I realized it was Dean's way of being extra cautious. There had been a dead body in it less than a day ago. "Uh, thanks."

"Honestly, it's disgusting. You should get it cleaned out more often."

I bit back the comment that wanted to follow, knowing it was his weird OCD talking.

"Okay," I said.

"Good." The conversation ended with a click of the phone, and I sent Kaylee a quick message to tell her he'd be in touch. Ten happy emojis appeared on my screen with her enthusiastic response. After reading it, I shut off my phone and leaned back on my oversized pillow. I closed my eyes, trying to bring back the visions of Vanessa. It was no use.

With a frustrated sigh, I pushed myself from my bed and retreated downstairs in search of alcohol. Anything to quench this thirst, this itch inside me. The voice cackled. Maybe alcoholism did run in the family. I shuddered at the thought I could share the same weakness with my dad.

Downstairs, the TV had been shut off and the couch vacated. My dad was gone, along with his shoes and the last bottle of vodka.

Fuck.

4

Courtney Faith

Sunday, July 9

I left my car down the street, unsure what I was about to find. My parents' house looked as it did when I last left it, with crumbling grey siding aged with wear, and the black door faded and chipped from too many visitors throughout our childhood. The brightly painted windowpanes used to welcome good memories. Now they only filled me with terror.

Mark was visible through the front window, stomping around the living room, anger written on his flushed face. I ducked behind the hedges, hopeful he wouldn't notice me, and made my way around the back to the patio door.

Before pulling the door open, I glanced down at my phone. Brett had answered.

On my way now.

I sucked in a breath and pulled open the back screen, dreading the squeak that had been there since my eighth birthday. It sounded through the back hallway, but Mark's drunken rage overpowered it. His heavy footsteps echoed through the downstairs, as he knocked over furniture and yelled his displeasure.

"Fucking bitch!"

I froze at the sound of his raspy anger. An image of his abuse flashing into my mind before I could stop it. A crash made me scamper to the back staircase leading to the floor above. Likely the coffee table being overturned.

I scurried up the stairs as he yelled again, "Goddamn useless woman!" Something shattered.

I winced.

My racing heart couldn't be calmed as I tiptoed towards my parents' bedroom. The door was ajar, and their room a mess with lamps knocked out of place and bedding strewn about. The anger had begun here and moved downstairs. At the closet I knocked carefully; the only response was my mother's pitiable whimper.

"Mom," I whispered. "Mom, it's me." I glanced back towards the bedroom door, straining to hear if there had been any change in Mark's anger. As far as I could tell, he still raged on the floor below. I allowed myself a moment of relief, hopeful Brett would arrive to distract him before he realized I was here.

The lock on the closet door clicked, and it opened enough for me to slide inside. I'd had Brett install it after the last time we picked Mom up. It was a place for her to escape when Mark's anger took over, since she refused to leave his side despite all the pain he'd caused.

She was exactly where I expected her, cowering against the back of the closet, fear written on her gaunt, pale face. Her thin, dark hair looked stringy and knotted, half in a bun, half pulled out, and her once-bright eyes were dark with misery. She cradled her left arm, wincing as she moved. Broken, was my best guess.

Rage bubbled up inside as I took in her swollen cheek, and the darkened bruises forming around her eye. Her shirt was torn where she held her limp arm in place. This was the worst I'd seen her.

"What did he do?"

Mom dropped her gaze, only allowing me to catch the shame for a moment. "It wasn't his fault."

"It's always his fault."

"You don't understand," Mom accused. "Your father works so hard, and it's not fair to him. I don't live up to his expectations."

My hands clenched at my sides. My patience with this situation had run thin. Time and time again I'd come to her rescue, and each time I hoped she would learn. The fact that she never would, filled me with a mix of rage and sadness.

"Mark is a no-good drunk. What kind of work has he done since he left prison?"

Mom winced at my harsh words. "Courtney, stop it. You know that's not true."

It was the exact conversation we'd had every time I found her in a situation like this. She always swore it would be better. It never was.

"Anybody home?" Brett's cheery voice filled the entrance hall, over-loud, to let me know he'd arrived. Almost immediately, my stiff shoulders relaxed. My fiancé had tamed my enraged father more than once. Maybe Mark had learned to respect the police's power when he was in jail. Or maybe he knew better than to challenge someone bigger than him. Whatever the reason, Brett always seemed to work magic.

Only muffled voices could be heard from then on, and I helped Mom to her feet, leading her out the way I'd come in.

She moved slow, cradling her limp arm, her face marred by worried glances. I didn't breathe a steady breath until we were in the yard, heading to my car.

Mom glanced around. "Don't let anyone see," she hissed.

I didn't answer, certain the neighbours already knew of Mark's violence, but I shared her sentiment. We didn't need the whole town to gossip again.

Once safely in my car, I texted Brett, letting him know we made it out, and asked him to get some of Mom's things. She'd be staying the night with us, as she had before. Together, we'd try to convince her to report it, and maybe this time she'd have some sense to trust Brett and let him take her statement. She never would speak against Mark in the past. I always hoped that would change.

Mom and I didn't exchange words as I pulled into the street and headed towards the Cedar Plains General Hospital.

"Where are we going?" Mom moaned when she realized we weren't heading back to my house.

"The hospital."

"Courtney, no," Mom protested. "I don't need to go."

I cast a sideways glance at her before shifting my eyes back to the road. "Your arm is broken."

"It's fine."

My grip on the steering wheel tightened. "You can't move it. You look like shit. We're going."

She huffed at me like a stubborn child but didn't say another word against it. Whatever her thoughts, she knew I was right.

We took a number when we entered the waiting room, disturbed by the warm, familiar greeting we got from the front desk nurse. She was an elderly woman, who had treated my brother and me for all our bumps and bruises growing up, and the few times I got Mom here, for damages caused by Mark.

The waiting room was small and sterile. Only two other patrons occupied the small space. Black, plastic chairs lined the white walled room and quiet, classical music drifted from the ancient wall speakers. For being the only hospital in town, the facility hadn't been updated since the early 2000s.

Mom sat clutching her fractured arm when a ping came from her pocket. Carefully, she pulled the device out and glanced at the message. From where I sat, I could see it was from Mark and immediately snatched the phone from her hand.

"Give it back," she demanded.

"No." I powered down the phone and tucked it into my purse. "I will not have you messaging him right now."

"Courtney, he's going to be angry if I don't answer him," she warned.

"He's already angry," I said. "You're not apologizing to him after he's beaten you."

"Shh," Mom hissed, glancing around at the two other patients. Neither even looked in our direction.

"What?" I asked. "Embarrassed someone will find out your husband broke your arm and you're apologizing for it?" I didn't want people to gossip about my family, but I wanted Mark back behind bars. It was the one aspect of my life that I couldn't keep squeaky clean. Well, that and Alexa.

"You don't understand," she said.

And she was right. I didn't understand, and I didn't want to. I wasn't about to enable her.

"Your phone will be safe with me." I zipped up my purse for good measure.

Mom looked to protest but was interrupted when the familiar nurse called our number. We'd been waiting only twenty minutes, and she took us into the first room to begin filling out paperwork. She was an overbearing woman, husky, with tight white scrubs. Her grey hair was pulled back, away from her round cheeks and wrinkled eyes. The only makeup she wore was on her lips, painted neon pink.

Mom's health card in hand, she began with the usual questions, "What are you here for?"

I motioned to Mom's arm. "We think it's broken."

The nurse nodded, though her eyes rested on the swollen cheek and forming bruises. "What exactly happened?"

I opened my mouth to accuse Mark.

Mom spoke first. "I fell." She forced a stilted laugh. "Down the stairs in my house. I'm so clumsy, right hon?"

I gritted my teeth and forced out the word. "Right." Mom never told the truth about what happened.

The nurse hesitated as she glanced between me and Mom, grimaced, and wrote down what she was told. She didn't bother to contradict Mom's excuse, and I imagined Mom's file likely outlined her refusal to speak to social workers in the past. And she certainly wasn't the only one this woman had seen. Brett often talked about the domestics he'd be stuck breaking up. When she finished, she stood and handed us the filled-out paperwork. "Take this with you when the doctor calls you in." Then she motioned us to leave and called the next number.

It was another twenty minutes before the doctor called Mom in.

When I was alone, I scrolled through my phone, seeing a text from Alexa. I'd left our meeting so abruptly, I hoped she hadn't worried too much.

It was Mark, of course. At the hospital with Mom. I think it's a broken arm. I'll call you later.

It was only a couple minutes before she pinged me back.

Glad you're okay.

I smiled at the message, thankful that despite our sometimes-rocky relationship, she really was my best friend. Then another text followed giving me pause.

Wheels threatened our friendship today. Ready to cut that needy accident out yet?

I read over the message twice and swallowed the lump in my throat. I'd never cut Savannah out. Alexa knew better than to suggest it.

Leave Savannah alone, was all I texted back. I hoped there was enough implication in the message for Alexa to know it was time to shut up. I closed the message app and switched over to my books app, letting my eyes focus on the ebook I'd been reading and trying not to think about the things Alexa could unravel with her closely guarded secrets.

Nearly an hour passed before Mom emerged with a soft cast on her arm, smiling at the young, handsome doctor.

"Thank you," she said.

The doctor nodded. "You take care."

"Well?" I asked, with a knowing tone as we walked to the car. "How bad was it?"

"Two small fractures. Not terrible."

I pursed my lips, keeping my mouth shut.

I helped Mom into my car, turned the key in the ignition, and steered toward my house.

"I can go home," Mom said.

"No, you can't." I wasn't about to leave her with him while she was healing. "Two fractures is a big deal. Worse, you're in complete denial about it."

"What's that supposed to mean?"

I shot her a cold look. "You fell down the stairs?"

Mom looked out the window. "It's no one's business how I got hurt."

"It should be the police's." I gritted my teeth. "He should be back in jail, but you keep covering his ass." It was hard on me and Brett. He had to watch her deny the truth and defend her attacker, knowing even with his position on the police force, we couldn't do anything. It didn't matter if we spoke against him when Mom wouldn't corroborate our story.

She reached out to pat my arm. I pushed her touch away.

"You can't understand, honey." Her voice was sad. "You were raised privileged. You have a wealthy fiancé. Your father has his struggles. That doesn't make him a bad person."

Mom always used that excuse when she wanted me to feel naïve. That my "privilege" made me starry-eyed and wishful. She'd been the one who raised us this way, giving us a sheltered life in a small, safe town. She was the one who created this so-called privileged life. As if she forgot about the abuse Miles and I suffered at Mark's hands when his drinking got worse. Growing up the way I did didn't make me stupid. It made me smart. I knew good people, and I knew bad people. The fact she thought I was naïve for allowing her husband to abuse her blew my mind.

"He's definitely not a good person. It would have been better if he'd died in prison." The words were out of my mouth before I realized what

I said. In my final year of high school, we'd heard Mark ended up in the hospital after getting stabbed by another inmate. Both Miles and I still wondered what could have happened if Mark had succumbed to his injuries.

Mom gasped. "How could you say that?" Her hurt expression was evident in my periphery, but I didn't regret my words.

"Because the world would be a better place."

"You don't know him like I do." She sniffed as she cradled her newly casted arm. "He doesn't deserve what he's gotten. Someone has to give him a break."

"You've given him a break, alright. So strong he snapped your arm."

"That's not what happened."

How could she defend him time and time again?

"You're in serious denial. You need help." I couldn't keep the accusation from my tone, though, like me, she'd never air her problems to a professional. I'd been raised understanding that what happened behind our front door was nobody's business. Until the cops came and took Mark away.

Mom looked out the window. "I don't want to talk about this anymore."

I opened my mouth to protest but as I did, my phone rang. I hit the Bluetooth on my car and Brett's voice filled the car.

"You're on speaker," I warned, casting a quick glance at Mom.

"How is everything?"

I huffed. "Arm broken in two places. I'm bringing her home now."

"Sounds good. I have a few of her things in the spare room. She can stay there for a few nights. Or as long as she needs."

"Thanks, babe."

His voice and consideration always brought a smile to my face, no matter how dire the situation seemed. I'd be lost without him.

"Uh, listen Court." His tone faltered. "You still okay if I go down to Toronto tonight?"

He and his friends had been planning this trip down to the city to watch the Blue Jays game for weeks, and it felt wrong to deny him, but I really wanted him by my side through this.

"I can get out of it," he added quickly.

I sucked in a breath. "No, you deserve this."

"You'll be okay?"

"Yeah. I'll call Alexa and see if she wants to crash for the night." Another glance toward Mom. "We'll make it a girl's night."

"That sounds good." He paused. "You'll be home soon?"

I turned the corner, heading towards our house. "Less than five."

"See you soon."

The call ended and Mom rolled her head toward me, never lifting it from the headrest. "Maybe it would be best to spend the night just the two of us."

"I want Alexa to come over." She'd be a good buffer between Mom and me. Further, I wanted someone else at the house in case Mark decided to show up. He had a habit of coming by whenever Mom was hurt. One too many drinks and he'd be knocking down our door. Usually, Brett was home to calm him down and send him away. With him gone, I'd have to be strong on my own.

"I don't want anyone to see me like this." She winced, cradling her arm closer.

"Alexa has seen you at your worst. It's my house. I'm inviting her over."

Mom pouted like a scolded child and turned her disappointed gaze away from me. Ever since Mark was released from prison a couple of years back our relationship had suffered. She had promised me she wouldn't let him back into her life. She lied. It was only a matter of weeks before they were together again, and he was moving back into her house. He'd been in prison for over ten years on assault charges, and while I hoped he'd learned his lesson and maybe gained some manners, as soon as he was free, the drinking started again, and soon, the well-known abuse followed.

For a time, I'd tried to get Mom out of there. I constantly came to her rescue and each time she made empty promises things would get better. Until there was another phone call, another violent outburst, and another lie to cover his tracks.

Brett was waiting out front on the cobblestone walkway, waving as we approached. He rounded the passenger side and opened the door for Mom, helping her out and up the stone steps to our quaint, two-story, brick home. I'd fallen in love with this house the moment I'd seen it. Located off the main roads in Cedar Plains, the red brick had been built in the early 1900s. We were in the process of completely renovating and restoring the inside. Our white door was freshly painted and welcomed visitors, and the windows were bright and calming, letting the sunshine in. Three bedroom, two and a half baths, it would be the perfect place for Brett and me to start our family once the wedding was done.

Inside, Brett helped Mom up to the spare room, and I made my way into the unfinished living room, taking my phone out. I texted Alexa and asked her to come stay the night.

My phone pinged with Alexa's answer as footsteps sounded behind me. I turned to face Brett's joyful eyes. He grinned as he reached up and touched my lower lip with his thumb, stopping my nervous chewing habit.

"You're going to get a canker sore if you keep that up." His dark hair fell across his forehead when he leaned down and planted a light kiss on my lips. Then his strong arms wrapped around me, pulling me against his firm, muscular chest. He held me in place with his hand on the back of my head. I closed my eyes and inhaled his spicy, vanilla scent. It had been my favourite since we were in high school.

"You okay?" his deep voice vibrated through his chest as he spoke.

I hummed my response, content in his arms and dreading the idea he was leaving me alone for the night.

"Court." His hold loosened.

I pulled back enough to look into his hazel eyes. I resisted the urge to reach up and run my hands through his thick dark curls. "I'm fine, I promise."

A grin played on his lips. "Fine is your response when everything's not fine."

I smiled because he knew me too well. "I'll just miss you." I untangled myself from his arms and grabbed my phone. "Lex will come stay with me. So, I'll be okay."

"You'll call me if you need anything?" Brett placed his hands on my hips and his forehead against mine.

"I will."

He kissed my forehead and gave me a smile as he pulled away.

"You're leaving so soon?" I hated how desperate the question came out.

He was dressed for the game, and his duffle bag sat by the front door. He ran a hand through his hair. "If I don't go now, I'll be tight to make the first pitch."

"Sure, of course," I said, unable to keep the disappointment from my voice.

"I won't be long. Only for the night." He moved toward the door. "I'll call you when I arrive."

"You better."

"You know I will." He moved to give me one more kiss and held me for a few moments longer than I expected. "Take care of yourself. I know you feel like your mom is your responsibility, but you're the most important thing in this house to me. Don't risk yourself for her when she won't help herself."

"I promise."

He kissed my cheek and gave me his winning smile before retreating from the house.

I watched from the front window as he climbed into his SUV, backed down the driveway, and sped out of sight. My phone pinged again, Alexa telling me she'd come by in time for dinner. I answered with my approval, then, with a final defeated sigh, went upstairs to see how my mom was doing.

5

Alexa Huston

Sunday, July 9

I climbed the steps to Courtney's front door and pushed it open, finding no one in the front hallway.

"Hello?" I called out.

"In here." Courtney's voice came from the kitchen, and I followed the sound. She was perched on a barstool at the counter, a large glass of white wine in front of her.

I paused at the threshold of the kitchen. "You okay?"

Courtney simply met my eyes and shrugged.

"How's our patient?" I asked, moving towards her. I let the backpack full of my overnight things fall to the floor below before taking the stool next to her.

"Resting." She shook her head then stood to fetch another glass and the opened bottle from the fridge. "I honestly don't know what to do with her anymore."

I reached into my bag, pulling out my sketch book and a couple pencils. It had been months since I'd been tuned into my art. Since before Dean. I'd been itching with inspiration ever since I watched Vanessa's lifeless eyes get buried beneath the ground last night. I shouldn't draw in front of Courtney, but the voice called me to document it. *Remember her.*

"You look better," Courtney said, placing the glass down in front of me. "Did you get some rest?"

I flipped open the sketchbook, ignoring the subtle dig in her words. "Yeah, I had a nap this afternoon. I guess I was pretty drained after last night." I didn't meet her eyes as I said it, worried my own gave away my dark thoughts that hadn't left my mind since.

Courtney hummed a clear disapproval of my wild Saturday night and sat back on the barstool. Then her eyes dropped to my artwork, and she watched as I began moving the pencil fluidly across the parchment, working on the sketch I'd started earlier in the day.

"Are you drawing again?"

I shrugged, keeping my eyes trained on the work. The pencil felt light, almost magical in my hand. As if the drawing was pouring out of me like water from an opened spout.

"Not really," I said. "Just using the inspiration as it hits."

"That's great." Her tone lightened, and I tried not to let it grate me. She used to bring up my art all the time, until I'd snapped at her to leave it alone. I should have known seeing me working would bring her some sense of peace. The idea I could still have an interest in something before Dean. That maybe I wasn't all lost.

"Maybe you can make me another masterpiece, this time for our living room when the renovations are done," Courtney said. A piece I'd done for her years ago hung in their spare room. A painting of the historical terminals—though unused—still graced the skyline of the Cedar Plains Harbour.

I glanced over my shoulder to the half-renovated room attached to the kitchen. "Whenever that is." I met her eyes, this time with a teasing grin.

"Don't get me started."

I glanced back at my sketch, seeing the image take shape. It was Vanessa, of course, as I couldn't get her out of my head. One half of the portrait showed how I saw her when we brought her home, young and quite beautiful. The other half was shrouded in darkness, her lips twisted into a gnarled expression and bruising on her neck. Her hair was long and luscious on one side, lifted with volume, the way it looked at the bar. The other was flat, lifeless, matted like it had been when the blood poured from her brain. I left her nude, though the image didn't show anything beyond bare shoulders. I wanted to capture her elegance, her beauty and her pain. In her ears I drew her many piercings, the small heart shaped spacers and the two metal studs. On the right side I sketched my treasure. The star stud earing had found a new home in my own second piercing. My trophy.

"That's a bit dark," Courtney said, eyeing my art.

"You know I don't really do light and happy." I forced a laugh. "Except when my bestie commissions it."

"I guess I do have a bit of a different taste." Courtney sipped her wine. "I was always partial to your mom's work."

That was one thing my mother and I shared. Her studio in our old house had been our sanctuary, though I'd been unable to create anything joyful since her death. The images that came to me simply encouraged the opposite.

"What did you want to do for dinner?" Courtney asked after a moment of silence. She pushed herself from her seat and started rummaging through the fridge, then freezer, looking unprepared and exhausted.

"What if we order something?" I asked, putting my pencil down for a moment and gently running my finger over the star stud. "Maybe sushi?"

Courtney grinned. "Sounds great. I'll go see if Mom wants anything."

She left me alone, and I resumed my drawing, darkening the right side of Vanessa's face, and obscuring the expression in shadow. I could hear their muffled voices on the floor above me, and the slight raise of Courtney's voice, before a door slammed and Courtney headed back down the stairs.

"Everything okay?" I asked when she reappeared in the kitchen.

"Fine." Courtney crossed the room and grabbed her phone from the counter beside me. "Just Mom wanting to call her abuser." She looked at me with a pinched expression that showed her exasperation.

"I'm sorry."

Courtney simply shook her head and pick up her phone to order dinner.

When the food arrived, Courtney went upstairs to give her mother a plate. Liv still refused to come down and face me, probably convincing herself the less people who saw her broken arm, the more likely she could continue to deny her reality.

"Will she eat?" I asked when Courtney sat down beside me on the cushions we'd placed on the floor. We sat in her partly renovated living room, where half the room and furniture were covered in plastic. Still, the TV worked, and we'd decided to sit on the floor and eat at the coffee table like we used to in high school. *The Fellowship of the Ring* played quietly in the background.

"Not my problem," Courtney said, but her tone told me otherwise. "All she wants to do is call him."

I reached for a spicy salmon roll and popped it into my mouth as Pippin asked about second breakfast.

Liv always wanted to go back to Mark, no matter how hurt she was. I was surprised she'd survived this long but knew she wouldn't forever. One day Mark would take it too far and Courtney would end up motherless like me. *How tragic*, the voice whispered.

"Doesn't she realize he's going to get himself too drunk and do it again?" Courtney said more to herself than me. "Like I guarantee he is already at the bar getting wasted." She shuddered. "I hope he doesn't show up here tonight."

I reached for my wine. "Agreed." Though the darkness inside me whispered that would be his mistake.

"I probably won't sleep at all tonight," she continued. "Without Brett, I don't know what I'll do if he shows."

I didn't answer her, knowing nothing I said would bring her peace of mind. I hated how much he frightened her, and I worried about what losing her mom would do. I grabbed my phone and clicked on my messages, bringing up Kaylee's name.

What's the scene looking like tonight? I was thinking a girl's night with Courtney.

The reply was almost immediate.

Not tonight. Your dad is here.

I frowned as I read the message. Irritation rose up inside me. Typical for my dad to take over the bar the first moment I stepped away. How much of our rent money would he burn tonight? At least Kaylee wouldn't let him drop too much. I'd complained about his habits more than once.

"Remember how it used to be?" Courtney asked, swirling her wine and pulling me away from my phone despite it chiming again. "Mom was distant, sure, but at least she was safe. Mark was in prison, and we had some semblance of peace."

"I know you're worried about your mom, but you can't let your peace rely on her if she won't help herself," I said carefully. *Something else could help her*, the voice whispered.

Courtney shook her head. "I know it's stupid. But it's Mom. She's always been there." She paused for a moment and shot me a playful smile. "Like when I got arrested for shoplifting because my *friend* had sticky fingers."

I averted my eyes, sipping my own wine. "I haven't the faintest idea what you're talking about."

"Of course." Courtney laughed. "I'm sure you barely remember slipping those stupid earrings from Claire's into my purse."

"Well, sure," I said. "But if you hadn't been caught by security for a single measly pair of earrings, I wouldn't have gotten out with the ten pairs that we proceeded to sell and make bank."

"You're lucky Brett's dad was chief of police," Courtney retorted. "Or I'm not sure we'd still be friends."

"You certainly know how to forgive." I offered my glass for a toast. "And I wasn't trying to get you in trouble, but you can't lie that putting the heat on you made it easier for me to get away."

"With shoplifting, with school projects, with family gatherings." Courtney ticked them off on her fingers, each one a reminder of when I'd thrown her to the wolves so I wouldn't get blamed.

"When you put it like that, I'm not sure why you're still my friend."

"That was years ago." Courtney laughed and reached out, placing her hand on my arm. "We were kids. Besides, despite your penchant for self-preservation, I won't be someone that abandons you. I told you that from day one, no matter how many times you tried to push me away."

I sipped my wine then to stop from answering. The voice whispered that her promise didn't matter. She was abandoning me. For Brett. For married life. I knew what came next. A family and time she no longer had for me. I should be happy for Courtney and the life she'd found, but it was hard to be happy when, once again, you were the one being left behind.

I reached for my phone, hopeful for a distraction but cringed when I saw another text from Kaylee on the screen.

Definitely don't come tonight. Mark just showed up.

I regretted texting her then, bringing Mark back to the centre of my mind. Even through the regret, something inside me cackled with glee.

"I'm sorry," Courtney said, drawing me from my phone. "I shouldn't bring up the past. It was a hard time in our lives. I worry whenever I think about what Mark has done. Despite my difficulties with Mom, I don't know what I would do if something happened to her. Especially If I could have saved her."

I glanced back at my phone. Courtney's dad had joined my own at the dive bar. For a moment I was brought back to our early teen years when my dad and Mark were regular drinking buddies. Before Dad had fallen deep into his depression and used drinking as a crutch. Before we knew the level of abuse Mark hid behind his front door.

A shiver ran down my spine. I couldn't let Mark show up here unannounced. I glanced over at my tired best friend. Her eyes were sad, and her shoulders slumped forward with defeat.

I reached out and placed my hand on her back. "It'll be okay. I'm here with you, and I'll make sure nothing happens."

Courtney turned to me a look of desperation in her eyes. "What if that's not enough? Mark is dangerous; he's proven that time and time again. Maybe I shouldn't have let Brett go tonight. What was I thinking? I can't handle him if he shows up here."

"Hey, hey, let's stop for a second and not fall into a hole of despair." I gently shook her shoulder. "Remember two summers ago when Mark was set to get out of prison, and we were sitting at the lookout and swore we'd never let fear rule our lives? I know you're scared of Mark and what could happen, but you're stronger than you know. You've already been through so much that scares you and come out better."

"I don't know if I can be brave in this case," Courtney said quietly. "It was easier to imagine when we were in the middle of nowhere, far away from the monsters that could hurt us. Now, it all seems too close."

I wrapped my arm around Courtney's shoulder and pulled her to me. "I swear to you. I will never let Mark hurt you." The voice cackled inside, swearing a promise. I would stop Mark by whatever means necessary. For the second time since it surfaced, I found myself understanding and agreeing with this thing inside me. I invited its thoughts and feelings. I wanted to feel its power.

Courtney had proven time and time again that she was the only one who'd ever loved me for who I was, no questions, no excuses, no matter what I did, nothing. Mark would die before I let him touch her. *Yes*, the voice agreed.

Courtney leaned into my embrace for only a moment before pulling away. She reached for her nearly empty glass of wine. "I guess I can't help but worry how far he'll take it. When someone dies?"

Again, the voice cackled with glee.

"Sometimes I wish he was dead." She looked at me then, her eyes shining with tears. "And I hate that he makes me that kind of person."

My heart ached as I glanced from her hopeless gaze to her shaking hand. I reached for her glass. "Can I get you more wine?"

"Thank you," she said, her words barely a whisper.

It would have been better if Mark died back in high school, because the only way this would end was in someone's death. I had to make sure it wasn't Liv or Courtney. I had to take control. *Good*, the voice cooed, *good*.

I reached into my backpack and carefully tipped out a doxylamine pill from the container in my bag. I'd been sleeping rough lately and had taken the sleep aid to help ward off the effects of drug use.

I carried the two glasses to the fridge, and with one last glance over my shoulder to be sure she wasn't watching, I quietly crushed the pill then let the powder settle into her glass. Then I grabbed the wine and topped it up, carefully swirling the drink until the powder dissolved.

"Here," I said, placing the glass down in front of her. "You definitely need this."

She sipped the wine then gave me another smile.

After dinner and finishing the bottle of wine, Courtney and I crawled into her king-sized bed and scrolled through Netflix before finding a cheesy romcom to watch. The voice whispered it was only a matter of time. And it was right. From the way Courtney yawned and her eyes drooped, sleep wasn't far off.

We were barely half an hour in before her breathing turned heavy, and she was out cold. I glanced at the clock. Now, the feeling pressed. It read

11:00 p.m. It was early still, maybe too early, but I didn't want to miss my chance.

Slowly, I lifted the covers and crept out of bed. Grabbing my pants and my hoodie, I exited Courtney's room and headed for the stairs. I stopped at the top, glancing down the hallway towards where Liv slept. I wondered whether she was out or not. The doctors had prescribed her painkillers, and she refused to come down to eat with us. I sucked in a breath, hopeful she would sleep through what was about to happen.

Downstairs, I felt like I was in a trance, following the commands of the darkness inside me as I grabbed my backpack off the floor and went to the knife block. I took the largest one and weighed the would-be weapon in my hands. It was a strange sensation, knowing what the voice wanted me to do. Knowing the intent behind these actions. It had to be done. No matter how awful Liv had been, no matter how much she denied the abuse and allowed her family to live through it, I couldn't let her die. I couldn't let Courtney die.

With the knife tucked into my backpack, I slipped out the front door, closing it silently behind me. *It's time*, the voice chortled with glee.

6

Courtney Faith

Monday, July 10

I woke to the sound of birds chirping through my opened window. I was groggy, though felt like I'd slept the best I had in days. Maybe having Alexa with me offered more serenity than I realized. When I checked, the other side of the bed was empty.

I crawled out of bed and walked down the hallway, looking for any sign of her. I was immediately hit with the smell of bacon. At the stairs, I hesitated, looking towards Mom's room. The door was still closed. I knocked twice before she answered.

"Come in."

I pushed open the door to find Mom lying in the spare bed staring out the large window overlooking the street below.

"Did you get any rest?" The plate I'd brought her last night was empty so at least I could assume she'd eaten.

"A bit," Mom said, still not meeting my eyes.

"How's your arm?"

She met my gaze with tired eyes. "Fine." She reached up to cradle it, trying to hide the wince that crossed her face.

I entered the room, taking her pain meds off the dresser. “You should take another one. Come down for some breakfast; it smells like Alexa has something on the go.”

Mom didn’t move, staring at me with pursed lips. “I want my phone back. You promised I could have it today.”

Damn, I’d hoped she would forget. Without a word, I retreated to my bedroom to fetch her phone from the bedside table. When I returned, Mom was seated on the edge of the bed. She held her hand out to me.

“I’ll give you a minute with it,” I said. “But if you don’t come down for breakfast soon, I’ll be back to take it away.” I left the room, exhausted from acting like the parent once again.

“Morning, sleepy head!” Alexa called as I entered the kitchen. She stood at the stove flipping bacon and stirring what looked like cheesy scrambled eggs. Her blond hair looked damp and was tied up in a messy bun. “Hope you don’t mind. I made myself comfortable.”

I sat on one of the barstools. “I definitely don’t mind. That smells heavenly.”

“You look rested,” she said as she placed a plate in front of me.

“I slept well.” I picked up the fork, spearing a chunk of egg before shoveling it into my mouth. “Best I have in ages.” I paused when I heard a noise. “Are you doing laundry?”

Alexa laughed, though it sounded forced. “Just put it in the dryer. There was a huge pile in the laundry room. I thought I could lend a helping hand.”

“You’re a saint.” I thought of the days’-old laundry I meant to put on but had forgotten once again. It really was my least favourite chore.

Alexa sat across from me with a plate of her own.

“How long have you been up?” I asked.

She shrugged. "A couple of hours. You know I never sleep in."

Alexa had been an early riser for as long as I could remember. I used to wake up during our sleepovers to find her scribbling away on a sketchpad or reading a new book, having woken up hours before I graced the day.

"I hope you got a bit of rest."

Again, Alexa shrugged and didn't meet my eyes. We sat in silence for a moment, each enjoying the greasy breakfast, warding off the slight hangover I could feel pressing into the back of my forehead. Maybe I'd indulged a bit too much last night. Mom's drama always made me want to drink.

"At least Mark didn't show up last night," I finally said, gracing the topic of my abusive father.

Alexa seemed to stiffen at the mention of him and immediately I felt stupid for bringing it up. We'd found some peace last night after our turbulent day, and I'd gone and ruined it. I wondered if Alexa and I would ever find the ease that used to define our friendship. Before adulthood, drugs, and drama. When all that mattered was being the best of friends, no matter how shitty the rest of the world was.

"Maybe he worried Brett was still here," Alexa said, pushing a piece of egg around her plate. She'd only taken a few bites, and I wondered if she was feeling more hungover than she let on. I tried to remember how much wine we'd consumed but found the memories hazy, shrouded in a dense fog.

"Whatever the reason, I'm glad we didn't have to deal with it last night." I would have called the cops immediately if Mark had dared step foot on my property, Mom's wishes be damned.

I glanced towards the entrance to the kitchen. Mom still hadn't shown her face downstairs since before Alexa arrived the previous night. I was dreading the idea I'd have to go back upstairs and demand the return of her phone again. I could practically picture her pacing the spare room with her phone pressed against her ear, apologizing profusely to her awful husband, blaming me for overreacting. The image was almost enough to have me storming up the stairs and throwing her bedroom door open. But I didn't. Instead, I resigned myself to leaving her alone, once again reminding myself I couldn't control my mother and her foolish choices. If only I could figure out how to put it all behind me.

My thoughts were interrupted when my phone sprang to life. A picture of me and Brett from our engagement shoot last fall filled the screen as the device buzzed on the countertop.

I reached for it then glanced at Alexa. "Do you mind?"

She waved off my question, finally eating the piece of egg she'd been toying with.

I stood from my seat and stepped away as I pressed the phone to my ear.

"Morning, Babe."

Brett immediately let out a long breath. "Thank god you picked up."

The hair on the back of my neck stood on end. His tone was rushed, nervous. What happened? "Are you okay?"

Brett sighed into the phone. But it wasn't a defeated one, it sounded worried. "Something happened last night."

I felt for the stool I'd abandoned and lowered myself back to the seat, exchanging a worried glance with Alexa who'd looked up when I asked my question.

"Brett, you're scaring me." My mind raced with a million ideas. Had he been in an accident? A shooting? He was calling me so at least I knew he was alive. I considered checking his location on our shared app to see if he was at a hospital.

"Courtney, Mark died last night."

The words hit me, and while Brett continued to talk, I could no longer hear the words he was saying. The way the blood in my ears pounded. My dad was dead.

It was a strange sensation—both a dream come true and a horrible nightmare. Hadn't this been what I was wishing for? My mom to get her freedom, my dad to disappear. Wasn't that what I told Alexa last night, that only death would stop him? My throat tightened as I considered the idea that my awful wish had come true.

"Courtney?" Brett's voice came through the phone firmly. "Did you hear what I said?"

I felt dazed. Confused. "Do you know what happened?"

The pause that followed told me that of course he knew; his cop buddies would have called him first.

"Brett," I pressed, the questions swirling around my head. Had it been sudden? Intentional? Suicide?

Brett drew a breath. "They think he was murdered."

My breath caught. Murdered. Someone had killed him. But why? Mark was no saint, having spent years in prison and having made countless enemies, though he'd been hurt before, he was a big enough guy that people generally didn't mess with him.

"How?" I asked.

"I don't think—"

"Brett, tell me how." I met Alexa's gaze again, and she studied me with confusion and curiosity. Part of me considered putting the phone on speaker as I wasn't sure I'd be able to vocalize what happened after the call ended.

He sighed with frustration. "Stabbed. Multiple wounds to his back. It looks like he was attacked from behind and once down the attacker cut open his throat."

My stomach churned as the breakfast I'd just consumed threatened to make its way back to the surface. This was my fault. I'd manifested this, hadn't I? Wishing he'd died all those years ago in the hospital when another inmate stabbed him.

"Why?" The word came out so softly I wasn't sure I wanted him to answer it.

"We don't know," Brett said. "But I'm on my way back to town. We will figure this out."

"Okay," I said.

"Courtney, I need you to stay put; they're sending over a couple uniforms to ask some questions. I should be home before they get there, but just in case I wanted you to know." He paused before continuing, "They will want to talk to both you and your mom. If Alexa is there, they'll want to talk to her, too."

"Okay, I'll let them know."

His voice softened. "It's going to be okay. I'm sure whatever happened was a random act of violence or a drunken bar fight."

He wasn't wrong. Still the idea a random fight could be the downfall of my terrifying father surprised me. Maybe because if it could happen so easily, why hadn't it happened before? Why did he die this time?

Brett told me he loved me before ending the call. I put the phone down on the counter in front of me and looked at my half-finished plate of food, appetite gone.

"What's going on?" Alexa asked.

I blew out a long breath unsure how to begin. I dropped my eyes to the counter between us. "Mark is dead."

I didn't know what reaction I expected, but Alexa didn't answer me and when I risked a glance at her face, she wasn't looking at me, but over my shoulder.

I followed her gaze to see my mother standing in the archway to the kitchen, clutching her phone in her good hand and tears filling her sad, tired eyes.

7

Alexa Huston

Monday, July 10

I sat in Courtney's kitchen, perched on a barstool, my elbows resting on the counter. Two officers sat across from me.

"Can you tell us what you did last night?" Detective Stevenson asked. A colleague of Brett's, with salt-and-pepper hair in an unflattering crew cut that was thinning on top. I placed him in his mid-forties. He had a light stubble coating his rounded jaw. While it seemed time and the job hadn't been kind to him, I could guess he'd been good looking in his youth. Clear lines of worry creased his oval face, and dark sunspots speckled his olive complexion.

"I came over around five, we ordered dinner, drank some wine, and went to bed," I said, reciting the night Courtney and I had.

"Did you see Mark at any point yesterday?" Detective Francis Day inquired. Her stern expression made her narrow cheeks and angular jaw striking and rigid in an intimidating way. She wore a navy-blue suit and little make up. Her jet-black hair was slicked back in a painful looking low bun. She'd been mostly silent through the questioning. She wasn't a local cop, Brett explained, but a specialist from the Criminal Investigation Bureau, called when they first identified Mark's death as homicide.

Yes, the voice whispered, so much joy in that single word.

I shook my head. "I came over after Courtney picked up her mom."

"But you didn't see Mrs. Faith?" Stevenson again.

"No," I said, trying not to think about what I thought I saw last night. "Not until this morning after we'd heard the news. Courtney said she was upstairs in bed and refusing to come down."

"Why's that?" Stevenson exchanged a look with Day, his eerily dark eyes darting from me to her and back.

"I'd be theorizing," I said. "Is that what you want?"

"Just tell us what you think."

"I think she was in complete denial about her abuse," I said. "I think that has affected her relationship with her daughter, and I think she was sulking."

"Do you think Courtney would ever hurt her father?"

"Excuse me?" I bit back on the laugh that wanted to follow. Inside, the feeling cackled mercilessly.

Stevenson exchanged another look with Day. "You mentioned their strained relationship. Courtney obviously has some resentment built up. Do you think she'd ever act on it?"

"Courtney wouldn't hurt a fly," I said, pushing the memories of the accident out of my mind. It *had* been an accident after all. "She may have hated him, but for good reason. Whatever happened to Mark was always coming. You've brought him into holding more than once. It's not like he was some upstanding citizen."

"You sound bitter," Stevenson said.

"And you sound like you're looking for someone to blame in the wrong place," I retorted. The darkness flared at my anger, and I drew a deep breath to silence it.

Stevenson pursed his lips. "You and Courtney were both here last night?"

"As I already said." Repetition of questions—meant to catch us in some sort of lie.

"Could she have left while you slept?"

I shook my head. "I was literally in her bed next to her. If she'd left, I would have known. I'm not a particularly heavy sleeper." I only hoped Courtney would say the same thing about me. Maybe I should have stayed in bed longer, held off on breakfast. But then the laundry would still be lying on the floor and my clothes still stained. Washing them here might have been a risk but necessary.

I glanced to the knife block where my weapon was stowed clearly in the police's peripherals. Inside me the darkness preened. Could they smell the lingering odor of bleach in the backyard? If they did, they showed no indication or interest in the block.

"And what do you think happened to the missing ring?" Stevenson asked. The police had noted Mark's ring finger should have held a wedding ring, clear from a tan line it had recently been removed.

So shiny, the voice whispered.

Like it was brand new. The hair on the back of my neck stood on end, thinking back to the golden ring lying at the bottom of my backpack.

I shrugged. "The hopeless in this town will take anything they think is worth a dime. Couldn't it have been taken by anyone?"

Stevenson pursed his lips again, regarding me in a way that said he didn't appreciate my tone.

Thankfully, Brett entered the kitchen before he could respond. "Are you two about done here?"

Stevenson looked to disagree, but Day stood, and he followed suit.

"We'll let you know if we need anything else." He stepped around Brett towards the front hallway.

Brett glanced at me. "All good?"

I nodded, then let my gaze fall back to the counter in front of me. His departing footsteps told me he was seeing the other officers out. I wasn't alone long before Courtney entered the kitchen. Her red-rimmed eyes gave away her stress, and she collapsed onto the barstool across from me.

"What happened?" she asked, though I wasn't sure why she did. The police had told us what happened. *Someone* attacked him and left his body in the park. The feeling swelled with glee.

"They'll figure it out." I folded my hands on my lap beneath the counter, hiding my fidgeting. I hoped they'd never figure it out. I pushed myself from the stool as Brett entered the kitchen.

"I should get going," I said. "I have to work tonight. Will you be okay?"

Courtney looked at me with tired eyes, asking how I could be so okay right now and I fought the urge to look away.

"I'm sorry, Court," I said, realizing I hadn't yet apologized for taking her dad from her, though I wasn't certain I needed to.

Courtney dropped my gaze and waved off my comment. "Don't be. He was an awful person."

Her words were flat, void of emotion, and weary from the trying day. From the kitchen, I could hear Liv's muffled sobs, vocalizing a pain Courtney would never understand. I only hoped with Mark gone, she could begin to heal.

I stepped out into the fresh afternoon air and hesitated. The sun was high in the summer sky, and I squinted in the bright light. I hadn't thought of Vanessa in hours, and now, with the high of Mark's murder waning and the urges silenced, I found myself mesmerized by the idea of her beautiful corpse again. It had been a full twenty-four hours. Someone must have noticed she was missing by now. I fought the urge to check the news again, something I'd been doing too much lately.

I grabbed my cellphone and powered it down for my walk home, knowing Dean would be in touch. He hadn't contacted me yet today, but Brett likely informed his best friend I'd be unable to chat for a while.

My body buzzed with excitement as I made my way through town and back to my condo. During the police questioning, I couldn't get the events out of my head. A part of me wanted to walk the opposite way through town, back towards the bar to the roped-off park, back to the scene.

Killers like to do that, right? Revisit the scene of their crimes. I'd never understood why those stupid people on crime shows would return to the scene and give themselves away, but feeling it, wanting to go back and relive the power, the control, again, made sense now.

Last night felt like a trance. Almost an out-of-body experience as I'd waited outside Big Shot for half an hour, shrouded by the shadowy entrance across the street. From where I waited, I watched the patrons filter in and out of the dingy dive bar to smoke. It wouldn't be busy inside. It was a Sunday night after all.

I'd noticed him the moment he exited the bar. Hard not to. He swayed on unsteady feet and laughed with the hulking bouncer. The feeling inside me jumped with glee when I first spotted him. Then he turned and stumbled down the street. I waited a moment, listening to the darkness inside me and noticing he took the turn that led to Courtney's subdivision rather than the route that would have taken him home. Had he known he was heading towards his daughter's home? Had he pulsed with rage, or was it subdued by the whiskey and the drunks he'd shared it with?

When the bouncer stepped back inside, the voice whispered, *now*. I moved from the shadows with my hood pulled over my head and hurried down the street after Mark. It was after midnight. And the evening was quiet. Most were comfortably home awaiting the week of work ahead. It was always a blessing to find the streets empty.

The way Mark stumbled and swayed made his inebriation obvious, and when he turned off the street and started walking through the darkened park, I swiftly followed, feeling like my hands weren't my own, they pulled the knife from my bag in the process.

He stopped in the centre and glanced around, causing the darkness inside me to hesitate and move into the shadow of a large willow tree. Had I been too noisy? I held my breath as his narrow eyes squinted in the darkness, looking for any movement. I swore he looked right at me, and I prayed the blade in my hand didn't glint or reflect in the moonlight.

When he turned and continued his path, I moved quickly. I ran up behind him and plunged the knife into his back with all my might. I met a brief resistance before the knife tore through his T-shirt and into his flesh. In a swift motion, I pulled it out and stabbed him again. He sputtered and fell forward, barely bracing his fall, and once on the ground, I stabbed the knife into the soft flesh of his neck. Once. Twice. Three times. Before I was sure he couldn't survive it.

"For Courtney," I whispered.As he died, the urging inside me waned, and there was a gentle purr of satisfaction. I'd fed the darkness that had taken root. It was pleased with me.

Straightening, I glanced up at the nearly full moon, clutching the bloodied weapon in my hand. I gave myself only a moment to consider the body lying at my feet. The man I killed. The lives I had saved with this decision. I found myself thankful for the current dry spell. The ground was firm, so none of my shoeprints would be recognizable around the body.

My eyes fell on his wedding ring. Of course, he still wore the jewelry tying him to Liv and Courtney. I pulled my sleeve down over my hand and yanked the ring from his finger.

Clutching the ring between my finger and thumb, I held it up in the moonlight and admired it, imagining this was how Gollum felt in *The Lord of the Rings*.

My precious, the voice cackled, and I laughed along with the idea, as I tucked the ring into my backpack, then turned and ran from the scene.

My quick pace made my already excited heart beat faster. I wanted to slow, to savour the kill, to breathe in the strangely fresh evening air. But I had to hurry.

The idea never panicked me; however, a sense of calm and joy made my body tingle with success. It was different from how I felt about Vanessa because this kill was right and only mine.

I still clutched the blood-covered weapon in my hand. If anyone were to see me now, there would be no denying my crime. Luckily, at this time of night, in this town, the sleepless raccoons and cloudless sky were my only company.

I turned onto Courtney's street, thankful for the few streetlights which were easy enough to avoid, but stopped when I noticed a light on in the upper window. From where I stood, I could see the outline of a woman—Liv—staring out at the empty street. My heart leapt into my throat. Her gaze was directly on me. My hand tightened on the bloody knife, ready to act, but I tried to silence the voice. I didn't want to hurt Liv.

Unsure what else to do, I held her eye contact, freezing like a deer in headlights. The only sound was my ragged breathing until she turned away from the window and the lights went out.

I waited a few moments more, knowing the longer I stayed on the street the more likely I would get caught. Drawing a steady breath, I tried to calm my nerves and moved forward with my plan.

I slipped into Courtney's backyard, careful to keep my movements as silent as possible. The darkness had ceded control to me, now ever silence, and I had to clean up. In the backyard, I glanced up at her bedroom window for only a moment before grabbing the bleach I'd left out. I placed the knife in a bucket and poured the bleach over top. Then I slipped through the unlocked backdoor and made my way into Courtney's laundry room. I stripped my clothes and tossed them in the sink, rinsing the blood that had splattered across me before throwing it into the laundry along with the pile of Courtney and Brett's things gathered on the floor. I loaded the soap and set the timer so the machine would start before Courtney woke up. I didn't want to risk turning it on now in case one of them heard my dangerous movements.

When I exited the laundry room, I paused at the base of the steps and listened for any sound of the women sleeping upstairs. If Liv had seen me, she didn't make any move to catch me in the act. Had I imagined her gaze on me? I only hoped the darkness had been enough to shield me from her wandering eyes. I tiptoed back into the kitchen and out the backyard to dump the bleach and returned my weapon back to its rightful place.

I crept downstairs to the mother-in-law suite Brett and Courtney were in the midst of renovating and removing, thankful the shower was still intact. I hesitated only a moment before stepping inside and letting the warm water cascade over my body, washing the rest of my crime away.

Excitement still coursed through my tired body as I relived the experience. I'd been so level-headed, so in control. I never realized I could be capable of something so brutal. A shiver ran down my spine. No drug could compare to the high I'd felt.

I shook the memory of the murder away as my condo appeared in the distance. When the police came to question us this morning, Liv hadn't mentioned my appearance on the street and didn't indicate she thought I'd done anything wrong.

I reached into my bag and pulled out the gold band I stole. Slipping it onto my thumb, I admired the soft glint from the sun. A perfect addition to my collection.

Something to keep the memory alive.

My joy was short lived as when I climbed the steps to my unit, I found something stuck to the front door. An envelope with my name on it. Inside were only two words.

I know.

I swallowed hard as the darkness flared with annoyance. I tried to rack my brain for some explanation, some understanding of what this note could mean, but as I did, my mind could only focus on two things. Could it be about Vanessa or Mark?

I crumpled the sheet of paper in my hand and thew open the door. Dad was nowhere to be found, though even if he was, I doubted he could provide any insight into the identity of whoever left the note. I stormed into the kitchen and tossed the scrunched envelope and paper into the trash bin before darting upstairs and grabbing my sketchbook. The adrenaline pulsed through me as I gave into the voice, urging me to recreate the glee of last night.

8

Courtney Faith

Monday, July 10

When Alexa left, I collapsed forward onto the counter, exhausted from the day. Brett came up behind me and put a hand on my back, gently rubbing in circles.

"You okay?"

My shoulders shook under his hand from my bemused laugh. "Is that an instinctual question?" I lift my head to gaze at my fiancé, who moved to sit on a stool next to mine.

"Definitely," he said. "I'm sorry about the formality. All the questions."

I shook my head. "That's not your fault. Someone's dead. They have to figure it out. Even if the man who died was a monster."

I didn't mourn Mark, as I didn't have a single good memory to apply to him. His abuse had been long and constant in my early years. I remember hiding with Miles in our shared closet on the days he came home angry. Mom had tried to protect us back then, still able to stand up to him, but in time, he beat her down. She was never the same after he was arrested. I was sixteen then and had already suffered his rage more than once when protecting Miles from his wrath. And now, he was gone.

"I feel like I wished this on him," I said, and Brett's gaze softened with sadness.

"Don't say that." He leaned closer to me, placing his forehead against my temple. "We all say things we don't mean in the moment. You were scared and angry. No one blames you for that."

"Mom does," I muttered, and Brett pulled back slightly.

"Your mom is grieving. She knows this wasn't your fault. Today has been a terrible day."

I swallowed the lump that had formed in my throat and turned towards him. "Who would take his ring?"

Brett shook his head. "Maybe whoever killed him. Or maybe someone who stumbled across his body. Unless we find it, we'll never know for sure."

"I didn't even know he still wore it." I couldn't imagine anything being sentimental to Mark.

"I know you don't believe it, but when he was sober and his mind clear, your mom was important to him." Brett placed a hand on my thigh, and I brushed him off.

"Please don't ever defend him again," I said. "Even if he was brutally killed, he does not have a redemption story. He was not a good person."

Brett put up his hands in defeat and said nothing more.

"I should try to talk to my mom." I pushed myself to stand when there was a knock at the front door.

Brett and I exchanged a glance, not expecting anyone, and for a moment I worried Stevenson had returned with more questions. Brett went for the door, and I followed him, hoping to present a united front.

It wasn't Stevenson, but an older woman with greying hair pulled back in a tight bun. She wore a pencil skirt and a crisp white blouse, tucked in with one button too many undone, giving an ample view of her cleavage. She was familiar, but I couldn't put my finger on why.

"Mr. Knight?" the woman asked. Her eyes found mine. "Ms. Faith?"

"Who wants to know?" Brett asked, clearly angling himself in front of me.

Her face broke in a smile, and she offered her hand. "Rita Rounds, Ceder Plains Today. I was hoping to ask you a few questions about Mark Faith."

Brett stiffened and I shrunk back from the door. No wonder she was familiar. I remembered seeing her name and photo on many articles in our local online newspaper. A reporter looking for details about my dad's death.

"It's an ongoing investigation," Brett said, his voice steely. "We have nothing to say to you."

Rita wasn't deterred. "I understand that, but I was hoping to get a more personal angle from the family."

"No," Brett said.

"I've had some sources tell me that Mark Faith had a history of violence," Rita continued. "That something happened within the family."

"Enough," Brett snapped as I stepped farther away from the door. "The history of violence can be noted from his time incarcerated. Everything else it's hearsay, and I won't have you harassing my family for any information."

I expected the woman to retreat after Brett's clear statement, but she didn't. Instead, she smirked, gave him a once over and waved off his comment.

"How like your father you are," she quipped. She tilted her head around Brett, getting a clear look at me. "Your type may like to bury the facts, but I can assure you, with or without your help I will find more."

She turned on her heel and stepped back to where she'd parked her Prius on our front curb.

"She knows your dad?" I asked, when Brett closed the door.

He shrugged. "Dad had a few run ins with the local reporters when he was chief. Most people know him."

I wanted to ask more, since Rita seemed to insinuate something about his father, when my phone buzzed in my pocket. I reached for it, realizing I'd not touched it most of the day. As soon as I did, a pit formed in my stomach. "Shit, shit, shit."

Brett stiffened. "What's wrong?"

I shook my head. "Savannah and I had a final dress fitting today. She opened the store for me and everything, and now I've left her waiting. Oh my god. I'm such an idiot."

"It's okay, babe," Brett said, reaching out and taking my arm. "You've been through some trauma. You can cancel. Savannah will understand."

I chewed on my bottom lip. He was right, of course, I could cancel, but I didn't want to. Seeing Savannah and focusing on my upcoming wedding would be a good distraction.

"No," I said. "I want to go." Then I hesitated and looked towards the front hallway to the stairs leading up to where Mom had hidden away in the spare bedroom.

As if reading my thoughts, Brett smiled. "You should go then. If you think it will help. Don't worry about your mom. I'll be here."

I hesitated still, feeling guilty about leaving her, about not being there for her after her husband's untimely death. But as I thought about it,

I felt worse about leaving Savannah hanging. I'd been there through everything for Mom, but consoling her over a death I couldn't mourn? I wasn't sure I was cut out for it.

"Thank you." I sprinted up the stairs to change into a sundress, then I whipped back into the kitchen to kiss Brett goodbye. "If Mom comes down, tell her I'll be home soon."

Savannah was waiting outside the dress shop when I pulled up. She waved from her wheelchair, and when I reached her, we entered the store together.

"I am so sorry," I said.

Savannah waved off my excuse. "Don't worry about it. You're busy."

I gave her a grateful smile and wondered if I should tell her why the appointment slipped my mind. Did she know about the murder that happened in town only a few kilometers from her shop? Word had a habit of travelling fast in this small town.

"Want to talk about anything?"

As soon as she asked it, the story came spilling out. When I finished, Savannah gazed at me with wide eyes.

"Oh my god, Courtney." Her mouth was open wide. "I'd heard the park was roped off with police presence, but I didn't know the details. This is awful. Go home."

I shook my head. "No. This is where I want to be."

"Okay," Savannah said. "If you're sure."

Before I could affirm my statement again, one of Savannah's sales associates entered from the back room.

She grinned, oblivious to the tension. "It's all set back there."

"Thank you, Jenny," Savannah said. "Is there champagne?"

"Already poured." Jenny beamed.

"Great. Bring in the bottle." Savannah glanced at me. "We're going to need it."

Once in the back room, Savannah passed me a glass. "You should drink this."

Jenny returned with the bottle. "Anything else?"

"Fine for now, Jenny. I'll call for you if I need anything." Then she shooed her out of the room.

I sat down on one of the plush chairs that lined the room. I'd done all my fittings at this boutique. Usually, it was me and a few of my bridesmaids. Alexa had only come once, but Savannah, she had been a saint.

"I'm sure they will figure out whoever did this," Savannah said when neither of us spoke for a moment.

I nodded, unsure what to say. We both knew the police weren't faultless. They'd try, sure, but if they couldn't find anything whoever did it might get away.

As if reading my mind, Savannah looked down at her hands. "I mean, we know they're not perfect. But from what you've told me, it was careless. And careless people don't get away with murder."

"You don't think your accident was careless?" The words spilled out of my mouth before I could stop them.

Savannah cracked a small smile. "Sure, but getting hit by a car is a little different than getting stabbed."

I shuddered. I didn't want to think about either situation. I still remembered Savannah in the hospital. The way the accident had shattered her legs and snapped her spine. The morning the doctors told her she'd be in a wheelchair for the rest of her life. It was nothing short of awful.

Lifechanging. I shook the memory away, choosing instead to remember Savannah's sunny attitude during the whole thing.

I jumped at the sensation of her warm hand on mine. And I looked up to meet her gaze.

"Do you want to talk about it?" she asked.

I shook my head. I'd talked about it endlessly today in front of the cops. With Brett. But I couldn't deny that Savannah's gentle smile and kind eyes calmed me. She'd been such a positive presence since we became friends after her accident. Looking at her now, I'd nearly forgotten how important she'd become to me. It was more than her loyalty. Such a different person than Alexa, Savannah was someone I could count on, an easy relationship I didn't have to continue to nurture or worry about. If Alexa and I met now, I was certain we wouldn't have become friends.

"I'm sorry you are going through this," Savannah said. "I know how confusing and scary not knowing can be."

The dread I'd been feeling since Brett's phone call grew.

"But it will be okay." Savannah squeezed my hand. "I know whatever happens, you'll be okay. You're a survivor."

She had no idea how right she was. I would survive. I always had.

9

ALEXA HUSTON

MONDAY, JULY 10

I scribbled in my sketchbook while I stood behind the bar at Big Shot. It was nearly eleven and only a few regulars were here, playing pool or seated at the tables. I pressed my pencil hard into the page, sketching the darkened park from last night's murder. I'd been working on the piece since I returned home this afternoon, taking a few creative liberties.

In the centre of the park, a man lay on the pavement. I took care to draw dark pools around him, grinning as I remembered the blood. The letter from earlier in the day still rested at the back of my mind. It put me on edge, thinking someone knew my secrets. But which one?

I jumped at the sound of the kitchen door swinging open as Kaylee pushed her way through. I flipped my sketchbook shut.

"What's up?" I asked, my voice higher than intended.

Kaylee paused, frowning. "Nothing." She shook her head, dark curls tumbling around her shoulders, and pushed by me to the opposite end of the bar. Kaylee had been avoiding me most of the shift, choosing to be holed up in the office, rather than on the floor. Not that I needed her support with this crowd. Mondays were rarely busy.

"Are you okay?" I asked, keeping my voice down as I stepped up behind her. We weren't the best of friends, but our shifts were usually warm and friendly.

She jumped in place and turned, putting distance between us. Her slight shoulders reached her ears before relaxing as she turned to face me. Her normally pleasant face was pinched, and her dark, worried eyes met mine for only a moment before she quickly averted them.

"I'm fine," she said, though her voice shook.

I reached out for her but stopped when the front door swung open and in walked a middle-aged woman dressed in a suit way too nice for Big Shot.

Kaylee took my moment of hesitation and moved around me, heading through the kitchen door again.

The woman glanced around the dingy bar, a clear look of disgust on her face. I eyed her carefully as she crossed the threshold. She was out of place.

Still, she gracefully slid onto one of the bar stools and looked pointedly at me.

"What would you like to drink?" I asked, tucking my sketchbook into my purse below the bar and out of sight.

She waved off my request with one of her own. "Are you Alexa Huston?"

"Who are you?" I demanded, leaving her question unanswered.

She clearly got the answer she wanted as she offered her hand. "Rita Rounds, reporter for Cedar Plains Today. I'd like to ask you a few questions about the murder of Mark Faith that occurred last night."

I stiffened, and the voice inside me growled. "I have nothing to say about it."

"I've been told you and his daughter are quite close," Rita insisted. "Friends for fifteen years I heard?"

"Something like that," I mumbled.

"Then certainly you have something to share." Rita poised her phone, her voice notes open, clearly ready to record any response I could give her.

"I don't have anything to share with you," I said, trying to keep my voice even. "I have no idea what happened last night."

For a moment her expression faltered, and her lips turned down. "Pity." But the disappointment only lasted a moment before she smiled again.

"I understand Mr. Faith was quite the monster to his family," Rita continued. "Can you comment on that? I understand he did time for it."

The darkness inside squirmed with displeasure.

"If you know he did time then you know all you need to." I glanced around the bar, looking for an excuse to dismiss her but none of the other locals were vying for my attention.

"Did you, as such a close family friend, ever experience this abuse firsthand?" Rita's question lingered as I thought about the things I had seen. The way Courtney had cowered. The times she ran to my house for shelter.

When I didn't answer immediately, she continued, "You must know something."

That put me on edge. "Look, I'm in the middle of a shift," I said. "Now isn't really a great time."

Rita frowned. "Would another time be better?"

Before I could answer her, Dean stepped through the front door and into the bar. His hands were pressed deep into his pockets and hair slicked back. Had he been working late? Or was it drinks and drugs with his buddies? I hadn't heard from him since the previous day. And he still had my car.

"Sorry, another customer," I said and hurried off, motioning to Dean to take a stool at the opposite end of the bar.

"Hey, babe." Dean plopped onto the bar stool I'd indicated. "Almost done?"

I glanced back to where Rita sat. She eyed me for only a moment longer before pushing herself from her seat and leaving the way she came.

I turned my attention back to my boyfriend, shaking off the strange encounter. "Where have you been all day?"

Dean's jaw tightened. "Busy."

The darkness growled again.

"Doing what?" I kept my voice low. He'd been practically MIA since we'd killed someone. Something inside me whispered the worst. He'd been securing an alibi. Making sure if somehow it all went wrong, he could pin it on me. I shuddered at the thought he could use Vanessa and her beautiful death against me. The darkness promised that he would.

He ran a hand through his hair, loosening the gel. "Making sure everything is handled." He reached into his pocket and dropped my keys on the bar in front of me. "Your car is spotless, by the way. You're welcome."

I clenched my jaw and swiped the keys off the counter. Then I drew a breath, forcing the darkness to silence and softened my shoulders before grabbing a pint glass and pouring him a beer. I slid it across the bar to him. "Thank you for taking care of the car."

Dean stared at me for a moment before his easy smile appeared, and he grabbed the beer, taking a big swig. "Are you ready to head out?"

I glanced around. "Kaylee hasn't given the okay yet." She was the manager on shift and should have told me to go home by now.

He sipped the beer. "Just leave then. It's not like they're going to fire you from this dump."

I rolled my eyes. He was right, but it was still my job. I wanted to be taken somewhat seriously.

"I'll go make sure she's cool I clock out." I didn't wait for his response before I darted through the kitchen door towards the office.

Kaylee sat in front of the computer, staring at the screen, though her fingers didn't move across the keyboard. She appeared to be doing nothing.

"Hey."

She jumped at the sound of my voice. "Alexa. What are you doing?"

"It's dead out there. You don't need me, do you?"

"Oh." She shook her head. "No, head out. I'll be out in a bit to keep the regulars thirsty."

"Great." I hesitated at the door.

"Something you need?" Kaylee asked, her tone short.

"No, I wanted to make sure everything is cool. You're okay?"

"It's cool." Kaylee waved me off. "Go home."

"See you tomorrow."

"Mhmm." Kaylee only stared at the computer again.

Back behind the bar, I poured myself a stiff vodka soda, clocked out, then took a seat next to Dean. He turned toward me, placing his legs on either side of mine and sliding his hand up my thigh. I wondered if he'd notice the star stud in my ear, if he'd recognize it as the same one Vanessa wore the night we took her home.

"You good, babe?" There was actual concern behind his words. We hadn't spoken about Vanessa since the *incident,* and he hadn't seen me since before Mark. It had only been a couple of days, but it felt like a lifetime. So much had changed in only a few hours. I didn't fully understand the urging inside me, only that it had been there since I looked into Vanessa's lifeless eyes. Could he see the new darkness dwelling behind my own?

Things between Dean and I were always a bit uneasy. Our relationship was never conventional, and now, we were locked in this awful secret together. Though the voice and I wished it could be ours alone.

"Yeah, fine," I said, keeping my gaze locked on his. He really was a handsome guy, a mask to hide the ugly buried beneath. The spoiled kid, the drug dealer, the self-obsessed. *Beast*, the voice hissed. And yet, I was drawn to him. Maybe it was the security his wealthy upbringing promised, maybe it was the distraction from my brutal home life and go-nowhere job. Or maybe it was the self-destructive part of me that knew we had no future, so the relationship was easy, fun, no strings attached. Really, it was all three.

He reached up and brushed my hair behind my ear, tracing his fingers down my jaw to my neck until he had a gentle hold of my throat. He held me there for a moment, his eyes searching mine for some reaction, and when I gave him none, he let his fingers slide lower, hooking the chain that now hung around my neck. The darkness was thrilled when I first slipped it on. Wearing my trophies for all to see and not understand. It excited the voice within, and I found I couldn't deny its desire.

"This is new," he said, sliding the chain through his fingers and grabbing the golden ring that hung off it.

The voice flared with anger at his invasion.

I reached out taking my souvenir from his hold, not wanting his touch to dirty my crime. "Not new. Old." I tucked the ring back beneath my shirt so only the top of the chain holding it was visible. "It was my mom's. I used to wear it all the time. Just thought I'd try it again." A half-truth. I did have my mom's wedding ring in my jewelry collection back home. Phoebe had found it amongst Dad's things one day and insisted I have it. It was the first time I'd considered my dad's girlfriend as part of the family. Only this particular ring wasn't it.

Dean raised an eyebrow, an amused glint in his gaze as he reached for his beer. "How cute."

I ran my hand over his arm, my fingers tracing the leather band of his Tissot watch. He barely wore it, claiming the expensive piece was too nice for our little town, but I'd noticed it more and more in the past few weeks. The value of the piece would have covered more than an entire month of groceries.

"I guess I'm sentimental sometimes."

The way Dean grinned told me he didn't believe it, but he didn't say otherwise.

Before either of us could say more, Kaylee pushed through the kitchen doors, stopping when she saw us. "I thought you were going home."

"After this." I motioned to my drink.

"Right." She frowned, walking past us and behind the bar, but before she could get too far away from us, Dean glanced up.

"Can I get another one?" He pushed his glass towards her. They made eye contact only once, then she averted her gaze. It hit me then why she'd been losing it tonight. Kaylee was one of the biggest cokeheads I knew.

"Let's go after this one." I leaned closer to Dean. "And do me a favour and leave Kaylee a bump. She's been a mess all night."

When Kaylee passed him his beer, he caught her hand and shoved something into it.

"On the house."

"Uh, thanks." She tucked it into her cleavage and turned away. I only hoped it would brighten her up a bit. I downed the rest of my drink, feeling claustrophobic in the stifling bar. "Let's get out of here."

Dean raised an eyebrow but finished his nearly full beer in a few quick chugs.

"Later, Kaylee." He waved to my co-worker as I grabbed my purse, and we exited the bar.

Dean immediately slipped his arm across my shoulders and pulled me close. We turned down the street, walking away from the bar and towards his house where he'd left my car. "You seem tense."

I'd hoped he didn't notice the way I flinched at his touch. The annoyance the voice felt. When I didn't answer quick enough, Dean groaned.

"Aren't you going to say anything?"

"What do you want me to say?"

"You haven't even asked about me," Dean said. "About *her*." The way he emphasized the word 'her' meant he was talking about Vanessa. It had been two days since we dropped her in the field and her body had yet to be found.

"You haven't texted me all day," I said. "I assumed you didn't want to talk."

Dean's grip on my shoulder tightened. "I don't want anything in writing, Alexa." Whenever he spoke my full name, it came with an air of condescension. "That's how they get you."

The voice cackled at his discomfort.

"Right," I said simply. "I didn't think about it that way." Then I lowered my voice to play into Dean's paranoia. "So, anything new?"

His grip on me loosened as he pulled away. "I haven't heard any news. Whatever happened to Courtney's dad seemed to have taken precedent over any missing person case. Though if there was, it's likely in the Toronto news."

"Has someone reported her missing?"

"I don't exactly know, Alexa." Dean's voice carried an annoyance, telling me I was stupid for asking such a question. "I can't really ask if anyone has reported her missing or toss her name in a Google search. That's a bit obvious."

"It'll be all over the news," I said. "Once someone uncovers her."

Dean's tone softened. "We covered our asses." Then he leaned closer to me. "And now we have to be diligent."

I nodded in response.

"Come on." He glanced at his watch then slipped his hand into mine, quickening our pace. "Let's get home. I'm dying for a bump and a lay."

I said nothing, letting him pull me down the street towards his waiting house. Weirdly enough, a bump was the farthest thing from my mind. My body no longer itched for the sunny high and instead craved something different. Something dark. Something scary and unknown. Something I could never tell anyone.

10

Courtney Faith

Tuesday, July 11

"Courtney, this is serious." I glanced back to the computer where Miles filled the screen. My younger brother had days-old scruff coating his chin and his blond hair was messy like he'd just rolled out of bed, though it was nearly dinner time.

"I don't know what you want me to say." I lowered myself back to the bed where my laptop rested.

"How's Mom, really?" Miles pressed. "I tried calling."

"She's not talking," I said. "It's been hard on her."

Miles' expression hardened. "It's been hard on all of us."

I knew Miles wasn't talking about Mark's death, but the affect his presence had had on all of us over the years.

"He's gone now," I said, unable to keep the resentment from my tone. Miles had picked up and left for university the first moment he could and never came back. I didn't blame him for it, but I'd been left to pick up the pieces, to care for Mom and watch Mark slowly destroy her. Now I would be left to deal with this too. And that nosy reporter who'd since tried calling. How she got my cell number, I'd never know.

"Thank god," Miles said.

"When are you coming back?" I was expecting him for the wedding but beyond that he hadn't formalized his plans.

"I'm still sorting it out with work." Miles looked away from the screen and rubbed his eyes. "It's been crazy busy, but I think I can wrangle some remote days so I can head over a few days earlier."

"I'd like that."

"Courtney!" Brett called from the floor below.

"Ah, it's time to go," I said, looking back at Miles.

He chuckled. "The dreaded in-laws. Good luck."

We bid each other goodbye, and Miles promised to update me on his schedule as soon as he could, then we exited the chat.

"Be right there!" I called back to Brett. He'd been spending the entire afternoon working in the living room, peeling off the old wallpaper and sanding down the walls. Stevenson, the lead on the case, continued to investigate Mark's murder, keeping Brett at arm's length stating conflict of interest.

I glanced in the mirror, tracing my made-up face and long maxi dress. Cancelling did seem like a great idea. Spending the night with Brett's parents was never a favourite activity of mine, but if we didn't go tonight, his mother would blame me and find some way to punish me for it later. Besides, Brett's mother, Missy, had already called three times to confirm we were coming despite the fact Mark had just been murdered. The woman was so pushy.

When I was ready, I went to our spare room to check on Mom. She'd barely left the bed since the previous morning when the police came to question us.

"Mom?" I knocked on the door before gently pushing it open. Mom lay in bed, facing away from the door. "Mom?" I said again, my voice low in case I'd disturbed her sleeping.

She rolled her head to gaze over her shoulder at me but didn't answer before turning back to look towards the large window. I moved into the room and perched on the edge of the bed, following her gaze to the blue sky outside.

"Are you okay?" I asked, though the question seemed pointless. Whatever hold Mark still had over my mother had hit her with a sadness I couldn't comprehend. Her eyes were red-rimmed and puffy. The bags beneath showed she'd barely slept. If she had, it was likely from the exhaustion of crying for hours on end.

"It doesn't make sense," Mom muttered. "Why?"

I grimaced. It had been something she'd been repeating ever since we heard the news. She couldn't fathom someone would want to harm Mark despite his ability to anger or hurt nearly anyone he met.

"The police will make it make sense," I said firmly. "Once they catch whoever is responsible. I know you don't believe it, but Mark had enemies. He burned a lot of bridges over the years."

Mom's eyes narrowed. "You have no idea what you're talking about." She spat the words at me like his downfall was somehow my fault.

I flinched away from her anger, unsure what else I could say.

"I'm sorry," Mom finally said. She reached out and placed her hand on my arm.

I covered her hand with my own and we sat in silence for a moment. "Brett and I are going to his parents' for dinner. Do you want to join us?"

Mom simply looked away without answering, and I knew getting her out of this bed and into something presentable was as impossible as understanding why someone would have taken Mark's wedding ring. I imagined it was in a local pawn shop by now, allowing whoever stole it to profit off the golden band.

When she still didn't speak, I stood and reached for the pain killers on the dresser. I gently shook the bottle, wondering if I should remove them in Mom's depressed state, but rethought it immediately. My mom didn't need me treating her like she was a suicide risk when she'd never given me reason to think she was.

"How's your arm?" I asked, still holding the pills.

"Fine," she said. "I'm taking the medication as prescribed. Last night the pain was okay, the night before it kept me up for a bit, but the medication helped numb everything in time."

I placed the pill bottle back on the dresser and moved towards the door. "We'll be back in a few hours. There are leftovers in the fridge. Eat something, please."

I hesitated outside the closed guest room door. In her grief, I worried I'd have to be the one to handle Mark's affairs. A will, if there was one, and whatever else went with handling the death of a family member. Maybe I could have his body incinerated and the ashes forgotten. Mom would likely disagree.

I met Brett at the base of the stairs where he now waited for me, car keys in hand.

"We can reschedule," he said with an amused expression. As he did, his phone jumped to life. He glanced down at it and grimaced as he silenced the ringer.

"Missy, again?" I tried to keep the irritation out of my tone.

Brett nodded. We were already a couple of minutes behind schedule. Only Missy would consider calling someone sixty seconds after they were supposed to arrive.

"We can still say no," he offered.

I shook my head. "No, we can't. I'll never hear the end of it. Let's get it over with."

Brett chuckled in response, knowing how much I dreaded spending time with his mother. He loved her but knew how overbearing she could be. He slid an arm around my waist and pulled me against him. I allowed my head a moment of rest on his chest, inhaling his sweet scent and listening to the gentle rhythm of his breath.

"How's Liv?"

I pulled away, letting his question linger, and led him out the front door to his waiting SUV. Once in the car, I let out an exhausted sigh.

"I don't know how she is," I said as Brett drove down the driveway. "It looks like she's barely slept. She keeps crying and wondering what happened. It seems like it's killing her."

Brett grimaced but didn't take his eyes off the road. "We both know your mom harboured a lot of confusing and difficult feelings for your dad. And his sudden death is bound to affect her." He cast a sideways glance at me. "I'm more surprised it's not affecting you."

I looked out the window. It *was* affecting me. I'd been restless, paranoid, worried. I spent yesterday in a bridal shop telling Savannah about the whole thing, then spent the entire ride home on edge, feeling like I'd told her my worst secret in the world.

I didn't mourn him, no; it was something else. Maybe guilt or a strange dread I couldn't explain. Like something in my gut told me this wasn't it, it didn't end here. Mark had been too terrible; how could we get off so easily?

"It does affect me," I said softly. "But I can't understand what she's going through."

Brett didn't respond as he turned the car into his parents' driveway.

"Can we drop this for now?" I asked. "I don't want your parents asking questions."

Brett frowned. "Court, they already know. It's in the news."

I'd seen the brief report Rita had posted late last night, the details were minimal as the police hadn't shared much, but she knew about the missing ring and of course our names were present. She was still looking for 'my side of the story' as she put it in her latest voicemail. I'd since blocked her number.

"I know." Everyone in town would know about it at this point. And even if it hadn't been reported, Brett would have shared it with his parents. Or maybe Mom would have. Once, she and Missy had been very close. "I just don't want it to be the central topic."

"I'm sure it won't be."

As we climbed the steps of the old stone house, my skin prickled with unease. This had never been a house I'd felt comfortable in. It was large, stark, and cold. A house meant to display wealth and privilege, not to entertain kids. All throughout high school, visiting Brett and his sister Nia at home was always awkward. That feeling never went away.

We entered the front door and were immediately greeted by Missy, who threw her arms around my neck and pulled me against her ample bosom. Her done-up face brushed against my shoulder, likely leaving a powdery residue behind, and her recently permed curls tickled my ear.

"Oh honey, I'm so sorry." She held me so tight I struggled to breathe, and being forced to inhale her potent, mothball perfume made me dizzy.

Brett quickly pried his mother's hands off me and intervened. "Mom, it's been a lot. Can we just have a nice dinner and let everything else go?"

Missy looked between me and Brett. "But this awful thing happened. Oh, your mother must be beside herself. Poor Liv."

I bit down on my lip, willing the words that wanted to follow to stay silent. Thankfully, Brett took the lead.

"She is." Brett grabbed his mother's elbow, directing her away from the front hall and back towards the kitchen. I followed like a lost puppy, keeping my mouth shut.

"It's horrible," Brett agreed with whatever his mother had said. "But not why we're here. Just drop it."

He was laying it on harder than he had to, but I didn't intervene. His push to keep his parents silent was only for my benefit. Missy was a busy body in her late fifties. Throughout high school Brett's sister, Nia, was often pushed aside in favour of Brett. It was no surprised she'd moved out of town immediately after, though they'd since mended fences and Nia moved back, buying a house close by.

Missy was the type who would smile in my direction, give me noisy fake kisses on arrival, and coo over how gorgeous her perfect son's bride-to-be was, but then came the backhanded compliments or the way she'd mock my wedding plans and play the victim on every occasion we went against her wishes.

Kevin, Brett's dad, was different. Tall, stoic, and perpetually proud of his family. A retired police chief. And he loved me like I was his own. Brett was his father, through and through.

The table was already set, and we settled down for a home-cooked meal. My cooking was shaky at best, and Missy took almost every opportunity to remind me of that. She expected Brett's wife to be the perfect homemaker. I was far from it.

Tonight was different. My tragedy was enough to nullify Missy's condescending ways and soon I found myself enjoying the meal with Brett's parents for once, until Missy couldn't help herself.

"I still can't believe it." She nudged Kevin. "Do you remember the last time we were all together? Oh my gosh, it was ages ago. When you two were still teenagers."

I stiffened at the mention. I knew the story well. It was the last time any of our parents gathered because later that night, Alexa's mom got into the accident that ended her life. And their friendships.

"Mom," Brett protested. "Can you not?"

"What?" Missy gazed around the table with wide, innocent eyes. "I'm just remembering the last time we really spoke to Mark."

"Of course," I said, unable to hold my tongue any longer. "You never hung out again because Bronwyn Huston died, then Mark nearly beat his family to death and ended up in jail. I can't imagine why you would want to remember it."

Missy's eyes widened, but she kept her painted mouth shut.

Kevin placed a hand on Missy's arm. "We agreed that we would leave that night in the past." His voice was low and firm. "Everything that has happened, doesn't matter now."

I didn't agree with his statement. The past weighed too heavy on me to forget it, but I appreciated the sentiment.

"I *am* ready to leave it in the past," I said, my tone more level now. I fixed my gaze on Kevin, hopeful to take advantage of the opportunity.

"But a local reporter came by desperate for answers. Some woman named Rita Rounds."

Kevin hesitated, his fork halfway lifted to his mouth. The utensil slammed to the table as he lowered it. When he spoke, he spit his words, "Do not say anything to that vile woman."

I leaned away from Kevin's anger, shocked by the outburst. I glanced to Brett, who looked just as surprised.

"What happened, Dad?" Brett asked, reaching under the table and placing a hand on my knee.

"Nothing, nothing," Kevin said, his voice lowering as he seemed to correct himself. "Just some nasty business from back in the day. She used to harass the force. I'd stay away from her if I were you. She has a way of twisting words."

I frowned but nodded. "We haven't said a word. Hopefully she'll get the hint."

"I'll make a call," Kevin said. "She'll stop bothering you."

I said no more, and Kevin was quick to change the subject. "Nia is very excited about the bachelorette. Next weekend, right?"

I reached for my glass of wine and sipped it as Brett answered.

"Yeah, ten days until the big weekend." He gently nudged me. "Hopefully one to rival my own!" Brett and his groomsmen had celebrated weeks ago with a trip to Vegas. I hated every minute of it. Dean was the last person I trusted to throw a respectable party. I never got the details, but to be honest, I didn't ask.

"And you're not concerned at all," Missy began, "about how that would look?"

"Mom," Brett hissed.

"What?" Missy asked, her tone light. "I only mean that with your dad's untimely death, doesn't a party look bad?"

"No," I snapped. "No one will think twice about the fact that I'm not interested in dwelling on Mark's death. He put me in the hospital more than once."

Missy opened her mouth but clamped it shut when Kevin growled a warning, "Miss, we talked about this."

Again, I was taken aback by his cold stare at his wife—not a look I often saw on Kevin's face but one that reminded me of his service. I had no doubt he'd been a formidable police chief in his time.

"The time away will be good for both of us," Brett said firmly. "And Courtney is right. No one will think twice."

For the remainder of the meal, Missy wouldn't meet my gaze, acting like a scolded child, and I avoided conversation. Finally, the meal ended, and Brett and I prepared to leave. I almost allowed myself to believe things would be okay, that despite Mark's death, we could move forward as normal.

Until I saw the text from Alexa that I'd missed in the hours I'd been eating. And the words she'd written filled me with dread.

11

Alexa Huston

Tuesday, July 11

I lay on the couch, scrolling through my phone. I'd be waiting to hear from Dean nearly all day, expecting to spend my shift-free afternoon with him. Things had been different since Vanessa, only three short days ago. Even when I lay in his arms last night, something felt off, changed. I couldn't be sure if it was him. Or both of us. Certainly, I was.

I wished I knew Vanessa's last name or where she was from. I considered Googling her name along with missing persons but thought better than to type it into my browser.

I was about to give up on Dean and find another way to spend my free afternoon when I saw the cruiser pull up, and panic seized in my chest. The voice growled as from the window I could see Stevenson sitting in the front seat, alone. I'd answered all his questions yesterday, so why on earth would he be here now?

Thankfully, Dad was gone, where to, I had no idea, but the last thing I needed was him talking to the cops. He was barely coherent on a good day.

I glanced down at my phone, scrolling over the unanswered texts and ignored calls I'd sent to Dean this morning. He was avoiding me, though

I couldn't be sure why. Again, the feeling of dread rose up inside me. Could he have said something to the police?

The voice roared with anger, and I felt its dark desire. I had to take several deep breaths, trying to calm my rapid heartbeat. I lived in a condo complex, so for all I knew Stevenson being here was a coincidence. My gut told me differently.

The image of Vanessa appeared in my mind again, and I darted away from the window and up the stairs to my room. My sketchbook lay open on my bed, the drawing of Mark's embellished murder on display. I quickly grabbed the book, shut it, and slipped it under my mattress, hiding the truth away.

By the time I made it back downstairs, Stevenson was at my front door, knocking hard. I drew one more breath to steady myself and went to answer it.

"Can I help you?" I gave the older officer a once over. He wore his uniform well, keeping fit in his position, but the scowl on his face made him look menacing.

"Ms. Huston," Stevenson said, his voice low and formal. "I was hoping we could chat."

I held the edge of the door, keeping it open only a crack. "What's this about?"

"Can I come in?"

I glanced behind me at the mess in my condo. A full ashtray, empty bottles piled in nearly every corner. The place stank of stale beer and lingering tobacco. That last thing I wanted was Stevenson in my house.

Let him in, the voice whispered. *Let's play*.

I shook off the desire.

"Got a warrant?" I raised an eyebrow and Stevenson frowned.

"I just want to talk." He shifted from foot to foot, clearly annoyed with how I was handling the situation. But he knew I didn't have any obligation to let him in.

"Then talk." I stepped outside, pulling the door shut behind me and leaning against it.

He eyed me carefully, then looked at my front door. "Something you don't want me to see?"

I forced a laugh. "Hardly, detective, I know my rights. Now, what do you want?"

Stevenson's brow furrowed he pressed forward. "There has been some surveillance footage from the night of Mr. Faith's murder."

The voice stayed quiet, but I could feel its presence, waiting, listening.

I tried to keep my expression neutral as my stomach twisted into a thousand tiny knots. "That's great. What does that have to do with me?"

"Someone followed him," Stevenson pressed forward, ignoring my pointed question. "Cameras outside the bank picked him up stumbling down the street and a hooded figure behind him."

The low growl buzzed in my ears, and I clenched my teeth, trying to keep my micro-expressions from being noticed. I hadn't thought twice about a camera. I should have known the bank we strolled past would have picked up our movement.

"Sounds like you've found your bad guy," I said passively. "Still doesn't explain what you're doing here."

"The figure was petite," he explained. "A woman, we think."

"A scorned lover?" I joked.

"Or a scorned daughter."

I frowned at the implication, pushing myself off the door and straightening in front of the detective.

"What exactly are you implying?" I asked, wanting him to outright say what he thought.

"Nothing," he said. "I'm simply stating a fact. You're certain Courtney didn't leave at any point in the night?"

No, I wasn't certain, because I hadn't been there all night. Then again, the drugs I'd put in her system had her out cold.

"I am one hundred percent certain." I crossed my arms. "You're looking in the wrong place."

"What's the right place then, Ms. Huston?" Stevenson asked.

I rolled my eyes. "I'm pretty sure that's your job to figure out."

Stevenson kept his gaze locked on me. "And then there is still the issue of the missing ring. Who else would take such a trinket but a daughter—or a wife?"

Or the deranged, the voice cackled.

The hidden chain around my neck felt heavy in a way I couldn't describe. Why hadn't I taken it off when I hid the sketchbook?

"Someone who thought there was money to be made," I said. "Have you checked the hock shop? Facebook Marketplace? Whoever took it would probably have unloaded it quickly." The voice praised my calmness. The weight of the chain grew heavier with each lie. I tried not to cave under its pressure.

Stevenson pursed his lips at my response. "Can you tell me more about the relationship between Ms. Faith and her parents? From my understanding it has been strained for some time."

"Why don't you ask Detective Knight these questions about his fiancée?" I snapped, losing patience with the stupid cop. "I'm sure he can fill you in on all the reasons Courtney may have hated her abusive father." If he really thought Courtney had anything to do with this, no wonder our police department was so useless. They couldn't even get a proper lead straight.

"I intend to," Stevenson said.

"Great, good luck." I turned towards the door. "We're done here."

"I can't help but feel you're being a bit hostile," Stevenson said, stopping my movements.

I turned back towards him. "And why do you think that is?"

"Why don't you tell me?"

I reached up and tapped my chin. "Maybe it has something to do with the fact my best friend lost her dad in a horrible murder, and the cops on the case can't find any viable suspects except the person who is most affected by it? With, may I add, no evidence to prove it? I can't imagine why I'd be hostile to that line of questioning." The sarcasm dripped off my words and Stevenson's eyes narrowed.

"We have to explore every angle."

"Of course, you do." I shook my head. "Forgive me for wondering why you're wasting your time on a terrible lead. But good luck with it." I reached for the door and pushed it open.

"I'll be in touch," Stevenson called after me. "We will find out what happened."

I glanced back over my shoulder. "I hope you do, for Courtney and Liv's sake." Then I shut the door and leaned against it, trying to calm my rapid breathing.

Stevenson stood at my door for a moment longer before making his way back to the car. I watched as he climbed into the cruiser, then headed out of my condo complex. I didn't breathe steadily until he was out of sight.

Then I reached for my phone and texted a warning to Courtney.

The police came by asking more questions. That Stevenson has his eye fixed directly on you.

12

Courtney Faith

Thursday, July 13

I nearly didn't believe it when I read Rita's newest article in *Cedar Plains Today*. It had to be the hottest topic in town for all my networks to be pulling me towards the story as soon as I logged online. A body found on the Cody farm. Vanessa Foster, a twenty-five-year-old from Toronto. She'd been visiting over the weekend for a friend's birthday and hadn't been seen since Saturday night. A missing tourist.

I stared at her picture. She was beautiful, or so the provided picture made her look. Long, dark hair, pin straight. It was almost a side profile shot as she was looking over her shoulder and grinning at the camera; it seemed candid. The photo was credited to her Facebook account. She was pale, but not nearly as pale as me. Her complexion looked silky smooth, and I wondered who would want to hurt this woman. Someone must have really hated her to dump her body in a field to be picked at by coyotes.

"What happened?" I asked Brett who stood at the counter, filling a to-go cup. He'd been assigned to Vanessa's case when they found the body yesterday and tight-lipped ever since.

He grimaced. "You don't need to know the details."

"You've never held off before."

Brett frowned. "The coroner said blunt force trauma to the head. Enough to crack open her skull. We suspect she died sometime early Sunday morning. She'd been missing since then. Disappeared from the Cape, though no one can say for sure what time she left or with who. So far, we haven't found any security footage of her, but you know the Cape, it's always jampacked. Analysts are reviewing all the footage we could get our hands on." He spoke about her tragic death so matter of fact, though he'd always been more desensitized to the things than me. I guessed being a cop he saw more than I could imagine.

She'd died five days ago. It was too surreal.

"This isn't supposed to happen here." No one killed in Cedar Plains. Especially not tourists. They fed the town!

"It may be a dumping ground," Brett offered as some sort of encouragement.

I scoffed at him. "Hardly, if she disappeared from the Cape. That sounds like a targeted murder."

He cleared his throat. "Don't let it stress you out. This is my case, I'll get some answers."

The suggestion was callous but not wrong. The big bachelorette bash—as Alexa kept referring to it—was only another week and a half away, and after the past few days I found I was dreading it. I'd already considered cancelling, too stressed with the upcoming wedding and overwhelmed by dead bodies, but knew it would devastate my bridesmaids, and after how much work I'd put them through for the wedding, they deserved to let loose. Then there were the deposits to consider, and I hadn't even floated the idea past Alexa.

Still, my eyes rested on the computer screen between me and Brett. I couldn't stop staring into Vanessa's dark eyes. Something about this woman was familiar, but I couldn't quite understand why. Maybe it was the way her complexion reminded me of an old friend from high school, or her pin-straight, dark hair and perfect centre part made her look very Kim Kardashian circa 2012.

Before I could consider it further, Brett carefully took the laptop from me and gently pressed the screen closed.

"Hey," I said, trying to grab for the computer he kept out of reach. "I was using that." I still had emails to answer. Some about work, but one in particular to my mother's lawyer.

"No, you weren't," Brett said. "You were staring at a murder investigation, and I could see you spiralling."

"I wasn't," I protested, but the conviction in my voice wavered, and Brett raised his eyebrows. "Okay, fine, I was." It felt like all I could do lately. The pressure of Stevenson's investigation had weighed heavily on me since his impromptu visit to Alexa's. Brett claimed he subdued his persistent colleague, but it didn't stop the nervous sweat that came from his invasive questioning. The last thing I wanted was Stevenson to drum up the past and shine a light on the one thing I'd kept buried deep for years.

Then there was the reporter who wouldn't leave us alone. She'd fallen silent in the past few days, but Alexa had shared about her visit to the bar. Her insistence that we *knew* something.

I was still thrown by Kevin's reaction and Rita's resolve that Brett and his father were hiding something. Though I didn't give it too much of my time. She was obviously devious and trying to get a rise out of us.

"It's because I can't believe it," I tried, pushing away the worries that could unravel my perfectly curated life.

"What's not to believe?" Brett asked. "Terrible things sometimes happen."

But *not* in Cedar Plains. And within a week, two murders had happened back-to-back. First Mark and now Vanessa. It didn't seem like an accident.

"I'll need my computer back to answer some emails." Although I worked mostly remotely, my emails usually piled up, and I'd have to make sure I had building tours scheduled for next week.

"I thought you were taking some time off."

I'd agreed to take a few weeks off work leading up to the wedding and the week following for our honeymoon. I had yet to actually ask for the time off. I hated the idea of being away for so long, of possibly losing clients to my shark of a co-worker. His smarmy ass was itching to get his hands on some of my larger lease accounts.

"I am," I said. "But I have time." The wedding was still a few weeks away, and I wanted to at least get caught up before my extended vacation. "After next week, I promise."

Brett frowned but slid the laptop back towards me. "Okay, but enough about the dead girl. If anything happens, I'll let you know."

I nodded as he stepped to my side and planted a kiss on my temple. "I'll call you later and let you know our plan." He was heading to Toronto to meet with Vanessa's family and learn more about her.

"Love you," I said as he headed out the kitchen. His muffled response was the last thing I heard as the front door closed.

When I reopened my laptop, the article was still front and centre, and I forced myself to exit the page. Brett was right—no reason to dwell on it.

I opened my personal email first, replying to the latest from the lawyers. Mark had no will, so everything would go to Mom, not that I wanted anything that had once belonged to my father. In her absence, I organized his cremation and would allow her to do whatever she wished with his ashes. No funeral for the monster that was now gone. After this, I could finally wash my hands of him.

In my work email I found only a few unanswered and started working my way through them. An hour passed before I had cleared out the bulk, and Mom meandered into the kitchen looking exhausted despite spending most of her time in bed.

When I met her sad, tired eyes, I closed my laptop again and waved to the stool across from me. Mom took the seat, clutching tightly to a porcelain mug of coffee I could guess was cold by now.

"How are you?" I asked. Our conversation had been stilted over the past few days. She had been a mourning, moaning mess, and I'd been unable to understand her pain. When it came to Mark and my mother, I could only see the good in his death. Now, she was safe.

Mom grimaced as she sipped the coffee. "I'm fine. Ready to go home."

I'd been dreading the day she wanted to return home. It felt safer being together. Having her here meant I knew where she was all the time, that she was okay.

"Are you sure that's a good idea?" My gaze rested on the hard cast wrapped around her forearm, newly put there on Monday to replace her temporary one after the swelling went down. "Maybe you should stay a little longer, until you have both your arms back."

"Courtney, that will be weeks." Mom's eyes widened. "I may be broken but I'm not helpless. I can do things with one arm, you know." She pursed her lips. "I don't need you to protect me."

I didn't mention I'd been protecting her since Mark returned home. "I like having you here."

Her gaze softened, and she reached out with her good arm, gently patting my hand. "And I like being with you, sweetie, but I have my own house. And my own friends."

I hesitated, understanding the need for comfort, and I wondered how many of her friends had tried to reach out. Before I could answer, Mom spoke again.

"Besides, I'm not comfortable here." She glanced around. "I feel like I'm being watched."

I nearly scoffed at the implication but instead pushed myself up from the bar stool. "Understood. Do what you want, Mom."

"Courtney, that's not what I meant," she called after me, but I didn't look back.

In our bedroom, I collapsed on the bed, wishing Brett hadn't left and I had his arms for comfort. Whenever he got on a big case, the overtime hours were tough.

Mom felt I was fluttering around her like an anxious hummingbird, but what did she expect? The past few years had been nothing but hard with her, and now she was under my roof, widowed and broken. Of course, *I* was watching her.

I allowed myself only a moment of frustration before pushing myself from the bed and entering the ensuite bathroom.

I'd arranged a luncheon for the bridesmaids to thank them for all their support over the last few weeks and prepare them for the weeks ahead. It was a thank you and a bribe, combined in one. In a few hours I would have to be presentable with a delicious meal ready. I needed to push Mom and her issues from my mind.

I stared at my tired reflection, unsure where to begin. I couldn't reconcile the strange feelings inside me. Two deaths too close together. It put me on edge, like with each new crime, there was potential for my own to be unearthed. Despite the death of my abusive father, my biggest fear still hung over my head like a waiting noose, ready to strangle the truth out of me.

My five bridesmaids arrived on schedule. My maid of honour strolled in ten minutes later. When Alexa entered the kitchen, we were all gathered around the counter and together we'd started carrying the meal to my back patio. I'd invited Mom to join us, but she hadn't bothered to leave her room.

I had pulled out all my best recipes, including my famous risotto primavera. The sun was high over head and promised a beautiful day.

"Thank you all for being here." I raised a glass of champagne to my guests. "I know some of you had to make arrangements to be here, so I want you to know how much I appreciate it, along with all the work you have been doing for the bachelorette."

"You're paying us back with a wicked party," Nia called from the opposite end of the table, and the surrounding ladies whooped their agreement. I smiled at the woman who'd been my friend since we were infants. She wore her dark-brown hair in perfect curls and had little makeup applied to her heart-shaped face, looking like the cherub she'd always been compared to. I was so grateful for her steady friendship, and for her quiet companionship in my marriage to her brother. The ease we now had as future sisters-in-law wasn't always this way. When we first started dating, Nia didn't speak to me for weeks. And when Brett proposed with the family ring, I worried Nia was done with me. Thankfully, she proved me wrong.

Nia emptied the bottle of champagne into her glass then waved it. "Looks like we need another."

Alexa was on her feet and inside the house before I could speak. I grabbed the empty bottle and rounded the house to toss it into the recycling bin. I stopped when I noticed it. There in the corner of my well kempt yard, was a circle of very dead grass.

I bent down, running my fingers over the dead area, wondering how this could have happened.

"Courtney, all good?" Alexa's voice came. She found me squatting before the brown patch.

"Yeah, fine," I said, standing and tossing the bottle into the bin. "Just noticed a weird dead patch." I thought about the living room in mid renovation. "Maybe something from Brett's work. Chemicals or paint, or what not."

"You should tell him to be more careful," Alexa joked, motioning for me to follow her back to where the women sat.

I took my seat next Savannah, and Alexa sat on the opposite side.

It was the first chance I really got to look at Alexa. Her hair was piled on top of her head in a careless knot and last week's manicure was chipped away in bits, a bad habit she had when something serious was on her mind.

"Are you okay?" I asked, keeping my voice low and trying not to draw the attention of the chattering bridesmaids.

Alexa waved off my comment. "It's nothing. I'm just ... distracted."

I forced out an uneasy laugh. "A distracted maid of honour. Just what every bride needs."

"That's why you have all of us," Savannah chimed in. I could always count on her sunny attitude.

Alexa pursed her lips. "Did you see the news about the body?"

I glanced down the table as she said it, suddenly all eyes were on us. Savannah's smile faded.

"I did," I said slowly, making sure to meet the eyes of every woman around me. "It's so tragic. But it's all a horrible and rare occurrence. This is Cedar Plains. It's safe here."

Alexa's eyebrows furrowed, and she tilted her head to the side in a way a dog would, trying to understand its master's gibberish. "You really think so?"

"I think Cedar Plains is safe," I said firmly.

"I hope you're right," she said in a low voice. "Or else what would become of Cedar Plains?"

"We're safe," Savannah insisted, jumping to my defense. "Besides no matter where we live, monsters are always hiding in the shadows, aren't they, Alexa?"

Alexa glared at Savannah, but it lasted only a moment, and the tension disappeared as Savannah shifted her gaze to me.

"Just because this has happened close by, doesn't mean it will happen to us."

I didn't respond, instead dropping my gaze to the table between us. In a way it had already happened to me. Savannah was right, bad things did happen, and I couldn't help but admire Savannah for seeing the good despite the things she'd been through.

Alexa gazed at Savannah for a moment. "Hopefully those monsters stay in the dark." The two kept their eyes locked for a moment longer than I expected, so I jumped in hoping to ease the tension.

"They will," I said firmly, but even as I did, that creeping suspicion I was wrong came back in full force.

13

Alexa Huston

Friday, July 14

The loud music thumped as my head swam from the mixture of booze, weed, and coke. I lay, sprawled on the leather sofa, my legs across Dean in the living room of his friend's house. Someone he'd known since high school. I didn't bother to remember the guy's name, as we'd only come to this house twice before on the rare occasion he had a party and Dean knew he could score some customers. The place was packed. Dean's fingers gently stroked my bare legs as people around us danced, snorted lines, or hooked up in the dark corners.

"Come here," Dean begged, his voice muffled by the heavy house beats. He pulled on my arm, forcing me against him, his lips finding mine. When he pulled away, his mouth trailed across my cheek to my ear. "Wanna play?" he whispered as his fingers threaded through my hair, tugging my head back so he could look me in the eyes.

The voice inside growled with frustration, and I was beginning to understand why. Days had passed since Mark's death. There was a desire inside me willing itself to be fed. I pushed away the feeling and kissed Dean again, trying to silence it.

When we parted, his gaze was dark, glinting in the low light, the lust clear in them. I stared back silent, waiting for him to tell me what he wanted. His eyes darted from mine as he loosened his grip on my hair, dropping his hands to my arms.

I'd been unable to get Savannah's implication the previous day out of my mind. The way she gazed at me like she knew I hid something deep inside. Did she know the truth that Courtney and I hid from her, or did she suspect something more sinister about me? I had to keep reminding myself there was no way that Savannah knew either truth.

Dean gave my arm a squeeze, and I forced myself to focus on him, following his gaze as he scanned the crowd. Maybe a plaything would be a good distraction, though even as I thought it, I didn't feel the same excitement I used to.

Through the throngs of people, Kaylee stood across the room, leaning against the wall, her small hands wrapped around two beer bottles. The way her hips swayed and her eyes were half closed it was clear she was as fucked up as the rest of us.

"We can do better than that little hoe." Dean's rough voice grated in my ear. My eyes darted back to him, and I saw he too watched Kaylee.

"She's my friend," I said. "We can't do that."

Dean held my gaze, and it was clear he didn't agree. To him, anyone was fair game.

"I didn't think you two were friends," Dean said, turning away from me. His hold on me loosened, and a clear coolness grew between us. His fuse had flipped in a matter of seconds.

The voice bristled with irritation. I pushed myself off the couch. "I need air." I didn't wait for Dean to answer me as I made my way through the crowded room to the deck out back.

The warm summer evening and quiet outdoor space provided an immediate release. The darkness found joy in the nighttime air. Outside, I could still hear the muffled thumping coming from the house. The deck held a few partygoers, smoking cigarettes or weed. As I walked to the steps, I glanced around, noting I didn't recognize any of them. I lowered myself to the bottom step, looking out into the grassy backyard, though it was too dark to see much beyond a few metres ahead of me.

I stared into the inky blackness of the yard, and the voice found calm where for days it had been anxious. I knew what it wanted, but I couldn't reconcile the feeling. Mark's death had been just. Vanessa's a beautiful, innocent loss. I wasn't sure I could live with the death of another innocent. If I had to feed the darkness, I had to find a worthy kill.

I thought back to yesterday afternoon, seeing the dead patch of grass in Courtney's yard. I hadn't thought twice about dumping the bleach, thinking I had gotten away cleanly, now only days later for my mistake to surface. I hoped she wouldn't think about it again, though knowing Courtney, she'd drill Brett for answers. The bottle of bleach in their laundry room was significantly emptier now, so it might only take them going to use it to realize something wasn't right.

And then there was the issue of Savannah ...

Expendable, the voice whispered. *And dangerous.*

"Lex?" Dean called, pulling me from the darkness's hold. His footsteps sounded as he crossed the deck.

"Down here," I said.

Dean descended the steps and lowered himself next to me. "What was that?"

"What do you mean?"

"You stormed off in front of my friends." His voice was hard.

The darkness growled.

"I was dizzy," I said, when really, annoyed.

He narrowed his eyes but didn't speak.

"I'm not feeling great," I said.

"I bet you're not," Dean snapped.

I frowned, unsure what he meant.

"Brett told me you'd been questioned by the cops," he said. "And that reporter."

"Why would he tell you that?" The last thing I needed was paranoid Dean to think Stevenson had been by the house to ask about Vanessa. And that Rita woman had only tried to be in touch with me one more time since, and I'd hung up on her. Though if he made the connection between Rita and the article about Vanessa yesterday, then I guessed I could understand his concerns. I'd like to pin the whole thing on him if only to remove this unending tension between us.

"Because you're my girlfriend and apparently he's the only one who thinks I deserve to know." He turned his glare on me. "I gave you all night to tell me about it."

"So, this was a test?" I asked, but Dean's glare didn't falter. I sighed. "I didn't think it mattered." It was about Courtney's dad, not Vanessa.

Dean's hands clenched into fists. "What did you tell them? What did they want to know?"

"Is now really the time to discuss this?" I lowered my voice, unsure if anyone who still lingered on the deck could hear us.

"Tell me," Dean demanded through gritted teeth.

I glanced from Dean's hard expression to his clenched fists and put my hands up in defense. Keeping my voice quiet, I said, "They were asking about Courtney's dad. It was days ago. Totally unrelated to finding ... the second body." I wanted to speak her name but thought better of it.

He didn't answer right away. Soon, his hands relaxed, and his face softened, though I still wouldn't call the expression friendly.

"Good," he finally said. Then he shifted and stood. "I'd hate to have to turn the story on you somehow."

An itch started in my palms as the darkness voiced its displeasure and desire. I bit back the fury that wanted to surface. He'd threatened me more than once now. No one would believe my story over his. Dean's dad had gotten him out of trouble in the past. Their money buried everything.

"Let's get back in there." He offered his hand. "I'm still up for it tonight, if you are."

I looked at his hand for a moment, then stood without taking it. "Not tonight. I'm going home."

Dean's chest puffed out, his anger evident, and instead of saying anything, he dropped his hand, then turned and stormed back towards the house. The sliding door opened, then closed behind him. I stood alone outside.

I hesitated, wondering if I should go back through the house, then turned to the yard and left through the back gate.

14

Courtney Faith

Saturday, July 15

Unease twisted through me when I opened the front door and saw Stevenson standing on my porch. He was dressed in uniform, holding his hat in his hands.

"Good day, Ms. Faith." He bowed his head. "May I come in?"

"Why?" I asked. "Do you have an update on Mark?"

Stevenson eyed me expectantly, and I stepped aside, inviting him in and to our kitchen.

"Can I get you water?" I asked out of politeness.

Stevenson shook his head. "This will be quick." He took one of the barstools and waited until I did the same. I tried not to squirm under his gaze. Brett was out and my mom was upstairs likely asleep. Part of me wished she would come downstairs, or Brett would be home soon to put an end to this invasive visit. Though he was on his way back from the city, I couldn't be certain when he'd arrive.

"How can I help?" I asked, trying to keep my voice level but my rapid heartbeat was nearly deafening.

"I understand your mother suffered a lot at the hands of your father," Stevenson said slowly. "He went to jail for ten years for assaulting you, correct?"

My mouth went dry at the thought of reliving our abusive past. "Yes." I forced the words out. "My mom took the worst of it."

Stevenson's expression remained impassive. "And when he got out, she let him move back in."

"She did," I said. "She had hoped he changed."

"But he didn't," Stevenson said.

"No, he didn't."

"That must have made you angry," Stevenson said. "I see you've been into the hospital with her a few times. From the reports it sounds like she could be pretty clumsy." He paused, searching my eyes. "Why wasn't anything ever reported?"

I gritted my teeth. "Because she refused to report him."

"Wow," Stevenson said, reaching up and scratching at the stubble on his chin. "I can only imagine how you would feel."

"What exactly are you getting at?" I asked.

"Tragedy seems to follow you and your friends," Stevenson suggested. "Your father and your history, that friend of yours, Ms. Savannah Torres, and her hit and run, then, of course, Ms. Huston and her mom's mysterious accident."

"What mysterious accident?" Bronwyn Huston had died in a car crash—it had been pretty cut and dry, according to Kevin who'd been the officer first on the scene.

Stevenson tilted his head to the side. "Let's just say the file is weak. Almost like someone swept the real truth under the rug."

I opened my mouth to protest. To tell him he was wrong. We'd all heard the story about Bronwyn and her tragic death. How could such a truth be kept hidden from us? Before I could ask, I heard the front door open.

"Hey, Court?" Brett called, moving towards the kitchen.

Stevenson stood, his posture less cocky and stiffer than it had been in the previous moments.

When Brett appeared in the doorway, he frowned at his fellow officer. He was out of uniform and looked exhausted. I imagined the two nights he spent in Toronto hadn't been the most restful.

"Stevenson." His voice was hard. "What are you doing here?" He glanced between me and his colleague.

"He was questioning me about Mark," I said quickly, hopping off the stool. "Back to imply Mom or I had something to do with it."

"I did no such thing," Stevenson said firmly.

Brett kept his glare on Stevenson and stepped aside, indicating he should leave.

Stevenson straightened his jacket, reached for his hat, then headed back the way we'd come only moments before.

"I'd appreciate you speaking with me before you interrogate my family with baseless accusations." Brett's voice followed Stevenson out of the house.

I waited in the kitchen, knowing he'd return after seeing the officer out. If Stevenson answered, I didn't hear what he said, and soon the door slammed, and Brett was back in the kitchen.

"Are you okay?" he asked, eyeing me with concern.

I nodded but couldn't stop the frown. What the hell did Stevenson mean by tragedy followed me? That I somehow had an influence on all these terrible events happening around me?

"Courtney?" Brett asked.

"Do you know anything about Bronwyn Huston's accident being a lie?" I blurted before I could stop myself, knowing I should ask him about Toronto and his time away instead.

Brett's brow furrowed, and he shook his head. The fatal accident occurred years before he joined the force, though at the time his dad was the chief. "Did Stevenson say something about it?"

"He seemed to imply something. But that's impossible. Your dad was lead on the case. First on the scene."

"Then it sounds like this guy is just blowing smoke. Trying to get a rise out of you." He clenched his jaw, his irritation at this colleague clear.

His words didn't sooth me. How could I be sure what Stevenson had said was true? Part of me wanted to rush over the Brett's parents' house and ask Kevin straight up. But I shook the thought out of my head. Clearly Stevenson was trying to bait me into telling them something I didn't want to share. Why else would he bring up Savannah?

I watched Brett retreat, phone in hand, as he mumbled something about putting an end to the harassment. I wanted to trust him, to believe that Stevenson was just throwing stones and hoping that one would land, but his insistence felt off. Why bring up something that was so easy to prove false?

Worse, I didn't want to bring Alexa into this. The death of her mother had been awful then. She'd been haunted after the fact, certain Bronwyn had been brutally murdered. It took months of therapy to silence the false nightmares, and the last thing I wanted to do was remind her of them.

15

Alexa Huston

Monday, July 17

When I woke up on Monday morning, I found another note tacked to my front door. The same plain envelope with my first name scrawled across it. This time the note was only a fraction longer. *I watched you do it.* I now lay in my bed with the ominous words in front of me. Watched me do what? With too many secrets, it was hard to know which one this note intended to threaten.

I dwelled on it for some time, until the dryness in my throat became too much to bear. Like a thirst I couldn't quench. A strange itch deep inside me was reminiscent of the cravings I used to have when I was desperate for a bump. Now, the thoughts of cocaine couldn't be further from my mind.

I'd spent the weekend trying to silence the voices in my head with too much alcohol and weed and was beginning to worry I was turning into my father. Still, the itch wouldn't subside and with the height of the summer in Cedar Plains, the heat stifled.

Now this from my mysterious messenger brought the feelings back in full force.

I hadn't heard from Dean since I left the party on Friday and didn't bother to message him beyond the single text I sent on Saturday morning. It was weird, having a Saturday off from the bar, and though I'd expected to spend it with my boyfriend, his lack of response didn't bother me. I was over our lifestyle. I didn't want to do the drugs anymore. I didn't want to play our games. I didn't even think I wanted to do him. Maybe I'd officially outgrown our relationship. Maybe something else was more intriguing now.

Dean and I had been hot and heavy when it started six months ago. He'd come back to town after a few years in Toronto. Rumour had it his dad made him move back here to curb his partying habits. I bet his dad had no idea how little moving to Cedar Plains had changed things.

A few months after he returned, I ran into Dean when a couple of the ladies from work went out in the Cape. We'd been drinking, and Dean asked if we wanted to party—a given for a group like us.

That's how the love affair began. Wild parties and kinky sex. Dean took a liking to me, and I took a liking to the attention, the sex, the drugs, and the distraction. The company was better than what I had at home. With Courtney planning her wedding and working on her house, I barely got a word in. Dean's attention gave me purpose, a freedom from everything out of my control.

In reality, I knew what solidified us as a couple. That awful day in March I didn't like to remember. The anniversary of Mom's death. Dad was on one of his usual benders, blabbering on about guilt and missing Mom or Phoebe. I wasn't sure which one he missed more. He spoke briefly about an accident, though in his state it wasn't clear if he meant the one that killed Mom, or the one that had broken him.

I found myself unwilling to stay with him in his depression, though I'd accepted Phoebe into our lives for Dad's sake, I never got over the fact she'd once been my mom's best friend. Plus, the months of therapy that followed her sudden death had given me my own coping mechanism. When the nightmares became too much, I had to remind myself they weren't real. They never were.

I quickly found my way to Dean's that day. It was the first time our relationship hadn't been about sex or partying. I'd been his girlfriend for nearly two months, but it was the first time he'd really comforted me and showed me he cared. It was easy to fall into a routine with him after, get comfortable in his lifestyle, even if his parents thought I was trash. We weren't conventional. Dean would disappear sometimes, ignore my calls and texts, but when we were together, it was easy, and fun. Plus, he'd been there for me when I needed him most.

Now, that feeling had vanished, and I didn't want the distraction anymore. I didn't owe him anything. The drugs didn't call to me. Something else did. And that something was hungry.

When I arrived at the bar that night for my shift, I was surprised to find Ashley working.

"Hey," I said. "Didn't know you were on today."

"I wasn't supposed to be," Ashley said. "I got a text from Kaylee begging me to cover."

"Is everything okay?"

"Who knows? She hasn't been around all weekend." Ashley rounded the bar, tossing the rag she'd been using to wipe up the spills on the counter. "You're good if I head out?"

"Yeah, of course," I said. "I can handle a crazy Monday."

Ashley flashed me a smile, then proceeded to gather her things and clock out. Soon I was alone in the bar, save for the two guys hiding in the kitchen. I glanced at the clock. Barely 6:00 p.m. It was going to be a long shift.

Where was Kaylee? It wasn't like her to dodge her shifts. I thought back to seeing her Friday night, clearly messed up and on a bender. Maybe she'd spent the weekend in a drug-induced cloud. If she did, I couldn't blame her. She was young and deserved a little bit of fun and irresponsibility.

I pulled out my phone, still surprised I hadn't heard from Dean. Maybe he was as out of our relationship as I was.

When midnight rolled around and the bar was dead, I decided to close early and see if I could talk to Dean. We should at least end things amicably since we would be in the same wedding in a few weeks. For Courtney's sake, if anything.

Dean's house was dark on the main floor when I arrived, so I used my key to let myself in. From the downstairs I could hear the commotion coming from the floor above. Loud music, a heavy *thump thump thump* reverberating through the house. Gripping the banister, I made the slow climb towards his bedroom. As I got closer, voices joined the sounds of the loud rock tunes. A female voice. I had the sudden urge to not be caught. To pretend I wasn't there, but my curiosity got the best of me, so I crept closer, careful to plant my feet quietly to avoid any unwanted attention.

The door to Dean's main bedroom was cracked open, and light spilled across the hall towards me. I didn't need to get any closer as someone passed by the door, bathed in light, swinging an empty bottle of rye over her head. Kaylee, dressed in nothing but a black lace bra and thong. The dark fabric cupped her petit breasts and hugged her narrow hips. Her milky skin looked nearly translucent in Dean's harsh lighting. She didn't seem to notice me. Her eyes were closed as she danced, lips mouthing the words to the familiar lyrics. While I'd heard the song before, my clouded mind wouldn't let me place it. Instead, I could only watch.

"That's empty." Dean's gruff voice pulled me from my trance of watching Kaylee's body sway. "I'll get another one."

My throat constricted, knowing he'd either have to seek liquor from the kitchen downstairs or the sex playroom across the hall. Without another thought I scampered back down the hallway and the stairs, finding myself outside in seconds.

Watch, the voice whispered, its desires mirroring my own. I wanted to. I didn't want to have to ask Dean about it tomorrow. I wanted to see it all for myself and know exactly what he was doing behind my back.

I glanced around me quickly and crept further into his yard. Dean had an older house in town. Most of these builds were over a hundred years old with expansive backyards and often modern renovations; keep it old and historic on the outside and modernize the crap out of the interior. It was the way of the Cedar Plains rich. I hated to admit Courtney was one of them with her nearly completed renovations on her classic house.

Like many of the older properties, Dean's backyard featured a large sweeping maple tree which cast a heavy shadow across the backside of the brick house. An old treehouse perched in it, left here by the previous owners. I'd been up it only a couple of times, knowing the aged structure was precarious at best.

I glanced up at Dean's bedroom window, brightly lit and swung open. Faint music could be heard from below. The voice growled and before I was totally aware of what I was doing, I grabbed the lowest rung on the treehouse ladder and hoisted myself up. I continued the ascent, remembering the first time I'd climbed to the ancient treehouse above. Dean and I had decided to do shrooms in the middle of the day. I was desperate to see the view from up high. Dean urged me to stop, but I couldn't hear him over the rush of the cold wind and my desire to reach the top. I realized my mistake when my hand slipped on a wet crosspiece, sending me plummeting four feet. I was lucky I only got that high.

I'd since climbed to the treehouse sober, with Dean joking how easily I could stalk him from up there. I hadn't really considered my view until tonight. Until I wanted something from him.

The darkness preened with pleasure. I listened to the quiet joy of the voice, allowing myself to push my worries about the structural integrity of the place out of my mind. I *had* to know what was happening.

Thankfully, the small window in the treehouse offered a prime angle to watch unnoticed from within the branches. The thought I was about to watch my boyfriend cheat on me with someone I thought was a friend wasn't lost on me. Another person proving how easy I was to leave behind or toss aside. But even as I thought it, I was aware I didn't even care about Dean anymore. Like a bad car crash, I couldn't look away. I wanted to see it happen.

I won't leave you, the voice whispered, and a warmth filled my body.

From my perch, I watched as Dean re-entered the room with another bottle in his hand. Instead of offering the bottle to Kaylee, he sauntered across the room to the crystal bar set he had in the corner. The one I always told him was so pretentious. He poured two glasses of amber liquid, then glanced behind him as he spoke. Kaylee entered the view coming from the direction of the bathroom.

My throat went dry as Dean passed Kaylee the drink. She grinned and prodded his arms, desire in her eyes. He smirked down at her, a look I knew all too well, and his eyes devoured her desperately as she sipped the drink she'd been given.

Dean turned and started fiddling with the plate on his dresser, using a card to form lines, another action all too familiar for me. A few lines for him, a couple for her.

A part of me wondered if I should try and stop them. If it would be worth it to try and fix this mess. Dean and I had been a good couple once, before everything happened with Vanessa, right? Maybe I was fooling myself. The darkness disapproved of my interference.

Still, I grabbed my phone and dialed Kaylee's number, listening as the phone rang. Then I watched as she reached for her phone, her face twisted, and she thrust the phone in Dean's direction. A simple shake of his head was enough for her to discard it. I lowered my own phone, trying to create saliva in my desert-dry mouth. Nothing I could say to her would pull her out of this scenario. She wanted to be here. Neither of them really cared about me.

Alone, the voice whispered, reminding me of my solitude. *So alone.*

Kaylee's head dipped down and she took a long line into her nose then she threw her head back with a wicked grin. Dean thrust the glass back into her hand, coaxing her into having another sip, which she did while her hips wiggled and her long brown hair swayed from side to side, brushing her lower back as she moved to the music.

He stood behind her, his hands on her hips, lips dipping down to kiss her collarbone. Her eyes remain closed, a gentle smile played on her face as her hips continued to rock back and forth to the beat.

His hands slid up her back and his fingers sipped under the lace bra, tugging at the hooks. He kissed her shoulder as the straps slipped down, one by one, and soon her bra was on the ground. His hands cupped her breasts, thumbs running across her nipples.

I squirmed as warmth spread through my abdomen. This was an act I knew well; a game I've been involved in several times.

Kaylee's lips parted, and I imagined a moan came out as she arched her back towards Dean, her round butt sticking into his groin, urging him to touch her more.

He didn't hesitate. His hands slid down her arms, then rested at her hips, plucking at the thin string holding her thong in place. His fingers hooked the fabric, and soon the scant piece of lingerie was tossed aside.

I leaned forward, taking in Kaylee's nude body. Dean slid his hand up her back, feeling every inch of her. How many times had they done this? Dean's voice in my ear from Friday reminded me he thought we could do better than Kaylee. Had he been doing her all along?

Kaylee stumbled, catching herself on the dresser in front of her. Her lips curled like she giggled, and she stumbled again.

Dean grinned, wrapping his arms around her and bringing her to his king-sized bed. She lay down willingly, tossing her head from side to side, and Dean stood back, drinking in her perfect body, flawless features. The body of a twenty-two-year-old in her prime.

I held my breath as longing filled my chest. She was exactly like every plaything we'd brought home before. Only this time, it someone I thought was a friend—and I wasn't invited.

He watched her for a moment longer before slowly discarding his clothes. It only just occurred to me while she had been naked, he had still been dressed. I hadn't even noticed. I'd been too focused on her.

Dean gently stroked himself, enjoying his own excitement as he often did, and slid a hand up her leg, dipping a finger inside of her. Kaylee moaned, tossing her head from side to side. He pulled away from her and his hands curled around her neck, squeezing until Kaylee reached up and clawed at his hold.

I told myself to climb down, to look away. To try and stop him, but I was paralyzed. I could only watch as he flipped her on to her stomach and put his weight on Kaylee's back, forcing her legs wide and burying himself inside her. He gripped her wrists, arching her back, and lifting her stomach off the bed in some sick yoga position, thrusting wildly from behind, like she was nothing more than a sex doll.

When he finished, he shuddered and rolled off her. He threw a blanket over her abused body, laced with drugs and alcohol, covered in cum and completely useless to him any longer, and strode into the bathroom. I didn't wait for him to return before making my descent down the tree, the voice growling the entire way.

I shook, trying to grip the ladder rungs tightly and keep myself from falling. When I hit the ground, the reaction was almost immediate. I buckled against the tree trunk.

I couldn't properly describe what I was feeling. I'd been wet with excitement watching Kaylee's clothes come off, watching Dean enjoy her, but within a moment the feeling changed into something sick, carnal. I no longer wanted to touch and taste Kaylee, but I wanted to stop it. To destroy Dean. *End him*, the voice cooed.

Back in my car, I headed to my condo still feeling twisted and confused. Was I into Kaylee or feeling protective? Was I angry she'd slept with my boyfriend, or too excited about her to care? I couldn't deny her body had turned me on. The idea of watching Dean and her together was too good to pass up. My own little porno, but the way Dean used her like she was nothing more than a toy made the anger boil up inside me again. Was that how he saw me? Considering how little he cared about me when I didn't want to play our usual games, it seemed true. A sick feeling welled up inside me again. How had I been so stupid?

Poor naïve, Alexa, the voice mocked. *Savour the anger,* it advised. I shook my head to clear the thoughts. I had only one desire pulsing through me now. I climbed the stairs to my bedroom and pulled out my sketchbook, my pencil began scratching out thick lines, tracing in the way I remembered Kaylee's body. The gentle curve of her perky breasts and firm buttocks, the way her long hair cascaded in ripples down her back. Then behind this perfect being, I drew a darkness, a beast emerging from the unknown, tiptoeing towards her, menacing. The figure that was Kaylee had her back to the beast, unaware of his approach.

When I finished the piece, sweat had formed in droplets on my brow line, and I gazed over the photo one time before ripping it out of my booklet, scrunching it up and tossing it towards the trash can.

The voice cackled with glee. There was a monster hiding in the darkness, and I wanted to snuff him out.

16

Courtney Faith

Wednesday, July 19

I barely slept as the days passed. When I did, I was plagued with nightmares of corrupt cops, mysterious accidents, and secrets never told. I woke up in a cool sweat, gasping for air. Beside me, Brett slept fitfully as he often did when he worked a new case. His coming and goings at all hours kept him woefully unaware of my fears or the implications. The few times I woke, his soft features, gentle snore, and mused hair gave only momentary peace to my worries.

The police had yet to find a lead in Mark's murder, and with the body of Vanessa now under investigation, I couldn't help but think about them. I'd done as Brett asked over the last few days and hadn't read the news, but often I thought about looking Vanessa up and trying to find out more about the mysterious tourist killed in our town. Brett had continued to keep his findings to himself, though he was barely around to ask about it.

Mom had been increasingly anxious in the days that followed Mark's death and, although she'd wished to go home, she had yet to make the move. As if a part of her wanted to stay. Still, with the bachelorette only a couple days away, I wondered what a weekend without me would be like for Brett and Mom. We'd all been through a lot.

Later that day, I went in search of Mom. I hoped I could catch her in a good mood and chat about my upcoming bachelorette. I had yet to ask her about what Stevenson said when he interrogated me, and I wasn't entirely sure why I'd waited. A conversation with Mom could make it clear Stevenson was lying about Bronwyn's accident and trying to get a rise out of me. Or worse, it could confirm it was true. Maybe that was why I'd been avoiding it.

When I found Mom, she was on the window seat in the living room, staring out the large window. The twisted expression on her face filled me with dread.

"Everything okay?" I asked, cautiously stepping closer to her.

She glanced up at me with wild eyes. "Fine," she said. "You never told me what the officer wanted. Did he have any news about your dad?"

I sat next to her. "No, he was asking a lot of the same questions. Though he did say one thing kind of weird."

Mom tilted her head. "What did he say?"

"He said Bronwyn Huston's car accident was likely a lie," I said. "That it seems like someone staged it, but you've always said it was bad weather, an unfortunate accident. You were there, right?"

Mom's face fell. "That awful night is not something we talk about. Bronwyn made a deadly mistake driving home after she'd had a few glasses of wine and during a snowstorm. Phoebe and Danny were never the same after it. None of us were."

"What do you remember?" I pressed, trying not to think about how poor of a choice getting behind the wheel after drinking was.

Mom pushed herself from the seat. “I said I don’t like to talk about it, Courtney. Why can’t you leave the past in the past?”

“Why would Stevenson bring it up?” I asked, following her steps from the living room. “It doesn’t seem like it will stay in the past. Did you lie to us?”

Mom turned back and regarded me, her expression cold. “What happened was nothing short of tragic. It was a terrible accident. Rehashing it now won’t change anything. We all regret letting her leave.” She stormed up the stairs, not giving me a chance to ask her anything further. I considered going after her but wasn’t up for another fight.

Instead, I grabbed my phone, hopeful to hear Brett’s voice if only for a moment.

The call rang through, and I thought it might go to voicemail until his soothing voice came through.

“Hey babe,” Brett said, obviously seeing my name on his screen before answering. “Everything okay?”

“Of course,” I said, but my voice came out too high, too unnatural.

When he spoke again his voice had lowered. “What’s wrong?”

“Nothing!”

He didn’t answer immediately, and I continued, “Just Mom spewing off her worries.” I didn’t know what to say about Bronwyn and her supposed accident. Mom hadn’t given me much to go on. Only more doubt.

“What’s up with Liv?” Brett asked, and I wondered if he was too busy to placate my worries.

“I’m not sure.” I chewed on my lower lip.

Brett was silent for a moment. “She’s been under a lot of stress. And grief. I think we’re all just looking for answers.”

"Yeah." I kept the creeping feeling inside me that said otherwise to myself.

"Is it about this weekend?" Brett asked after another moment of quiet between us.

"No." I'd considered cancelling the bachelorette more than once. But with Stevenson's invasive questions and Mom's clear unease, Brett encouraged me instead of deterring me, perhaps as aware as I was that I needed the weekend as a distraction. "Besides, we can't really cancel." Except we could. Alexa hadn't been worried when I brought it up once, insisting we sic Brett's lawyer sister—Nia—on the rental for the refund despite the date of cancellation already long past.

"You shouldn't cancel," Brett insisted. "Even if you could."

A weekend in paradise with a wine tour and my best girlfriends was probably what I needed right now.

"I'm worried about you," he said when I didn't answer.

"I'm okay," I whispered, though the words rang false. I hadn't felt okay in over a week, since even before Mark turned up dead. "I'm sorry, I shouldn't have bothered you at work." I could imagine him sitting in his car with his partner pretending to ignore him while I spewed off stupid worries.

"It's fine," he said. "I'm always here for you."

"I'm more worried about Mom," I said.

"Nah, don't. She'll be okay while you're gone," he reassured me.

"You'll call me if anything goes wrong? I'm only a few hours away."

"Of course," he said.

I closed my eyes for a moment. "I love you."

"I love you too." He ended the call, and I smiled, thanking god this man was soon to be my husband, and remembering why—despite

Stevenson's implications and the chaos clouding my mind—things had to stay exactly the way they were.

17

Alexa Huston

Friday, July 21

Brett and Courtney were waiting out front of their large house as I pulled into the driveway. Courtney's flaming-red hair was pulled back from her face, and around her sat too many suitcases for a weekend away. Classic Courtney, the over-packer. I glanced over my shoulder at my measly duffle bag, wondering if I should have brought more.

Once her many bags were loaded into the trunk of my sedan and they'd said their goodbyes, Brett waved from the front stoop. "Have fun and don't worry about Dean. I'll keep an eye on him."

"Pretty sure we both know that's not possible." I tried to keep my tone light. I hadn't seen Dean all week, spending the days dodging his calls and ignoring his messages. I'd taken more than one extra shift throughout the week, always finding an excuse and now with the weekend away, I was thankful I wouldn't have to confront the monster that lay beneath for a few more days at least. I still wasn't sure what to do about the whole Dean-and-Kaylee scene. Though the voice whispered otherwise.

We took the backroads out of Cedar Plains towards the waiting cottage. Courtney's clear excitement pushed the worry away. This weekend would be like old times with my bestie, an easy comfort we hadn't had in a while.

Still, I couldn't resist asking her one last time, "You sure everything is okay for this weekend?"

"For the final time, yes," Courtney said. "I want to have fun this weekend and god knows if I canceled my bachelorette, it would be another thing for Missy to comment on."

"Wasn't she hassling you for not canceling?"

"You know I can't win with that woman," Courtney said, though her tone was light.

I snorted with laughter. "And everyone thought the father of the bride was the scary one, no one ever talks about the mother of the groom."

The voice cackled at the thought of Mark, but I regretted the words as soon as they left my mouth. How careless could I be to bring up Mark so casually? Courtney turned away from me and I quickly apologized.

"I'm sorry, Court, I wasn't thinking. No more dad talk from here on out."

"From either of us," she agreed.

We were the first to arrive since I booked the cottage, which gave Court and me a moment to ourselves. We chose the biggest room with the ensuite bathroom and quickly poured our first drink. Courtney's famous but way-too-sweet paradise sangria.

"Cheers to you," I said. "And to your big weekend." One I hoped would prove to be a good distraction from all the mess I'd made back in our hometown. For me and for Courtney. I'd been doing my best to keep the worries from the forefront of my mind, but every time I heard a siren, I jumped. The police were circling. Reporters were circling. And then there was my unknown messenger whose intentions had yet to be made clear.

Courtney knocked her glass against mine. "And to you for putting it together for us."

"I hope it's what you want." I glanced at my phone as a message from Dean popped up on the screen. I flipped my phone over and ignored it, turning my attention back to Courtney.

She'd stood and started pacing the large bedroom, sipping her sangria between steps. "Honestly, I needed to get away."

"From Brett?"

Courtney paused her pacing and shot me a tired smile. "Of course not."

Still, I couldn't stop my hackles from rising at the thought. "I had to ask."

Courtney laughed. "Brett has been a saint. He's the only thing that makes sense in my life. Except for you and the girls, of course."

If only she knew the truth, then I probably wouldn't make the cut. The darkness agreed."What does he think of everything going on?" I asked. Brett's in at the police department hadn't kept the nosy Stevenson off our back.

"He's as confused as we are," Courtney said.

"But he can't stop the cops from questioning us." It came out harsher than I intended, and Courtney's smile faded.

"Look, I know Brett hasn't always been your favourite person," she said slowly. "God, I can't forget you throwing him out of my house that summer after first year university. I swear I thought he was going to dump me on the spot."

"He deserved it," I said, still standing by my decision to make him leave that party. I'd seen him with another girl who'd gone to our high school, getting way too close. Courtney insisted I overreacted. I had, I knew that now, understanding that my anger at the time was less about Brett and the girl and more about the fact that since Courtney had returned from university for the summer, I'd barely seen her. She spent all her time with Brett. I'd hoped to cause a bit of a rift between them. I'd wanted my best friend back. Obviously, it didn't work.

"He didn't, and you know it," Courtney said pointedly. "But I can't fault you for being overprotective."

I sipped my sangria, keeping my thoughts to myself. I still didn't fully trust him despite how our relationship had changed. Sometimes I wondered what Brett had been doing with that girl, or if he'd tried something with someone else behind Courtney's back. As I glanced at my best friend, I doubted my worries. Courtney wouldn't be naïve enough to let Brett get away with it. She demanded perfection from those around her. She'd curated a picture-perfect life in the years following university. Brett would be a fool to try and ruin that.

And part of me knew he loved her too much to do so. I guessed I couldn't fault him for something that happened nearly ten years ago, but I'd never forgive him for stealing Courtney away from me.

In my silence, Courtney resumed her pacing, the worry still etched on her face. "It's not Brett. It's everything. I've been feeling off, like ever since they found that girl's body, it's felt like I'm being watched." She met my gaze. "I know I'm being stupid."

The mention of Vanessa sent my insides turning and the darkness grinning. It had been nearly two weeks since I'd killed Mark and I felt suffocated, desperate. The voice wanted to do it again.

I forced a cautious smile on my lips. "You're not being stupid. I think it's natural to feel disoriented after everything you've been through."

"Maybe." She shook her head. "And then there's Mom. She's getting more withdrawn by the day."

"Your mom is grieving. That messes with people."

Courtney placed her glass on the dresser and wrapped her arms around herself. "I'm happy to be away from it all at least for a few days."

"Me too."

"There's more," Courtney said, pulling me from my scrambled thoughts. She gulped her sangria then plopped on to the bed next to me.

I frowned, "What do you mean *more*?"

"Stevenson," Courtney moaned.

I jumped to my feet, fetching the pitcher of sangria and refilling her glass. Immediately, I was annoyed by Brett's inability to rein in his coworker. "What about that nosy pig?"

Courtney grimaced at the choice of nickname but didn't comment on it. "He came by my house last weekend."

"Why didn't you say anything?" I'd seen Courtney only once this week, but we'd texted consistently. Why wouldn't she mention our favourite neighbourhood police officer before now? He hadn't been by my house since the last time he questioned me, but I doubted he was done with me.

"I don't know," Courtney said, looking away from me. "Maybe I thought if I pretended it didn't happen then maybe he would go away."

I snorted with laughter because Court should know better than anyone that cops didn't just go on their merry way.

"What did he want?"

Courtney avoided my eyes. "Asking the same questions. He clearly thinks Mom or I are involved in Mark's death."

"He's an idiot." The cops were stupid if they thought Courtney or Liv had anything to do with it. I wore the dead man's ring around my neck, and they couldn't locate it. I'd find it laughable if I wasn't so on edge by their constant intrusions.

"And he made a comment about Savannah," Courtney added quietly.

"What about Savannah?"

Before Courtney could answer, the front door creaked open, and someone called from the hallways. "Heeeeeeeellllooooooooooooooo. The party has arrived."

Courtney stood, exiting the bedroom and leaving my question unanswered. I begrudgingly followed her steps, finding Nia and Savannah in the front room.

"Let's get this party started!" Nia cried, shaking a bottle of champagne and letting it spray all over the front entrance. Lawyer by day. Party girl by night. I took a mental note to tell her to cool it. It was my name on the damage deposit, after all.

Courtney giggled and threw her arms around Brett's sister, then moved to hug Savannah. I eyed the girl in the wheelchair, wondering what Stevenson could have said to make Courtney worry. With their arrival, I might not get a chance to find out.

"We have a surprise for you," Savannah squealed when Courtney pulled away from her. Nia already busied herself with pouring glasses of bubbly.

"A surprise?" Courtney's eyes sparkled with excitement.

I allowed my stiff shoulders to fall. At least her fears had seemed forgotten for now. Courtney was right. She deserved a weekend of distraction. We could rehash Stevenson on the way home.

A high-pitched shriek erupted from Courtney the moment she saw him. The exact reaction I'd expected when I'd convinced Miles to join us for the bachelorette. At the time he'd made a sour face, hating the idea of being the cliché gay guy at the ladies' bash.

Miles stood in the doorway, all six feet of him, his blond hair the perfect mix of fell-out-of-bed-this-way and too many minutes spent perfecting it. Classic Miles. He was clean shaven, unlike when we'd video chatted last week, and his bright green eyes shone with excitement, a look akin to that of his older sister. He wore fitted jeans and a casual navy button down. Even I paused to admire how he'd grown into himself in his years away from Cedar Plains. This wasn't the same teenage punk that used to follow Courtney and me around.

Courtney hugged her brother for longer than she held any of the women, and soon, the five of us were seated around the coffee table with champagne flutes in hand.

"Okay, okay," Nia called. "Can we please do a quick toast before anyone else arrives? The OGs?"

Courtney beamed at the prospect and soon all our glasses were clinking together. I tried not to stare at Savannah who was the furthest thing from an original friend of our group. Nia, Courtney, and I had been friends for years, but Savannah? She'd been an unfortunate addition five years ago. I supposed it did make us old friends at this point, even if I hated to admit it.

"Where are the rest of them?" I asked, glancing back at the door. At least three more women needed to show up.

Nia waved off my concern, filling everyone's glass again. "They'll be here."

"It's going to be such a fun weekend!" Savannah's excitement nauseated me. Still, I forced a smile. For Courtney's sake, I hoped it was an amazing night.

By 1:00 a.m., after hours of food, bubbly, and silly party games, we began to fade. Starting with the icebreaking *Never Have I Ever* and followed up with a particularly rowdy game of *Cards Against Humanity*, we were soon settling into the king-sized bed in our shared room.

Courtney was rosy with intoxication and joyful in the attention.

"This is exactly what I needed," she murmured.

"I'm glad." I pulled the covers up to her chin and reminded her we had a tour pick up at noon the following day. Then I slipped out into the hallway in search of a glass of water to help ward off any hangover rearing its ugly head in the morning.

Out in the main room, Nia sat with two other women, unwilling to shut the party down.

"Join us, Lexie," Nia called with a grin on her face. "We're keeping this going until sunrise." She waved a baggy in the air. That beautiful white powder that once called my name. Except this time, I didn't see the point.

"What does Brett think about this particular habit?" I joked, entering the open-concept kitchen and reaching for a glass.

"What my big brother doesn't know doesn't hurt him." Nia waved off my concern. She formed a line on the table and was quick to snort it up. Her expression shifted as the high hit her, and for a moment, I felt a stir of desire inside me. She glanced back at me. "Want one?"

"I'm okay," I said. "I promised the bride I'd be a good girl this weekend. But you guys enjoy. Don't forget the tour tomorrow."

"Suit yourself," one of the others responded before dipping her head to do a line.

I filled up my glass and exited the scene. Back in the room, Courtney snored peacefully. I settled in beside her and lay back, watching the gentle rise and fall of her chest in the moonlight.

Beneath my skin the darkness hummed with impatience.

I wanted to wake her up, to ask her about Stevenson and his suspicions. The nosy cop had been at the forefront of my mind all night. An itch began in my palms. Why wouldn't he leave us alone? Brett should be handling it, keeping him away from his family. Though he was busy looking into Vanessa. The darkness bristled at the thought.

The muffled conversation of the women in the other room and quiet thump of the remaining music, had me considering the last time I'd done coke. At a party. Over a week ago with Dean. I hadn't really wanted it then but didn't know how to explain my lack of interest without sounding crazy.

I struggled to get Kaylee's body out of my mind, the way his hands pawed her. The way he used her. The anger I felt every time I thought about it. The way the darkness crooned.

I glanced back at Courtney, gazing over her closed eyes, her parted lips, her milky complexion. There was beauty in her peace, one I hadn't seen in a long time, and I worried what Stevenson could do to her. What the truth could do to her. I clamped my palms closed, trying to will the itch to stop.

The last thing either of us needed was Liv to talk or Stevenson's investigation unearthing a truth we'd kept hidden for too long.

18

Courtney Faith

Saturday, July 22

"Goooooood Morning!" Nia's perky voice rang through the house when the clock struck 9:00 a.m. I'd been up for over an hour, relaxing in bed and scrolling my phone. I'd messaged Brett and told him about the little surprise Alexa had planned. I still couldn't believe she'd convinced Miles to join us.

Alexa stirred, groaning. "How is she so chipper? I swear she was up until sunrise."

I laughed my response, because Alexa knew as well as I did Nia had always been overly positive and excitable. A late night of partying wasn't about to change that.

"I guess it's time to get up." I swung my legs over the side of the bed and grabbed my robe, tossing it over my negligee before padding out into the hallway. Alexa mumbled something after me along the lines of "be right there." She'd always been an early riser ... except when we had too much to drink.

In the kitchen I found Miles, Savannah, and Nia cooking up a storm. My other bridesmaids sat waiting on the couch, mimosas already in hand.

"Can I help?" I asked, looking from my brother to my friends.

"Nuh uh, no way," Nia chastised. Then she pushed a champagne flute into my hand, filled to the brim with a nearly transparent orange, bubbly liquid.

I laughed, taking the drink. "Does this even count as a real mimosa? It looks like you put only a drop of orange juice in it."

Nia winked. "My specialty. A Nia-mosa as I like to say."

Miles pushed the orange juice towards me when Nia turned away. "In case you want more."

"Thank you," I mouthed so as not to draw Nia's attention.

"Sit, sit," Savannah said. "Food will be ready in a minute."

With no other option, I went to the couch to join the others, and soon after my arrival, a dishevelled Alexa emerged and plopped onto the couch next to me.

"Rough night?" Savannah quipped.

Alexa shot her a glare but didn't answer. Thankfully, Nia intervened.

"And a Nia-mosa for you!" She pushed the drink into Alexa's hand then sashayed back to the kitchen.

Alexa watched her go with clear irritation.

"Lighten up," I said softly, with a playful grin. "The day is only getting started."

Alexa turned her gaze on me and forced a smile. "I'm light. I'm breezy."

"Sure, you are." I laughed, then I placed my mimosa down and went to the kitchen. "Is there coffee?" That would be the thing to bring Alexa back to life.

"Of course." Savannah produced a mug and pushed it towards me, pointing at the carafe on the counter.

I returned to the couch and passed Alexa the mug. She quickly abandoned her mimosa and sipped the warm drink, a grateful smile on her lips.

"You know me way too well." She chuckled.

"Better than most." I winked and retrieved my abandoned drink, ready for the day.

The tour picked us up at noon following a decadent breakfast of pancake eggs Benedict. I squealed when I saw the stretch limo out front.

"You didn't!" I gave Alexa a big squeeze.

"Only the best for you," she said, waving me out the front door. Our driver met us outside the limo. He set out a long red carpet from the back door and grinned as he held the door open and invited us to climb inside. He was an older gentleman, likely in his mid-fifties, and soon explained the carpet was his added touch to the tours. It would come out at every stop. Today we would be treated as royalty.

Once the door closed behind us, Alexa hooked her phone up to the Bluetooth speaker and started the tunes.

"Alright, I know you had your own tour outfits planned, but I've got something better," Alexa said, producing a bag and throwing tank-tops at each of us.

I cackled when I read over mine, featuring a Lord of the Rings slogan, "The One Ring to Rule them All" while all the bridesmaid's read "Fellowship of the Bride." She'd even gotten Miles a matching T-shirt. The throwback to our early high school years and our obsession with the fantasy series made me nostalgic. Alexa really did think of everything.

By the third winery, the party started getting rowdy. We were waiting for our tasting when I glanced around, and Alexa was nowhere to be found. I leaned closer to Miles.

"Have you seen Lex?"

Miles nodded to the door behind us. "She went outside."

"I'll be right back." I squeezed his arm and slipped away from the crowd, heading out the back entrance where I found her leaning against the building, cigarette in hand.

"You're hiding," I said reaching for the smoke.

"And you're drunk." She tried to snatch it back from me. "You hate smoking."

I stayed out of her reach and took a drag. "Only when I'm sober."

Alexa snorted a laugh as she took the cigarette back. "You'll regret it in the morning."

I motioned toward her hand. "So much for quitting." I didn't mean to sound critical.

Alexa looked at the smoke and shrugged. She took a long drag.

"Are you not having fun?" I asked, pressing my back against the wall next to her and looking out at the vineyards that stretched before us. The property was expansive and beautiful in full bloom.

"I am," Alexa insisted. "I only needed a minute."

I pursed my lips, annoyance creeping up inside me that she couldn't table her distaste of some of the company for one weekend. This was supposed to be about me. Before I could vocalize my irritation, Alexa flicked the cigarette and grinned at me.

"Should we head back?" she asked, clearly trying to make her voice light. She turned to the door, but I reached out, grabbing her hand and stopping her.

Before I spoke, my gaze fell on a patch of dead grass outside the winery. Brown and dry, much like the one in my backyard I'd discovered last week. Brett had insisted it wasn't his fault when I confronted him. I'd barely thought twice about it until now.

"Earth to Courtney." Alexa's voice came through, her gaze following mine.

"Sorry," I said, tearing my eyes away. I still gripped her hand from when I'd grabbed her, and I shook my head, remembering what I'd wanted to ask her. She'd seemed off since she picked me up yesterday afternoon. "Is something going on? This morning you said I know you too well, and I do. I feel like something is wrong."

Alexa's grin vanished, and she eyed me with clear suspicion. "Nothing. Everything is fine."

"That was convincing."

She turned away from me.

"Hey," I said, trying to coax her back to looking at me. "I get it, things around town have been crazy. First Mark dying, then a dead tourist. And now Stevenson won't stop asking questions." Or reporters for that matter.

"About that," Alexa said. "Last night you mentioned he brought up Savannah."

I nodded. "Tried to imply bad things like to happen around me and my friends."

"Nothing else?" Alexa's eyebrows raised.

"No," I lied, unwilling to tell her what he'd implied about her mom.

Alexa stayed silent, so I asked her the one thing on my mind since we left Cedar Plains. "Is it Dean?"

Alexa's head snapped in my direction. "What about Dean?"

"Did something happen?" I pressed. Her response to Brett had been abnormal yesterday, but maybe I'd imagined it.

Alexa sighed and looked away, her eyes scanning the rows of grapevines. "I don't know. Maybe. I think we've outgrown each other."

For a moment, I allowed myself a breath of relief. Maybe Dean was some horrible phase in Alexa's confusing life. Then another worry assaulted me. A wedding where the maid of honour was exes with the best man. That was some drama I didn't want to handle.

"It sounds like something happened."

A look crossed her face as if something was plaguing her, a dark glimmer in her eye I didn't recognize, but it was gone in a moment, and she simply shook her head. "I haven't seen him in a week," she said. "That's weird when you've been dating someone for six months, right?"

It was weird, but nothing about their relationship had been normal.

"Busy schedules?" I suggested.

Alexa tilted her head from side to side as if weighing the idea. "Maybe." Then she was quiet for a moment, and before I could ask more, she forced a smile and said, "No matter what happens with us, I won't cause any problems at the wedding."

I nodded, glad she'd acknowledged the elephant that had entered the room. "I'm only looking out for you."

"Enough about me, bride-to-be," she said, pushing me towards the entrance. "Let's get some more wine in you. I think this serious conversation sobered both of us up a little too much."

After the wine tour, the limo left us, and we grabbed Ubers to head to dinner and out on the town. When the night rolled to a close, I was thankful for Miles, as he escorted me back to the Airbnb.

In the back of the Uber, I rested my head on his shoulder. "Thank you so much for coming."

"Happy to, sis," Miles said. "I admit Alexa's idea did feel a bit cliché when she suggested it."

I grinned at the prospect of Alexa calling my younger brother to propose the surprise. They'd never been close, but this weekend they'd been friendlier than usual. "I'm glad she did."

"Me too." He leaned over, resting his head against mine. "How's Mom doing?"

"Bad," I said. "I don't know. She's functioning but she's miserable." I puffed out a long breath. "She was so brainwashed by him. Like the guy beat her more than once, and she's mourning his death. Is she losing it?"

"Grief can conjure up a lot," Miles said. "She will get better with time."

"When did you get so wise?" I teased.

He simply smiled his response. "Is there something else? Is it the wedding?"

"Just a nosy cop poking around and a reporter asking questions," I said. "Something I'm sure Brett will handle."

"Then why are you so worried?"

I pulled away from my brother, scrutinizing him in the back of the Uber, glad only the two of us had climbed in this one.

"They've both implied something about Alexa's mom," I said. "Like, maybe all those years ago, her accident wasn't exactly what they told us."

Miles didn't answer, but I didn't really expect him to. He'd only been eleven when Bronwyn died. Our parents and their group of friends wasn't something he would have paid any attention to.

"Why does that bother you?" Miles finally asked.

"Because they seem to be implying that something nefarious happened, and I don't know what to believe," I said simply. Kevin couldn't have been corrupt. And I had no idea what this theory would do to Alexa. She'd been through a lot with her family, so she really didn't need the past unearthed and her reality shattered. I thought about the months of therapy she'd endure that only ended when she could face the truth about her mother's death. Would dredging up the past unearth all her progress and send her spiralling once more?

"What did Mom say?"

"She didn't give me a firm answer," I said. "Only said they don't like to talk about it because it was a horrible night."

When Miles didn't respond again, I nudged him. "What are you thinking?"

"What will it change?" Miles asked.

"What do you mean?"

"What will knowing the truth change?"

I pondered his question for a moment. It wouldn't change the fact Alexa's mom had died and our parents fell out. It wouldn't change that Danny had dated Phoebe or she'd left them behind. Even if the report had been a lie, would knowing what really happened change anything?

"I don't know," I said finally. "I guess I wonder why they'd lie about it. If her being drunk was a part of the original story, why did they leave it out?"

"I don't know," Miles said as the Uber pulled up outside the cottage. "But if knowing the truth doesn't have a bearing on your life now, what's the point in dwelling on that past? What's done, is done."

I followed him as he scooted out of the car, and we made our way into the cottage. He was right, what was done, was done, but nothing stopped the twisted unease from swirling around inside me. Our parents had omitted a part of the story for a reason, and I wanted to know why.

19

Alexa Huston

Sunday, July 23

The itch didn't subside by the end of the weekend. Throughout the bachelorette I tried to drown the cravings with alcohol and weed but without success. And back in Cedar Plains I felt stifled by the heat. After dropping off Courtney, I returned home to find my dad supine on the couch, unresponsive. His loud snoring indicative of a bender. I could only guess how he'd spent the weekend.

I trudged up the stairs to my room, throwing open the door that had likely remained shut all weekend long. The room held its usual musty smell, but something was out of place. In the centre of my bed lay a single envelope. My name was scrawled on the front just like the others. I tore it open expecting another taunting message but instead something fluttered to the floor. I reached for it, realizing it was a photograph before I flipped it over.

The image made my body run cold. Staring me in the face was something that could easily implicate me in one of my crimes. The photo was dark, blurred figures surrounding the two women in the centre.

It was Vanessa, seated on the barstool at Weave, the martini bar we'd snatched her from. Standing beside her, though dark, was clearly me. I could make out the top I'd burned in Dean's parent's hearth and the jeans I wore. My blond hair was long and straight, and I even seemed to be glancing at the camera, a coy smile on my lips.

My hand was clearly around Vanessa's arm, tugging her to her feet, as if this photo captured the moment she agreed to leave with us.

The darkness inside growled with uncertainty. Someone was fucking with me. I wondered for a moment if it was Dean. The way I gazed at the photographer, seemed to imply I'd known them or at least been looking at them. Who else would take such a precise shot that implicated me in her murder?

Without thinking, I tore the photo multiple times before dropping it in the trash then scurried down the stairs to where my father rested. I violently shook him awake. If the note was in my room, either he'd put it there or someone had come in while he slept. Either way, I had to know.

Dad grunted, trying to push away my hold, but I didn't let up until he opened his eyes, and his gaze focused on me.

"Lex?" he groaned. "Did you just get home?"

"Did you put a letter in my room?" I demanded, ignoring his question. "An envelope with my name on it?"

He seemed to consider my question then he frowned. "I haven't been in your room." A moment passed between us as my heart rate ramped up. Had Dean walked into my house to plant the photo? Had someone else?

"Did anyone come by this weekend?" I asked, urging my dad to rack his booze-riddled brain for some recollection of a visitor.

"No," he rasped. Then followed up with, "Wait. Some reporter came by asking questions about Brett and Courtney. When I told her you weren't here, she went on her way."

I frowned. Rita Rounds had tracked down my address and been at my door. Had she slipped back into my house with the threatening photo after she realized my dad's inebriated state? But if she had the photo, why hadn't she turned me in?

I turned away from my dad, unable to look at him any longer. Disgusted that his negligence could allow someone to just walk into our house unnoticed. It sent a chill through me. It made the darkness angry.

When I went for my next shift the following Tuesday, I arrived to find Ashley instead of Kaylee. Worry washed over me. I'd tried calling her over the weekend but without an answer. Even my texts hadn't garnered a response. Clearly, she was avoiding me.

The picture I received when I returned from the bachelorette and everything it meant distracted me. There was evidence of me with Vanessa. Something that would be more than enough to get Stevenson on my case. The only thing I didn't know was why it hadn't been shared with them. What did this anonymous watcher want from me?

I had heard from Dean more than once in the past couple days, and I wondered if he could be the cause of the photo. I didn't linger long on the thought. Dean wasn't one to keep his blackmail secret. He'd threatened me outright. If he had this photo, he would have made sure I knew ages ago.

Around eleven, I was working away in my sketchbook when Lou, a nightly regular, stumbled in with a handshake to the bouncer and several "Hi, hellos," on his way to his usual barstool.

"Ahh, Alexa Rose." He threw me a playful smile as he used his nickname for me. He told me it came from a novel he loved as a boy. A girl with long blond hair and rosy lips. He swore I looked just how he imagined her. I'd reply that he was just an old man trying to flirt.

I didn't ask for his order, only sliding a beer across the bar to him. The regulars in this town didn't do complicated. Everyone was a bottle of beer, a carafe of wine, or a stiff rye (rail only). They came to get drunk, not to spend money on something ostentatious.

"Where's Scarlett tonight? Is she feeling better?" he asked, referring to his nickname for Kaylee, claiming she took his breath away like *Gone with the Wind*. Kaylee now joked with him saying things like, "Tomorrow is another day" and "Frankly, my dear, I don't give a damn." He ate it up.

"Haven't seen her since I got back." I busied myself clearing the glasses piled up in the dishwasher. "Not sure when I'll see her next."

Lou nodded, though he looked melancholy. "She was in a right state on Saturday. Must have done like twenty shots over the course of the night."

"Sounds like a wild time."

After another swig, Lou said, "But she looked like she was having a time with some fella. I couldn't recognize him from where I was, but she looked upset."

We dealt with a ton of drunk people daily. No surprise someone got under her skin, but as I offered Lou a polite smile and told him I'd let Kaylee know he was concerned, my mind went back to Dean's house. He could have easily been the guy Lou saw. Maybe there was more to Kaylee and Dean than drugs and sex. What if this had been going on for a while? Maybe I really was an idiot. The darkness growled at the thought.

Near the end of my shift, Dean strode into the bar. He nodded at a couple of the regulars and took an empty stool in front of me. He tried to catch my attention, but I barely glanced his way. When I finally didn't have a choice, I looked at him. His expression pinched. We hadn't seen each other in over a week. The voice urged me to reach for the paring knife we kept under the bar. I rung my hands together to keep the itch at bay.

"Something wrong?" Dean asked, sipping the beer Ashley had served him.

"Just busy." I brushed off his concern.

"For a week?" Dean cocked an eyebrow at the suggestion. "You've barely answered me."

"Honestly, Kaylee kind of ghosted, so I've been slammed." I hesitated, gauging his reaction. "The owner is seriously pissed."

When he didn't make any incriminating response, I continued, "You haven't seen her, have you?"

Dean shrugged. "Saturday, I think. Last I can remember at least."

"Selling?" I asked, my voice low.

Dean's expression hardened. "No, she hasn't gotten anything off me in days. I sent her another contact. I'm dried up."

"Seriously?" I eyed him for a moment, unsure what to think. Dean hadn't been without drugs for as long as I'd known him. To be dry seemed out of character.

He leaned forward with a wink. "For you, though, obviously I'm open for business."

"But not Kaylee," I said slowly.

"You done soon? I'd love to get out of here." It was nearly 1:00 a.m.

Not wanting to go anywhere with Dean, I shook my head and lied, "Without Kaylee, I'm on the hook to close up. Another couple of hours at least, I think."

"Why can't Ashley do it?" He asked.

"Because it's my night," I said. "And she took on most of the work over the weekend."

Dean let out an exasperated groan. "Fine." He placed his beer down with a heavy clunk and pushed away from the bar. "Call me tomorrow, then? It would be nice to actually see my girlfriend." The voice promised he'd seen me soon.

I offered a curt nod but nothing more of substance. I wasn't particularly interested in spending any time with him. *At least not like that,* the voice cooed.

I needed to figure out how to end it.

As he moved to leave, he hesitated and looked back at me. "Come by tonight, if you want to." Then he was gone without another word.

Once he was out of sight, I looked to Ashley and asked, "Mind if I head out? I'm beat." The regulars were winding down, and soon the bar would be empty.

"Yeah, of course." Ashley offered a friendly smile, which was all I needed as conformation to turn and leave her to handle the regular closures.

When the cool night air struck my face, the voice urged me to turn towards Dean's house, but I pushed the temptation aside, knowing he wasn't who I wanted to see. I left my car in the bar's parking lot and headed down Marie Street towards Kaylee's apartment, a couple of blocks away.

The lights in her living room were on, visible through the large front windows, but since she lived on the second floor, I couldn't see anything inside. First, I knocked, hoping she'd be up, but when I didn't get an answer, I tried the knob. It was open so I let myself in.

I slowly climbed the stairs, aware of my heavy footsteps and trying to listen for any sound.

"Kaylee?" I called as I pushed the door open. "Kaylee?" I made my way to the front room where the lights were on, but no one was there. My skin prickled. It was silent, but something told me I wasn't alone. I turned towards her bedroom at the back of the unit and noticed light coming from behind a partially closed door. My body shook as I made my way toward it. When I pushed open the bathroom door, my breath caught in my throat.

Kaylee lay on the floor, head tilted back, mouth agape. She was pale and her lips a slight shade of blue.

"Fuck, fuck, fuck," I muttered, as I leaned down to check her pulse; it was barely there. Her breathing was practically non-existent. As I straightened and reached for my phone, I noticed the needle. *Pity*, the voice whispered. *She died so peacefully.*

"Kaylee, what have you done?" I whispered, ignoring the mocking darkness and trying to steady my shaking hands as I punched 9-1-1 in my phone. When the operator picked up, I quickly gave Kaylee's address. "I found my friend unconscious in her bathroom. I think it's an overdose."

I touched her neck again to reassure myself she still had a weak pulse. Her chest rose slowly with whatever life remained in her. *It won't be long now,* the voice murmured.

I heard the sirens in seconds. The paramedics station was around the corner. Emergency response would be knocking down her door any moment.

I glanced at the needle, unsure when Kaylee started shooting up. Had it been something she'd done all along? I couldn't pin-point a single thing about her that implied she was a heroin addict. Dean had stayed away from dealing those drugs in the past, and he'd also made it clear he wasn't interested in selling to Kaylee anymore. Maybe she'd had another dealer all along, though the desperate texts I often fielded implied otherwise.

The sirens, loud now, were outside the apartment and things happened quickly then. The EMS workers pushed me aside and carefully lifted Kaylee from the floor onto a waiting gurney. I stood there, helpless, as they administered the naloxone then whisked Kaylee's limp body out the door. I hoped they could save her.

Then a police officer took me outside and asked a hundred questions. What was I doing there? When did I find her? How long had she been out? Did she have any family they should contact? I answered to the best of my ability, then the policewoman offered to take me to the hospital. I refused. My car was close by, and I'd get myself there.

The entire time I couldn't get my mind off Dean and Kaylee. Something had happened this past weekend between them. Something bad enough for Dean to cut her off and Kaylee to end up like this. The voice whispered its desires. *A life for a life.*

I hurried to the hospital, hopeful to find out more, but the nurses offered me no information beyond the fact that she wasn't dead—yet. My only glimmer of hope. With nothing more for me to do, I split, needing a reprieve from the busy hospital staff and scent of illness.

I climbed into my car, glancing up at the looming hospital one last time. I couldn't silence the doubt and worry that swirled around inside me, or the creeping feeling that told me Dean had something to do with this.

20

Courtney Faith

Wednesday, July 26

It didn't take long for me to hear about Kaylee. Brett arrived home early in the morning after a hectic night shift. While he hadn't answered the call, he told me what happened and that Alexa had been there.

I texted her quickly, a million questions running through my head. Worse, I never considered the crowd Alexa hung out with did heroin. Cocaine, sure, it was a party drug, but the other was harder than anything I'd ever expected of Alexa.

For the entire morning, I was on edge, waiting to hear from Alexa, trying to not wake up Brett from his well-deserved rest to get more answers. Finally, around noon, Alexa responded.

Hey, sorry. I was beat. I'm heading to the hospital now for an update.

Is she okay? I typed quickly.

I had to wait another minute for a response, watching the little dots appear and disappear three times before a message came through.

Not sure. They wouldn't give me much information last night, but at least she's alive.

I shook my head as I read the message. I didn't know Kaylee well. She'd been Alexa's friend, not mine. My thumbs hovered over my phone, considering the question I wanted to ask, knowing I'd hate to get an affirmative answer. Still, I asked it anyway.

Did you know about the heroin? Is it a regular thing?

No idea. Alexa's swift reply allowed the tightness in my chest to subside. *Hopefully I'll find out more soon. I'll keep you posted.*

I messaged my thanks but continued to pace around the house aimlessly. I didn't want to wait around. Alexa needed my support. I could practically picture her sitting in the hospital waiting room alone and distraught. I grabbed my purse and headed for the car, determined to meet her at the hospital. She shouldn't have to go through this alone.

I tried not to speed through the quiet streets. How awful it must have been for Alexa to find Kaylee nearly dead last night. With everything that had happened over the past few weeks our perfect town was falling apart.

I arrived to find Alexa waiting in the third-floor nurses' area, head down while she wrote on something in her lap. It took me a moment to register she was drawing. As much as the hospital made me wary, seeing Alexa hard at work offered a bit of calm. Her artwork had always been an outlet she shared with her mother, and seeing her sink so deeply into her work allowed me to believe she still held tightly to a part of her mother that wasn't haunted by the past.

She didn't notice me approach so I got a look at what she was drawing before she could snatch it away. The sketch was clear, and I wagered a guess it was the scene she'd stumbled into last night. A nude woman lying on what looked like a tiled floor. A needle was apparent in the image. She had no face, shielded by a mess of dark hair. The stark lines and dark shading gave the sketch an ominous feel. It creeped me out, causing all calm I'd felt when I first saw Alexa working to dissipate.

"Court?" Alexa asked when she registered my presence. She quickly tucked the drawing away. "What are you doing here?"

"I couldn't sit in the house anymore." I took the vacant chair next to her. "Brett was still asleep, and I wanted to be with you. To know what happened and support however I could."

Alexa eyed me with a suspicion I didn't expect, but she said nothing, and as quickly as it appeared, the look vanished. "Thank you," she murmured, reaching out and putting a hand on my own.

"What were you drawing?" I asked, hoping to get her to open up about the dark scene she'd been in the midst of scribbling.

She raised an eyebrow but didn't move to show me the work. "Nothing in particular. Just something that came to me."

"Can I see it?"

Alexa released my hand and moved the sketchbook out of reach. "It's not done yet."

I didn't care if it was finished, I wanted a chance to analyze it a bit more. I didn't push her and instead asked, "Have you heard anything?"

Alexa grimaced. "Her mom and sister are here. I left her room when they arrived to give them some privacy." Alexa fiddled with her phone. "Honestly, I was thinking of leaving if they didn't come out soon."

I nodded, not sure what to say.

Thankfully, Alexa continued, "She's made progress. She's been under observation since she came in. Her pulse and breathing have returned to nearly normal."

"Will she be okay?"

"They seem positive."

"What happened?" I asked directly this time, hoping Alexa would clear up the confusing events from the previous night. How did she find Kaylee? What was she doing at her house?

Alexa didn't get a chance to speak before a woman approached. She was middle-aged with dark hair tied up in a messy knot on the top of her head. There were prominent lines around her eyes. Giving her a once over, she and Kaylee were nearly identical.

"Mrs. Wen," Alexa said, greeting Kaylee's mother. "Is everything okay?"

"Alexa, dear," The woman said. "I've asked you to call me Carole. You know I hate all the Mrs. stuff." Carole looked around Alexa at me. "You have a friend?"

Alexa waved back at me. "This is Courtney. She's my best friend. When she heard the news, she wanted to come by."

I stood and approached them. "Nice to meet you." I nearly slapped myself for the words as they came out of my mouth. There was nothing nice about meeting someone in a hospital. "... Just so sorry about the circumstances," I quickly added.

Carole offered a tight smile and turned back to Alexa. "She's asking for you. Would you like to see her?"

"I would." Alexa tucked her sketchbook under her arm and looked back at me. "I'll call you later?"

I hesitated, wanting to follow her into Kaylee's room.

"Would you like to see her too?" Carole asked. "She can have more than one visitor."

"It's okay," Alexa said before I could speak. "Courtney just stopped by to check on me." The look she gave me told me to keep quiet. Of course she would want a moment with Kaylee alone after finding her last night.

"She's right," I said. "I should go, but I'm glad Kaylee is feeling better." I looked at Alexa then. "Call me when you have a chance."

Alexa nodded then she and Carole turned back the way she'd come. I watched them go before making my way towards the exit.

"Ms. Faith? I didn't expect to see you here."

I glanced at the familiar voice, locating Stevenson standing near the entrance.

"And who might you be visiting?" Stevenson asked. An amused smile played on his lips. "It wouldn't be Ms. Kaylee Wen, would it? My, my, that would be quite the coincidence."

The way he gazed at me made my skin crawl, like he knew all my secrets and was only toying with me.

"Brett told me about last night," I said, hoping my voice was steady and didn't give way to the panic I felt upon seeing him. "I wanted to know she was okay."

"So thoughtful," Stevenson said. "Yes, I've heard that about you. Didn't you spend days at the hospital after Ms. Torres had her accident?"

I tried not to react to the mention of Savannah. I *had* spent days by her bedside. "I was worried about my friend."

"Interesting," Stevenson said. "Ms. Torres has said her accident was really what solidified your friendship. I wonder why."

"I hear a lot of things from Brett," I said, trying to keep my voice firm. "I can't help it; I worry about people I know. One would think it was the empathetic human response."

"Or guilt." Stevenson grinned in an unfriendly way. "I suppose it could be empathy. It's funny how those two things can seem so similar."

I bit down on my lip, willing myself not to react.

"I suppose I can expect to see Ms. Huston here?" Stevenson asked, standing in the doorway and blocking my way.

"She and Kaylee are friends," I said. "And given what she found last night, I wouldn't expect her to be anywhere else."

"Right, she found her, nearly dead." Stevenson scratched at the stubble on his chin. "What was she doing there anyways? Indulging herself?"

"Is this an interrogation?" I retorted, ignoring the twist in my stomach as Stevenson mentioned the fear I'd had when I'd first heard about the heroin.

"Of course not," Stevenson said, putting his hands up defensively. "I'm simply trying to be friendly."

I glared at him. "She was worried about her friend. Stop acting like normal human responses are nefarious for some reason."

"I can assure you, Ms. Faith, most of what happens when any crimes are committed is nefarious." He tipped his hat at me. "I'm surprised it has taken you this long to realize that."

He shook his head and stepped around me. "I must be off. Especially if I hope to catch Ms. Huston for a much-needed explanation."

I watched him go, then grabbed my phone and sent Alexa a quick text warning her of Stevenson's impending arrival.

21

Alexa Huston

Wednesday, July 26

I hesitated at the door into Kaylee's room. Carole had taken her other daughter to the cafeteria, leaving me alone with Kaylee for a few minutes. After everything that had happened in the past few weeks, I wasn't sure how to approach her. The voice had fallen silent in the hours that followed finding her. As if the joy it found in death was lost on Kaylee.

Kaylee rolled her head towards the door, gazing at me with glassy eyes, exhausted. She had an IV connected to her arm, but otherwise, she simply looked like she had a rough party night. There was another bed in the room, currently unoccupied. It was the closest to privacy Kaylee would have for a while, I imagined. Carole would likely send her daughter to rehab after this.

"Thanks for coming," Kaylee said as I pulled up a chair and sat next to her. Her voice was raspy and strained.

"Of course," I said. "How are you?"

Kaylee offered a weak laugh. "That's a terrible question."

I frowned. "How about, what happened?"

She turned her face away from me. "It's complicated."

I waited a moment, unsure what to ask next or how to approach the topic I wanted to breach. Kaylee spoke again.

"They said you found me."

"It wasn't great."

Shame washed over her expression, and she struggled to look me in the eye. "It was stupid. I'm stupid."

"Don't say that."

"I did something," she whispered, and tears slid down her cheeks. "Something bad—to you." She looked at me. Her red-rimmed eyes laced with guilt and sorrow.

The voice returned with a low hum, as if anticipating her confession.

I beat her to it. "I know about you and Dean."

Her eyes widened and she shook her head in wordless. "Alexa, I—"

"Don't," I said quickly. "I'm not looking for an apology. I don't want you to explain yourself. I need to know if this was his fault."

The darkness already decided it was.

Kaylee shook her head, more tears spilling down her cheeks. "This was my fault."

"Kaylee, what happened?"

She looked down at her hands and fidgeted with the thin sheet covering her. "He cut me off. Something happened. Something went wrong, and he cut me off. So, I used another guy, but he offered heroin." Her eyes found mine. "I was desperate."

Pity bloomed inside me. She was a drug addict Dean used and threw away. She was in less control of herself then I was. The thought made me shiver.

"Why would he cut you off?" I asked.

"He told me I fucked up. He didn't want me anymore." Kaylee sniffed. "From now on, I'd be paying and because of our arrangement, I owed him some serious debt."

My mind spun as she divulged the arrangement she had with Dean. Sex for drugs. An arrangement he had with more than one person, though how many, I couldn't be sure. While I wasn't surprised, I felt stupid. How had I not known what he was doing behind my back?

Beast. The darkness bared its teeth.

"I tried to fight him on it," Kaylee said. "I told him I'd paid my debts and if he couldn't keep up his end of the bargain then I didn't owe him anything. I threatened him, said I could tell you and everyone else I knew about our deal and how shady he was. He got angry then."

"What did he say?" I asked, knowing Dean didn't like to be challenged.

When she spoke again, her voice was lower. "He said I had nothing on him and if he wanted to, he could make me disappear. Said he'd easily gotten rid of a girl like me before."

The voice hissed with anger. The small hairs on my neck lifted as I thought about Vanessa's lifeless eyes. Was that the girl Dean believed he'd made disappear?

"The look in his eyes," Kaylee said. "He was serious. He wanted to hurt me."

"So, you hurt yourself?" I asked.

"No," Kaylee said. "It wasn't supposed to happen this way. The dealer, he promised it wasn't too much." She shook her head. "It was stupid, but I wasn't trying to kill myself. I was trying to numb the pain."

Her eyes found mine again. "Do you think he would have hurt me? Has he hurt people before?"

"Yes," I said. "I think he would have hurt you. He's never been one to control his anger." Dean was becoming a liability. The voice told me I knew what to do.

"I'm sorry," Kaylee said.

"It's okay," I said. "I'm not mad. I'm scared for you."

Kaylee looked up at me through her tears. "Why don't you hate me?"

I reached out and touched her arm. "People like him are used to taking and always getting what they want. He took advantage of you, and you nearly died because of it. Don't worry about the past. Just get better and stay the hell away from people like him."

"I already talked to Mom about rehab. She's been in contact with a facility nearby to get me a room. It's time to figure out what my life looks like without all the partying and the drugs."

"I'm glad," I said, forcing a smile. I still couldn't clear what she'd said out of my mind. Dean was getting sex in return for drugs. Dean treated people like they were objects. Dean was threatening people, using Vanessa as an example. How long before he spilled the full secret and turned the cops on to me? The darkness purred with excitement. A desire. A release.

My phone pinged with a message, and I reached for it.

Heads up. Stevenson is on his way there.

I stiffened.

"You okay?" Kaylee asked.

"Yeah," I said, tucking my phone away. "But I have to head out. I'm sorry. Call me, though, let me know how things are going."

Kaylee nodded. "Of course, and Alexa, thank you, again."

I gave her a small smile then darted out of the room. I turned down the hallway, away from the elevator and dashed into the back stairwell, hopeful to avoid the nosy detective and another round of invasive questions. Thankfully, I escaped the hospital without seeing him.

Back in my car, I turned Kaylee's words over in my head. She'd been Dean's plaything. How many others did he have and how hadn't I noticed? Maybe I had and I chose to ignore it.

Whatever it was, I knew it had to end.

My car revved to life, and I pulled out of the hospital parking lot. I turned towards my house but as I headed down Main Street, past all the same stores I saw every day, something in me felt changed.

Vanessa had been an accident, something I couldn't take back, and Mark had been justified. He deserved to die.

And now, the voice whispered, *Dean deserves it too.*

22

COURTNEY FAITH

FRIDAY, JULY 28

Alexa agreed to meet me the Friday afternoon following her visit with Kaylee. I'd been distracted the previous night when Brett came home and considered telling him about Stevenson's surprise visit to the hospital, but the implications still swirled around my head. Stevenson was suspicious about Savannah and her accident, and as much as I wanted to tell myself there was nothing to worry about, each time he brought it up, I could see my world crashing down around me.

I sat on the patio of a restaurant down the street from Big Shot. I ordered drinks for both of us as soon as I arrived, knowing Alexa's choice.

The restaurant was a small place with everyone's favourite nineties hip-hop as the theme music and crafty cocktails as exotic as they sounded. Not to mention the ramen was to die for. I noticed when Alexa rounded the corner on to the restaurant's street, eyeing her carefully as she approached. She looked more put together then I expected, though I might have been too used to seeing her post-parties with Dean.

"How's Kaylee?" I asked.

Alexa reached for the water glass placed there by the server only a few minutes before. "She's okay. She agreed to go to rehab."

"Did she say what happened?" I asked, my voice low, hoping she'd give me some more details. She didn't answer as the server placed the drinks I ordered on the table between us. The young woman asked about food, but I shooed her away quickly, wanting to know what Alexa found out.

"She overdosed," Alexa said matter-of-factly.

"It was an accident?" I asked, taking a sip of my drink.

"Seems like it." Alexa scrolled her phone, likely reviewing the menu, though it didn't look like her eyes were focused on anything.

I watched her for a moment, but she didn't look up to meet my gaze.

"Alexa?" I asked, my patience wearing thin. "Did she say anything?"

She met my eyes then, chewing on her lower lip. The way her eyes narrowed and scrutinized me made it clear she didn't know what to say.

"Well?" I asked.

Her eyes darted away from mine then back. "Dean."

"What?" I frowned, unsure what she was saying.

Alexa tapped the table then pointed over my shoulder. "Dean and Brett are here."

I turned and sure enough my policeman fiancé and Dean were sauntering across the street towards us.

"Did you invite him?" I asked quickly, still unsure where they stood in their relationship.

She didn't say anything, only pursed her lips and shook her head.

"Hey babe," Brett said as he pulled the chair beside me out and settled down with a warm kiss on my cheek. I watched Alexa's stiff posture as Dean slid into the seat beside her and mimicked Brett's movements.

"What are you guys doing here?" I asked, my voice higher than usual, getting the sense Dean was the last person Alexa wanted to see.

Brett immediately regarded me with a raised eyebrow. "I told Dean you guys were here, and we thought it would be fun to meet you guys for a post-work-out drink." He flexed his bicep playfully.

"So fun," Alexa said, her voice flat.

Dean's expression tightened, but he didn't say anything.

"Didn't mean to interrupt," Brett said as he waved down the server, then proceeded to order two beers and two of "whatever the girls are drinking." "Continue with your conversation. What's the hot gossip?" He meant it jokingly, of course, like we were the same high-school girls tittering about Susie's horrible hair cut or Heather's bad nose job, but it was the wrong thing to ask.

"Kaylee's drug overdose," Alexa said so bluntly Brett's jaw dropped open. Dean's eyes darted to Alexa, his gaze suspicious.

It took Brett a moment to recover. "I'm glad she's doing okay. Have you been in to see her?"

"Yeah," Alexa said. "I'm glad I got to hear it straight from her." She shot a sideways glance at Dean before looking back at me and Brett. "She's going to rehab."

Brett shook his head in disbelief. "Poor, Kaylee, but good for her. Always a tough choice to make." He didn't know Kaylee beyond his boys' nights to the bar. He certainly didn't know his best friend helped supply her drug habit.

"I hope she gets the help she needs," Dean finally chimed in.

Alexa abruptly stood. "I have to go. I forgot I was supposed to pick up my dad from his appointment this afternoon." She glanced at her phone.

"And now I'm going to be late." She motioned to the drink she hadn't touched. "Let me know what I owe you."

"Lex," I tried but she only shook her head and walked away. As she left, Dean stood and moved to follow her. "What's going on with you two?" I asked, stalling him.

He ignored my question, instead following Alexa as she darted across the street.

Brett slipped his arm around my shoulder. "Is there something I missed?"

I cast a sideways glance at my fiancé and shook my head. "Alexa said a couple of things at the bachelorette, but I've barely seen her this week. Maybe their relationship is over."

"Too bad," Brett said, reaching for his beer. "I kind of liked the idea of our best man and maid of honour being together."

I gave him a small smile but kept my eyes trained across the street where Dean chased after Alexa. The last thing I saw before they disappeared around the corner was the look of pure hatred on Alexa's face saying more had happened than she let on.

23

Alexa Huston

Friday, July 28

"Want to tell me what is going on?" Dean snapped as he came up behind me. I hadn't even gotten to my car before he reached my side and grabbed my arm. The darkness flared. Everything that had happened over the past few weeks came bubbling to the surface. The murders. The affairs. The blackmail. The anger.

I pulled my arm from his grip. "Why don't you tell me?"

His eyes narrowed. "I don't know what you're talking about."

"Oh really?" I snapped, placing my hands on his chest and shoving him backwards. "Kaylee didn't spend the last year sucking your dick for cocaine? Cock for coke, is it a special you offer or something?"

"You seemed pretty happy with it." He sneered.

"You're disgusting." I moved to push him again, but he grabbed hold of my wrists.

"Watch it," he said, his voice quiet, menacing. "You have no idea what you're talking about."

"I know enough." I glared up at him, not backing down. "I know you're a cheating asshole and you nearly killed Kaylee."

He released his grip on my wrists and stepped back, running a hand through his hair. "I didn't make her OD. Whatever she did is on her." He matched my glare. "And you and me were never in a faithful, loving relationship, Alexa. We shared randoms. Sex is a game to you."

"I think I would have felt differently if I knew you were fucking my friends on the side." I gave into the darkness in full force, letting the anger and desire guide me. I'd grown to hate Dean, that much I knew for sure.

"What happened with Kaylee wasn't about you," he said, as if any explanation he offered could make what he'd done better. "She happened long before you did."

"And what now?" I asked. "You're done with her, so you've thrown her away?"

"It was always going to end." Dean scoffed. "I don't fuck trash for life."

I stepped back as the words fell out of his mouth. "Trash."

The darkness bared its teeth, willing me to end him.

"Yeah, Alexa, trash, that's all you and girls like Kaylee are." His words were low and hard. "Girls willing to jump on any dick for a sniff." He shook his head, a smug look on his very hittable face. "Kaylee was a dirty slut who got passed around. Once she let four guys fuck her back-to-back because I told her I'd give her an eight ball. Then she crawled on the floor like the dog, sniffing up whatever she could find."

I slapped him square in the face before he could continue. The voice cackled. *More*, it whispered. *More*.

"You're as crazy as she is," Dean snapped, moving away from me. "Trash that deserves each other." Then he said in a low tone, "Don't you forget who I am. You and Kaylee think you have stories, you think they actually matter, but I'm the one who will always come out on top. No one would believe you over me."

He turned and walked away without giving me a chance to respond. The sad thing was, he was right. I had nothing on him, no proof. Only my word against his, and on paper, he was the better one. It only made me hate him more. I thought back to the photograph I'd received, the clear evidence of my tie to Vanessa. Could that have been Dean's doing? A threat he could finally carry out.

When I climbed into my car, rage boiling over, I knew I had to do something. I couldn't let him get away with it. The hateful words, the things he proudly claimed to have done. The bile in my throat threatened to spew across my car as I considered it. *It's time*, the voice whispered. And a plan began to form in my mind.

24

Courtney Faith

Saturday, July 29

"You look good, Mom," I said honestly as I sat at our old kitchen table with a coffee mug in hand. Mom moved about the kitchen preparing her own cup, something she insisted I not help with. Even I had to admit she was mastering this whole one-working-arm situation.

She'd been back at home for under a week, and while the first couple of days had been a cause for worry, seeing her back in her house now, I knew it was the right choice. Time for her, for us, to move on.

"Thanks, honey," Mom said, sitting next to me. "It's been different trying to figure out how to manage. But I'm glad to be home."

I glanced around the kitchen where I'd grown up. It hadn't changed much over the years; the same linoleum floor, rounded oak table, and old chairs. The wall was still decorated with artwork from when Miles and I were in grade school. I'd tried to convince Mom to replace it with something more wall-worthy but never succeeded. She loved our juvenile paintings.

It felt strange sitting in this room and taking in all the good and terrible memories. The idea Mark was gone and he could never darken the doorway again wasn't lost on me.

"You've been busy." I'd been trying to visit her all week, but timing never worked out. Not that my week was particularly open or free.

"Getting back into things," Mom said. "I didn't realize how much I'd missed over the last few years."

I grimaced but didn't comment. It had been Mark who kept Mom locked at home and away from all her friends and loved ones. She'd let him do it.

"I'm glad." I forced the smile. After the bachelorette weekend, I'd been unable to stop thinking about Bronwyn and her accident, and without confronting Kevin, Mom was the only source I could think of for answers. Whatever Stevenson knew, he wasn't sharing.

"Is something wrong, honey?" Mom asked, tilting her head and regarding me like she used to do in high school when I came home upset over a bad grade.

"Actually, yes," I said, putting my coffee down harder than I intended. I turned to face Mom and locked eyes with her. "I want the truth, and I want to hear it from you."

Her eyes dropped away from mine as if she were found guilty from my statement alone. "I'm not sure I know what you mean."

I reached out and shook her arm, making her look back at me. "I need you to tell me about the night Alexa's mom died."

Again, Mom's eyes darted away from mine. The guilt shone clear now. They'd lied to us all those years ago. A feeling made my throat tighten, telling me how lucky I'd been, even though I didn't feel it.

"I don't remember a lot, but I'll tell you what I do know," Mom said slowly. "It was a really strange night. We'd been having a great time, then suddenly Bronwyn ran off. Danny tried to follow her, but she was gone before anyone could stop her. When Kevin found her the next day, it was too late. The car was totalled, and she was gone." Mom kept her eyes locked to the table as she spoke. She sniffed, and I was unsure if she was crying as she relieved the memory.

I frowned as this all sounded very routine. What did Stevenson know?

"That's it?" I thought back to the day we learned the truth and the way my mom sat Miles and me down to tell us. "You'd said it was a snowy night, and she hit a patch of ice. It sounds like nothing out of the ordinary. Just a bad accident."

"That's all it was, honey," Mom said.

"Do you know why she stormed out of the party?" I asked.

Once again, Mom looked away. A clear indication that she wasn't telling me something. I waited, certain she would continue.

"I will only tell you this if you promise to keep it to yourself," Mom said. "It was a very long time ago and everyone has suffered enough."

I stiffened, unsure what to expect, and Mom blew out a long, tired breath.

"Bronwyn discovered that Danny and Phoebe were having an affair. I don't have the details of how it came out. Missy told me years ago, long after Phoebe had left Ceder Plains." Mom sighed. "It was the reason she left the party, apparently claiming she was going to pack up Alexa and get them out of Danny's house. Obviously, that didn't happen."

I frowned at the mention of Alexa's pseudo-stepmother Phoebe and Danny's apparent affair. She had been Bronwyn's best friend. I shuddered to imagine that level of betrayal.

"And she died?" I asked, barely able to get out the words. How awful to discover a terrible truth about the people you love the most. An unforgivable betrayal that caused Bronwyn to make a poor decision and Alexa to lose her mom.

"We all wish we could have made her stay," Mom said.

I chewed on my lower lip, unsure what to say. If it was so simple like Mom implied, then where did Stevenson get his intel? I still wondered if Brett's dad could offer more information having been the first on the scene. Kevin had always been protective of us kids. He'd always felt like the dad I never had, and now with my upcoming marriage to his son, it would be official. His integrity was everything, and I struggled to imagine he'd do anything to compromise that.

"And you all fell out after?" I asked, remembering what Missy said about it being the last night they'd all spent together.

Mom nodded. "It was never the same after we lost Bronwyn. It all felt tainted. There was so much secrecy around that night and her decision to leave. It was awful. Keeping secrets ruins friendships."

I grimaced, remembering when Alexa and I believed our secrets were what made us close and kept our friendship strong. Now I realized maybe the secret we'd been harbouring for years was slowly tearing us apart.

When I left my mom's, I headed straight to Alexa's place uninvited. I'd texted her more than once, but she'd left the messages unanswered, and I needed to know what happened between her and Dean after she left yesterday.

When I arrived, I didn't bother knocking, knowing if I did, neither her dad nor Alexa would leave whatever they were doing to answer it. Knockers were rare here, at least for the past five years. Now they regarded any unexpected visitor as unwelcome. Considering Stevenson had made visiting the condo complex a regular occurrence, I didn't blame them.

I didn't announce my presence to Danny, who I could guess was in the living room watching TV, as the sounds of the afternoon baseball game echoed through the front entrance. Alexa and I had been friends since we were fourteen, but I'd been in this house only a few times. She and her father had lived here for the past seven years, and I never made it a habit to visit, considering her dad was usually occupying the only shared space in the condo.

The condo was nothing like her old house. The classic Victorian in the centre of town had been a favourite hangout of ours when we were teens. Even after Bronwyn died, Danny and Phoebe still hosted the girls for their sleepovers or encouraged Alexa to bring her friends over. The Danny I knew now was barely a sliver of the man he once was.

I made my way to Alexa's room on the floor above. Her bedroom door was cracked open, and I entered slowly, pushing it only enough so I could see her lying on her bed.

"Lex?"

Her eyes found me as I stepped in and closed the door behind me. She pulled the earbuds from her ears and flipped over the sketchbook she'd been scribbling in. I didn't get to see the drawing before she hid it from view.

"What are you doing here?" she asked, a blank expression on her face. I wasn't welcome, but she wouldn't kick me out.

I perched on the edge of her bed. "I tried messaging. I know you probably don't want company, but I had to check on you. What happened yesterday?"

Alexa looked away from me, her signature move for considering how much of the truth she wanted to tell. Also, a clear indication she was ready to lie.

"Nothing. He was an asshole when I told him we were done. I guess it was to be expected. It's not like we had a solid, loving relationship. But maybe I thought he'd be a bit more understanding." Alexa gave me a weak smile, so half-hearted it was barely there. "I'm an idiot."

"You are not," I said. "You are the furthest thing from an idiot. You are a genuine, caring person who gives people the benefit of doubt. You let Dean in even when he didn't deserve it, you gave him a chance, and I will not let you feel stupid for it."

"You always told me I was dumb for giving him a chance," Alexa said, this time with a more teasing smile. Still the sadness sat in her eyes.

"I've known Dean a lot longer than you." We'd been in elementary school together, then his parents whisked him away to Europe for his teenaged years. When he'd returned to Cedar Plains after university, he was a changed person from the shy kid we'd known before. Our lives were so different. But Brett never broke away from him, they'd stayed in touch by email all throughout high school, and Brett had visited him abroad more than once. He'd been Brett's first friend, something my fiancé could never let go of.

I had to imagine Dean was a different person with Brett, not a self-obsessed drug pusher I thought I knew. I never understood how Brett could stay friends with him once his career choice was clear, but Brett seemed to turn a blind eye to Dean. Like he didn't see him for who he was—or didn't want to.

"It's funny how hindsight is always so clear," Alexa said. "If I knew the things I know now, I'd never have started dating him."

"We live and learn," I said. "Have you talked to Kaylee?"

Alexa shook her head. "Not yet, but I'm sure I'll hear from her at some point."

"And Stevenson?" I stood up and started pacing through the room, unable to stop myself in the discomfort of it all. Alexa hated when I did this, and I couldn't blame her. It was a habit I adopted from Brett, and it still drove me crazy when he paced. Today, however, Alexa seemed unfazed by my irritating movement.

"He stopped by here after I left the hospital." She glanced around her room. "He's certainly getting comfortable with his questions."

"What did he ask you?" I paused at Alexa's dresser and started fiddling with the different jewelry on top; I'd always said she needed an organizer for all the pieces she inherited when her mom passed away, but she rarely listened to me when it came to organization. She loved her "organized chaos."

"Nothing really. Just about the night and if I had any more information about what happened to Kaylee," Alexa said, now watching my movements closely. "It's not even his case, but he's a nosy bastard."

I turned away, feeling scrutinized under her gaze. I searched for a distraction to lock my eyes on and found something out of place. A wedding ring, one I couldn't remember seeing before. It was a gold band with an engraving on the inside, barely legible, attached to a silver chain. It made me think about Mark's missing ring and I wondered where it ended up.

"Is this new?" I asked, though the aged piece clearly wasn't. I reached for the ring, sliding the chain through my fingers.

Alexa jumped to her feet and snatched the ring from my hands. "It was my mom's."

Then, with a look akin to a possessed Frodo, Alexa slipped the chain around her neck, letting the ring fall beneath her shirt, hidden from view.

I scrutinized her strange reaction. "I didn't know you had your mom's ring."

She smiled as she returned to her spot on the bed. "Yeah, you did. Phoebe gave it to me years ago. And here I thought you were the one with the good memory."

"Oh," I said, unsure how I could have forgotten. No wonder she was so possessive of it.

"Yeah, one good thing Phoebe did for me."

I nodded, unsure how to respond. I lowered myself back to the bed and eyed my best friend. "Tell me what's going on with you."

Alexa gave me a look. "Nothing. I'm fine. How many times do I have to say it until you believe me?"

"Maybe once more?" I cracked a smile.

"Don't worry about me, Court," Alexa said with a shrug. "I can handle myself in this tiny little town filled with *terrible* secrets." There was a joking tone to her voice, but I couldn't deny what she said. I thought back to what Mom said about Danny and Phoebe's affair and wondered if I should tell Alexa what I'd found out. As I considered it, I thought against it. Alexa didn't need to know the whole story or the choices her father made. Like Miles had said, it wouldn't change anything. Or it would make things worse.

"Are you going to make it to Nia's party tonight?" I asked, shifting the subject away from the things I wanted to forget and the secrets I was keeping.

"Yeah, I'll head by after work," Alexa said. "I shouldn't be off too late."

I hoped she'd be off earlier than later, but with Kaylee hospitalized, I wasn't sure if the bar was short-staffed. "It'll be fun!"

"Oh yeah." Alexa rolled her eyes. "A big Nia blow-out. Like last weekend wasn't enough."

I pushed myself from the bed, taking the hint she'd like to be left alone. "Text me if you need anything. Otherwise, I'll see you tonight."

I turned to leave and by the time I reached the door, Alexa had already picked up her sketch book again and gotten back to work.

"See ya," she said, without looking up.

I sat in front of my computer, chewing on my lower lip, as Brett got ready on the floor above. I'd been staring at Facebook for a few minutes, unsure whether I should type her name into the search bar. Alexa mentioning the recent crimes had put Vanessa back into the forefront of my mind. Her death, like Mark's, remained unsolved, but a sinking feeling told me something about it hit closer to home then we realized.

I typed Vanessa Foster into the search engine and began scrolling through the pages, looking for a recognizable photo. When I found the profile featuring the photo in the newspaper, I knew I'd found the right person. I flipped through her pictures, unsure what I was looking for when I landed on a profile of her. A life cut too short.

I stared at her for a moment, tracing every part of her face, one that would never see daylight again, when I noticed something strange. Two piercings in her right ear. The second was a star stud. A sense of déjà vu washed over me, like I'd seen this earring, or this picture, before. But where?

"Court?" Brett called from the stairs as he descended them. "All set?"

I jumped at the sound of his voice, then quickly closed out the browser and shut my computer.

"Yeah, all set." I shook my head, trying to clear the confusing thoughts from my mind. There'd been a series of strange, seemingly unconnected events over the last few weeks, but I wasn't convinced they were unrelated. Something in my gut told me I wasn't imagining things, that there was a danger lurking in Cedar Plains, and it was closer than I thought.

25

Alexa Huston

Saturday, July 29

I pressed the pencil firmly on the page, darkening the nearly finished sketch. Courtney's arrival had interrupted my work, and her unneeded conversation only intensified my desires, causing an uncomfortable itch in my palms and a dryness in my throat. The voice refused to be silenced. I would do as it wished. There was no alternative.

When I finished the sketch, I downed the remaining water in the glass beside my bed, but it didn't help to quench the clawing thirst. I glanced to the full waste basket, where I'd thrown away the sketch over a week ago. Drawing Dean's inner beast felt so surreal. Like my hands acted with a mind of their own. In the bin rested the ripped-up picture that my mysterious messenger left nearly a week ago. I hadn't heard from them since, but their watchful eye was ever in the back of my mind. They'd seen me with Vanessa. They knew too much.

Tearing my eyes away, I stood, hurried to the kitchen, opened the freezer, and found the ice-cold bottle of vodka I'd hidden near the back, thankful my dad hadn't been smart enough to look there for his latest fix. I poured a bit and shot it back, hopeful the gentle burn would do the trick and make the itch go away.

Still, nothing.

I threw the bottle into the sink allowing the remaining alcohol to spill out. Frustration bloomed. My palms itched. My throat ached. Nothing would clench this desire. Nothing but *him*.

The voice cackled with glee, knowing I had finally given in. I would do as it wanted. And tonight, my former boyfriend would give me the release I needed, as he always had before.

I walked into the small storage room in the back of our house. It was cluttered and had cobwebs everywhere. My father hadn't stepped foot in here for years.

His tool kit sat wide open, as I had left it days before when the cabinet door had come a bit too loose. The silver hammer was buried below the screw drivers, and when I picked it up, I felt the weight of the would-be weapon in my hands. The darkness smiled. This would be perfect.

After midnight, Ashley waved me over. The bar was packed and the four bartenders kept bumping into each other in a rush to get drinks.

"You wanna take off?" Ashley yelled over the loud music.

"You sure?" I asked. "It's a zoo in here." I scanned the people leaning over the bar trying

to get our attention. Some waved bills or clutched their credit cards in view.

"Yeah," Ashely said. "We're tripping over each other back here—it's getting inefficient. Take off, three of us can handle the rest."

I hesitated another moment until I felt Ashely's hands on my back pushing me away from the bar area.

"See you next shift," I said as I left her and the others to the chaos of the late-night partiers. I glanced at my phone as I made my way back to the staff area to grab my things. I had ten texts from a definitely intoxicated

Courtney begging me to get to the party soon. She'd be wasted when I arrived.

I got to Nia's before 1:00 a.m. and the party was in full force. From the street I could hear the muffled music. The curtains and low lighting obstructed me from seeing anything happening inside.

I found Courtney in the kitchen with Nia and a few of the other women from her friend group.

"You made it!" Courtney threw her arms around my neck and squeezed me tight. "I'm so glad you're finally here."

When she pulled away from me, I forced a smile, trying not to scrunch my nose at the stench of the tequila coming off her breath.

"Nia!" Courtney hollered to the hostess. "Get a picture of me and Alexa." Courtney shoved her phone into Nia's hand and drew me closer to her. Nia snapped a bunch of pictures as I tried to hold my false smile. Then Courtney grabbed my arm and dragged me towards the opposite end of the kitchen. "Here." She took a beer from the fridge and pushed it into my hand.

"Thanks," I said, cracking it open and taking a sip. Then I leaned closer so I could speak into her ear. "I'm going out back for a smoke." I turned and slipped out the door before letting her respond.

Wearing only a thin tank top, I shivered in the cool summer air but revelled in the silence away from the party. For working in a busy dive bar, I was never one to be in a crowd. At least at the bar I had a counter between us, something to stop the bodies from pushing up against me or the stumbling drunks from clumsily dumping their drinks all over me.

The creak of the door came from behind. I turned to see who had stepped out onto the deck. My palms itched when I lay eyes on him. The voice growled with anticipation. Dean shifted uncomfortably, his eyes cast downward to the deck below our feet. He held out a sweater—I assumed his—with purpose.

"You looked cold."

"I'm fine." I didn't take the proffered sweater or say anything further, only continuing to scrutinize him while I took another drag.

"What, you're going to be weird with me now?" Dean tossed the sweater over his shoulder and ran a hand through his hair. "In a few weeks we're walking down the aisle together, we're celebrating our best friends. We have to figure out some way to be normal." He took a step closer, and the stench of whiskey wafted from him. The voice cackled, finding amusement in his concerns. He was so worried about how we'd be seen together, and all the voice murmured was how he wouldn't be a problem anymore.

"Don't," I said defensively as I stepped farther from him.

"Alexa, I'm asking if we can figure out a way to be civil. I shouldn't have said the things I said yesterday, but I was angry."

"I'm angry too." I didn't offer him any compassion. I didn't have any.

"You aren't going to get over this, are you?" His entitled tone returned, his annoyance surfacing.

"My friend nearly died, Dean, that isn't going to change." I stared at him coldly, and his expression hardened.

"Your friend?" he scoffed. "You weren't friends with Kaylee, you were coke fiends. If you think she cares about you at all, you're wrong. Not once did she ever have any remorse for being with me when she knew I was with you."

I continued to smoke my cigarette, my silence saying all I needed to.

"Fine, see if I care." He turned back towards the door, his back facing me now. "No one else is ever going to give a shit about trash like you.

You're the one losing here." The door slammed shut behind him, and I turned away from the house.

The darkness simmered, making my palms itch and my mind fuzzy. The anticipation was numbing, and I was desperate for the release. I closed my eyes and let myself enjoy the slow burn of the tobacco. Only a few more hours and it would be over.

When Brett scooped Courtney up off the couch and left the party, it was nearly 3:00 a.m. The festivities had wound down, and only a few people lingered. I glanced around the crowd, a mix of those too drunk and others too wired.

I'd had little to drink but felt strangely intoxicated. Like another addition was fueling my feelings. The voice whispered its need. It urged me to finish the job.

With Brett gone, Nia found a place on the couch with two other women and dispensed a pile of powder. I caught her eye and gave her a wave, letting her know I was heading out. Dean was still there, chatting with a couple of guys I didn't recognize. I caught him staring at me as I slipped outside.

"You sure you don't want to come home with me?" I turned around at the sound of his voice. He hovered in the doorway, his words slurred and his expression droopy. I hadn't seen him do any cocaine all night. How unlike him.

I cocked my head as I regarded him. "I'm sure."

The voice whispered, *See you soon*.

He shook his head. "I don't get you."

"What's to get?" I asked. "You've made it very clear how you feel about me. I'm not sure why you'd think I'd go home with you."

"I could find someone else." He mocked. The darkness flared, an odd giddiness at the thought of two victims. I shook my head reminding the inner voice that Dean was deserving. He was the one who would fulfill its desire. No one else.

"Then do it," I said, trying to keep the irritation out of my tone. My passivity would bother him more than anger.

He stared at me hard for a moment, then turned and retreated to the party without another word.

I made my way slowly through town, heading away from my condo complex and instead to Dean's house. The streets were silent, typical for this time of night. Streetlamps gave off dull light, and a heavy cloud cover shielded the moon from view.

When I got to his house, I slipped around back and climbed the treehouse, sitting in the familiar spot from only a couple weeks ago, watching and waiting. The darkness simmered with joy. Its release was coming. It could feel it.

It was 4:00 a.m. when Dean finally returned home. I squinted for a moment at the sudden bright light of his bedroom. He stumbled into the room, and I held my breath, hopeful no one would follow. As luck would have it, he came alone. He sat on the edge of his bed, then stared at his phone. I wasn't sure what was happening until I felt the vibration in my pocket. I reached for my phone, seeing Dean's name on the screen. I placed it aside without answering, waiting for the call to be directed to voicemail.

"Fuck, Alexa," I heard Dean's muffled swearing from the open window as he chucked his phone across the room. Maybe he'd liked me more than he let on. *He's an idiot*, the voice mocked.

He sat on his bed, staring at the place he'd thrown his phone for a moment before standing and retrieving it. Then he stripped and went for the lights. Why did he come home alone? He could have found someone else, attractive and charming when he wanted to be. Something *had* drawn me to him months ago. But my mother had always told me the most dangerous wolves wore sheep's clothing. Dean was one.

I closed my eyes for a moment, and a new feeling took over. When I opened them again my movements felt predetermined like another hand guided my path.

I descended the tree when I was certain there was no movement in the darkness of his room and made my way to his front door. There, I pulled on the gloves from my backpack, slipped my key in the door, and silently let myself in.

In his front hallway, I took off my shoes and placed them in my backpack before sliding my feet into his oversized sneakers and pulling the laces tight. A couple sizes larger than my own, if any prints were left behind, they wouldn't be tied back to me. The anticipation hummed under my skin.

I laboured slowly into his bedroom, trying not to trip over the large footwear as my eyes adjusted to the darkness. His sleeping form was only feet away from me. I carefully reached into my bag and pulled out the hammer, weighing the tool in my hands.

"Who's there?" he asked, his speech slurred. I startled, stepping away and hiding my gloved hands and hammer behind my back. When the light flicked on, he rubbed his eyes, until they adjusted to the light. Soon his gaze was focused on me and a smirk appeared on his face.

"Alexa." He breathed my name, then he lifted his hand to me. "Does this mean you've forgiven me?" The confidence in his tone made the darkness angrier.

"I guess you could say that," I whispered.

Before he could answer I swung the hammer over my head and brought it crashing down against his temple. The sickening crack and warm splatter against my cheek confirmed the deadly blow as Dean's hand fell back to the bed.

I swung again and again and again, until I was sure my work was done. Then I stepped away from him, seeing the bloody mess before me.

The voice crooned with pleasure. The burning desire that had been forefront of my mind for weeks finally subsided. I'd fed the darkness, and it was happy with me.

I glanced to the light, wondering if I should turn it off, but knew I should avoid touching anything, even with my gloved hands. Forcing myself to turn away from the gruesome murder, I went to his dresser. I reached into my bag, pulling out the tissue I'd placed there earlier in the evening. I let the tissue unravel, and the star stud earring fell to the top of the dresser with a light clunk. Earlier, I'd sterilized it and cleaned off any evidence of my DNA on the piece. I was sad to part with it, but Dean seemed like the best keeper of our secret. After all, two can keep a secret if one is dead. The darkness agreed with my logic.

I turned to leave but hesitated when I saw Dean's Tissot watch sitting on his dresser. I stared at it for a moment, then swiped it. The voice cackled with joy. One trophy for another. I shoved the watch into my bag, then made my descent from his room, careful to pull the front door shut. Outside, I swapped his sneakers for my own shoes, then, with the hammer in hand I smashed the front window, making it look like someone had broken in and had their way with Dean. The noise was loud, so I moved quickly then, getting myself out of the street and onto a darkened path away from the house.

Under the cover of darkness, I stripped off my bloodied gloves and clothes then used the latter to wipe away the blood that had splattered on my face before changing into the extras I had brought and beginning my long trek home.

26

Courtney Faith

Sunday, July 30

Brett and I made love in the early morning, groggy from the night of partying and joyful in each other's company. I snuggled into him, wanting to stay in bed all day on this lazy Sunday. We deserved this.

It was bliss, until Brett's phone went off, and I envisioned him being called into work. He frowned when he picked up the call.

"Hello?"

The voice on the other end sounded rushed, though I couldn't hear what was being said.

His eyes went wide. "When? How?"

I straightened, gazing over at his stunned expression. What had happened? Brett swung his legs over the edge and pushed himself out of bed. He began pacing the floor as the call continued.

"Yeah," he said. "No, I get it. Call me if anything else comes up."

When the call ended, he looked to me, his face pale. "Dean is dead."

I went cold. "What?"

"They think he was murdered," Brett said. "That was the station." He continued to pace as he filled me in on the details he'd received. Someone had broken into Dean's house and brutally killed him, the method yet unknown. The police were called to his house after what looked like a break in and found his bloodied body. My stomach twisted at the idea Dean had been beaten.

"Are you okay?" I whispered, knowing the question was dumb but unable to think of another thing to say to him.

Brett shook his head. "I don't really know what I'm feeling right now. I can't believe he's gone. I can't believe he was murdered. These last few weeks have been nothing like what I thought our life in Cedar Plains would be."

I knew exactly what he meant. It was beginning to look like we had a serial killer in our midst. Why weren't the cops taking this more seriously?

"Did they say anything else?" I asked. "Was anything stolen? Could it have been a random break and entry that ended tragically?" I hoped there was more information to clarify the reason. For a moment, I wondered if Alexa had been involved. The recent break up and her strange behaviour had me on edge. I shook my head. Obviously, Alexa had nothing to do with it. She'd been with us all night.

"No details yet," Brett said. "All they said was someone broke in and killed him last night."

His phone jumped to life again, and we both looked at it. "Shit. It's Dean's mom."

I bit down on my lip as Brett answered the call, having no doubt Mrs. Miller would be hysterical. I slipped out of bed and went to our attached bathroom to give Brett privacy while he talked to her. I glanced up at my tired, hungover face in the large mirror. I'd seen Dean last night at Nia's but couldn't remember much, especially leaving. I placed my hands on the counter and drew several deep breaths, but when I closed my eyes,

I saw *them*. Vanessa, Mark, and now Dean. Three dead in less than a month.

Shaking the images from my head, I brushed my teeth, then headed back to the bedroom. I found Brett seated on the bed, his phone in hand.

"How is she?" I asked weakly.

He shook his head. "Not good. They'll be home later this afternoon, and I think I have to go over there. I need to help them, or something. But first, I have to go to the station."

"Of course," I agreed. "He was friend for years. You should be with his family. Honestly, I think I have to check on my own friend at this point." Alexa had been my first thought when Brett mentioned Dean. Did she know her ex-boyfriend was dead? I vaguely remembered seeing them together last night at Nia's, though whether it had been positive or negative I wasn't sure.

Brett nodded. "Be careful. The police probably went right for her house after they found him and made the connection between them. I'll let you know if I hear anything."

Of course, the police would go to her first. She was his girlfriend, actually a very recent ex. A lover scorned. A part of me wondered it, too, but as the thought crept into my mind again, I shook it free. This was my best friend I was thinking about. She would never do anything like this.

"I will," I said. I left Brett alone in the room and headed downstairs. When he followed, he was dressed casually in jeans and a T-shirt. "I'll message you in a few when I have an idea of what's going on."

He walked over to me and planted a firm but comforting kiss on my temple. Then he took me in his arms and held me tightly, a longer hug than usual, as if unable to let me go. When he did release me, I could see the tears forming in his eyes. There'd been so much death over the past month when these days were supposed to be happy ones. The countdown to the most-important day of our lives was on, but all we could think about was what had been lost. Mark, Vanessa, nearly Kaylee, and now Dean. I was beginning to feel nothing good was coming of our impending marriage. Maybe this was the universe's way of telling us we weren't meant to be.

Ugh. Foolish thoughts. None of these tragic events had anything to do with Brett and me. We were innocent bystanders who were tragically connected to troubled people. It didn't say anything about us as a couple, though I had to admit I felt self-centred considering my wedding plans with everything going on. In less than two weeks, out-of-town guests would start arriving, my brother Miles would be back, and I'd be walking down the aisle only a couple of days later. And we had the whole weekend planned. Different places for guests to stay and to visit, with activities and get togethers to celebrate everyone coming together. I was having a tough time wrapping my head around the whole ordeal when it seemed like locals were dropping like flies.

I got to Alexa's quicker than intended, my foot pressing extra hard on the gas pedal to match my ever-growing anxiety. When I saw the cop car outside her dad's condo, I didn't stop, unwilling to face Stevenson and his accusations. I had no doubt he was interrogating my friend and her invalid father.

Instead, I pulled over and sent her a text.

I saw the cop car. Let me know everything's okay. Let me know you're okay.

I drove home, hoping I'd have an answer from her by the time I pulled into our driveway, but there was nothing from either Brett or Alexa. An hour passed before I got anything. An abrupt and short text from Alexa.

It's cool, Court. Don't worry.

The cryptic text set me on edge. Too calm. How could I not worry? We'd had a nosy cop on our butts since Mark died, and now he had more he thought he could tie to us. Alexa's nonchalant attitude was strange. I texted her to ask as much but she didn't respond.

I opened my laptop and logged on to Facebook. I found Vanessa's profile and clicked over to her page. It had been converted into an in-memoriam page. A new post from who I assumed was a friend drew my attention. It was a picture of Vanessa and another girl arm in arm. The post expressed sadness and regret, implying Vanessa had left the bar that night with a guy, and the friend wished she'd been more attentive. I wondered if this guy had been identified or was just another mystery.

As I gazed over her joyful face, I was hit with the same feeling of déjà vu. This time, however, it came to me. I knew why both Vanessa and the star stud were so familiar. Alexa had been drawing something that reminded me of her. I recalled telling Alexa I found the picture quite dark but hadn't thought twice about my friend's taste for darker images. I was certain then Alexa had been sketching a star earring in the very piercing Vanessa had. I shook my head at the strange thought. How had she known to include this detail?

Darkness inspired Alexa—that had always been part of her artistry—and this time it was no different. She likely looked up the dead girl the moment she found out about it. Anything to inspire a bit of art. I clicked out of the profile and shut my computer, unsure how to describe the strange feeling I had.

I moved to head upstairs when there was a knock at my front door.

I opened it to reveal Rita Rounds, and it took all my effort not to close the door in her face.

"What do you want?" I snapped at her.

"I've been trying to get in touch without success," she said. "I'm still looking for a comment on your father's unsolved murder of course. And now I hear there has been another."

I narrowed my eyes at her. Dean had been dead for less than a day and this woman was already sniffing out the blood.

"Probably because I've blocked every number you've called from."

Rita was unfazed. "That sounds like you have something to hide. Only the guilty are afraid of questions."

"I'm not afraid of questions, but I'm also not stupid. Reporters like you aren't looking for the truth. You don't want the real answers. You want something you can spin and sensationalize. Trying to profit off someone else's tragedy."

"I'm sorry you feel that way, Ms. Faith," Rita said, her posture stiffening. "I only report the truth as it's given to me." She lowered her voice then. "But if someone isn't willing to share ... well, I can always fill in the blanks."

"Fill in whatever blanks you like," I said. "Because I have nothing for you and if you don't stop harassing me, I'll file a complaint."

An amused smile spread on her face despite the threat. "I take it you learned well from the cop fiancé of yours. So, like his father he is." She stepped back from me. "Very well, Ms. Faith. I'll leave you alone. However, given what's going on in this town, I suspect it's only a matter of time before you come to me with questions of your own."

Without another word, she turned on her heel, leaving the way she came. I watched her go, doubt whirling around inside me. For a second time she had implicated Kevin in something, and while a part of me was curious, the other part was desperate to protect my family.

As she climbed into her waiting car, Brett pulled up and climbed out, with takeout bags in hand. He hesitated, watching her disappear down our street, his glare following her. Then he saw me standing on the stoop and he came towards me.

"Hey." I went to him, taking the bags from his hands.

"What was that about?" He asked, glancing back over his shoulder to where Rita had been.

"The usual," I said, leading him into the kitchen. "I guess she's already heard about Dean."

"Did you say anything?" Brett asked.

"Of course not." I couldn't believe he'd suggest I would. "I told her to leave us alone or I'd file a harassment complaint."

For a moment his stern face broke into a small smile. "Sorry," he mumbled. "It's been a tough day."

"No doubt, how are you?"

The look on his face said it all. He was exhausted. Visiting Dean's family had surely been emotionally trying.

"His mom started crying the moment she saw me," Brett said. "They returned from their friend's cottage only a couple of hours before I arrived. I think they're both in shock." He reached into the bag and started putting the takeout containers on the table. Thai food, from one of our favourite spots.

"The coroner said he died around 4 or 5 a.m.," Brett said, and didn't notice when I frowned. I'd been pretty wasted. I couldn't even say for sure what time we went home.

"A neighbour called the police at 7:00 in the morning when they saw the broken front window." Brett shook his head. "Police found his body." His shoulders sagged. "I should have been there."

"Oh, c'mon, Brett." I moved to his side and stopped his busy movements of getting things out and ready for dinner. "Do not put any of this on yourself. It's a terrible tragedy, but it's not your fault."

Brett looked down at me with sad eyes but nodded to acknowledge he'd at least heard the words I'd said. He untangled my arms from around him and went to the cupboard, coming back with two plates and cutlery.

"His head was smashed in with a hammer."

I flinched as he said the words so bluntly.

"We don't know who did it," Brett said. "We're looking for any leads." Then he hesitated. "They wanted to know more about Alexa. And about their breakup." He turned his gaze to mine. "I know they seemed rough on Friday, but you didn't mention a breakup."

"She told me yesterday. It happened right after they left us."

"Why didn't you tell me?"

I shrugged. Why hadn't I? Because I was glad Dean was out of Alexa's life, and because I didn't want to stress Brett out with a complicated relationship between our maid of honour and best man. I guess the latter didn't matter anymore.

"What did you say about them?" I asked when Brett didn't continue.

"I told the truth," he said. "At least what I know. They'd been together only a few months. They spent a lot of time partying. Dean and I have been friends since we were kids. Standard stuff."

"What did they say?" I asked.

Brett drew a breath. "Apparently, Dean had a history of cheating on Alexa. And they found a lot of cocaine in his house when they searched it. They think he was dealing." Brett shook his head. "I believed him when he told me he wasn't. What an idiot I am."

"Brett, no—" I tried to cut in, but he continued.

"Then they asked if I had any information on what happened to Kaylee." He lifted his eyes to mine. "Implying Dean had something to do with it. It was weird to be questioned by my own guys."

"What about Kaylee?" I asked.

"They didn't say." He lowered himself to the bar stool next to me. "I know Dean's parents were never huge fans of Alexa, so who knows what they said to the police about her and her dad. I'm sure I'll find out more tomorrow." He reached for the Pad Thai. "Did you see her today?"

"No," I said, following his movements of putting food on my plate, though my appetite was gone. "There was a cop car out front of her condo, so I kept going. I didn't want to speak to any police, and considering how they drilled you, I'm glad I didn't."

"She hasn't texted you? Called?" he pressed.

"Just once, to tell me everything was fine." I shrugged. "She told me not to worry."

Brett snorted a laugh as he shoveled the first forkful in his mouth. "She knows who she's telling 'not to worry' right? All you do is worry."

I glared at him but knew he was right.

"You'll tell me, if you hear any more from her?" Brett asked, keeping an intense gaze on me.

"Do you think she had something to do with this?" I asked. Dean wasn't a good guy. I had no doubt he'd pissed off one too many people in this town.

Brett rubbed at his tired eyes. "I don't know."

We ate in silence, and I considered his words. Alexa couldn't have had something to do with Dean's death. She was an ex, sure, but she wasn't violent. She was a girl who'd been in a bad relationship. I prayed with Dean gone, Alexa would start to straighten out her messy life.

But as I sat there regarding my fiancé and chewing aimlessly on chicken satay, a quiet suspicion crept into my mind. Alexa had a darkness inside her, one she'd worked to quiet, though I'd always known about it, but in recent days it felt like it was clawing its way to the surface, and maybe I was too quick to dismiss her as wholly innocent.

27

Alexa Huston

Sunday, July 30

I sat at the kitchen table with Stevenson across from me. I hated the smug look on the detective's face, like he was a cat that caught a mouse and was toying with it.

"Was it a bad break up?" Stevenson asked. He'd been drilling me about Dean for several minutes. My barely coherent father sat on the couch, watching. Stevenson had tried questioning him, but his answers were jumbled at best.

"Aren't all break ups bad?" I asked, unwilling to give him any more ammo against me. At least there wasn't any evidence tying me to his murder. Well, almost. I'd ditched the hammer in the stream I crossed on my walk home. If they ever found it, I doubted they'd tie it to me. The bloodied clothes had been bagged along with Dean's sneakers and tossed in an industrial garbage bin miles from Dean's house, careful to check for cameras first. With any luck, it would be picked up first thing tomorrow morning and lost in a dump.

What Stevenson didn't realize was the expensive watch wrapped around my wrist put me at the scene of the crime. My eyes darted to my sleeve, making sure it was covered.

“Tell me about yours, specifically.” Stevenson steepled his fingers and placed his chin on top.

“Dean was a cheater,” I said simply. “I found out and decided we weren’t a good match.” I thought back to the sketch I’d scratched out late into the night. The fever dream trance when the darkness took over. Sweat had formed on my forehead as the adrenaline from Dean’s murder allowed me to recreate it on the page. The bed, the hammer, and the mysterious figure that was us, me and the voice. We’d finally snuffed out the monster in the dark.

It had since quieted to a gentle purred, sated in the aftermath of Dean’s murder.

“Sounds like you were angry,” Stevenson said.

“Not angry, not really.” A lie. “I felt stupid. How could I not have known?”

“Known he was a cheater?” Stevenson clarified.

“Yes.” I kept my eyes locked on him, resisting the urge to fiddle with the chain around my neck, a habit I’d caught myself practicing ever since I’d given up Vanessa’s earring the night before. The plain stud now occupying my second piercing was such a letdown compared to my trophy. At least I’d gained one in the process. I’d thought about the earring more than once since I left it last night. Had they found it and made the connection to the dead girl in the field? Or was it nothing but a lost treasure I should have kept my hands on?

My phone buzzed on the table between us, and both our eyes looked to the screen. It was a message from Courtney.

“It’s Courtney, do you mind?” I asked, reaching for the phone, irritation dripping off every word.

“By all means,” Stevenson said. “What does Ms. Faith want?”

I glanced down at the phone reading Courtney's text. "She's worried about me."

"And why's that?"

"Oh, I don't know," I said sarcastically. "Maybe because there are cops at my house and my ex-boyfriend was murdered. Seems like a valid reason to be concerned."

"Why would a police presence concern her?"

I looked at him pointedly. "You're an oblivious cop if you have to ask. You should know better than most a police presence can make even the most innocent person feel guilty."

Stevenson raised his eyebrows, amused. "What do you feel guilty about?"

"Making my best friend worry." My thumbs slid across the keyboard in response to Courtney, telling her all was okay. When I placed the phone down, I crossed my arms and looked back at the cop.

"You'd been together about six months?" Stevenson asked, though we'd covered the topic already.

"Yeah, pretty much."

"And during this time was Dean ever violent with you?"

I pondered his question, hoping the expression on my face didn't give way to my inner thoughts. Violent, sure, but was I ever scared of him? No. His violence was in the form of pleasure. Pulling my hair, choking, spanking. Nothing this particular cop needed to know about. Our sex games were our own.

"No," I said. "He wasn't a particularly violent guy. Though people like him don't need to be violent. They have other ways of causing harm."

"Like?" Stevenson asked.

"With money."

Stevenson pursed his lips but didn't ask me to expand. He didn't need to. I had no doubt Dean's wealthy father had already put pressure on the police department. He'd probably threatened them in a way similar to Dean's tactics. It was a learned skill after all. Dean had seen his family's money manipulate one too many people. Anyone who expected him to be different was an idiot.

"He'd never threatened you?" Stevenson asked.

"With violence? No."

"With something else?"

I looked away, thinking about the mysterious messenger who'd been silent since I received the picture of me and Vanessa.

"Ms. Huston?" Stevenson asked. "How did Dean threaten you?"

"Reputation," I said simply, looking back at him and tilting my chin up. "He made sure I understood with his money and his family's power, he could make me a social pariah, if I didn't do what he wanted."

Stevenson's lips quirked, clearly trying to hide this smirk. "Sounds like motive."

I scoffed. "Motive for what? Wanting out of a bad relationship?"

"Maybe murder was your only way out."

The voice flared with anger, and I glared at him, spitting my words. "If I had wanted to murder Dean, I would have done it long before now."

As quickly as the rage came it vanished, and I clamped my lips shut, realizing my mistake. The outburst made me look guilty. The darkness growled, deafening in my ears.

Stevenson simply grinned.

"That's enough!"

I jumped at the sound of my dad's rough voice; the growling in my head ceased. He'd pushed himself off the couch and lumbered towards the detective on unsteady feet. When he reached the table, he stood behind me and placed a heavy hand on my shoulder.

"You're looking for a confession in the wrong place," Dad said. I was surprised his words came out clearly, instead of slurred and garbled. "I have half a mind to get Geoffrey Miller on the phone and let him know how you are handling his son's murder." He glowered down at the detective who remained seated. "I'm sure he'd be interested to hear that you'd rather question a young woman with no evidence than actually do you job and find the killer."

"Mr. Huston, with all due respect," Stevenson said. "It seems tragedy befalls anyone who gets too close to your family. Dean, and the terrible incident with your late wife."

"Enough," Dad snapped, his eyes flashing. "If you aren't here to arrest one of us, then you can show yourself out. I won't have you harassing my daughter any longer. She's been through enough."

I sat, stunned, as I watched Stevenson slowly gather his things. I hadn't expected Dad to move, let alone defend me.

"Very well, Mr. Huston," Stevenson said. Then he looked back at me. "Ms. Huston, it's likely we will have more questions for you. With three unsolved murders in this town, a potential serial killer is not off the table."

"You know where to find me if you have more to ask," I said, keeping my arms crossed.

Stevenson tipped his hat, then found his way out of our condo. When the door closed behind him, I let out a breath.

"What was he implying about Mom?" I asked, turning my focus on my dad. "Why even bring that up?"

Dad regarded me for a moment, then reached up and rubbed his tired, unshaven face and retreated to the kitchen.

"Dad?" I asked, following his steps. "What about Mom?"

In the kitchen, Dad went to the cupboard and pulled out a bottle of whisky. He dropped an ice cube in the glass then filled it more than a single shot before tipping it back.

"Dad!" I said, harsher this time.

His glassy gaze found mine and he shook his head. "Nothing, Alexa. Your mom is gone, and it was a terrible accident but nothing more." He didn't wait for me to respond before he pushed by me with the glass and bottle in hand and returned to the couch. I watched him for a moment, unsure what to think. Mom's accident had been horrible. I still remembered the night like it was yesterday, how Dad came home in tears. The numbness that followed. The night of no sleep. The months of therapy. *It wasn't real. It wasn't real.* The nightmares and the awful realization that the mother I loved was gone.

Brett's dad had been there, telling us what happened, explaining the turn where her car went into the ditch, how she'd spun out in the snowy terrain. I'd hated the snow and winter ever since.

Now the alcohol plaguing my dad was the reason I was an orphan. Knowing I wouldn't get another answer out of him, I retreated upstairs to my room.

The following morning, I woke to my phone ringing. Courtney's profile picture lit up my screen.

"Hey," I said as I accepted the call and popped her on to speaker phone.

"Alexa," Courtney sounded winded. "Are you okay?"

"Yeah, I'm fine." I was getting tired of answering that question. I had been answering it since my mom died and now with Dean's demise. For some reason people never got tired of hearing I was fine. Maybe it was their sick way of getting comfort in the fact their life wasn't mine.

"Brett told me they think we might have a serial killer," Courtney said.

I slid the chain around my neck through my fingers, considering what she said. Was I a serial killer? The voice whispered, *Yes*. I'd murdered three people, well two, as one had been an accident. *Sweet Vanessa.* The darkness didn't care about her innocence. I still did.

"But the MO is different for each one."

"You've been watching too much *Criminal Minds*," Courtney joked. "Three murders in quick succession and no real leads, it's sus, and without any answers, they have to assume the worst."

'The worst' being Cedar Plains had a serial killer. I didn't answer right away, considering the label for myself. Serial killer. I was one of the disturbed people they chased down on some of my favourite TV shows. I was the bad guy. As I mulled over the word and the concept, I couldn't see myself as the evil person shown on TV. Sure, Vanessa had been a tragic accident, but despite the notion of murder being wrong, killing Mark and Dean had been the right things to do. When all the drama died down and their terrible ways faded into the past, the world would be a better place. I was sure of it.

The darkness agreed. *More*, it whispered. It liked the justice I sought.

"Alexa? Are you still there?" Courtney asked.

"Yeah, I am, sorry," I said. "Just wasn't sure what to say."

"This all must be so hard for you," Courtney said, sympathy in her tone. "I know you and Dean split on bad terms, but this isn't what any of us wanted."

Little did she know it was all *we* wanted, and *we'd* gotten our way.

"Did you see him at the party?" Courtney asked. "Did he talk to you?"

"Briefly," I said, thinking back to when Dean came outside and tried to give me his sweater.

"How did he seem?"

"I don't know, Court, drunk." I couldn't keep the edge out of my tone as I said it. "He tried to apologize, only to chastise me when I didn't give him what he wanted."

"Sorry," Courtney said quickly. "I didn't mean anything by it; I don't remember a lot of that night or seeing him, really."

I chastised myself for being cruel to her. She only meant well. "I'm sorry," I murmured. "I didn't mean to snap at you. The coward was probably avoiding you. There were enough cops at the party to keep his drug habits in check, but otherwise, he probably thinks you hate him since I hate him, you know, girl solidarity."

"*Thought*," Courtney corrected. "He's gone now."

"I know." My voice hardened. Why did she make this so hard? "What did you call for?"

"I was worried about you."

"I told you not to worry."

"I know," Courtney said, sadness in her tone. "But Brett came home last night from the Miller's place and told me the police were asking questions about you. I didn't know what to expect."

"Do you think I had something to do with it?" I kept my voice low, the darkness enjoying the game. The thrill.

"Oh my god, Alexa, no." Courtney gasped. "Never."

"Then why worry?" I could only guess it had something to do with what the Millers had said about me. Those WASPs hated me.

"Because you're my best friend." She sniffled, and I was sure tears had started rolling down her cheeks. Courtney had always been a crier.

"I'm okay," I said, my voice softer now. I hadn't meant to upset her. "It'll all be okay."

Courtney softly sobbed on the other end of the phone, and I didn't rush her. I was certain the Millers spoke poorly of me. They certainly didn't try to tolerate me and were quite good at making others feel less than. To them, I was trash their perfect son would be rid of one day. Too bad, I took out the beast first.

I was the lowest of the low when it came to their wonderful, perfect, industrious son. If only they'd known the real Dean. If only they'd known the games we'd played and the horrible person he'd truly been. To his parents, Dean had been a saint. No wonder he'd been so rattled over Vanessa and so rattled over me. I could have stained his perfect image. That had never been my goal. I didn't want to ruin him. In the end, I only wanted to be rid of him.

"Can I come see you?" Courtney asked. "I really want to give you a hug."

"Okay," I said. "You can come."

"I'll be there in an hour," she said. "And Lex?"

"Yeah?"

"I'm so sorry, for all of this." She disconnected before I could answer her, so I had to accept her apology in the silence of my house. She had nothing to be sorry for. Courtney wasn't to blame.

I stared up at the ceiling, running Mark's wedding ring between my fingers. A nosy cop unable to leave me alone. A mysterious messenger who knew too much. And three dead bodies tied to me. I needed the police to make the connection between Dean and Vanessa. It would help take the investigation in another direction. A thought prickled at the back of my mind. If they searched through Dean's things, would they find the incriminating photo? Would my hope of a distraction end up putting me back in the line of fire?

I sat up in bed considering my mistakes. I'd have to figure out how to play it cool. I couldn't have another outburst like the one I'd had before.

I moved to my dresser, removing the ring from around my neck and unclipping Dean's watch. I gazed over both my trophies, feeling the joy of the darkness inside. At least I knew, when it came to Dean and my choice to kill him, I'd picked right.

28

Courtney Faith

Wednesday, August 2

I finished up what I was working on in the morning and passed my clients on to my assistant to manage during my time off. Brett was on his last round of shifts before his extended holiday, and I felt the squeeze of the slow yet quick approach of my wedding date.

Savannah and I met at the bridal shop, the first thing on our to-do list, and she quickly ushered me into the changing room to try on my dress one last time. Only ten days to go, so it had to be perfect. The dress fit like a glove. An A-line gown with a sweetheart neckline, the long train, and the lace sleeves added to the originally strapless dress I'd picked out. I reached up and ran my hand over the cap sleeves. My something new.

After we headed downtown to pick up the printed table numbers, menus and place cards from the local printer, we then agreed on a spot for lunch before we would head to the venue one last time.

As we settled down for lunch at one of my favourite gourmet sandwich places, I found myself grateful for Savannah's steadiness. With all the drama surrounding Dean and Alexa the past few days, Savannah had proved to be a safe space for me.

"Thanks for all your help," I said. "I know it's not exactly the role you signed up for when I asked you to be a bridesmaid."

Savannah smiled. "You mean, because typically one's maid-of-honour takes on these duties?"

I laughed, "Yes, but Alexa has been through a lot the last few days."

Savannah's smile faded and she looked away from me. "We all have. These last few weeks."

I was quiet, because I couldn't argue with her.

"Has she seemed off to you lately?" Savannah asked, catching me off guard. "Like, not herself?"

I eyed my friend, considering her question. Thinking about the odd conversations, the sometimes-quick anger, and that strange gleam I'd seen in Alexa's eye.

"She's been through a lot," I said again, firm in my belief that the past few weeks had put us all on edge. "And all this suspicion from the police is making everyone uncomfortable."

Savannah reached across the table and place her hand on my own. "If you needed me to step in as maid-of-honour for you, I absolutely can."

I was stunned, not having expected this offer. Savannah had never hinted her desire to take over the role, only to support me when I asked.

"Thanks," I said, trying to keep my voice steady as I pulled my hand away from her and reached for my phone. "I'm sure Alexa will be okay, but I really appreciate how you've been there for me."

Savannah's pleasant expression faltered for a moment but was quickly replaced with her usual sunny smile. "Of course, Courtney. All I ever want to do is help."

Later in the evening, I was curled on the couch in my pajamas sipping a lukewarm cup of tea and wondering if I should crack the wine stashed in the fridge. It had been an odd day with Savannah. A new tension in the air after her clear desire to take over Alexa's role in my wedding. She was only trying to be helpful, I knew that, but her suggestion that something was off with Alexa had made me reconsider the last few weeks.

My suspicions were put on temporary hold when Brett arrived home. He'd texted a vague message earlier saying there was a new development in his case. I hadn't expected him home that night, so when he came in close to eleven, I wasn't sure what to expect.

"What happened?" I asked.

Brett fell to the couch beside me with an exhausted sigh, running a hand through his gelled hair and loosening it.

"I'm not sure I should say," he said, though I knew he would spill. Brett rarely kept secrets well when it came to work, though he'd never really had to. Besides, he knew me better than anyone. His secrets never left my lips.

I didn't answer, only continued to sip my simply underwhelming tea.

Soon he sighed again. "We believe Dean murdered Vanessa, the tourist."

The cup nearly fell from my hands as the words hit me.

"What?"

Another sigh. "A witness came forward, placing him at a club in the Cape with her the night she died. They swear they saw her leave with him."

I bit down on my lip. "Just him?"

"Yeah," Brett nodded. "I guess Kaylee isn't the only one Dean took advantage of." The strain on his tired face made my heart hurt; he'd known Dean for so long and now ... he was just another creep. Another convict. I wanted to comfort him, to tell him he couldn't have known, but I couldn't will myself to do it. Instead, my mind wandered. Dean was spotted in the Cape alone with a murder victim. Where had Alexa been?

A few months ago, when Dean and Alexa first started dating, I'd noticed the drugs getting out of hand. And then when we'd gone out for Nia's birthday at the martini bar in the Cape, I saw them leave with a skinny brunette. After, I didn't see them for the rest of the night.

When I asked Alexa about it the next day, she tried to shrug me off, push away the question. But I wouldn't let it go. Eventually she confessed her dirty little secret. She and Dean liked to play, with strangers. Tourists were easy—seduce them with the idea of drugs and a good time. Then never see them again.

It was harmless, she told me. Now, I wondered how harmless it really was. I rejected the thought as quickly as it crept up inside me. Alexa couldn't have been involved. Dean was a cheating creep. Vanessa was probably another random lay for him. Still, Savannah's words lingered in the back of my mind. Was I trusting the wrong person?

"There's more," Brett said, another audible sigh escaping his lips. He reached up and rubbed his bloodshot eyes. "We found an earring in Dean's house, one that could have been hers."

I went cold. "What kind of earring?"

"It's a small silver star stud," he explained. "It's circumstantial, but Vanessa wore one in many of her online photos."

I thought again about the star stud and the drawing I'd seen Alexa sketching weeks ago. The star stud was so prominent in my mind, almost like I'd seen it before. But, of course, I had noticed it in Vanessa's online photos.

"Is that all?" I asked.

"There were traces of blood," Brett said. "On his bedside table, the bedroom floor and in his bathroom. It was cleaned up, but not well enough."

"Can you match it to Vanessa?"

Brett shook his head. "At this point, no. He must have used bleach or something because the sample was tainted, but it's enough with the earring and the eye-witness account to close my case." They didn't need to convict a dead guy.

"I'm sorry, babe," I finally said to my fiancé when I forced myself to push the nausea aside. Dean was dead, but something told me it wasn't the end. "Nobody would have ever guessed what Dean was capable of."

"Except you, right?" The question sounded bitter, but his tone was simply defeated. "You've been telling me forever how little you thought he contributed to my life." Then he paused and asked me something unthinkable. "Are you relieved?"

I gasped. "Oh my god, Brett! No. Of course not. I would never have wished for this on anyone, let alone someone you loved."

Brett stood and started pacing the floor before me. His uniform was wrinkled from a long day's shift, pushing sixteen hours, and his nervous habit was in full force.

I nearly rolled my eyes and tried to coax him to sit but thought better of it. Instead, I stood and caught his hand, halting his movements and turning him towards me. Then I wrapped my arms around his waist and pressed my cheek into his chest. His rapid heart thudded under my ear as I breathed in the scent of his day. Old, lingering cologne, musty dried sweat, and cool evening air. Soon his arms found their way around my shoulders, and he bent down, placing a soft kiss on my hair.

"I didn't mean that," he murmured softly. "I know you didn't wish this on Dean. I guess ..." He trailed off and untangled himself from my hold. Then he ran his hand through his hair again. "I think I feel stupid. Like I should have known something had happened right under my nose." His shoulders drooped. "Some cop I am."

"You are a great cop, but when you care about someone, it's easy to have blinders."

"How can I go to his service tomorrow?" Brett asked. The Millers had organized a small service to commemorate their son. So small, they'd asked that only Brett attend, though I was grateful I didn't have to be a part of it.

I slipped my hand into his. "You don't have to go."

The frown on his face said otherwise. I gently squeezed his hand and led him to the stairs. "You also don't have to decide right now. Go get changed, have a shower. I'll bring up a snack and you can rest. Maybe tomorrow you'll feel differently."

Brett hesitated at the base of the stairs, looking me once over, then trudged up the stairs towards our waiting bedroom. When he disappeared into our room, I reached for my phone.

Something felt strange as I clicked into my photos and started to scroll, unsure what I was looking for. I started at Nia's party, swiping through the photos of me and Alexa. I looked way drunker than she did with my squinty eyes and wide grin. Alexa simply stared at the camera with a forced half-smile. With two fingers, I zoomed in, scrolling over our faces and trying to make out anything in the background. Nothing seems suspicious. Still, the unsettled feelings wouldn't cease. I swiped back to my bachelorette party and the shared album Alexa had created so all the guests could share their photos. The idea had been sweet, but chaotic, given that half the photos uploaded were blurry or haphazard, the result of too much wine and a mass upload. As I continued to swipe, I landed on a photo of me and Alexa in the limo, one I hadn't seen before. It was candid, as we were facing one another, talking about something hilarious by the looks of how Alexa's head leaned back in a laugh.

That's when I saw it and froze. Of course, I'd seen the star stud earring before. Carefully, I pressed my thumb and index finger to the screen and zoomed in on the side of Alexa's face. There, in her second piercing was a star stud earring. A forgotten conversation sat at the back of my mind.

A lump formed in my throat. A random girl. A club night. Dean's involvement and now this earring. Too much of a coincidence.

I swiped back to the photo of Alexa and me at Nia's party and tried to see if I could place the earring. If Alexa was still wearing it, then my theories were as farfetched as they sounded. But the photo revealed nothing.

I exited the photo app and tucked my phone away. I was being crazy. I was making a connection based on circumstantial evidence. Nothing told me the truth. Alexa was my best friend. If she was involved in this, if she'd had anything to do with Vanessa or with Dean, I'd know. Still Savannah's accusations whispered to me.

I tried to will myself to believe Alexa really was innocent, that she'd not been a part of any of this. The turmoil in my gut said something different.

I went to the kitchen and pulled together a bit of the leftover dinner I'd made and brought it up to Brett. My mind ran with all the possibilities. Could Alexa be involved in Dean's crimes? Or was it another person Dean had taken advantage of, like Brett implied.

When Brett emerged from the bathroom, I drew a deep breath and tried to push all my worries about Alexa aside. I didn't have proof. I didn't know for sure.

I slipped out of bed the next morning, leaving Brett sleeping soundly. I scribbled a note and left it on the counter for him to find. He was off today, and after the night he'd had, I expected he'd sleep for a while longer.

I was across town in minutes and outside Alexa's door before I really considered the time. Would she even be awake?

The door was locked, so I had to knock, and when a dishevelled Danny answered the door, looking overtired and groggy, I realized my mistake. He eyed me through narrow slits, ready to shoo me away until he registered who I was.

"She's not here," he said gruffly.

I stepped back, "Where is she?"

He shrugged and moved to close the door in my face.

I reached out and stopped him. "Did she come home last night?"

Danny frowned. "She stays where she wants to." This time he closed the door before I got another word in. I listened to his retreating footsteps, unsure what to do next. I considered texting Alexa to find out where she stayed last night but wasn't certain I'd get the answers I sought. Would the earring still be in her ear where I expected it, or did she have something to do with it being in Dean's room?

I reached out and tried the door, wondering if Danny had locked it behind him. The knob turned easily, and the door pushed open. I glanced around the front hallway, found it empty. Danny had likely made his way to the TV or had gone back to bed, though Alexa always made it sound like the two were one and the same.

I held my breath as I slowly closed the door behind me and crept up the stairs and slipped into Alexa's room.

The bed was made up and unslept in. I glanced around the immaculate room, wondering when Alexa would have cleaned up. She was never a particularly organized person. A strange sense of dread washed over me as I glanced around. The unease had been so present since yesterday. What had I come here for? It's not like Alexa's room would have a big sign saying, "Yes, your best friend is a murderer."

I glanced to her dresser, noting the ring I'd pointed out only a few days before was gone. Likely still hanging around her neck. For a moment I wondered if the ring reminded her of Bronwyn or of Phoebe. The latter had given it to her, after all.

The remaining jewelry was nothing fancy. Joe Fresh bulk earrings, a few necklaces. Nothing resembled the star stud she wore to my bachelorette. Wherever that earring was, it wasn't here.

The garbage can beside her dresser was empty, but as I turned away I noticed a crumpled piece of paper tossed carelessly behind it, nearly wedged between the wall and the dresser. I reached for it and flattened out the drawing. My chest tightened as I took in the crude artwork of the nude woman about to be attacked by a monster behind her. The picture was darker than anything I'd seen Alexa draw, and I quickly scrunched it back up and tossed it in the bin where I imagined Alexa had intended it to land. A sick feeling washed over me, and I forced myself to push it away. It was only art, right?

On my knees I searched for her sketchbook. I'd been unable to get her sketch of Vanessa out of my mind. I found the book tucked under her mattress between the bedframe and started flipping through. They were sketches of unfamiliar people or places but as I flipped further, the drawings began to darken in style and theme. Thicker lines, harder angles, intense shading.

I hesitated only a moment on an image I didn't recognize. It featured a car and three girls. I quickly flipped the page, shielding it from my view. My heart rapped a nervous beat against my chest. Why would Alexa draw *that* night of all things?

I continued flipping until I found the page from my memories. It featured a beautiful girl who could easily be the tourist whose picture had been shared in the news. They weren't identical but their features seemed similar. And I had been right. She did have piercings, two in her right lobe. The hard lines of a clear star stud stood out in the second hole.

I drew a deep breath and flipped to the next page. This one featured a body. Someone lying on the pavement, what looked like blood pooling around them. A discarded knife on the ground beside them. A clear line on the left hand, a tan line or maybe a ring.

My throat went dry. Was this supposed to be Mark?

When I flipped the page, I noticed the rips along the spine and glanced to the trash bin. I quickly retrieved the crumbled sketch and flattened it out, a perfect fit to the tears. Alexa had torn this page out for some reason.

I set it aside and stared at the picture after it. It was the one I'd seen Alexa drawing in the hospital. Kaylee's accident. The nude, nearly dead woman with a needle on the floor. As I glanced between the two, it was clear the girl about to be attacked by the monster in the shadows was also Kaylee.

My hands trembled as I looked to the next drawing. This time it looked like a bedroom, and a figure lay on the bed. As I glanced over the image, I realized it wasn't a person on the bed, but a beast. There looked to be blood splatted across the body and the wall, and what looked like a watch around his wrist. I looked back to the torn drawing. Was Dean the beast behind Kaylee?

In this new drawing, the beast wasn't alone. Instead, there was a figure in the shadow and a hammer in their hand. I flipped to the next page but found it blank.

I blew out a long breath, flipping slowly through the previous four. Alexa had documented each one of the murders, some with eerie accuracy. Sure, Mark had died in a park, not on a sidewalk as it looked in the image, but the night, the ring. The bloodstain.

A creak sounded in the hallway, and I jumped at the sound of someone climbing the stairs. I stood stock still, skin prickling, listening for approaching footsteps. My eyes fell to the sketchbook, still flipped open on Alexa's bed. I reached for it, closing the book then shoving it back into its hiding place.

The footsteps halted in the hallway, and I held my breath, waiting for Alexa to push her way into her room and catch me snooping. As I ran over a million excuses in my head, the sounds of a door opening then closing, snapped me into action.

I threw open her bedroom door and clambered down the stairs, dashing through the front door as quickly as possible. Outside, I sucked in the air, trying to calm my rapid heartbeat. Alexa had nearly caught me going through her things. Things I couldn't make sense of. Why had Alexa documented each murder? My imagination ran wild with pieces that didn't exactly fit.

Dizziness overcame me, and I lowered myself to the steps leading to the upper condos and willed my heartrate to slow.

"Courtney?" Her voice cut me like a knife, making me nearly topple over. Hadn't she just been inside? Her hands pressed into my arms, holding me steady. "Court, are you okay?"

I opened my eyes to meet Alexa's concerned green ones. I quickly pushed her away from me.

"I'm fine," I said, putting distance between us. She looked well rested, no bags under her eyes, no sign of drug use. She carried a small duffle bag, and it looked like she wore fresh clothes. She'd brushed her hair. It was down, straight and shielding her ears from view. She looked normal.

"What are you doing here?" she asked.

"Looking for you."

"I stayed at Ashley's last night," she explained. "We had a long shift then figured a split bottle of wine was better than one alone. What's up?"

"Something happened with Dean's murder," I said. "Something I shouldn't know about."

"But Brett told you because he can't help but share everything with his precious Courtney?" She didn't mean it as an insult, but the words were harsh. Again, Savannah's words came back to me. This wasn't the Alexa I knew.

"They think Dean killed the tourist. Vanessa," I said bluntly. "The one they found in the field."

For a moment I thought I saw her shoulders go rigid, but it was so quick I wasn't sure if I imagined it.

"Wow," she said, surprise in her voice. "Seriously?"

"Don't sound so surprised," I said.

Her brow furrowed, and she regarded me with confusion. "What are you talking about?"

"They found an earring in his room," I said. "A star stud that matches the one you wore to my bachelorette."

"You aren't making any sense." She tucked her hair behind her left ear, revealing the place where the star stud earring had been a few weeks before, now a plain silver ball rested in its place. Her sleeve slipped down, revealing a watch I'd never seen her wear before. "You know I never take out my earrings."

"There's a photo of you wearing it," I snapped. I reached into my pocket and pulled out my phone. Quickly I flipped through the shared album trying to locate the picture I'd seen the day before, but it was gone. I looked up at her with accusing eyes. "Did you delete it, to cover your tracks?"

I hadn't come here to accuse her of murder, but the strange coincidences were too much. The detailed drawings, the missing earring, Savannah's suspicions and the things Stevenson implied.

"What exactly are you trying to say?" Alexa demanded. "You're acting crazy."

I forced myself to look her in the eye. Was I acting crazy? It made my mind fuzzy with confusion. I wasn't sure what I knew anymore.

Before I could answer, her gaze softened and she said, "Consider what you are saying." She drew a slow breath. "Do you think I killed a tourist, took the earring, kept it, only to murder my ex-boyfriend and frame him with it? A piece of metal. Really think about this. Why would I do it?"

When she laid it out, it did sound crazy, but what sounded crazier at this point? A random earring that was a perfect match now mysteriously gone and a missing picture I was certain I'd seen. My head couldn't make sense of it anymore.

"What about the drawings?" I asked. "The girl with the star stud earring, the dead bodies, the monsters." The images I'd seen upstairs for only a few moments still burned in the back of my mind.

Alexa's eyes narrowed. "Have you been snooping?"

"I saw what you drew," I said, ignoring her accusation. "Each murder, meticulously sketched out."

"Oh my god, Court." She laughed. "It's art. You know I venture a bit dark. I used the deaths as inspiration."

"No," I said. "Vanessa wasn't found until after you started the picture of her. You were drawing it at my house the night Mark died." I was sure of it now. I remembered her sitting at the table, carefully sketching a woman's face. It had to be Vanessa's.

Her mask of confidence slipped for only a second before righting itself. "I was drawing a picture of my mom at your house. Do you even know what you're talking about anymore?"

I frowned. Had I misremembered? I squeezed my eyes shut, trying to force the memory to come forward. Trying to remember what I'd seen her sketching.

"The portrait of Vanessa came before Mark's death," I said. "He was found first. They're out of order."

Again, Alexa laughed. "I honestly don't know what to say, Courtney. I never thought my bad artwork would be grounds for you to think I was a murderer. I started Vanessa's drawing when I saw her picture in the paper. She was beautiful, a piece of art. After I began, the rest followed."

I chewed on my lower lip but didn't answer.

Alexa spoke again, her voice calm and soft. "Court, really think about this. Do you think I'm capable of murder?"

I looked up at her and considered the question. I'd known Alexa for over fifteen years. Of course I didn't think she was capable of murder. But even as I considered it, I realized, like Brett, I couldn't really know what my best friend was capable of.

I had no real proof. The picture was gone. The sketches were just sketches. I made my accusation, and she told me otherwise, so I conceded, and said, "No, I don't."

Alexa shook her head with an amused smile. "Jeez, Brett needs to stop telling you about his cases. You're going out of your mind."

"Isn't this perfect," a voice said, coming from the parking lot behind us.

Alexa and I turned to see Officer Stevenson standing only a few feet from us, smiling, though it didn't look friendly. I immediately went cold. How much had he heard?

"What do you want?" Alexa said, glaring at the officer.

"I was in the area," Stevenson said, tucking his hands into his pockets. "And I saw what looked like a rather heated argument." He glanced between us. "Everything okay?"

"Fine," I said, hoping my voice didn't shake. Had he heard me accuse Alexa of murder?

He continued to glance between the two of us, but neither of us offered any further explanation.

Stevenson reached up and tapped his chin. "This wouldn't be about a certain accident, would it? Arguing about Savannah." He paused, glanced between us then added, "Or Bronwyn."

Alexa's hands tightened into fists at the mention of her mother. A look crossed her face I couldn't describe. She almost looked like a stranger in her rage.

I stepped forward, putting myself between Alexa and the officer. "We're fine. Mind your own business."

Stevenson produced an easy grin. "Why, peculiar crimes *are* my business. Like a hit and run, or a snowy accident."

I inwardly cringed and forced myself to keep my eyes on Stevenson, hopeful he wouldn't expand on his suspicions.

"We said we're fine," Alexa said, her voice hard. "Or do we need to report you for harassment?"

Stevenson's eyes narrowed, and he put his hands up to feign innocence. "I can see where I'm not welcome." He took a step back but eyed us with suspicion for a moment before he turned on his heel and walked away.

Alexa and I remained silent, watching him go.

"What the hell is he on about?" she snapped when he was gone.

I shook my head. "I don't know. He's been implying things about Savannah ever since Mark's accident."

"And my mom?" Alexa asked.

I hesitated, knowing if I didn't want to tell her what Mom had said, then a lie was my next choice. "Nothing. It's the first I heard him mention her."

When I met her eyes, she gazed at me with suspicion but soon her glare shifted to the spot where the officer had been standing. "Bastard."

"He doesn't know anything," I assured her, though it was more for myself. "Just tossing a line out and seeing if anything hooks." Trying to catch us in a lie.

Alexa fixed her gaze back on me, her hardened expression was gone. "Are we okay?"

I forced a smile. "Yeah, I'm sorry I jumped to conclusions."

She reached for me and put her arms around my shoulders, pulling me against her. "Good, because I'd be lost without you."

I let her hold me, trying to silence the twisting inside me. Despite her words, I couldn't forget her strange drawings. Or the missing picture. I tried to force myself to see reason, to agree with the things Alexa told me, but something inside felt wrong. Like I was missing something right in front of me. Something big.

29

Alexa Huston

Sunday, August 6

It had been weeks since I'd seen her; I had to double take as she walked into the bar. Rita Rounds was still dressed far too nicely for a dump like Big Shot, but she seemed unfazed as she passed by Sunday drunks on her mission to where I stood behind the bar.

"It's good to see you, Ms. Huston," Rita said, sliding onto a barstool and placing her phone on the bar between us. "I've been hoping to catch you for a minute alone."

"I'm kind of in the middle of a shift," I said, waving around at the few patrons gathered about.

"Yes, well, you've been difficult to track down," she said. "I've been by your condo, tried calling."

"Have you ever considered that maybe people don't want to be featured in your articles?"

Rita pushed forward. "But wouldn't you like a chance to comment? Dean Miller has quite the reputation and being his girlfriend—"

"Ex-girlfriend," I said through gritted teeth. The darkness growled.

"Right." Rita smiled, like she'd gotten the reaction she hoped for. "*Ex*-girlfriend. You must have something to say about this suspected murder."

I glared at her, willing the anger inside me to stay quiet. To not give into the darkness.

"No?" Rita asked, tilting her head when I didn't answer her. "Such a shame." She pushed herself from the barstool and shrugged. "Well, I guess I have others to speak to. Ms. Wen will certainly prove helpful, I'm sure." She was out the door before I registered that she spoke about Kaylee. I was beginning to hate this nosy woman.

When I returned home, it was after eleven, and I found another note tacked to my front door. The same envelope. The same scrawl. My mysterious messenger had returned. I guess it hadn't been Dean after all. I cringed upon seeing it, glancing around, feeling as though a hundred eyes were fixed right on me.

I snatched it from the door, noting the seal and hoping that whatever was inside was still secret. After the photograph of me and Vanessa, I couldn't be too careful.

In my room I tore open the envelope to review a note with only one word.

MURDERER

The blood red letters were capitalized and messy across the page. I crumbled it up and threw it against the wall, watching it tumble into the trash. The darkness raged, demanding answers. Someone knew my secret, but what did they want?

The following morning, my mysterious messenger and the nosy reporter were temporarily pushed from my mind when the ad popped up on my Instagram feed. *Brand-new tell-all memoir from best-selling romance author, Phoebe Dawson, out August 8.* Nausea whirled around inside me. I'd been avoiding Phoebe's pages, finding myself uninterested in her with my new hobby taking over. That didn't stop her information from showing up on my feed. I should have unfollowed her ages ago.

In the last seven years, Phoebe made quite the career for herself, writing steamy romances and torrid love stories, novels other women in my age bracket devoured but of which I wouldn't even flip a page. I could barely look at her name on the cover, let alone support her career. After all, my dad's money had funded it all.

And now ... she was releasing a memoir—*The Hardest Part of Love*—to tell *her* story of love, loss, and life. The post advertised a juicy little tidbit: how it felt to be with someone who had everything and then lost it all. It didn't outright say it, but I knew it was the story of my dad's accident.

I nearly threw my phone against the wall as I read through the comments of her avid fans. So many expressed excitement to read about the author's love life, something many romance authors kept to themselves. Could it be as good as her novels? Could it be better? It was real life, after all.

In two days, my dad's story, the *wrong* story, would be out in the world for all to read. She wouldn't sugar-coat it, as that wasn't Phoebe's style, so it would be embellished and drawn out. I wondered for a moment if she'd even bother writing me in. We'd been close once, early in my dad's relationship with her. She'd been Mom's best friend. A constant presence around the house. It was weird when she first started dating Dad, but the relationship brought him light in the darkness of Mom's passing.

As if my body were acting separate from my mind, my finger clicked on the link to her profile, and soon I was scrolling her Instagram page. Seeing her painted, smiling pink lips while holding her precious novels caused anger to course through me. She was blond now, something I hated to admit suited her more than her dark strands ever did.

She'd milked Dad for all he was worth: lavish trips, luxurious clothes, late-night dinners, the most expensive bottles of booze, and then one day, when they'd stayed out too late, indulged too much, he was clumsy on the job. He fell and was never the same again. Soon, he was laid off and put on workers' compensation, followed by the long-term disability cheques that kept his habits afloat today. I'd since taken on the responsibility of the bills.

I scrolled back up and went to click off her page before the pink circle around her profile picture caught my eye. She had a posted story. I clicked on it and nearly gasped at what I saw. It was an older shot; she looked younger than her other pictures and her hair was dark like I remembered. When the time ran out and the picture exited, I clicked the story again. I knew this picture. Too well. Dad took it nine years ago. Phoebe stood outside our old house with the familiar white framed windows in the Victorian home. The house where I'd been a teenager, where Mom died, where we lost everything ... thanks to Phoebe.

The short text she'd written over top put a sour taste in my mouth.

Find me back in Cedar Plains where the juiciest part of my story took place. Cedar Plains Public Library. August 11, 2:00 PM.

The darkness awoke from its short rest, unsure how to process this new information.

Phoebe was coming back to town in five days. The day before Courtney's wedding.

I clicked out of the app and set my phone down on the bed beside me. I was overcome with desire, something I didn't expect. I felt drawn to the library, like I needed to be there, needed to lay eyes on her for the first time since she broke my dad. I didn't know what to expect, or what I even wanted from her.

I opened my messages and sent Courtney the link. We'd barely spoken over the weekend since she came by with her accusations, though I tried not to think about it. Every time I did, the darkness growled. I didn't like the way it felt about Courtney.

Worse, I worried how much Stevenson had heard and what he'd begin to investigate. I hadn't seen the nosy cop since, though his comments about Mom still whirled around my head. Courtney denied he'd mentioned her before, but the way she looked away from me, the guilt written on her face, made it clear she was lying.

The message Courtney returned was short, *Did you know she was coming back?*

I answered her inquiry with a shrug emoji, hoping to avoid any further discussion on the matter, but it was no good. Why did I bother sending it to her in the first place? I knew better than to think she'd let it go without an inquisition.

Now she had my attention and peppered me with questions. What did I think? What would I do? Would I tell my dad?

The latter was easy. No. Dad didn't need to know about this mess and the last place he'd ever show up was the library. For once in my life, I was thankful he'd run his life into the ground. At least he didn't have any friends who could put Phoebe's impending arrival on his radar. No, Phoebe's surprise visit would pass right by Dad which was for the best. If he knew she was coming ... I couldn't even imagine what he'd do. Would he try to see her? Beg for her? Be over her? Or would it break him further? All I knew was I couldn't try to pick him up again after seeing her. She'd broken him worse than the bones in his back, and he'd never recovered from that wound. This was something better left unsaid.

I lay back against my pillows, unsure what I wanted. It had been so long since we'd seen each other. Phoebe left so abruptly. I'd been away when she had the gall to walk out the door. I came home to a nearly empty house and a drunk, broken father who couldn't verbalize what happened through his slurred speech and sputtering tears. No longer the excited, spirited, joyful man who raised me and played in the nearby park and carried Mom up the stairs after their date nights. He'd been so full of life and love, but Phoebe had changed that.

The idea of seeing her rolled around in my head as my phone chimed again, this time with question marks for the questions I still hadn't answered. Hoping to silence Courtney for the night, I texted back quickly.

I don't know what I'm going to do.

It was a moment before Courtney replied. Her message was short and sweet, followed by a heart emoji.

I'm here for you. No matter what. ❤

Me too, the voice whispered. *No matter what.*

30

Courtney Faith

Tuesday, August 8

I sat at the table with Mom to my right and Savannah and Missy sitting across from me. Alexa was supposed to be here. The wedding was only four days away, but my maid of honour was having an emotional crisis with the impending arrival of Phoebe. Savannah had stepped in once again.

Missy and Mom were discussing the wedding, gushing over how beautiful the day would be and planning out the morning when we'd be getting ready. Missy and Nia would be joining the bridal party until they needed to be carted off for family photos with Brett's side.

Savannah gave me a sympathetic smile as another bottle of bubbly was dropped on the table and Mom and Missy helped themselves. It was the third bottle, and between the four of us, they'd consumed the most.

"It's going to be such a great day," Missy gushed, sipping the bubbly liquid. The way her speech had begun to slur told me this lunch needed to end soon.

Mom gave my hand a squeeze. "Perfect."

"Oh, Liv," Missy said, lowering her voice. "I've been meaning to ask you. Did you hear about Phoebe Dawson?"

I straightened at the mention of Phoebe and glanced between my mom and Missy.

Mom looked down at her glass. “Yeah, she actually reached out to me.”

“What?” I asked, too quickly.

“I didn’t talk to her,” Mom said, shooting me a sideways glance.

“She’ll be at the library on Friday. I guess some awful book she wrote came out today,” Missy continued, sipping her champagne again. “I can’t believe she’d show her face around here again. After what she did to Danny.”

I bit down on my lip.

“Phoebe saved Danny,” Mom said. “After Bronwyn died, without Phoebe, Danny would have struggled.”

Missy scoffed. “He struggled anyway. Besides, she’s the reason Bronwyn died in the first place.”

“What?” I demanded, glancing from Mom to Missy.

“Miss,” Mom said, urgency in her tone. “We don’t know that.”

“*You* don’t know,” Missy said, sipping her drink again. “But I do. If Phoebe hadn’t been sleeping with Danny, Bronwyn would have never left us. And to think people just accepted her after Bronwyn’s death.” Missy shook her head. “It’s awful, is what it is. And that woman has no business coming back here.”

A coldness swept over me, and I glanced at Savannah. She kept her eyes trained on the plate in front of her, as if she hadn’t just heard Missy’s confession.

“Miss,” Mom said again. “Don’t go spreading those rumours. It was a long time ago.”

"All I know is that snake is making a mistake coming back to our town." Missy raised her eyebrows as she took another sip, downing the rest of the liquid in her glass.

I agreed. It made me think of Alexa again, and I wondered how she was coping. We'd been barely communicating for days, and I was starting to worry. Part of me wished I hadn't confronted her with my accusations, but the other part of me couldn't get the strange sketches or conflicting facts out of my head.

"Court?" Savannah prompted, drawing me back into the conversation. "We're about to settle up. You want to stop by the boutique to grab that bracelet you wanted?"

I eyed her, unsure why she'd suggest I grab it now when she'd planned to bring it to the wedding, but the look she gave me implored me to say yes. I nodded as Missy grabbed the bill, insisting lunch was her treat.

Then Savannah and I said our goodbyes and started down the street towards her waiting store.

"Sorry about that," I said. "Brett's mom tends to get a little too gossipy after a few drinks. You'll keep what they said between us? I don't think Alexa needs to know."

Savannah cast me a sideways glance but voiced her agreement. "Everyone has secrets in this town, don't they?"

"You have no idea," I said before I could stop myself and wonder what Savannah could mean by that. How much did she know about mine?

Savannah kept quiet after, and I realized she'd been silent most of the meal. With Missy gabbing on at every chance possible, it didn't surprise me. Still, something was off.

"Is everything okay?" I asked as we reached her store.

She didn't answer me right away, instead, sticking her key in the lock and leading me through the front entrance. Once I was through, she locked the door behind me. The store was usually closed on Mondays and Tuesdays so she wouldn't be expecting customers today.

When she turned back to face me, her expression was ashen.

"You're freaking me out," I said, my mind running wild with the possibilities.

She wheeled closer to me and shook her head. "I don't know. I feel like the police are giving me the run around."

Nausea twisted through me at the mention of the cops, remembering the way Stevenson implied I had something to do with Savannah and her accident. "What do you mean?"

"Some officer, Stevenson, I think," Savannah said. "Called a few days back to say they think they may have found the car that hit me and asked if I could remember any details."

My throat went dry, and I rasped out my next words. "How could they have located it after all this time?"

Savannah shrugged. "He wouldn't say. Just kept pressuring me to remember." She paused then looked up at me. "He mentioned you. Implied you might know something."

"How could I know something?" I tried to ignore the pit of guilt forming inside me, threatening to swallow me whole.

Savannah shook her head. "That's what I said. Do you know this guy?"

I grimaced. "He's handling Mark's murder. He's been invasive with his questioning. Like he is looking to blame us since he can't find a suspect."

"What an ass," Savannah muttered. "The last thing I need is to dredge up the past."

"You don't harbour any anger for the person who did this to you?" I glanced over her wheelchair, wondering who Savannah would be if she'd never been hurt.

She glanced back at me. "Sure, I'm a little angry. Someone's poor decision completely changed my life. But harbouring any ill will towards them won't change what happened to me. If whoever hit me was human at all, I have no doubt the accident has haunted them for as long as it has me."

She had no idea how right she was.

"You're such a good person," I said and meant it.

Savannah offered a small smile. "I'm just trying to live the life I have." Then she let out a long breath and wheeled towards the front counter. There she opened a locked case and pulled out the diamond bracelet she promised me. The one she wore to her wedding. My something borrowed.

I reached out to take it from her, then glanced around the closed store. "Thanks for this. And again, for coming with me today. Alexa was having a hard day."

Savannah looked to retort but instead smiled and said, "I'm always here for you, Court. Whenever you need me."

I glanced to the large clock on the wall. It was mid-afternoon, and I was itching to go home. The conversation had put me on edge, and the last thing I wanted to do was remember that night while Savannah sat with me scrutinizing my behaviour.

"I should head home," I said, trying to remain as casual as possible.

"Call me if you need anything," Savannah said.

I glanced back at her. "Yeah, you too."

I stepped out into the afternoon sun as a car whipped by, and I was immediately taken back to that night.

It was dark, past midnight. Alexa and I had been out in the Cape, drinking for longer than I'd planned.

"Let's grab a cab," Alexa said, pulling me away from the parking lot toward where the line up for the cabs waited.

My car keys jingled in my hands. It would cost a fortune to leave the car overnight and the line up for the cabs was already around the block.

"I'm fine," I insisted. "I can get us home."

Alexa studied me. "We've been drinking for a while."

I waved her off, feeling more sober than I was. "You've been drinking for a while. I didn't have nearly as much." The truth was, she'd only passed me by a drink or two.

She continued to gaze at me, not responding, so I reached out and grabbed her arm.

"Come on," I said. "It'll be fine."

Soon we were in my car, speeding towards town, blasting Miley Cyrus and singing at the top of our lungs. When we reached the main street, it was empty, so I kept my speed and made my way towards our turn. I barely slowed, and as I wrenched on the wheel to make the turn, it all happened quickly.

A flash of colour to the right in the beam of the streetlight. A sickening sound of something solid hitting the front bumper of my car. My foot slammed on the brake, throwing Alexa and I forward in our seats. The fabric of the belt pressed hard into my shoulder. The taste of bile and traces of vodka made my already-dry mouth pastier as I looked over at Alexa, certain her wide, panicked eyes matched my own.

"What was that?" She turned down the music, glancing over our shoulder. My heart thumped in my chest as I pulled over and we both climbed out of the car. I squinted in the darkness, taking a couple hesitant steps towards the street corner.

When I saw it, my muscles tensed.

"Oh my god," I said, nausea overtaking me. "Oh my fucking god."

Alexa glanced from me to the body and back. I took another tentative step towards the person I'd hit. They lay motionless on the asphalt. The night air was crisp, fresh from a recent rainfall and slick with humidity. Could I smell the metallic tang of blood? My legs went weak, and I fumbled in my pockets, trying to find my phone.

"Courtney, get back in the car," Alexa said, her voice flat.

"Did I kill—" I couldn't finish the thought, instead I continued to search for my phone. Where was it?

"Get back in the car." Alexa's words were firmer this time as she interrupted my thoughts. I still didn't follow her instructions. "Now."

Then I booked it back into the driver's side. I gripped the steering wheel, unsure what to do next. My eyes fell to the centre console. My phone. I reached for it as Alexa climbed into the passenger side.

She reached over and took the phone from my hand. "Drive."

"We can't leave them there," I protested. "I have to call someone."

"We can't." Alexa closed her eyes for a moment. "Courtney, we're drunk. This is going to ruin your life. We have to go, now."

Still, I hesitated, unable to imagine leaving the person behind.

Then she spoke again. "Brett is a cop. This will ruin his life too."

Brett. His career. Our life together. I could see every door to the life I'd imagined closing in my face if this got out.

I slammed my foot on the accelerator and got the hell out of there.

I shook my head as I cleared the memory from my mind. Afterward, the night was a blur. Alexa rarely spoke of it again. And when I checked the car the previous morning, there was no clear indication anything had happened, no damage, no scuffed paint. We let the secret be buried between us.

I later learned it had been Savannah I'd hit as she was leaving her store, working too late on a last-minute gown. It had put her in the hospital for months. She didn't die, but her life was never the same. And neither was mine.

By the time I stepped foot in my house, my arms had begun to itch, and blotchy hives had formed. The stress was overwhelming. The secrets began to take their toll. Between the wedding, Phoebe's return, our parents' secrets, Alexa's strange sketches, Savannah's suspicions, and now my skin breaking out with disgusting craters, strung-out didn't begin to describe how I was feeling. My hypersensitive body went into full panic mode.

When Brett saw my distress, he was quick to run me a bath and start his typical soothing methods. I tried to protest but couldn't deny it when the itch moved from my arms, up my neck. A full out reaction happening. I settled into the oat-bath and Brett hesitated, perching against the bathroom counter with his arms and ankles crossed, it was clear my stress was affecting more than my hormones.

"Is it the wedding?" Brett asked, his tone strained. I'd been on edge since he came home with news of Dean. For him, the case ended there. For me, I was in some weird sort of limbo trying to convince myself my best friend had nothing to do with it and fighting with my gut seeming to think differently. I'd been sick for what felt like weeks when it had only been a few days. I hated lying to him.

"No," I said sincerely. The wedding was the only thing in my life making sense now.

"Because you know Miles stepped in to be best man," he said, trying to reassure me as if all my worries depended on the fact his former best man was dead.

"Of course, he did," I said, forcing a smile and trying not to rub the small red bumps on my skin. The bath soothed the itch. If I could calm down, the hives would vanish by tomorrow.

I didn't need him reassuring me about my brother's new role. Mom was going to walk me down the aisle now, like I'd wanted all along.

"Something's still bothering you." Brett looked down at the floor, uncrossing his ankles and shifting in place. The urge to pace was nearly overtaking him.

I sighed, stirring the bubbles in the tub aimlessly. "Do you remember the woman Danny Huston started dating back when we were still in high school? After Alexa's mom died?"

Brett's blank expression told me he was clueless.

"She's back in town," I explained. "Or she will be. It's been years since she walked out on Danny and Alexa, and to be totally honest—"

He cut me off before I could say more. "You're worried about Alexa." There was exasperation in his tone, but I wasn't sure if he meant it. He'd been seeing me as Alexa's saviour since we were teens. I had no doubt my worries exhausted him.

"Yeah," I said, though felt shameful for feeling it. "It's just ... she left Alexa without a word and for a long time Alexa looked for her. And now ..." I shook my head. "Her coming back, it's opening old wounds." Seemed like that was happening a lot lately.

"Alexa is stronger than you give her credit for," Brett said simply.

"Phoebe wrote a book about them," I said, thinking of the memoir. "I couldn't imagine someone taking stories from my youth and repurposing them as entertainment." Phoebe had been a lot of things, fun, playful, outgoing, but self-aware was not one of them. She would paint the story exactly how she remembered it. I didn't think it would bode well for Danny or Alexa.

"I don't know," Brett said playfully. "Sometimes I think it would be good for you to relive some of your youthful indiscretions."

"I know *you* would love it," I teased back. He likely remembered my last year of high school and all the shenanigans we got into around town.

He pushed himself off the counter and bent down, planting a kiss on my head. "Don't worry about Alexa. She's a big girl, and you have other things to think about."

"You're right," I conceded, then he slipped out of the bathroom, leaving me alone.

I sank lower in the warm water unable to stop myself from remembering the day we returned from Montreal to find Danny a drunken mess and Phoebe gone.

I'd dropped Alexa off that afternoon, helping her get her bags through the front door. As soon as we entered her house, I knew something was wrong. Stuff was missing. Pictures smashed. Chairs overturned.

Alexa found Danny in the main floor bedroom, draped over the bed with his cane tossed aside and an empty vodka bottle discarded beside it. In the following days, we found out Phoebe had emptied the joint bank account she'd gotten Danny to apply for the year before and taken nearly all their life savings. For a time, I thought there might be a civil suit, but the cost of lawyers would prove to be too much, and soon, with Danny off work, the bills piled up and the Victorian house Alexa's mother had loved had to go.

Alexa changed after that. It was like as soon as Phoebe walked out, she knew she couldn't count on her dad anymore. She had to be the adult from then on. Alexa worked and cared for them both. No choice in the matter, nowhere else to go, no other family to love. Danny had failed her, but Alexa would not fail him. She never went to college. She got the job at Big Shot and never left the bar. She stayed in Cedar Plains despite her life only beginning and despite having no real future here. If she left, no one would care for Danny. She wouldn't abandon him, no matter how used to abandonment she had become.

I took several steadying breaths and closed my eyes. I felt at a loss. I wasn't sure if I expected Alexa to spiral or if she would cope like Brett implied. Maybe she'd brush it off entirely. She wasn't a confused, lonely teenager anymore.

When I opened my eyes again, another thing came to me. Maybe I didn't actually know Alexa as well as I thought, and that idea scared me.

31

Alexa Huston

Friday, August 11

Being here was wrong, but I couldn't stop myself. Courtney had been called away on a last-minute wedding disaster her "less than helpful" wedding planner (as she described her) couldn't handle. She tried to take me with her, her obvious intentions very clear, but I had my own agenda. The voice urged me to go.

There was a line-up at the library, longer than I expected, and it occurred to me many of these people likely weren't locals. They'd probably flocked from around the province to get a chance at a meet and greet, or to scope out the places mentioned in Phoebe's memoir. I'd tried to avoid the stupid book, but I had to know what she wrote.

I shamefully bought a copy from the local bookstore and skimmed through it this week. I had been mentioned, though she called me Lexie, as if that would be enough to hide who she was talking about. She painted me as a tragic character, confused after the devastating loss of my mother, harmed by my father's lack of interest, and clearly mentally unwell.

The way she painted my dad was more pleasant, at least at first. She wrote about their lavish vacations and intimate dinners. She penned their erotic sex life which I could have done without, and she shared intimate details about him, like how he said he finally felt alive for the first time in years with her. She called him Huss, as if no would know who he was. As if figuring out 'Huss' referred to the drunken Danny Huston and Lexie, his troubled teen, Alexa, would be hard for anyone to figure out.

People in Cedar Plains knew Phoebe Dawson, as she wasn't some mythical author writing about a town she didn't know. She was a local at one point.

It was the reason she left that did me in, her book painting a dramatic, violent outburst from a broken Huss. He'd lost his job and was struggling with his mobility. Vodka became his friend and his temper took over. I didn't know the real truth behind their ending and why Phoebe walked out. My dad had never told me, and I never wanted to know. I didn't remember him as a violent drunk in all my life. When the alcohol took over it was sadness that breached the surface, not anger. The state of my house that day might imply otherwise.

I trudged to the end of the line, pulling my ball cap down to try and hide my face from view. I didn't want her to see me before I had a chance to see her.

When I first glimpsed her now, memories made my blood boil. I neared the front of the line, knowing that if she looked up, away from the avid fans before her, she could catch my eye. Dressed to the nines in a long flowing sundress and golden necklace, her face was caked with makeup, trying to hide the wrinkles that had formed over the past eight years. She was no longer the young woman who had seduced my dad. She was older, and according to her naked ring finger, unmarried.

She never met my eyes, always smiling at the person in front of her who offered her praise and affirmation. It wasn't until I dropped the book on the table before her, and she flipped it open to sign.

"Who should I make it out ..." her words trailed off as she looked up at me and her overly pleasant expression faltered. "Alexa?"

"Why don't you make it out to Danny," I snapped. My gaze hard.

"I-uh-I'm so ... surprised to see you," she stuttered, the sweet tone in her voice wavering as she glanced around at the crowd, clearly wondering if anyone noticed her shock.

"Are you? Then you really are as stupid as I thought you were."

Phoebe frowned. "Alexa, that isn't what I meant. Did Missy tell you?"

My anger faltered, the mention of Brett's mother catching me off guard. "Why would Missy know?"

Phoebe glanced away. "No reason."

I held my gaze on her.

"Because I was there yesterday," she said with a sigh. "I hear Courtney and Brett are getting married tomorrow. You must be really excited."

I grit my teeth. "How dare you?" The darkness growled with me.

"Alexa," Phoebe said. Each time she spoke my name it sounded more condescending than the last. "I'm not trying to upset you."

"What are you trying to do then?" I asked. "You wrote a tell-all book about my dad and me, and our life. You disappeared one weekend never to be heard from again. I called you. I emailed you. You shut me out. I couldn't imagine why I would be upset about seeing you again." I couldn't stop my voice from raising. The crowd behind me started to sway with discomfort.

"Alexa," she said again. "This isn't the place to have this discussion."

"You don't get to decide that," I snapped. "You left me. You ignored me." I hesitated, trying to stop the way my chest tightened, forcing the impending tears to stay at bay. I wouldn't cry for her; she didn't deserve it.

"After everything," I said, my voice quiet now. "The last thing I needed was another person to walk out on me." I waved to the book. "And you wonder why I was so 'mentally unwell.'" I snarled those words at her.

Phoebe gazed at me, her pen hovering over the book, unsure if she should go ahead with the signature. I didn't wait for her to decide; instead, I swiped the book off the table and stormed off, dropping the book into the trash on the way out. I didn't look back to see her reaction.

My palms itched with anticipation, and the voice whispered its desires. A thirst clawed at my throat, and I threw open the doors, gasping for the outdoor air. I steadied my rapid breathing and glanced at the time. It was midday. I didn't exactly know where to find Missy, but I'd try their house. Wherever Courtney's future mother-in-law was, she'd better have some answers for me.

Outside Brett's parents' house, I ambled up the front step and pounded on the door. I waited only a minute before it swung open, and Missy stood in the entrance way.

"Oh, Alexa." She placed a hand over her heart. "You startled me."

I didn't wait for her to invite me inside before pushing my way into their front foyer. I'd only been in Brett's parents' house a few times. It was stark white and felt more clinical than homey. No wonder Courtney felt uncomfortable under Missy's scrutiny here.

"Alexa," Missy said, her voice firmer this time. "What is going on?"

I glanced expectantly at the door, waiting for her to close it. When she didn't move, I said, "I'm sure you heard Phoebe was back in town."

Missy's furrowed brow lifted briefly, but she quickly regained her composure. "I didn't know."

"Bullshit," I growled. "She told me she came here. She visited you."

Missy sighed then waved towards the kitchen. "Can we sit?"

I hesitated, wanting to refuse and have it out with her in the hallway but thought better of it. Maybe if I sat her down, she'd be more willing to talk.

In the kitchen, I settled on one of the bar stools, watching Missy as she bopped around the kitchen and filled two glasses of wine.

"I thought we might need these," Missy said, sitting beside me then angling herself towards me. "Yes, Phoebe did come see me yesterday."

"And you welcomed her with open arms," I grumbled. The darkness hummed with irritation.

"No," Missy corrected. "I told her she made a mistake coming back here. This town wasn't what she left all those years ago. And writing that book was dreadful."

"I don't believe you." I gripped tightly to the wine glass, hoping Missy couldn't see the way my hand shook. The way the darkness was trying to claw its way to the surface.

Missy grimaced. "I can't change that. All I can do is say everything that went down between Phoebe and your dad wasn't just between them, and I have a right to tell her how I really feel."

I frowned, allowing my anger to wane. What was she talking about?

Missy pressed on. "All those years ago, I thought Phoebe saved your dad. After your mom's death, your dad wasn't doing well. Phoebe was Bronwyn's best friend. She picked up the pieces. That's all we saw."

I scoffed. "If that's how you saw her, then I'm surprised you threw her out."

Missy looked away from me. "Have you talked to Courtney about any of this?"

I frowned. Courtney had her own things going on. A wedding to worry about. Phoebe was my problem.

"Why would I talk to Courtney?" I asked.

"I didn't ever want you to know this," Missy said. "But Phoebe is the reason your mom died."

"What?" I nearly choked on my wine mid-sip.

Missy drew a breath. "Phoebe and your dad were having an affair. Bronwyn found out. I don't know exactly what happened the night of her accident. All I know is that she stormed out of the party and hours later, Danny called Kevin for help."

My head spun. An affair? That was impossible. Dad would never cheat on Mom. I met her gaze, ready to deny her accusations when I saw the softness of her eyes and the pity behind them. The truth they'd all deprived me of.

Liars, the voice whispered. Everyone around me had lied.

I swallowed hard. "What party?"

"We were all here that night," Missy said. "Having a dinner party, and we'd had a bit too much to drink. Phoebe and Danny disappeared. No one noticed really, though your mom and I did. Soon, she also disappeared, and the next thing we knew, they were screaming at one another, Bronwyn and Phoebe, then your mom stormed out. Danny followed quickly after and Phoebe behind him. The next morning, Kevin told me they found her body."

"You said my dad called Kevin for help," I said slowly. "Did he see the accident happen?"

Missy shook her head. "I don't know. That night has weighed heavily on your father and my husband for years. I never asked about it again."

My stomach twisted with nausea. I leaned forward, placing my head in my hands, as dizziness overtook me. Images plagued my mind of a bloodied body. A woman screaming. A man carrying me away. Nightmares that haunted me for months after my mom's death. *It wasn't real. It wasn't real.* I came out of my trance when I felt Missy's warm hand on my back, rubbing gentle circles as she cooed like a mother shushing her baby.

I stayed like that for a moment before I lifted my head and gazed at nothing in front of me. My dad had been there for me. Loving me. Letting Phoebe love me. Giving me permission to let her into my life. To begin again and be a new family. And now, to find out they'd been doing it behind my mother's back all along. Phoebe had ruined my family and killed my mom.

"Please tell me it's all a lie," I said, my voice quiet and defeated despite the rage and turmoil that toiled around inside me. The darkness inside cackled at my naivety. Of course I believed them.

Missy looked at me with sympathy. It had been a lie all those years ago. A coverup. A sham. Everything I knew about my dad was wrong.

I abruptly stood, leaving my wine unfinished, and turned for the entrance.

"Alexa!" Missy called after me, her hurried footsteps following me to the front door. "Alexa, I didn't mean to upset you."

I turned back to face her. "You didn't upset me. You're the first one to tell me the truth in a while." Then I turned and left, not giving her a chance to respond.

In my car, I let out a scream, slamming my hands into the steering wheel as I pictured Phoebe in our family home. The way she'd inserted herself into our life. How she'd completely replaced my mother until we weren't good enough for her anymore. The darkness cursed her, raging along with me, the anger unbearable.

When my throat tired of screaming, I drew several steady breaths and shifted into drive, punching the accelerator and speeding down the side streets. My palms itched and the dryness in my throat became unbearable.

Back at my condo, I found the place empty, my dad off to who-knew-where. Alone and shaken, my next solution wasn't a great one. Thankfully, the bottle I'd stashed in the back of my closet still hadn't been found, and soon, I was in the kitchen with a shot glass, letting the burning sensation of vodka trickle down my throat. When the first shot was finished without quenching my unbearable thirst, I had another, then another.

By the time my dad strode into the house, I was five shots deep and feeling the buzz. He gazed at me with glassy eyes and made his way to the couch.

"Where have you been?" I snapped, ready to fight.

He glanced over his shoulder at me then shrugged. "Out." He fell to the couch and pulled out a mickey of vodka from his pocket, half gone.

"Casual drinking at Mom's grave?" I couldn't help but sneer as I said it. Did he think about how Phoebe drove a wedge between them whenever he went to see her grave? Did he visit her out of guilt for what happened?

"You know I don't drink when I visit your mother." Dad tipped the bottle back as he flicked on the TV.

"Oh, an alcoholic with a conscience. How quaint. Where else do you have to go but the bar or her grave?"

He stiffened but he didn't acknowledge my comment, instead he lit a cigarette and continued to stare at the TV.

Anger over taking me, I stormed across the room and stood in front of the TV, glowering down at my dad. He sighed and met my eyes; his gaze held a sadness I'd never really noticed before.

"What is it, Lex?" Dad said, his voice empty of feeling. A defeat that had come to define him.

"I know about the affair," I hissed. "I know you lied to me."

Dad looked away from me and shook his head.

"Don't try to deny it," I snapped. "Have the decency to look at me and tell me the truth for once."

When his gaze found mine again, his eyes were wet with tears, and he shook his head sadly.

"It's all my fault," he mumbled.

"You're damn right it is," I yelled, unable to stop the anger from rising, trying to silence the babble from the TV behind me. The darkness rose inside me, making the rage burn hotter. "You cheated on Mom. You ruined this family. And for what? For her?"

"I made a mistake," he said softly. "I thought I was doing the right thing. To protect you. We all did."

I swallowed hard, remembering what Missy had said about my dad calling her husband. About them finding my mom. I told the darkness to quiet, to let me learn more, and to my surprise it shrank back with a patience I didn't expect.

"What happened that night after you left the party?" I said, trying to keep my voice level so as not to frighten him into silence. "Was it really a car accident?"

"Lex, please," he begged.

"Tell. Me," I said through gritted teeth. The darkness flared.

Tears fell from his eyes now, in a steady stream down his cheeks.

"When we got home, your mom stormed upstairs and started packing. She told me she was leaving and taking you with her," Dad said. "I begged her to reconsider, to stay, to talk to me, but Phoebe had followed us, and as soon as your mom saw her, she started screaming at her.

Calling her a whore, a homewrecker. Phoebe tried to defend herself, but your mom wouldn't hear it. Bronwyn charged at Phoebe and slapped her hard. Phoebe grabbed her and they started fighting. I tried to stop them, but it was like I wasn't even there. Then your mom fell down the stairs." He closed his eyes. "I still remember looking over the railing and seeing her body, bent from the fall, bleeding from her head where it had collided with the stairs over and over."

I sucked in a sharp breath as an image came back to me. Mom's body twisted and broken. Her head wrenched in an awful direction. And blood. So much blood. *It wasn't real. It wasn't real.* The very image that had played over and over in my head when I was fifteen. The apparent dream they convinced me wasn't real. Only it had been real. All along.

"You told me it was a nightmare," I whispered. The darkness overtook me then, layering a protection around me as I realized all the lies he'd told me. "That I imagined the whole thing." My body went cold as I thought about the hours spent across from a shrink. The denial that I'd seen anything. The delusion I was fed. *It wasn't real. It wasn't real.*

Liars, the voice screeched.

"I couldn't let you remember your mother that way," Dad said. "You were inebriated. Phoebe was certain you wouldn't remember a thing."

"And then you made sure that if I did then I thought I was crazy," I snapped. An urge inside me began to form, a deep itch in the palm of my hands. The voice promised revenge.

"She swore it was an accident," Dad said. "That Bronwyn had slipped when she tried to push Phoebe. It was self-defence. A mistake. So—"

I didn't need him to explain it to me anymore. "So you called your buddy on the police force, and with his help, covered up the murder of my mother."

"Alexa, no," Dad whimpered.

"And proceeded to invite her murderer into our home," I said, my voice cracking at the memories of Phoebe and our once-strong relationship. So many lies.

I stared at the pathetic man that was my father. This shell of a human who let his weaknesses rule his entire life. I shook my head and turned away from him, disgusted. Retrieving the bottle I'd been drinking from, I turned for the stairs. Before I climbed, I hesitated and looked back at him.

"Did you believe her?" I asked.

Dad tilted his head, as if unsure what I was asking.

"All those years ago when Phoebe told you it was an accident, did you believe her?"

Dad nodded. "Back then, I did."

"And now?"

He looked away. "Now, I'm not so sure."

Without another word, I trudged up to my room. Everything was spiraling out of control. I couldn't reach myself beyond the darkness that clouded my mind. My anger, my frustrations. I felt dizzy with unrequited desire.

Mom was dead because of her once-best friend, Phoebe. Did Courtney know about the affair? Brett's mom implied as much.

Speak of the devil, my phone buzzed with a message from Courtney, asking to meet at her house. The darkness growled as I tossed my phone aside, unwilling to face her and desiring only one outcome.

Glass abandoned, I drank straight from the bottle, begging the burning liquid to numb my feelings, silence the darkness and rid me of my pain.

I didn't know whether it worked. I only knew the next day when I woke up, the itch remained and the bottle was nearly gone.

32

Courtney Faith

Saturday, August 12

I eyed Alexa from where I sat in the salon chair. We'd booked out the small boutique with my local hairdresser and celebrated the morning with mimosas while my bridal party was forced into chairs for hair and makeup.

My best friend had been suspiciously quiet all morning, barely glancing my way. She'd been all but unreachable the previous evening and had bailed on our plans to spend the night before my wedding together. This morning when she had the decency to show up, she reeked of booze, had messy hair, and looked like she'd slept in a dumpster. To say it annoyed me was putting it mildly.

When the stylist finished my hair, I grabbed another mimosa then dragged Alexa outside with me. The sun was already high in the summer sky. Mother Nature blessed us with the most beautiful day, another indication my marriage to Brett was meant to be.

"What's wrong?" I asked pointedly, unwilling to beat around the bush on my special day.

"Nothing." Alexa wouldn't meet my eyes.

"Something is clearly bothering you," I said, trying to keep my voice low and not give way to the irritation swirling around inside me. "You ignored me last night, then bailed on our plans. Honestly, I'm surprised you showed up this morning." Maybe I should have taken Savannah up on her offer to take over the role.

She turned her glare on me. "I almost didn't."

"Why?" I asked exasperated. What could I have possibly done now?

"I saw Missy yesterday afternoon," Alexa said.

I frowned. Missy had been with us all morning, Nia too, until the photographer whisked them off for photos with Brett. "Why would you do that?"

"Something Phoebe said."

I rolled my eyes. "Of course, I should have known you'd go see her the first chance you got. I thought you were smarter than that."

Alexa ignored my comment. "Missy told me about my mom's accident."

My anger dissipated. My throat went dry.

"What about it?" I asked.

"Cut the bullshit, Courtney," Alexa spat. "I know you've been hiding it from me. Phoebe and my dad were having an affair and Missy believes Phoebe is the reason Mom died."

I considered lying, to keep up the ruse, but I knew she'd see right through me.

"I didn't want to upset you."

Her eyes narrowed further. "Because finding out you're a liar is so much more comforting."

"I didn't think it mattered," I protested. "It's all in the past."

Alexa tossed her hands up in frustration. "Right, because I wouldn't want to know my dad is a colossal asshole who ruined our family because he wanted to get laid. My mistake to think I could trust my best friend."

"Alexa," I said, but she cut me off.

"Don't you ever forget I know the truth, and I could easily share it with Stevenson. With *Savannah*." Her eyes flashed with a darkness that caught me off guard. It wasn't an empty threat. She meant it.

I swallowed hard. "You wouldn't." The accident had been our secret, and she was implicated too. Surely, an empty threat.

She turned her back on me, heading towards the entrance to the salon. "Who knows what *you* could drive me to do." She disappeared through the door, leaving me feeling cold and afraid.

The photo session at my house went quickly, and I tried to keep my panic under wraps. Alexa played her part well, but she barely looked at me except when instructed by the photographer. My red hair was up in a braided up-do, with a sapphire crystal embellished piece added to the back. My something blue. My bridesmaids wore powder-blue dresses, long and low-cut. Completely flattering—the style suited each of them, a rarity with bridesmaids' gowns.

"That's a wrap," my wedding planner called, waving us towards the front door. "We have to get to the venue now."

We climbed into the limo, Miles and I entering first as he helped me with the train of my dress. When we were settled in the seat against the partition window, I leaned my head against my younger brother's shoulder.

"I really wish you were walking me down the aisle," I said, looking over my chattering wedding party. I'd wanted Mom to do it, but she'd been so distant the past few weeks.

Miles gave my arm a gentle squeeze. “I know, but I’ll be at the end waiting for you. If you get nervous, you can look at me.”

“I’m already nervous.” I glanced to where Mom sat near the door to the limo on the opposite side of the vehicle. “I hope Mom is up for it. All the attention.”

Miles didn’t respond.

“That’s not very comforting,” I said, lifting my head from his shoulder and looking him in the eye.

“Sorry.” He grinned sheepishly. “Just distracted.”

“Like everyone, it seems,” I said. Then I asked, “How has Mom been?” Miles had been staying with her since he came to town a few days before.

“I’m not sure,” Miles said, looking away from me. “Strange. She’s been talking in her sleep, up all hours of the night, exhausted during the day, and kinda paranoid.”

I cocked my head towards him. “Paranoid?”

“Yeah.” Miles reached up and scratched the back of his neck. “Constantly peeking outside. She keeps the curtains closed all day. Last night, she asked me if I saw someone standing across the street, but there was no one there.”

“It’s the grief. And probably lack of sleep.”

“Yeah,” Miles agreed. “She burst into tears when she first saw me, telling me how much I looked like Mark. Ever since then, I’ve caught her staring at me for long periods of time. I tried to ignore it at first, thinking maybe she was happy to have me home, but it’s weird, Court.”

“I’m sorry,” I said, not sure what else to say.

Our mother gazed out the window at the opposite end of the limo, uninterested in my celebrating bridesmaids or her two children seated in eyesight. She looked exhausted, as Miles said, the heavy makeup caked under her eyes unable to hide the purple bags. Tormented was the only way I could think to describe her.

"You can come stay with us, if you want," I suggested, though I hoped he wouldn't take me up on it.

"No, thanks." Miles grinned. "I don't need to be around when my sister and her fiancé become newlyweds." He made a fake gagging noise.

I nudged him with a giggle. His face shifted quickly back to concern.

"Besides, I don't think she should be alone," he said. "Last night I found her pacing the hallway outside my room, muttering something about Mark."

I glanced back at Mom, now finding her looking directly at us. Her eyes weren't on me but on Miles. I tapped his leg, drawing his attention to our watcher.

"See what I mean?" he said, waving to mom who seemed to realize she was staring and tore her gaze away from us with a small smile.

"She's been through a lot," I said.

"It shows."

The ceremony and reception were at a vineyard outside of town, a popular spot for Cedar Plains weddings. The long fields of grapes seemed to stretch to the waiting skyline, making the venue seem expansive and intimate at the same time. A picturesque wooden barn had been strung up with fairy lights and outfitted with sleek furniture.

The wedding went off without a hitch and soon the reception began, and the drinks were flowing. We had a five-course meal, followed by a DJ and dancing. The head table featured me and Brett, Mom, Miles, and Brett's parents. Missy had been gushing over me all day. I tried to keep my sour attitude from spoiling the night. I was still angry she'd told Alexa the truth about the affair. Maybe I was angry I hadn't told her myself.

The speeches went quickly, and when Alexa stood up to make hers, something she'd tried to get out of, she still seemed sullen and withdrawn.

"Courtney has been a staple in my life for as long as I can remember," she began, keeping her eyes locked on the paper in front of her. "From the moment I stepped foot into Cedar Plains, Courtney latched on to me. She was always the friendliest, most-welcoming student at CPHS, and I know I wouldn't be the same person without her."

I watched her careful, unsure the implications behind her words.

"She brought me into the 'cool' crowd." Alexa made quotations with her fingers as she said it. "If you call overachievers the cool kids." This earned a laugh from the guests.

"And always kept a lookout for me." Alexa paused and looked at me. "We've done everything together. Including keeping each other's secrets."

I swallowed hard, trying to keep my steady smile in place. Her eyes said more to me about those secrets than anyone in the room would understand.

Alexa looked back out at the crowd. "When Brett and Courtney started dating all those years ago, I'll admit I didn't like him. He was this older, dreamy football player who made all the girls swoon, but he only had eyes for Courtney. And damn, did I feel like he was stealing my best friend."

Again, another chuckle from the crowd.

"I kept a close eye on him for a long time," Alexa admitted. "I was afraid. I couldn't let him hurt her in any way, because if my champion got hurt, who would save me?"

She allowed a small smile to slip through her rigid demeanour.

"That's where I was wrong," Alexa said. "Brett didn't break Courtney down, Brett built her up. Together they made the best versions of each other. With Courtney's encouragement, Brett pursued his dreams, and no one can handle Courtney's constant anxiety quite like Brett does." She looked at my husband with a playful smile. "You beat me there, brother."

This was met with sporadic claps as Alexa turned her gaze to the crowd.

"So, please join me in raising a glass to my best friend and her white knight. To Brett and Courtney!" Alexa lifted her wine glass and shot back the remaining contents before stepping down from the platform.

I stood and rounded the head table, pulling her into my arms.

"You surprised me," I whispered before she could pull away.

"I will always surprise you." Her voice was flat and when I pulled back, her lips were pursed. Clear irritation still in her eyes. She returned to her seat before I could say anything else.

Back in my chair, Brett leaned over and planted a gentle kiss on my cheek. "That was sweet."

"It was." I watched Alexa as my brother stood to make a toast. She stared at her plate, clearly uninterested or trying to avoid the attention.

When Miles began to speak, I tore my eyes away from where Alexa sat, and the next time I looked back, she was gone.

33

Alexa Huston

Sunday, August 13

I zipped my dark hoodie as the cool wind blew down the narrow street. The crescent moon provided little light. I'd changed from my bridesmaid dress and left the reception after the dinner concluded and the dancing began. Most of the guests were heavily intoxicated, and Courtney was too busy to notice. Dressed in my dark street clothes, I drove back to town unable to control my urges. I should be staying at the wedding, supporting my best friend, and enjoying the lavish party, but I wasn't in control anymore. I gave into the whispered desires, following the need that pulsed inside me.

Dad had once believed Mom's death was an accident, that Phoebe wasn't truly to blame. The darkness and I weren't so sure, and this time, she would tell us everything we wanted to know. Then we would take what we came for.

Phoebe had rented an Airbnb from one of the local cottagers. Places like these were often vacant during the off seasons. No snow on the hills left little for the apres-ski crowd to do, and so they returned to their McMansions in the city, leaving their second homes empty and waiting.

Some offered rentals, like the one Phoebe found. It had been easy enough to find her, the owner boasting about having a famous author stay on their social media pages. Her fame was miniscule when really considered, but celebrity, no matter how minor, was big news in a small town.

As I got closer to the house my hands began to shake. Like an addict suffering from withdraw, sick with desire and desperate for a taste. We were dying to get our revenge on the woman who ruined our life.

From afar, the house looked empty. It was late, but not late enough Phoebe would be sleeping. She once told me she did her best work in the wee hours of the night, the silence allowing her mind to truly take control of the story. Of course, this was years before her publishing dreams came to fruition. I could only hope that things hadn't changed. The darkness promised it hadn't.

I considered surprising her and getting the job done quickly. But that would mean giving up on the answers I deserved. So, I walked to the front door and knocked, my gloved hand muffling the noise, but I heard footsteps cross the front hall.

"Yes?" Phoebe asked as she pulled open the door only enough to look out. When she saw it was me, she stepped back, opening the door wider. "I thought I might see you again."

She motioned for me to enter. Trusting idiot. The darkness cackled with gleeful anticipation.

Phoebe led me into the large, picturesque sitting room where a grand piano sat in the corner. Across from the piano was a large colonial fireplace with a golden grate and pristine tools, both looking like props instead of having any actual functionality. The long leather couch was easily worth several thousand dollars. A luxury I no longer knew, thanks to the woman standing in front of me.

"Do you want water?" Phoebe asked. Then followed up with an afterthought. "Or maybe something stronger?"

I shook my head. "I'm not here for a drink." Only one thing would quench our thirst.

Phoebe let out an exhausted sigh, as if I were the last person she wanted to see. I found myself wondering why she'd stayed in this town a day longer than necessary. Did she hope to find some sort of solace here?

I could have told her this town wanted nothing to do with her. No one here cared about her. They weren't her starry-eyed fans.

"Will you sit?" She perched on the edge of a red velvet armchair and motioned to the leather couch.

I only shook my head.

"Then how can I help you, Alexa?"

The makeup from yesterday was no longer there; instead, her face was bare, the bags under her eyes were prominent, and her previously-styled hair was pulled back, casting her thin cheekbones with harsh angles. Living a constant lie must be tiring.

"You can't help me," I said, my voice low and quiet, sounding so unlike my own. "Thanks to you, I've been helping myself for years."

"Then what do you want?" she asked. "Here to have another go at me? Tell me again how awful I am?"

"Do you deny it?" I asked. The voice said she couldn't.

She folded her hands on her lap. "Of course I would. And I'm sure most people would agree with me."

"Probably because most people don't know you're a murderer," I retorted, keeping my hard gaze on her face. The darkness swelled with glee waiting for her confession. Waiting for our release.

Her brow crinkled as she considered her next words. "I'm not sure I have any idea what you are talking about."

"My dad told me everything," I hissed. "About the affair. About mom's death."

Phoebe squared her shoulders and lifted her chin, clearly unwilling to be intimidated by me. "Honestly, Alexa, I really don't know what you're talking about. Your mother's death was a terrible car crash."

"Liar!" I yelled as the darkness grew angrier, and Phoebe flinched, leaning away from me. "I know about the cover up. I know everything."

"Alexa, please," Phoebe tried.

"No wonder you took off the first chance you got. Did that house have too many memories of what you did? *Murderer.*" I felt out of body, watching the interaction unfold. My voice haunting and deep. The darkness guided me, and I wanted nothing more than to give in, submit and take the release we both desperately needed.

She didn't answer and I scoffed.

"I tried to contact you. How you must have laughed when I reached out." The darkness shook its head in disgust. "Poor, pathetic Alexa, desperate for approval from her mother's *murderer.*"

"Stop calling me that," Phoebe cried. "I didn't kill Bronwyn."

I turned my cold gaze on her. "Even if you didn't push her, which I'm certain you did, your affair with my dad is enough of a crime."

"Alexa," Phoebe said, standing and putting her hands up in defence. "There is so much about your father and me you don't understand—"

"She was your best friend! And you took her family from her. Her life!"

"That's not what happened," Phoebe said. "When I first met your mother, she was this beautiful and kind woman. I honestly didn't know how someone could be so giving and humble. It wasn't until we got to know each other I realized it was a front."

My hands clenched at my sides. The darkness growled.

"And then I met Danny." The way she said his name made me pause. There was a dreaminess behind it, making my sick stomach turn. She was a villain in my story, how could she still have a romantic vision of my alcoholic father? "And he was brilliant. A doting father, a great husband, and your mom did not appreciate him."

I narrowed my eyes. "How dare you."

She looked at me with confidence. "If you would say otherwise than you've let your memories of the two of them fade. They used to fight all the time. You and I were both present for a lot of those."

"Everyone fights," I said.

"Not like this," Phoebe said. "They were miserable, but they had you. Bronwyn couldn't imagine leaving Danny and ruining anything they had built together as a family. No matter how she struggled with Danny, she wouldn't leave you behind."

"So, you seduced him," I spat. "You inserted yourself into his life and took him from his wife?"

"Your father made his own decisions," Phoebe said. "I was only there to pick up the pieces your mom left behind."

I took a threatening step towards her, and Phoebe threw her hands out between us.

"I didn't want to hurt your mom," she said. "Danny and I talked about it constantly, about how to tell her and how to move forward. There was just never a right time, but then she discovered the truth, and it was too late."

"So, you pushed her down the stairs," I growled, my voice sounding strange.

"No," Phoebe insisted. "It was an accident, that's all."

"If that was true then you had nothing to cover up," I said. "You wouldn't have to stage a car accident. You wouldn't have to lie."

"Alexa, the situation looked bad," she said. "And when you stumbled home, we panicked. You were so out of it, mesmerized by the scene. It was eerie. Dry-eyed, you reached for your mother's face, tilting her head to look at the blood. Danny scooped you up before you could do anything further, and it was then we knew we had to make sure no one found out and that it never affected you."

I thought about Vanessa in that moment and the way her brain hemorrhaged. The strange feeling of familiarity that washed over me. The way it resembled my mother's death. The desire to touch the blood and the trance I felt in. The darkness it had awoken.

"Accident or not, you tried to steal her husband," I said. "You ruined them. You *killed* her."

"They would have split up without me," Phoebe said, standing now and matching my anger. "It's not my fault any of this happened."

I took in her wide eyes, the guilt behind her assertion. And I laughed, hollow and cruel. "Oh my god, you've been telling yourself that for years, haven't you?"

She clamped her mouth shut.

"You're pathetic," I said it softly, and Phoebe bared her teeth.

"You got your answers," Phoebe said. "Now, go."

I looked to the door. I could leave her here, allow her to live out the rest of her days in the lonely, guilt-ridden misery. When I looked back at her again, I saw it. The golden necklace around her neck. It was the very one my dad had given her on their first anniversary. I remembered the dinner well, the three of us out at a steakhouse, and Dad presenting Phoebe with the gift like it was the fucking holy grail. And she still wore it now.

My palms began to itch wildly as the urge crawled up inside me, begging for a release. The knife in my bag suddenly seemed too good for her. My gaze found the fireplace tools. I walked over to them and picked up the heavy golden poker, sharp, pointed. I shifted the would-be weapon between my hands, trying to gauge the damage I could do with it. All the while, Phoebe watched me closely.

"What are you doing?" Her voice shook.

"It did affect me, you know," I said softly, the hollow voice of the darkness coming through. The memories I'd believed to be false. The belief I'd been losing my mind. It all had an impact, and this was the crossroad.

"What?" she asked, backing away from me.

"Seeing what you did," I explained. I moved quickly then, charging her and swinging the weapon fast and hard. Her hands flew up, trying to stop my assault, but it was no use. The curved, pointed end lodged itself into her side. Her breathing faltered, and she fell forward as I pulled the rod from her side. Blood quickly soaked through her shirt.

She clutched her side as she gasped for air. When she looked up at me, her eyes shone with fear. She knew she was going to die.

I didn't give her much time to consider it before I brought the weapon crashing against her temple, knocking her unconscious. Then I hit her again, and again, and again, until I was sure she was dead. All the while, the darkness cackled with an unhinged glee.

My heart raced as I stepped back from her mangled body, her face barely recognizable and covered with blood. It pooled on the clean hardwood floor as it spilled from her wounds. My eyes wandered over her bloodied corpse and a sense of relief washed over me. In a few minutes I'd avenged my mother's untimely death. Phoebe was no more.

I reached down and grabbed hold of the golden chain, tearing the necklace from around her neck. Then I held the blood-splattered piece to the light; it still shone after all these years. The voice approved of our new trophy.

I tucked the chain into my pocket and returned the poker to its rightful place, seeing no reason to take it with me. There wouldn't be any fingerprints, nothing to tie the crime to me. It was another dead-end for the useless police department.

I didn't cast her bloodied body another look before heading to the opposite end of the house and slipping through the backdoor. I found myself in the small backyard and exited through the fence before making my way to my waiting car. I'd parked it two streets over and moved quickly, hoping to go unnoticed.

Across the street, a drunken man swayed as he walked, seemingly unaware of my presence. I stood in the dark and waited for him to pass. Then I pulled off my gloves and climbed into the car. I sat still for a moment, steadying my breath and allowing my rapid heartbeat to slow.

When I returned home, I scampered up the stairs, not bothering to check if my dad was passed out on the couch and closed myself in my bedroom. Before the high wore off, I grabbed my sketch book and started drawing the scene I'd left behind. A strange sense of euphoria took over my body. Phoebe was gone and she could no longer hurt me. She had ruined my life, and I got to end hers. The darkness purred with contentment.

34

Courtney Faith

Monday, August 14

Phoebe's body was found the evening after my wedding by the owner of the Airbnb. Brett received the call first thing on the Monday morning following, a co-worker keeping him up to date. Apparently, her body had been mangled.

A sick feeling hadn't left me since. I tried calling Alexa the moment Brett headed to the station, but her phone went straight to voicemail. He'd been informed Stevenson was already enroute to Alexa's house, intent on questioning the people who'd once been closest to Phoebe—the ones most harmed by her, certain one was to blame.

Maybe it was Danny's doing, an ex-lover finally able to get his revenge. The state of the body implied anger, Brett said, giving me the details with a frankness I'd never get used to. He described her as practically unrecognizable. I tried not to think about the countless shows I'd seen where makeup and special effects were used to brutalize a murder victim or someone engaging in swordplay or war. I imagined seeing such damage in real life put any special effects to shame.

Even as I tried to convince myself it was Danny's doing and not Alexa's, my wishes were shaky. It would be clear to Stevenson upon arrival that Danny wasn't able to overpower any murder victim, even one caught by surprise. The man's disability was apparent in the cane he leaned on everywhere and a high blood-alcohol level that seemed to be his norm. Danny was on death's doorstep; he wasn't killing people.

When Nia and Missy arrived at my house, the dread inside had made me sick. They found me in the front hallway bathroom, on hands and knees, leaning over the toilet. I jumped when I saw them, not having heard them enter.

"I'm sorry," I muttered, flushing down the remnants of my lunch. My insides still twisted and turned with the strange reality. Alexa had looked me in the eye and told me she wasn't capable of killing anyone. But now I no longer questioned it. My best friend had committed murder. The thought was enough to send me spiraling again and wishing I could reach for the toilet once more. My empty stomach offered nothing but dry heaves.

Was Alexa responsible for the others? Could this be a one-off, an unfortunate coincidence, or was she really the psychopath the news described?

"Hey," Nia said, her voice quiet as she took me by the elbow and led me into the living room where she pointed to a couch and told me to sit. She and Missy sat on the couch across from me. They'd come to help me organize the gifts and thank you cards, ensuring I'd have everything set before Brett and I were to leave on our honeymoon next week. Now the whole idea seemed pointless. I couldn't focus.

"Are you okay?" Nia asked.

I shook my head, unsure what to say. The words Brett had spoken still ran through my mind. I struggled to come to terms with the idea Alexa could be capable of something so brutal. Our wedding had been perfect, and now it was shaded with the dark crimson of Phoebe's blood.

"Oh my," Missy teased, a lightness to her tone. "Could my daughter-in-law be experiencing morning sickness?"

I eyed Missy, wondering how she could suspect pregnancy at a time like this.

"Oh my god, Mom," Nia chastised. "Don't be stupid. Courtney is clearly distraught by the shit going on in this town. We all are."

I wouldn't tell them what the true source of my anxiety was. My once-trusted best friend had become unhinged. I racked my brain trying to remember when Alexa had left my wedding. Had she stayed during the dancing, or disappeared the first moment she could? How could she be in two places at once, my wedding and nearly thirty minutes away at Phoebe's rental? I'd been too distracted to say for sure when she went. If the police questioned me, would I say she was there the whole time? I wasn't sure if I could protect her, but as the thought surfaced, I knew I would. If I couldn't keep her secrets, why would she keep mine?

"Courtney?" Nia asked, eyebrows drawn together.

"Are you even listening, dear?" Missy asked, the roll of her eyes unwarranted but not unexpected.

I hadn't been listening. Their lips moved, but their voices wouldn't reach my ears.

"Maybe we should do this another time," Nia said, looking at her hands folded in her lap. She looked smaller than usual, her shoulders hunched over and a slight tremor to her voice that was so unlike her. Still, she gave me a firm nod. "Mom, I think we should let Courtney go lie down and we can go for tea."

"Nonsense." Missy waved off her daughter's concern. "Courtney invited us here."

I placed my hand on my forehead. "Actually, I wouldn't mind a rest. I am feeling a bit under the weather."

Nia needed no further encouragement and quickly shuffled her mother out of the house, insisting they stop by the new café that had opened off the main street. I watched them climb into her car from my front window, willing the turmoil inside me to relax.

In a few short weeks my entire life had changed. I reached for my phone, trying Alexa's phone again, but after a few rings I was directed to voicemail.

I sat staring at my phone for a moment, wondering what I should do next, when Rita's voice appeared in the back of my mind. Unsure what the reporter could actually offer, I unblocked the first number she'd called me from and promptly dialed it.

"Rita Rounds." The familiar voice came through the receiver.

"Ms. Rounds, it is Courtney Faith," I said, my voice shaking. "I'd like to talk."

I planned to meet Rita at a café outside of the downtown area, a place I hoped wouldn't be busy. I arrived early, drumming my fingers anxiously on the table and leaving my coffee untouched.

When Rita finally showed up, she didn't bother ordering, instead she sauntered across the café and plopped down across from me. "I wondered when you would call."

I eyed here carefully, unable to fully trust this woman, but desperate to know more. Despite Alexa's anger at Phoebe, the brutal murder seemed over the top, and I found myself wondering if there was more to the story of Bronwyn's death.

"You mentioned something about my father-in-law," I said. "I want to know what you meant."

"Many years ago, Chief Knight worked very hard to silence a few of my stories," she said keeping her voice low. "He nearly cost me my career when I tried to get more information about a local car accident."

"Bronwyn Huston," I said and Rita nodded.

"He was angry because I'd pulled some strings and gotten my hands on the coroner's report. And the injuries I saw there had been inconsistent with a car crash."

"How so?" I asked.

"The reports indicated that she died on impact, brain damage from her head colliding with the dashboard, but the coroner indicated the blunt trauma was to the back of her skull."

I frowned. "So you're saying the car accident was a lie?"

Rita shrugged. "All I'm saying is the reports were falsified, and when I tried to get more information and dig into the story, Chief Knight worked hard to shut it down. I was cut off from all my police contacts, and my editor-in-chief put me on temporary leave, assigning the story to another. I was a rookie at the time, and I had dug into some corruption, but no one believed me."

"What happened if not a car accident?" I asked.

Rita shook her head. "I never found out. I was told in no uncertain terms to drop it if I wanted to have a career. So, I did, but that wasn't the last time I questioned the integrity of our former police chief."

My head spun with questions. If Bronwyn hadn't died in the car, then did someone stage it? I couldn't imagine Kevin putting himself in such a compromising situation. He was supposed to be a pinnacle of hope and integrity in our town. How much of it had been a lie?

"What do you know about this new murder?" Rita asked, clearly done with sharing. "She was a friend of your family?"

I shook my head, pushing myself from the table. "I don't know anything." I moved away from her, but Rita reached out and caught my wrist.

"Be careful, Ms. Faith," she said. "Sometimes people are not what they seem."

With those words haunting me, I dashed out of the café and didn't look back.

35

Alexa Huston

Monday, August 14

Stevenson sat at my kitchen table in the same spot he'd sat over two weeks ago when he'd all but accused me of Dean's murder. He held me under a clear gaze of scrutiny as his partner attempted to question my drunk dad.

"Mr. Huston," the young cop tried again. "Did you know Phoebe Dawson was in town?"

Dad looked at him with glassy eyes, fresh from a morning of drinking—after a long night of drinking. Come to think of it, he likely never stopped. Maybe passed out but then started again.

"You do realize how useless this is, right?" I asked, my arms crossed over my chest, eyebrow raised.

"Why do you say that?" Stevenson asked.

"Do you really think that man is capable of murdering someone in his state?" The idea my dad could be the one who wielded the fire poker was almost laughable.

"You seem capable," Stevenson said.

"Then I guess it's a good thing I have an alibi," I said. My attendance at Courtney's wedding had been good for that in the very least. I hadn't talked to my best friend since Saturday, but after she'd felt it necessary to keep secrets from me, I wasn't sure I wanted to. Besides, she was suspicious already. Once Courtney heard about Phoebe, her once farfetched theories wouldn't be far off. I thought about the broken necklace I'd shoved into my top drawer, the one I tore from Phoebe's dead body. Or the sketch hidden away in my notebook, the one detailing the gruesome crime.

"We will have to confirm it," Stevenson said.

"It was a cop's wedding." I laughed. "There will be more than a few people you'd considered good sources who will say I was there."

Stevenson raised an eyebrow. He doubted it. A part of me doubted it too. I'd left the wedding when the dancing began. Most people were heavily intoxicated already, and the booze would have continued to flow. I made sure Courtney was distracted, and despite her suspicions of me, I was sure my best friend would vouch for my attendance. I knew too much for her to say otherwise.

"Mr. Huston," the young officer tried again. "Is it true you were having an affair with Phoebe Dawson before your wife died?"

I stood, anger written on my face now. "What the hell?" I snapped, looking between Stevenson and the other officer.

Stevenson stood to meet me, wearing a smug expression. "We believe this was a crime of passion," he explained. "Not planned but carried out in anger. Who would be angrier than your own father? After all, there was a memoir out recently. I understand it painted both of you in a rather negative light."

My hands clenched at my sides as I glared at the officer. Before I could snap back at him there came a knock at the door.

Stevenson looked at me expectantly and the caller had to knock again before I moved to open it. There in the doorway stood a familiar woman.

"Detective Frances Day," she said, though I remembered her from my first interview with Stevenson. She didn't wait for me to invite her in before stepping through my door. Her nose scrunched with disapproval as she made her way towards where my father sat. "Daniel Huston?" she inquired, staring down at him.

Dad grunted his response.

"You're under arrest for the murder of Phoebe Dawson," she said, motioning to the younger officer. "You have the right to remain silent, know anything you say can be used against you in a court of law."

Dad didn't struggle as the younger officer reached for his arm and hauled him to his feet. He seemed subdued, almost not present.

"What the fuck is going on?" I demanded, my eyes darting between Day and Stevenson.

Neither answered me as Day continued to dictate Dad's rights as the young officer cuffed him behind his back. When she finished and Dad voiced his understanding, the young officer led him out of the condo.

Seething, I turned my hard glare on Stevenson. "You have no proof!"

Day's cold, dark eyes found mine. "We found fingerprints at the scene. And a letter. It's enough for an arrest." She turned on her heel and left me standing alone with Stevenson in the kitchen.

"You're stupid if you really think he did this."

Stevenson wore a knowing smile. "In the very least, maybe he'll sober up and we'll get some straight answers." He stepped around me and disappeared through my front door.

From the window, I watched as he ducked into his police car and sped off with my father in the backseat.

When they were gone, I flopped onto the couch my dad had vacated and put my face in my hands. Had Dad been by to see Phoebe on Friday? I wondered what drew him in his drunken state, the desire to rekindle what they lost or his belief she lied about Mom's accident. I couldn't be sure. Either way, going to see her had been stupid.

Alone, I climbed the stairs to my room and pulled open my top drawer. I reached for the golden necklace still speckled with blood and ran my finger over it. Then I grabbed my sketch book and shoved them both in my backpack. After, I slipped the Tissot watch off my wrist and removed the ring hanging around my neck. Each trophy I shoved in my bag along with the sketches of my crimes.

My dad had been arrested, and I had no doubt they'd be by with a warrant to search the place. I was lucky they hadn't yet. With the only evidence pointing me to these crimes packed away, I slipped out into the evening air and made my way to the beach at the front of the condo complex.

Seated at the base of the large maple tree with freshly laid soil, I carefully dug into the loose dirt feeling it build up beneath my fingernails. Once the hole was wide enough, I dropped each treasure into it, then pulled out my sketch book and looked over the artwork. I sucked in a sharp breath as I tore out the pages one by one, folded them tightly, and dropped them into the hole with the trophies. They'd be ruined if the rain came too heavy before I could retrieve them, but it was a risk I had to take to get rid of the proof until it was safe to have them again.

Once I buried everything, I glanced around quickly then jogged back to our condo. I was grateful the clothing I'd worn when I disposed of Phoebe had long been torn, bleached, and destroyed. The only remaining evidence had now been relocated and hidden.

When I returned to my condo, a new envelope was taped to the door. My heart rapped an anxious beat in my chest as I reached for it.

I glanced around as I tore it from the door. The person who left it couldn't have gotten far, but the parking lot surrounding my condo building was mostly empty, and nothing stood out as misplaced. Had they seen me hide my secrets?

Back in my bedroom, I ripped open the letter, finding a note similar to the others, this one however was longer. *I guess you'll let anyone go down for your crimes.* I glanced over the words, finding the message eerily timely. Dad had just been arrested for my actions. Though I doubted they would actually charge him. His incontinence was clear to any who looked at him. I crumbled up the note and tossed it into the waste bin. This person was too close, and I still didn't know what they wanted from me.

I lay on my bed, staring at the white ceiling, and forced the messenger from my mind, allowing myself instead to consider Phoebe. I'd felt relief when she died, like a part of me had been set free. I'd gotten my revenge. I'd taken an undeserving life. I'd gotten my high. I'd given into the darkness. But this time, the feeling wasn't sated. The darkness wanted more.

Phoebe deserved everything she got, but I'd been careless.

The darkness bristled at the accusation. Careless, it wasn't.

I tried to shake my head free of the heavy feeling, but the darkness didn't seem to wane like it had in the past. It whispered its desires, telling me how much it wanted more. I thought back to Dean and how the darkness had quieted, purred almost with pleasure at the release. Why hadn't Phoebe made it satisfied? What had I done wrong?

I sat up as I came to this realization, conflict brewing inside me. Killing had given me a release. Except this time, it didn't work. Was this like any other drug? Take too much and you only needed more, more, more?

Vanessa had birthed the darkness I'd buried inside me. Mark fed it and Dean ... he'd been the prize I desired the most. Then why, after everything Phoebe had done, did she not offer the same feelings?

An itch began in my palms. A desire for more. To act again. The lives I'd purposely taken had been deserving, but now the darkness sang to me in a way that I wondered why that had mattered before. Maybe it wasn't about justice. Maybe all I wanted was to kill some more.

36

Courtney Faith

Wednesday, August 16

The week had been hell, and it was only halfway through. Alexa remained unreachable. I'd driven by her condo, knocked on her door, called and texted countless times, but no response. Not even when I heard Danny had been arrested, only to quickly be cleared of the charges, leaving the police floundering.

They'd searched the condo, finding no evidence or proof of his crime. The bar staff working at Big Shot on Saturday night were quick to vouch for Danny, claiming he was seated at the bar most of the night. Cameras in the place confirmed it, and he was released within twenty-four hours. He claimed to have visited Phoebe the night before with a letter detailing his feelings for a reunion he hadn't wanted to share with Alexa. I wondered how much my best friend knew about it and if she did, how far she would take it?

I couldn't really know because Alexa still wouldn't speak to me.

Savannah waited by the kitchen table as I paced aimlessly in front of her. She'd arrived claiming she had something to tell me, but I'd been unable to take my mind off Danny.

If he was innocent, then what did that mean about Alexa? The idea my friend could be a murderer was still too difficult to grasp. I waffled between wanting to see her and pull her into a tight hug, knowing she must be innocent, then quickly reminding myself that the coincidences were too much, that I didn't really know this person who'd been my friend for years. What was stopping her from taking her rage out on me?

"Courtney?" Savannah asked. She wheeled closer to me and caught my arm, halting my movements.

I glanced down at her, allowing my eyes to focus and register her concerned expression but before either of us could say more, there was a gentle knock at my front door. I ripped my arm from Savannah's grasp and dashed to it, wondering if it might be Alexa coming to her senses to talk to me, but when the door swung open, Stevenson stood on my stoop. Damn it.

He was dressed casually, in baggy jeans and a dark polo top, out of the stiff uniform I was used to seeing him in. He wore a sheepish grin on his face, and his eyes pleaded with me, though for what I wasn't sure.

"Brett isn't here," I said stiffly, still gripping the door, ready to close it in his face.

He bowed his head. "I know. I hoped I could speak to you alone." He risked a glance at me. "Off the record."

I hesitated, unsure if I should trust him. "Brett told you not to come by here anymore without cause."

He put his hands out, palms up, like a peace offering. "I'm off duty. I just want to talk."

"I'm not alone." I let the door slide open further to show Savannah behind me.

Stevenson looked to her before focusing back on me. "Please."

Curiosity got the best of me, and I stepped aside letting him enter. "If Brett finds you here, he'll lose it."

Stevenson nodded, following me and Savannah from the front hallway to my kitchen, where he perched on a bar stool. "I won't be long."

I leaned against the counter, staring at him with my arms crossed over my chest. Savannah waited beside me, eyeing the officer with suspicion.

"What is it?"

"I need your help," he said, his voice had an edge of desperation to it. "I need to know what Alexa is hiding."

Savannah noticeably stiffened at the mention of Alexa.

I drew my shoulders back maintaining my previous statement. "I don't know what you're talking about."

"We searched the condo," Stevenson continued. "We couldn't find anything tying either Danny or Alexa to the murder of Phoebe Dawson."

Savannah sucked in a breath, her eyes finding mine. I shook my head, urging her to keep quiet. I wasn't sure I wanted to incriminate my friend, let alone it be my statement that caused her arrest.

"Then you're looking in the wrong place." A part of me still tried to convince myself it was true. Savannah's eyes had found her hands that wrung together in her lap.

Stevenson shook his head. "This isn't a coincidence. Three of the murder victims have a direct tie to Alexa."

"Couldn't you argue the same thing about me?" I protested.

"Or me," Savannah chimed in, though I felt that was a bit of a stretch.

Stevenson ignored us. "She's hiding something. She knows something. And I think you know it too." He held eye contact and didn't bother glancing at Savannah. "Tell me again when she left your wedding."

I tore my gaze away from his. "You already have my statement about my wedding. As far as I know she was there all night."

"As far as you know."

"Yes," Savannah said firmly, placing her hand on my arm.

I glanced at it for a moment before forcing myself to look back at him. "Yes." I didn't know, in fact, I couldn't remember seeing her beyond the speech she gave. I'd been so busy all night, constantly pulled in every direction by adoring guests. Had she stayed for the entire meal or the dancing? Or had she skulked off in the middle of the festivities to commit a heinous crime?

"Please," Stevenson begged. "You are the only one who can give us something to go on. All the evidence we have found is circumstantial at best. We know Alexa is involved, but without you telling us what you know, we can't stop this from happening again."

Savannah's hand on my arm tightened as I grappled with his words, unsure if I should give in. Alexa denied killing Dean, Mark, and Vanessa. The words she said to me after Dean's body was discovered rolled around in my mind. She'd painted me as crazy when I came at her with accusations. She made me feel like everything I was imagining was unbelievable, impossible, insane, and yet ... now it seemed clear. Had she killed Vanessa too and used Dean to cover it up? Did Dean know her secret and plan to reveal it, so he had to die? And what did that say about me and the secrets we shared?

I wanted to believe my best friend hadn't been involved in the brutal murders, but when Phoebe turned up dead ...

No. I had to believe Alexa was the same girl I met fifteen years ago.

I shook my head. "I don't know anything."

Stevenson gazed at me for a moment longer before he huffed out a long breath and stood. He wiped a hand over his tired face then turned for the door. Before leaving he hesitated, looking back at me. "If you hear anything, or something changes. Call me, please."

I nodded, but I wouldn't call.

From the front window, I watched Stevenson climb into his personal car and slowly head down my street. Savannah came up behind me and I turned to her.

"I'm sorry about that," I said. "I have no idea what he's talking about."

Savannah grimaced. "Come sit down. I need to show you something." She led me back into the kitchen then reached for her purse. Methodically she began pulling things out of her bag. A wedding ring on a chain, an expensive watch, a broken gold necklace, and several pieces of folded paper. All dirty with stains of mud or dirt caked into the pieces.

The last things she pulled out was a photograph which she put face up for me to examine.

The items all felt out of place until I realized what stared me in the face. It was Alexa and the dead woman, Vanessa, but here she was very much alive, and they were together at what looked like a bar. I remembered what Brett had said about Dean being spotted with the victim, and I immediately knew that she'd been a pawn in Alexa's games.

My eyes raked over the folded papers, and I reached for one, carefully laying out the drawing of Vanessa I'd seen earlier that month. I didn't need to unfold the rest to know what they held but I did anyway, knowing eventually I'd get to one I hadn't seen before. I guessed it was Phoebe by the context. Brett hadn't sugar-coated it when he told me about her murder. In the sketch, there was a clear heart necklace on the victim, and I placed the drawing down, picking up the broken necklace.

I dropped it almost immediately when I realized the speckles weren't dirt but blood. My eyes scanned over the other items. Mark's ring. Dean's watch. Phoebe's necklace. My insides twisted with nausea.

"What is this?" I whispered, unable to meet Savannah's eyes.

"Two months ago, I started to have Alexa followed," Savannah explained. "Nothing major. Just with the wedding coming up, she was distant and acting strangely, and I wanted to make sure that everything was okay."

I looked at my friend then, trying to understand her decisions.

"I didn't think I'd catch her doing this," Savannah said. "I only wanted to show you how destructive she was. That she couldn't be trusted. That I would have been the better choice. That maybe you were better off without her."

I swallowed hard.

"I planned to show you the photo and explain about her and Dean's weird sex parties," Savannah said. "But by the time I got the photo from my source, Vanessa's body had been found, and Alexa had already moved onto deadlier things."

"You knew she killed Mark?" I asked, my mind still frazzled with the news.

Savannah gave a firm nod. "I didn't at first, and when I realized the connection, I didn't want to say anything. Mark threatened you. He deserved what he got."

"But the others?" I asked, my voice breathy.

"I didn't predict how Alexa would act," she said slowly. "I thought if I threatened her with exposure, it would be enough to deter her from causing any more harm. Obviously, that was the wrong approach."

She waved over the stolen items. "I was ready to come clean to her. To admit I knew about Mark and Vanessa, when I saw the police arrest her dad. Maybe I was wrong about Dean and Phoebe. I had no proof of those. Until she panicked and buried everything that tied her to them."

Her tired eyes found mine. "I left her one last message, and I dug up everything she'd hidden. I had to tell you the truth, because I'm not sure she ever will."

I didn't respond, unsure what to say as I stared over the evidence in front of me. This was exactly what Stevenson was asking for, and Savannah had it right under his nose. Did I call him now and turn her in? I wasn't sure that was what I wanted. This woman I'd known for over fifteen years was a murderer. Did I owe her a chance to tell me why?

I jolted out of my thoughts when Savannah reached out to touch my arm.

"Are you okay?" She asked softly.

"How could I be okay?" I asked, my eyes gliding over the evidence again.

Savannah moved to gather the things up, but I stopped her.

"Let me keep this," I said. "I don't want Alexa to know you were involved." I didn't know what she would do to Savannah. It had become clear that Alexa was unpredictable.

"I can take care of myself," Savannah said. "I'm not scared of Alexa."

I gave her a small smile. "I know, but I don't even know what to make of all this."

"I should have said something earlier," Savannah said. "Maybe it wouldn't have come to this."

I didn't answer her, instead moving to grab a plastic bag, then I swiped everything off the table and into the bag, hiding the evidence from sight under the kitchen sink.

"I'll handle it," I said. "I'll make sure Brett takes it all in."

Savannah gave my arm a gentle squeeze, then excused herself, leaving me alone with my thoughts. I wouldn't pass it on to Brett. Not yet.

I grabbed my phone and sent Alexa a message.

Please. I need to talk to you.

When I put my phone down, I told myself I wanted answers, and then I would tell the police. I was protecting my friend, doing whatever I could to keep her safe. But the sinking feeling inside me told me otherwise. It wasn't her secrets I wanted under lock and key. It was my own.

37

Alexa Huston

Thursday, August 17

As I climbed the front steps to Courtney and Brett's home, I didn't realize I was walking into an ambush. I'd ignored most of her messages, until the final one when I decided to answer her desperate pleas to see me. I could guess why she wanted to speak. Her suspicions only days ago must seem so much more plausible. I didn't know whether I'd admit anything to my best friend, but I knew I'd remind her that secrets kept us safe.

The darkness hummed in my ears. Its once-silence presence comforting, but now its constant need had begun to feel stifling.

Courtney greeted me with a closed smile, my first indication something wasn't right, and led me into the kitchen. There was no food in sight, another indication, as Courtney had always been an entertaining queen when it came to hosting. The discomfort the darkness felt made me squirm. It didn't want to be here. This wasn't right.

"Everything okay?" I asked as I settled onto a bar stool. Courtney didn't sit. Instead, she leaned against the counter, gazing at me. She looked tired. Haunted, though I supposed we were all haunted these days. Being surrounded by death had that effect.

"Yeah, I'm fine," Courtney said, turning her gaze away from me. "Why wouldn't I be?"

"You seem … off." She still wouldn't look at me. I tried a different approach. "Is it Brett?" With a playful grin, I added, "Trouble in paradise already?"

When she looked back at me, her eyes were narrowed, her once-smiling lips a straight line.

"Brett isn't the problem." Her voice was hard.

"Okay," I said slowly. "But obviously something is bothering you."

"Maybe it's because my best friend is a murderer."

I stiffened at the accusation but tried not to let it show. "Back on this theory again?"

"Phoebe Dawson is dead," Courtney said.

"I'm aware."

"She was brutally murdered the night of my wedding," Courtney said. "They predict around midnight."

Again, I said, "I'm aware. Police questioned me, and they arrested my dad. Why are you speaking to me like I wouldn't know this?"

She continued to glare at me. "But your dad didn't do it."

"Of course not," I said.

"Did you?" Courtney's head tilted as she gazed at me with scrutiny. The look on her face caught me off guard. She stared at me like I was a stranger, not the friend she'd known for half her life.

"No."

Courtney shook her head. "I'm tired of all the lies, Alexa."

"I'm not lying," I tried again. The darkness growled at the insinuation.

"It would be one thing if you'd shot her out of spite," Courtney snapped. "I understand how horrible she was. How much she hurt you. But you didn't. You brutalized her. You beat her to death."

My hands began to shake as she described my work to me. *It wasn't brutal*, the voice whispered. *It was just*. Phoebe deserved what she got. Who was Courtney to say otherwise? She didn't know what Phoebe had done. She hadn't had to live with the fallout. She didn't understand my struggles.

"You're a monster." She'd said the words so softly for a moment I thought I imagined them. But her gaze held mine, as if to gauge my reaction.

Monster, the voice mused, as if it enjoyed the label.

"She got what she deserved." The words slipped out before I even considered them. My tone was dead pan, matter of fact, no feeling. Like the words were not my own. I thought I would see triumph on Courtney's face. She got my confession, what she wanted.

Instead, her face twisted in horror. Her mouth dropped open, and fear filled her eyes. She'd hoped I would continue to deny the truth. The darkness cackled at her misfortune.

I stood, and she stepped back from me.

"Phoebe murdered my mother," I said in low tone. Maybe If I explained my reasons, it would make her see that, although I'd done bad things, I wasn't a bad person. The darkness disagreed. "Phoebe destroyed my dad. She ruined my life, and she wasn't sorry. She didn't apologize, she didn't concede. And she did the one thing she never should have. She came back to the place where she started all the fires. All I did was put them out."

"What are you talking about?" Courtney asked. "Your mom died in a car accident."

"That was a lie," I whispered, my voice sounding foreign to my ears. "My dad covered the whole thing up. With the help of your dear father-in-law." I was glad Phoebe was dead. The darkness agreed. She didn't deserve to continue living the lavish life she'd made for herself. She made it off my dad, my family, my mother's blood, *my* loss. And she left us behind to pick up the pieces. My dad never did.

"No," Courtney said. "Kevin wouldn't do that."

"Oh, of course," I mocked. "Because such an upstanding family like the Knights would never be involved in something like that. Maybe you don't know your new family as well as you think."

Courtney frowned while she processed what I told her; whether she chose to ignore it or didn't believe me, I wasn't sure.

"And what about Dean?" Courtney's voice held steady, but the tone was weak, frightened.

"I didn't kill Dean," I said, the practiced lie feeling robotic. The darkness chuckled at the audacity of it all.

Courtney glanced towards where my hands rested at my sides. "What happened to his watch?"

"What are you talking about?"

"For days you've been wearing his watch," she said. "After he was murdered. Do you think I'm stupid? I know you couldn't afford it, and I highly doubt he handed it to you before you killed him."

"No," I said. My palms began to itch as my plans spiraled out of control. Anger rose up inside me. I drew a steady breath, trying to keep the need at bay. Not here. Not now.

She pulled something out of her pocket and slammed it on to the counter. Dean's watch, dirt still caked around the dial and the band. I'd buried it the day they arrested my dad. How did Courtney have it?

She didn't give me a chance to respond as she continued, her face written with horror. "Dean's head was smashed in, and Phoebe mutilated. This is the work of someone insane; this isn't about revenge."

I'd never considered the methods to be any more than what they were, a means to an end. Sure, the blood had been a strange fascination, and the idea of death had drawn the darkness in for weeks, but brutal? *No,* the voice whispered. *Just.*

It was clear Courtney didn't see what we did.

"No," I said again. The itch, the need, grew. The darkness growled, its desire overpowering.

"So, what?" Anger replaced the fear in Courtney's tone. "You dumped the guy, so you had to murder him? Then what?" She withdrew something else and slapped it down next to the watch. It was the photograph from my mysterious messenger. "Did you murder the missing tourist too and plant the earring? I *believed* you."

I grabbed the photo off the table, Courtney flinching at my movements. "Where did you get this?" I turned my glare on her. Had she been the one following me?

"From someone who actually cares enough about me to tell me the truth," she shot back. She held her head high, clearly trying to show me how little I frightened her, but even her confidence couldn't hide the way her hands shook.

For a moment, my anger waned. My actions were never meant to scare her. She was the only one that mattered to me. I ignored the flare of irritation the darkness felt at my sentimentality.

"Vanessa was an accident," I said softly, my gaze still on the very alive Vanessa in the photograph. "Dean pushed her when he was playing rough. She hit her head. It all happened so quickly. We didn't mean to kill her."

Tears welled in Courtney's eyes, and she took a step back from me, clearly unsure how to process all I was telling her.

"I don't do the things I do out of irrational anger," I tried to explain, though the darkness protested. "When Vanessa died ... it entranced me. I couldn't explain it. It woke up something inside me. Something broken that had been long hidden away."

I took a careful step towards Courtney. This time she didn't flinch, but she watched me closely.

"When Vanessa died, I didn't know how to handle it," I said. "This feeling urged me to take the earring as a reminder of how I'd felt in that moment when she died. It quieted the voice in my head. It felt right."

"Voices in your head?" Courtney snapped. "A broken thing awoken inside you? Do you know how insane you sound? There is no justification for what you've done. No matter how you try to rationalize it."

My palms began to itch again, and for a moment, I envisioned myself wrapping my hands around Courtney's skinny neck and squeezing, squeezing until something snapped. The darkness cackled as I unsuccessfully tried to clear the feeling.

"You got dealt a shit hand," Courtney said. "No one disagrees with you, but that doesn't give you the right to do these things, to take this revenge."

I swallowed hard, the darkness speaking for me. "It was only what they deserved."

"No one deserves to die."

I almost scoffed at the naïve comment so typical of well-wishing Courtney. Tons of people deserved death; hell, I was one of them.

"Dean was a no-good drug dealer who took advantage of addicts and prostituted them. The things he told me about Kaylee, and the way he felt he was right ..." the voice inside my head coming out as my own. "He's lucky I didn't stab him on the spot at Nia's party."

Courtney flinched. "When did you become so callous?"

"Around the time I realized you wouldn't fight your own battles," I whispered, letting the darkness dictate my feelings. "Mark would have killed you and your mom. He was supposed to die in prison. I was only making sure that this time it happened the right way."

"And you stole his ring," she whispered, not meeting my eyes. From her pocket she produced another of my treasures. The chain I wore around my neck for weeks. Already I missed the weight of the trinket. I reach up, rubbing the back of my neck where the phantom chain rested.

"Yes," I said. "I *had* to."

Courtney steadied herself against the table. The realization hit her like a bus. I'd been a murderer for weeks.

"When we spoke that night, you were terrified," I continued. "I gave you something to ensure you'd sleep through the whole thing. I only wanted to save you and your mom. I didn't want you to end up like me."

"I would never end up like you," she whispered, gazing up at me with a hatred I'd never seen before. I straightened as she moved away from me, putting distance between us.

"I had to do it, Court." There was no other choice.

Courtney shook her head. "You *wanted* to." As she said it, she deposited the rest of my hidden items on the table. The broken necklace and my artwork, all laid out for me to see. I stepped closer to the table, the desire to touch my trophies overwhelming. The darkness had wanted to kill them all, and I had let it, driven by my sense of right, but really by the desire-filled voice inside me.

"You've been watching me," I said, my voice low as I reached out and slid my finger over the golden ring. "Maybe you're just admiring my work." My finger grazed over the drawing of Vanessa and her once-perfect face.

"Oh my god, Alexa," Courtney said, disgust clear in her eyes. "You're going to get caught."

"No," I said, my voice hard, unfamiliar. The itch in my palms returned in full force. "No one knows ... but you. And you won't say anything."

She bumped the table in her haste to put distance between us, causing my trophies to dance and flutter. My fist clenched. My throat felt raw.

"Even if I don't say anything, it wasn't hard for me to figure out the truth," she said. "They already suspect you. Stevenson practically begged me to give a statement, anything to tie you to the circumstantial evidence."

My arms tingled as the desire grew. No, I tried to shake my mind free of the voice, but the darkness refused to be kept at bay. My secrets weren't safe. I wasn't safe. *We* weren't safe.

"And did you?" My voice was low, deadly serious as I dug my nails into my palms, trying to calm the burning itch crawling its way up my arms.

"Of course not," she said.

"I keep your secret," I said slowly, trying to push off the fogginess that wanted to cloud my mind. The darkness begging to take control. "You keep mine."

The terror in her eyes told me all I needed to know. This secret wasn't safe with her.

She was going to tell Brett. She would give in to Stevenson's wishes. Like with Dean, two could only keep a secret if one of them was dead. I *had* to stop her.

Feeling like my hands weren't my own, I reached for the knife block on the counter, pulling out the large chef knife we'd used to murder Mark. The darkness overpowered any rational thought. *Kill her*, it whispered, *or she will ruin everything*.

"What are you doing?" Her voice shook. Her words penetrated my resolve, forcing me to drop the knife on the counter and dart for the door. I had to get away before the darkness did something I regretted. Despite what she knew, I didn't want to hurt my best friend.

"Alexa," she called after me, but I didn't stop. I only continued to run.

The voice urged me to go back, to gather my prizes and leave with something new. That sparkling engagement ring had always been pretty. Imagine it splattered with blood. *It's not real, it's not real,* I whispered to myself about the voice in my head, hopeful my old coping mechanism would keep the murderous desires at bay.

I threw myself into my car, turned on the engine, and sped off. My blood boiled, my palms itched, and desire scratched at my dry throat. I shook my head to try and clear the cloudy thoughts overtaking me.

This wasn't a game anymore. I wasn't some vigilante taking the lives of those who deserved it. I considered killing my best friend to save myself. I was out of my mind, and I didn't know where to go from here.

38

Courtney Faith

Friday, August 18

The night following Alexa's confession, violent nightmares plagued me. Waking up to Alexa towering over our bed with a knife in hand. In the dreams, it was never me she harmed. I'd been certain that was what ran through her mind when she picked the knife out of the block in the kitchen. But after she fled so quickly, I couldn't be sure. Now, in my dreams, she plunged the blade into Brett's stomach. Alexa's emotionless face stared down at me, splattered with his blood, and soon a slow smile spread across her lips, and she licked them hungrily.

"He had to go," she said, her voice monotone. "He was going to ruin everything."

I screamed.

The dream ended there, with Alexa's harsh words and my blood-curdling shriek. Worse, I woke up crying, ripping Brett from his night's rest and causing him to worry.

Brett wasn't stupid. He asked what was wrong, but I brushed him off, unable to tell him my true fears.

I found myself pacing the house aimlessly, unsure what to do. We were leaving for our honeymoon in Turks and Caicos in a week. I should be excited, looking forward to the life we had been planning for years but instead found myself sick with worry over what Alexa had done. What she could do.

Alexa was unstable. It was clear by the crazed look in her eyes and the way she confessed her crime. She murdered three people in cold blood. She had been responsible for another death out of carelessness. There wasn't anything to understand beyond the fact she'd taken lives when she wanted to. And a part of me wondered if she'd wanted to take mine too. My eyes found the knife she'd held so confidently the previous day. It could have been so easy for her to plunge the knife into my chest.

Could her instability mean the end of my life too? If not in death, then in my lifestyle and relationships? If Alexa were caught, would she spill my secret? Would she tell the police about Savannah's accident and how I'd been at fault.

I thought of the way people would view me. Of how Savannah would feel, of Brett's disgust at my choice to drink and drive, then to cover up a crime. The life I'd planned out so meticulously would come crashing down around me.

The logical part of my brain said there was nothing to be done about my crime. Too many years had passed, and without the proper evidence, they couldn't truly convict me. I wouldn't go to jail; hell, I probably wouldn't even be arrested. Socially, though, it would ruin me. No one would trust me again. I could lie, sure, tell them Alexa was clearly grasping at straws, looking for anything to take the heat off her. I could even say it was her behind the wheel if I wanted to.

I didn't know if I was capable of living with another lie for the rest of my life. Worse, it would put doubt on me, doubt that Brett or Savannah had never had. I might not go down for my crime in the eyes of the law, but I would lose everything I'd built.

I couldn't get the things Alexa had said out of my mind. That Phoebe had murdered her mother, and Kevin had played a hand in covering the crime. One of many as Rita had implied. Could my father-in-law be capable of such corruption? I couldn't wait until Brett came home. I needed to know the truth. So, I hopped into my car and went across town to Brett's parents' house, hopeful I could get a moment alone with Kevin. He was the only person I hadn't gone to for answers, and now I was certain he was the only one who could tell me for sure.

At their house, I noticed Missy's SUV wasn't in the driveway, so I took her spot and hurried up the front step, letting myself in.

"Hello?" I called into the empty front foyer. "Kevin?"

Footsteps sounded upstairs, and soon Kevin came into view on the top landing, leaning over the railing and peering down at me.

"Courtney?" He asked, his eyebrows raised. "Were we expecting you?"

"No," I said, kicking off my shoes and hurrying up the stairs. "But I was hoping to talk to you."

He frowned, drawing his bushy eyebrows together. "Is everything alright?"

I waved towards his office, assuming that was where he came from. "Can we sit?"

He seemed hesitant but after a moment led me into the small square room and motioned to the seat at his desk.

"How can I help?" he asked when he'd sat in the chair on the opposite side of the desk. He folded his hands before him, and suddenly I felt foolish being here. Did I really believe what Alexa had said? I couldn't imagine this kind man capable of any treachery.

"Honestly, I feel a bit silly coming to you," I said slowly. "But it was something Alexa said." I thought twice about bringing up Rita's accusations since the last time he'd heard her name it hadn't gone over well.

"Danny's girl?" Kevin asked, his frown deepening.

"Yeah," I continued, lacing my fingers together to avoid fidgeting. "About her mother."

Once again, his eyebrows shot up. "Bronwyn?"

I nodded. "She said the accident was a lie, and that you and Danny set it up all those years ago."

Kevin pushed off the desk, leaning back in his chair. The present frown had grown, and I could see the worry in his eyes. Eyes that reminded me of Brett. My husband was so like this man, following in his footsteps on the force and priding himself on his beliefs and integrity. For a moment I considered getting up, leaving that room and never hearing the whole truth. Instead living in ignorance of his involvement. But I had to know the truth. For Alexa's sake, and my own.

When Kevin finally spoke, he released a long sigh. "It was a long time ago. Sometimes we make rash decisions in the heat of the moment. I thought I was protecting a friend."

"Protecting him from what?" I asked.

Kevin reached up, rubbing at his tired eyes. "When Danny called me about Bronwyn's death, he was panicked. Swearing it had been an accident and cursing because Alexa had come home to see it. Danny and I knew each other back in high school, before I met Missy and moved here to be with her. He's my oldest friend. I had to help him."

"Cover up a crime?" I cringed as the words came out of my mouth, having not intended to be so blunt.

"That wasn't how I saw it," Kevin said. "It was an accident."

"What about the reporter?" I asked, remembering Rita's words and needing to hear it from him. "You tried to ruin her career over this."

Kevin's eyes darkened. "That woman schemed her way into the coroner's office to review a confidential report; she was lucky I only tried to have her fired."

"This is corrupt," I said, unable to stop myself. "How can you justify it?" He played a role in Bronwyn's death, whether he believed it or not.

"I did what I thought I had to for the people I loved," Kevin said, his voice softened. "What would a drawn-out investigation have done to Alexa and Danny? It would have been an awful affair with invasive questions and scrutiny. Maybe Danny would have ended up in jail, and then Alexa would have been truly alone. When he called me that night, I believed I was doing the right thing." He reached out and touched my arm, adding softly, "For family, always."

I chewed on my lower lip, unsure how to process what he'd told me. It had been a cover up years ago. Alexa's nightmares were real. My heart hurt then for the girl I'd known back in high school. Before the loss of her mother. Before all the bad that had seemed to shape her in ways I couldn't fully understand. But when I gazed back into Kevin's eyes, so like Brett's, I was reminded about who my family was and the life I was fighting for. It seemed that Alexa was no longer a part of that future, and I wasn't sure what that meant in the end.

39

Alexa Huston

Saturday, August 19

The itch didn't subside after I left Courtney's, and I'd avoided her ever since. The darkness inside me had gone on the defensive, determined to keep her from spilling my secrets. I didn't have control over a part of me, and that notion frightened me. I never intended to cause harm to those I loved, only to rid the world of those undeserving of the life they'd been given; only those who caused harm themselves were meant to be a part of our twisted games. It was clear the darkness didn't care who it made a victim.

When Courtney confronted me, angered me, judged me, it took over. I didn't know what would have happened if she hadn't brought me back. I never wanted to hurt her, but I also couldn't let my secrets get out. One way or another, our friendship was bound to end. Maybe secrets didn't keep us close. They tore us apart from the inside out.

Nearing the end of my Saturday shift, I was overworked and tired. I'd spent yesterday wondering if the cops would show up any minute, if Courtney had turned in my trophies, but none came. She kept quiet, whether through loyalty or fear, I wasn't sure. Did it even matter?

The end of summer crept ever closer, and the bar was busier than normal. I was getting tired of drunken patrons spilling beer and breaking glasses. Security had been up to their ears in rowdy partiers they'd had to remove for fear of fights breaking out. And the darkness simmered below my skin, making the itch, the desire at times unbearable.

One of the regulars, Lou, became particularly unruly. I usually liked him, but tonight he made inappropriate passes at all the bartenders, but most had brushed him off as a lonely old man. I'd done the same until I watched him fawning over a young girl in a skimpy party dress.

The itch grew as he pawed at her with his fat hands and tried to kiss her. She was clearly intoxicated and trying to fend off his advances, but the attempts were futile and weak at best.

The darkness whispered its desire as I waved down security and motioned in the direction of Lou. "Probably should do something before the guy gets arrested for assault." I didn't need to add that an assault arrest wouldn't be good for business, no matter how common those things were in this dingy little bar.

Exasperated, the bouncer approached them and took Lou aside to speak with him. In the time he took Lou, the girl slipped away and out of sight. I hoped she'd gotten far enough away from Lou's advances.

Lou looked angry as they talked, glancing around for the girl then fixing his eyes on me. When the bouncer left him, Lou came to the bar, eyes blazing.

"You have something to say to me?" He puffed out his chest as he spoke. The button-down shirt he wore strained across the front of his stomach and sweat beaded along his brow line. His face was bright red, likely a mix of embarrassment, anger, and alcohol. The darkness bared its teeth. It wasn't words it wanted.

"Not a thing." I turned away, but he reached across the bar and grabbed my arm. I turned on him with a hard gaze, my voice no longer my own. "I suggest you let go of me."

He released his grip immediately and stumbled backwards. "Stupid bitch." Though nearly drowned out by the DJ, I still caught what he said. The itch in my palms grew.

When last call passed, the music died, and the lights turned on, there were only a few left in the bar, including Lou.

Ashley, on a managerial shift, let her shoulders droop as she cashed out our tips then sent us on our way, claiming she would close the bar. From Ashley's tired scowl it was clear she was over the busy season. I was thankful, knowing I could use the rest. Except I couldn't leave. Lou was slumped at the opposite end of the bar, drunk and mumbling, and each time I looked at him and met his beady-eyed stare, the darkness growled. Before I left, I went to the kitchen and tucked one of the butcher knives in my bag. If he came after me, then at least I'd be protected, or so I told myself.

Outside the bar, I didn't go to my car. I hesitated as desire clawed at my throat and my palms itched with anticipation. I stepped into the alleyway and waited. It wasn't long before Lou emerged, stumbling. He came in my direction, turning down the alley, then placing a hand on the wall. Keys jingled in his hands as he steadied himself, unzipped his pants, and let out a sigh of relief as he urinated.

The darkness took over then, moving on the vulnerable and unwitting drunk.

I came up behind him and swung the butcher's knife, lodging it in his neck. His cry was silenced by gurgling blood, and he fell to the ground writhing. For good measure I stabbed him several more times, feeling the resistance of his fatty flesh with each cut. Soon, his movements ceased. I reached for his keys that had fallen to the asphalt and slipped them into my pocket.

The itch subsided and the desire vanished. The darkness hummed with pleasure as my skin tingled. The scent of metal and death filled my nostrils. I dropped the knife next to his mangled body as I realized what I'd done and ran for my car.

Back at my house, I remembered the keys in my pocket and pulled out the new trophy. The darkness preened with pleasure, but I couldn't stop the sick feeling swirling around inside me. I attacked someone unprovoked. The darkness had taken over. An out-of-body experience. My mind disconnected. I hadn't planned to kill him. I hadn't wanted to kill him, had I?

In my room I lowered myself to my bed, wondering if Courtney had been right about me. Maybe I was a monster.

In the chaos of my addled mind, the darkness cackled with pure joy.

40

Courtney Faith

Sunday, August 20

All hope of coping and normalcy came crashing down in the morning when Brett took the phone call. His handsome face contorted with worry and panic. And when he pulled the phone away from his ear, I knew what he was going to say before the words left his mouth.

"There's been another body."

"No," I said. "Who?" Who had Alexa killed now? Guilt turned inside me, making my stomach flip-flop. This was my fault. I knew she was guilty, and I kept her secret. Was this how I'd feel for the rest of my life? Nothing was worth this.

"Lou Garrett," Brett said, lowering himself to the couch in our living room. "A retiree."

I frowned. He was a Big Shot regular.

"Found outside Big Shot in the alleyway. Pants down and brutalized."

Alexa's signature style, it seemed. When had my best friend gotten so cruel?

"This is getting out of hand," Brett said, placing his forehead on his palm. He glanced up at me and his expression fell. "Sorry, Court, I shouldn't have said anything."

"Why is this happening?" I whispered, and I leaned against my husband. He wrapped an arm around me, comforting me in my sadness.

"I don't know, babe," Brett said. "But the murder weapon was found. The kill was careless. We will figure it out."

His words filled me with dread. Alexa left something behind that could implicate her. There were cameras in Big Shot, would they show her leaving the bar or following the murder victim? Somehow, it seemed impossible she could get away with this.

As I thought it, panic rose inside me. If she was caught, then I had no idea what lies she would tell, what secrets she would spill. Would she tell them I'd known the truth? That I was an accessory to her crimes? She'd been in my house only days ago, and I still held all the evidence that tied her to the bodies. Was she vindictive enough to send the police my way? If my best friend was arrested for murder, I was convinced there was no way I wouldn't be caught up in the drama of it all. My life would never be the same.

I glanced at the picture of Alexa and me stuck to the front of the fridge. We were young, barely eighteen, seated at the Cedar Falls lookout on one of our favourite trails. Her arm was thrown around my shoulder and she wore a huge grin. The good days. Before Phoebe had left. Before Alexa's life changed. We'd promised to be friends forever, no matter what, and now I wondered if maybe we would have been better off without each other all along.

I knew only two things then: I couldn't keep Alexa's secret for the rest of my life, and I couldn't let her get caught.

41

Alexa Huston

Monday, August 21

The steady buzz pulled me out of my dreamless sleep as my phone toppled from the dresser to the waiting floor below. Groggy, I reached over the edge of the bed, feeling around for the incessant device. Mackenzie Health flashed across the caller ID, and I hit the green button to accept.

"Hello?" I sat up and rubbed my eyes, unsure of what time it was.

"Hey, Alexa," the voice came through the receiver. It took me a moment to register the voice belonged to Kaylee.

"Hey, Kaylee," I huffed out a long breath. "How are you?"

"Fine," she said.

I grimaced. Fine didn't sound good.

"Look, Alexa ..." Kaylee trailed off, leaving me in silence once more.

"What's wrong?"

She drew a deep breath. "I spoke to the police. I'm sorry. They came to me yesterday to get another statement about Dean's death."

I closed my eyes knowing what would follow.

"They know what Dean did to me," she said. "And they know you know."

"Did you say anything else?" I asked, keeping my voice calm.

"No," Kaylee said. "But they seemed suspicious. Like they knew the answer before I said it."

I tilted my head back against the wall behind me, eyes closed and drawing slow steady breaths. I wasn't surprised. A part of me knew the case would eventually tie back to me. The darkness was taking over. Courtney knew the truth. Eventually I would be caught.

"They asked a lot of questions about you," Kaylee said. "I didn't say anything untrue." She paused. "They asked if I thought you killed Dean ... I said no."

"Thank you." I didn't know how else to respond.

"I'm sorry," Kaylee said again. "I really am. I don't know what they want with you, but I thought you should know."

"Don't be sorry," I said. "Nothing that happened is your fault. Just forget about it and get better."

Kaylee apologized again before she hung up the phone, but by then, I'd stopped listening. The police were building a case against me. Had Courtney tipped off her white knight about our conversation?

The darkness simmered, anger rising again.

All I knew was what would happen if they came to arrest me. There were four unsolved murders in our little town and the police were on the verge of connecting them to me. Eventually, it all would begin to make sense: the people that had died, the choices they'd made. It wasn't serial, it was justice. The darkness and I agreed on that.

While the voice inside me plotted its next release, I found my mind wandering to the consequences of my actions. If I was arrested, my dad would be alone. No one would care about the invalid Danny Huston. He'd be dead before I got out.

Even as I considered it, there was no way I was ever getting out. Courtney hadn't been wrong. There was a monster inside of me, one that awoke the moment I saw Vanessa's blood on Dean's floor. And it grew with each decision. When I saved Courtney from her sadistic father. When I saved other women from Dean. At times, the desire had been unbearable, but each kill had been just, more than just: their suffering hadn't compared to their victims'.

The darkness whispered that there was only one thing to be done. I popped open my email, glancing over the note I'd started writing to Courtney. The one that would explain everything to her better than I could explain it myself. It was unfinished, but I'd have time to complete it.

Then I clicked over to my messages. Feeling like I was in a trance, I sent one last text. The final one before my world would change.

42

Courtney Faith

Monday, August 21

I woke up the next morning feeling unrested and distraught. I'd all but lied to my husband the day before when he spoke about Lou's death. The carelessness of the murder would eventually point to Alexa, still, I couldn't bring myself to confess her crimes to Brett.

I couldn't forget what she'd said about Mark. That he should have died in prison. Had she meant it literally or had it been a wish like the one I made the day before his death? A feeling sat at the back of my mind that maybe it was something more.

When I stretched and reached for Brett, I found the bed empty, void of the morning snuggles I'd received every day since we got married. Dread filled me as I tossed the covers off and clambered out of bed. Dressed in sweatpants and a T-shirt, I hurried down the stairs to find Brett hunched over his computer at the counter, brow furrowed and eyes concentrated.

"Is everything okay?" I asked as I stepped to his side.

"Yeah, completely fine." He closed the computer, hiding what he'd been working on from view.

"What's going on?" I reached for the laptop, but he slid it farther away.

"Nothing really," he said. "Just following up on some emails. I really shouldn't have checked it. I think I've let myself fall into a rabbit hole of work."

"We're supposed to be on vacation," I teased, trying to keep my suspicions out of my voice.

Brett grimaced and ran a hand through his messy hair. "I know, I'm sorry." He grabbed his phone off the table. "Let me shower and we can go for a walk or something. Looks like a nice day."

I glanced to the living room where the sun streamed through the large window.

"Sure," I said.

He grinned, kissed my temple, then disappeared back upstairs.

I reached for the coffee pot, filled to the brim with steaming, rich liquid, but hesitated when I lay eyes on his laptop again. I couldn't shake the feeling he was hiding something from me.

I flipped open the laptop, keeping an eye on the front hallway. I tapped the table impatiently as the screen took a moment to load, and soon, I was staring at his work email. First, I clicked around aimlessly, unsure what I was looking for, until I found one of his read emails confirming my suspicions.

My throat tightened as I read over the email contents. It was from his captain, responding to an inquiry Brett asked. Yes, an arrest warrant had been issued for Alexa. They were charging her with four murders and one accomplice charge for Vanessa. They thought they had enough evidence to close the case quickly. He would let Brett know when they brought her in.

My heart raced as I slammed the computer shut and grabbed my phone. Without a thought, I dialed Alexa's number. It rang several times before it went to voicemail.

"Alexa, please call me." I couldn't keep the pleading from my tone. Instinct told me I had to warn her. Guilt made it certain. I couldn't let her go down without knowing how she'd handle my secrets. I couldn't risk she'd ruin my life as hers was destroyed.

I tried calling again, but once more the call clicked through to voicemail. Before I could dial again a text message came through, and I knew what I had to do.

Without a thought to my husband upstairs, I grabbed my purse and car keys and darted out the front door.

43

Alexa Huston

Monday, August 21

The sun shone high in the clear blue sky. It was a weekday, so the trails were nearly empty as I made my way to the lookout. It gave a great view over the provincial park and the hiking trails below. Those high rocks had once been my salvation, an escape whenever I needed a break from the trials of home and the exhaustion of work.

I hadn't been in ages, but today it felt right. A fuzziness covered my thoughts, as if I were high without smoking anything. My phone buzzed in my pocket as I made my way through the forest following the marked trail. Courtney again. The fourth time she'd tried to reach me, but I hadn't given her the courtesy of taking her call.

I knew how this would all go. Soon the police would come for me, it was only a matter of time now, and when they did, it would all be over. Everything I'd thought I'd wanted, everything I'd thought I'd gained. It would be for nothing. I'd be another name in the system, another person forgotten in a numbered cell.

There'd be infamy when the truth came out. Some people probably wouldn't be surprised, like Dean's parents. I had no doubt they'd thought me guilty since day one. Others would have never seen it coming.

When I rounded the next turn, the lookout stretched before me. There was a young couple, tourists likely, carrying a selfie stick and snapping photos of themselves standing on the rock that offered the incredible view of the town I called home.

They smiled at me before snapping one last photo and moving on. It was a great photo op. It had once been a favourite of mine and Courtney's.

When I was alone, I sat on the large rock and let my legs dangle over the cliff, looking at the long drop stretched down below me.

I closed my eyes and breathed in deeply; the air was fresh, clean, and better here than anywhere in town. Tourists coming up from the cities were always blown away by the clean air. No smog, no city pollution. It was freedom here.

Once, I'd numbed my pain with drugs—like father like daughter—looking for any sort of out to make my mundane, depressing life seem less so. It was a ruse, of course, but one I could bear when I let the highs numb all feeling. That was why I flocked to Dean. That was why I played his games. The freedom in letting go, forgetting.

Then Vanessa died and everything changed.

Now, everything would change again. The darkness whispered there was no going back.

My phone jumped to life again, and this time I glanced at the screen. A photo of me and Courtney making goofy faces in selfie mode. Once, it had been my favourite photo; when we were still young and carefree, before all the bad. I hit ignore and tucked my phone away. It would take some time, but I hoped Courtney would one day forgive me. The darkness softly laughed at the foolish desire.

The rustle of bushes drew my attention away from the steep fall in front of me. I glanced around, certain I was alone with only my thoughts and wildlife. I pushed myself to stand, swaying in the cool wind, feeling the gentle breeze on my cheeks, breathing the clean air again.

There was only one way for this to end. I was going to do the right thing. What better way to end than on my own terms.

As I was about to turn back the way I'd come, the sound of rustling drew my attention again and steady footsteps hurried up behind me.

The darkness cackled mercilessly.

44

Courtney Faith

Monday, August 21

When I arrived at Alexa's condo, there were two empty police cars outside her unit. I hurried to the door, wiping the sweat away from my forehead and knocked hard. Danny answered, and to my surprise, he looked put together. His usually bloodshot eyes were almost clear, and he wore clean jeans and a button-down. Far different than the sweats and bathrobe I'd gotten used to in the past few years.

"Courtney," he said, stepping aside and letting me enter the foyer. "Come in."

The tension in the house was thick, and I tried to steady my heavy breathing. Four police officers stood around the small room. I only recognized Stevenson, who'd been a fixture in my life these past weeks.

"What's going on?" I asked, turning to Danny. "Did she run away?"

"We don't know," Danny said, his voice barely a whisper. "I arrived home to find the place empty." Then he waved to the table. "And this left for us to find."

I glanced around Stevenson at the mess on the kitchen table. Dirt covered drawings and little knickknacks. Alexa's trophies. As I took in the items that had been in my house, I didn't think long on how they'd ended up here.

I stepped around Danny and reached for the drawings, slowly spreading them out and looking over the crimes. While the pages had been dirtied and ruined by wherever she'd stashed them, the brutal images from before were still clear. Vanessa, Mark's death, Kaylee's overdose, Dean's smashed face, and the newest one. Phoebe's murder, featuring the darkened figure clutching the fireplace poker in the background.

I put a hand to my mouth to silence the screams or keep the bile at bay, I wasn't sure.

"We found these in her room," Stevenson said, tossing a set of keys on to the table. I wondered if they belonged to Lou.

"Where is she?" I glanced from Stevenson to Danny.

"Wherever she is, we're looking for her," Stevenson said. "She won't get far."

Tears formed in my eyes as I thought back to the girl I knew before this terrible summer. The awkward teenager who lost her mom too young but knew how to make me laugh when things got tough at home. The sweet girl who would lie in my bed, whispering secrets in the middle of the night when we were supposed to be sleeping because we had school in the morning. My best friend who worked hard to keep her father afloat, a roof over their heads while I was a carefree university student. The young woman who'd witnessed my worst moment and vowed to keep the secret as tightly as I'd held it. When did it all change?

"Is there anything you can tell us? Anything at all?" Stevenson asked

I shook my head, unsure what I could share they didn't know or suspect already.

Stevenson eyed me for a moment, then conceded. "There will be an officer stationed in the parking lot in case she comes back." He glanced between me and Danny. "If either of you hear anything, call me immediately."

Danny nodded and the officers left, leaving Danny and me standing alone in the silent condo.

He lowered himself to the couch, and I shifted awkwardly; should I leave or wait around and see if he was okay? He only stared at the TV, so I turned away from him, but before I got too far he called out to me.

"Courtney," he said. "Did you know ... about what she's done?"

I walked back into the living room and sat on the opposite end of the couch.

"Yes," I said.

Danny found my gaze. His eyes were now glassy with tears. "Is it true?"

I bit down on my lip considering what to tell him. Should I lie and preserve his daughter's memory no matter what came out on the news in the coming days, or should I be honest with him, a man who had suffered so much?

In the end, the truth would be kinder.

"Yes," I said.

Danny closed his eyes, and a few tears escaped, rolling down his cheeks. "Why?"

I reached out and took his hand in my own. This man had once been like a father to me. He'd been full of life and love. He had me over for personal pizza nights and Monopoly, even when Alexa and I outgrew family board games and wanted instead to drink vodka or get stoned. He always forced game night, and it always turned into a competitive night of laughter. It used to be so important who won those nights, and now

I couldn't even remember who'd been the best. I could only remember the good and the fun.

"I wish I knew," I said.

He shook his head. "All I ever did was ruin her life."

"She loved you," I told him. "She wanted you to be happy."

"And now I have nothing," he said. He stood and went to the kitchen. I followed him, watching as he pulled the vodka from the freezer and took a long swig. For a moment I considered stopping him, telling him this wasn't what Alexa would have wanted, but there was nothing I could say to help this man with his grief. His wife was gone, his life was non-existent, and his daughter was a murderer.

Instead of chastising him for drinking, I turned without a word and let him sink into his grief in privacy.

At the front door I hesitated, glancing up the stairs. With Danny distracted, I crept up towards Alexa's waiting bedroom, my mind focused on one sketch. In her room, I reached between her mattress and boxspring, pulling out the hidden sketchbook. I flipped through it, finding the one she'd drawn of Savannah's accident, and tore the page from the book before returning the sketchbook to its hiding place. Gripping the last real evidence of my crime in my hands, I hurried down the stairs and slipped out the front door.

Back at my house, I found Brett standing in the front hallway, his eyes wide with worry.

"Where have you been?" he asked, his voice frantic. "I got out of the shower, and you were gone."

"I saw your work email. I'm sorry," I said. "I went to see Alexa."

His brow furrowed. "Seriously? Courtney, what were you thinking?"

When I didn't respond, he held up his phone. "I tried to track you, but your location didn't show up."

"Weird," I said, brushing him off, trying not to think about the crumpled drawing in my purse. I'd burn it the first chance I got. "I was at Alexa's. I spoke to Stevenson."

"Did they arrest her?" Brett asked, following me into the kitchen.

"They can't find her."

The rest of the day passed in a blur. Brett was on and off the phone, and still no word from Alexa. I suspected the worst. When we crawled into bed, my sleep was plagued with nightmares, and I woke up the next morning feeling groggy and unrested.

I reached for my phone, hoping there would be word from Alexa, only to find a new email appeared in my inbox overnight. When I clicked on the notification, I was surprised to see Alexa's email address in the sender line. Then I noticed the fine print at the top of the email. *Scheduled message.*

I swallowed the lump in my throat and read my best friend's words.

45

Alexa Huston

Tuesday, August 22

It's always at the end when we question the beginning. It's then we wonder how we got there. It's a weird feeling, wondering if you made the right choices, if you'd done something different, how things would have changed.

I never intended for it to go this far. When Vanessa died ... I was entranced. It was a sensation I'd never felt before and one I struggled to explain. It awoke something long dormant inside me. Suddenly, the drugs didn't cut it. The alcohol didn't quench the thirst. Maybe I was always supposed to be this way. Maybe the lies only kept the monster at bay for so long.

Courtney, I hadn't gone to your house with the intention of hurting anyone. I hadn't thought about killing Mark before then suddenly it felt like the only option. For a while it was quiet, but as time passed I couldn't deny this darkness inside me.

I didn't want to harm people for the sake of harming them. I didn't need to cause anyone the grief I'd felt and lived with my whole life. I had to find the right person. The right release.

So, I waited. And the itch grew worse every passing day.

Then Kaylee hurt herself and I found out the truth about Dean. When he told me what he'd done to her, the monster inside me knew there was no way out of this. He wasn't meant for this world.

Again, the darkness quieted, content in the release that Dean had offered though short lived.

Phoebe should have never come back to Ceder Plains. She was the reason my mom was dead. The monster was all too happy to unleash on her.

I expected quiet following it. The monster sated and put to rest, however temporary. But this time it didn't. There was no reprieve. No quiet from the whispering voice. No break from the desire. The monster tempted me to turn on you.

I knew then something was wrong. That I was losing myself. Though perhaps I'd been all but lost the moment it awoke.

I never intended for this to get out of hand. I never intended for my instinct to take over and do harm to someone who maybe didn't deserve it. Lou was a dirty old drunk but an unfortunate victim.

I'm sorry you had to find out these things about me. I'm sorry I lied to you. I'm not sorry I did it. I know I made some mistakes but I also know I did some good.

If they haven't figured it out already, I've gone to our spot. It seemed like a fitting place to end it all. I know you'll probably be angry at me for it, and I know you'll probably never forgive me. But I couldn't face the consequences of my actions. I couldn't let the system take control of my life in ways I'd never be able to escape.

This way it ends quickly. There's no need for a drawn-out trial. There's no need to cause anyone else further pain as my crimes come to light and the courts argue to lock me up for life.

This way the monster dies too.

Everything is so final in death.

I love you, Court. I always have and I'm so sorry I couldn't be better for you.

Take care of Dad. Don't let my mistakes destroy him any further. Don't let him get too far gone.

Love always,

A.

46

Courtney Faith

Tuesday, August 22

Tears poured down my cheeks as I stared at the email, cursing all that had happened between us.

"Babe?" Brett's voice cut through Alexa's words, and I tore my watery eyes away from my phone. "What's wrong?"

I didn't speak, instead I passed the phone to him to read what she said. Brett's eyes widened as he read my best friend's confession. Things I'd kept from him for days, but now she shared her full story.

"Where's your place?" Brett asked, when he finished reading and handed me back my phone.

I hesitated for a moment. "Cedar Falls Lookout."

The picturesque place had been a regular escape for us after Alexa's mom died. We'd skip the odd class at the end of the day and head out to the point with a joint. Together we'd sit on the large rock overlooking our small town and smoke. Sometimes we'd talk, sometimes we'd sit in silence, and sometimes we'd finish and get up and keep walking. One time she spoke about death on those cliffs, though I'd been quick to silence that discussion and move on.

Brett nodded and left the room. From where I sat, I could hear him in the hallway on the phone. Presumably giving his colleagues a tip as to where to locate Alexa's body. When I glanced down at the message again, I realized he'd forwarded himself her final note.

I sat in bed, unsure what to do next. I mourned my lost friend. The girl who'd been with me for all my firsts. A support and kinship I'd never know again. Or maybe I merely mourned the fact she wasn't that person anymore.

Brett returned to our room and perched on the edge of the bed. Close enough to touch, but far enough we weren't.

"If she's out there, we'll find her," he said.

I said nothing, knowing her body rested below the lookout, broken and battered from the terrible fall.

We sat in silence then, unsure what to say to one another. I was sure Brett had questions. Did I know the truth about my friend? Had I known all along? Answers I would never give him. With Alexa gone, my secret was finally safe, and I wasn't about to put further strain on the life I'd been working towards.

Brett moved closer to me and pulled me into his arms. He reached out and swiped at the tears trickling down my cheek and held me tightly.

"It will all be okay," he said, though what he was referring to I wasn't sure. A part of me would never be okay again, but I'd learn to live with it. As I had before.

"I'm sorry," he whispered into my hair, and all I could do was close my eyes and know I was sorry too.

The police found her body quickly. She'd been exactly where I'd expected her to be. With the email confession, the trophies and the drawings, it was quick work to close the open cases. For days, Brett worked finishing paperwork and cleaning up the mess Alexa had made of our small town. Our honeymoon had been put on hold.

I visited Danny often during the first week, helping him make the arrangements for the funeral and organize what Alexa left behind. While there was clear evidence he'd been drinking, he seemed more put together then I'd seen him in years.

The funeral was a week after her body was found. By then, every news outlet had gotten hold of the story, and Alexa's name had been blasted through the media and there was a clear opinion of her in our town. Nobody really knew the girl behind the monster, except for me and Danny. Though reporters like Rita Rounds pretended otherwise.

The story would die down in time, as there was no impending trial, no case to argue, and no one living left to blame. Once the novelty wore off, Alexa and her story would be forgotten by most.

The funeral was small, only a few locals attending, Danny, Savannah, and a few others from her job at Big Shot. Now that Alexa was a known murderer, it wasn't a surprise more hadn't shown. She wasn't popular to begin with and now the media had cast her as a mentally deranged psycho who killed without thought and ended it all when the truth was revealed. It didn't help that murders were brutal. I didn't blame people for thinking of my friend the way they did. I'd thought it once too.

Savannah and I agreed to keep what we knew about Alexa's crimes quiet. We felt secure in each other's friendship, and I was right to trust her. Afterall, secrets kept friends close.

When the funeral ended, people dispersed, but I stayed behind, asking Brett for a moment alone with Alexa. I knelt at her grave and carefully rearranged the flowers brought by guests.

I was proud of Danny, for his strength and the words he'd spoken. Today, he'd almost been the man I had known back in high school, but it wouldn't last. Alexa's death was hard on him, and now he had nothing to live for. He blamed himself, and he would never let it go. I wondered if his own dark secrets haunted him like they had his daughter.

I looked over the grave erected for her. She'd been put to rest next to her mother, and they'd be together forever.

I placed a hand on her gravestone. "I'm so sorry, Alexa. I wish this could have been different. At least now you are with your mom. I hope you two are painting together wherever you are."

I turned and left the silent graveyard, trudging toward the parking lot where Brett waited. All there was left to do was figure out how to live with this secret, knowing what I'd done. I got into the passenger seat of our car and Brett leaned over to kiss my temple.

"You okay?" he asked.

I wasn't but I smiled at him anyway. "I will be."

"You gave a beautiful tribute. I think you really helped her dad."

I studied him for a moment as he started to drive down the long graveyard driveway. I wondered about our secrets, his and mine. I wondered about the past and the things that were better left buried. I thought about our future and his father's mistakes, wondering if one day he might be driven to the same action for the love of his family. But I'd forget about all that in time. I'd picked him. I'd picked this life, and I would be happier for choosing it, no matter the price I paid.

I turned and looked out the window, staring at the passing tombstones and couldn't help but realize Alexa had been right. Everything was so final in death. And now with my secret buried alongside her, I would make sure it stayed that way.

EPILOGUE

COURTNEY FAITH

One Week Ago

My lungs burned as I ran down the wooded path towards the lookout. When Alexa had asked to meet me, I was surprised she'd wanted to hike out this far but knew it would only work to my advantage. I'd tried calling her before I left my car, but she didn't answer. One way or another, this had to end *now*.

As I stepped out into the clearing, I saw her looking over the long drop down to the trail below. The shining sun outlined her silhouette, as it was mid-afternoon now. There was a warrant out for her arrest, and I wondered why she'd have come this far out of town. She had to know what waited for her when she went home. Did she suspect I'd gone to her house before meeting her? I'd left it all out on the table to be found.

She must have heard me approach because she turned to regard me, a passive look I didn't recognize in her eyes.

"I'm glad you came," Alexa said. Her voice sounded different, not right. She didn't step away from the edge, she only beckoned me closer. I wasn't sure I wanted to approach her.

"I'm surprised you texted me." I crossed my arms over my chest, looking over the woman who'd been my best friend for years.

"I'm surprised you came," Alexa said. "I didn't think you'd want to be in the middle of nowhere with a monster that could hurt you."

I shuddered as she repeated my words back at me, thinking of the many times we'd stood at this edge together feeling safe in our company. How much had changed in only a matter of weeks.

"I don't think you'll hurt me," I said, trying to sound firm in my words, but my body trembled at the idea. Alexa had contemplated killing me if only to save herself days ago. I wasn't naïve to her self-preservation. It had gotten me in trouble more than once throughout our friendship. I had to play this cautiously.

"You know this was never about you." Her voice sounded hollow, as if it wasn't really her speaking. "Not really."

"You didn't kill Mark to save me?" I asked. She'd basically implied as much when she'd all but confessed.

Alexa tilted her head slightly. Her eyes were darker than I'd ever seen, a callousness that felt wrong. "Sure, if that makes you feel better about it."

I pursed my lips, unsure how to read this monster standing before me. She looked like my friend, but she was the furthest thing from it.

"You said he was supposed to die in prison," I said, remembering the words she spoke when she admitted the truth to me. "What did you mean?"

She cackled, a foreign sound I'd never heard come from her before. "You have no idea, do you?" She looked me dead in the eyes then laughed again. "My dad let it spill one night when he was particularly drunk. Going on about how all of us must make hard decisions."

I swallowed, unsure where she was going with this.

A sick smirk turned up her lips. "After Mark's arrest, and the truth about what he did to you and Miles came out, Kevin made a choice. And he convinced my dad it was the right thing to do."

"What does Brett's dad have to do with this?" I asked, the sinking unease about Kevin's corruption returning in full force.

"Don't you get it? Kevin has connections everywhere. Including the prison where Mark was held." Alexa tilted her head. "Did you really think it was a coincidence that another inmate stabbed him?"

I shook my head. "Kevin wouldn't do that."

Alexa gazed at me for a moment, then shrugged. "Maybe." Then she glanced back out at the view of Cedar Plains. "Or maybe not. He covered up the murder of my mother after all." She drew a deep breath, as if savouring the country air. Then said, "You know I enjoyed my time with Mark."

My stomach turned. "What, stabbing him?"

"Ending him," she said plainly. "I wore his ring around my neck for weeks after. The damn thing was the subject of a murder investigation, and it was right under the cops' noses the whole time." She laughed, not cruelly but with amusement, like this was the funniest thing about the whole situation.

"How can you talk like this?" I asked her. "Don't you care that you killed people?"

The look she gave me then was passive, like she couldn't comprehend what I was saying. This wasn't someone I recognized.

"Murder, Alexa," I said taking a step towards her. "That's not something one usually does lightly."

"It wasn't done lightly," she said, her face darkening. "It was meticulous, planned out, purposeful. It was an art, even if you can't see it."

"An art?" I snapped. "Brutalizing people, smashing them to death, was art to you?"

"You saw the sketches," Alexa said quietly. She turned her back to me again, and I remembered the reason I'd come. Alexa was no longer the person I knew her to be. I wasn't sure who stood in front of me now, I only knew that she couldn't be trusted.

"Did you ever see the one of Savannah?" Alexa asked, seeming to be speaking to herself more than me. Her voice was airy, almost dreamy, eerie. "It was one of my favourites. If only she had died. Then it would have been perfect."

As she turned back to regard me, I charged at her, placing my hands against her and shoving her towards the edge. She staggered from the force, and her hand reached out trying to grasp me in vain. Her foot tripped over an uneven section of the rock, and she was sent careening down, her shoes the last thing I glimpsed as she tumbled headfirst over the edge. A scream echoed faintly from her throat. Then, nothing but the chirping birds and gentle wind.

I fell to my knees, tears blinding my vision as I crawled to the edge of the cliff and looked over at the treetops below, unable to see her body. What had I done?

I sat back then, my heart racing. I'd killed my best friend after she'd taken so many lives herself. I told myself I did it to save everyone around me. To save Brett from the truth, to salvage any hope of Savannah and my friendship surviving, but most of all to stop the killing.

I sat for a moment, unsure what to do or how to explain why I'd been out in the middle of nowhere. I'd turned off my location and was quick to discard any messages from Alexa inviting me to meet her. Then, I noticed the phone lying in the dirt. I reached for it, realizing it was Alexa's, and swiped it open, typing in the passcode I knew by heart.

I clicked on her messages, wiping any communication from the last few days and did a force backup, hoping they'd never resurface. Then I clicked into her email, which was where I found her unfinished confession. I read her words detailing the crime and finished the message with her *suicide* confession before scheduling it to arrive in my inbox the following day.

Then, I wiped the phone clean with my sleeve and tossed it over the edge of the cliff, hopeful it would land close to Alexa.

Back in my car, I began to shake. I looked to where my powered-down cell phone rested in the centre console. I wondered if Brett had noticed my absence, or if he tried to check up on me. I swallowed hard, thinking about what Alexa said about his father and all I'd discovered in the past few weeks.

Drawing a deep breath, I carefully turned my car towards town, knowing while I'd saved the life I'd built, Alexa and our secrets would haunt me until the day I joined her in death.

Acknowledgements

What do you say about a book you first started writing almost twenty years ago? Other then it's changed. A lot. This book started as a very weird love story about three very close friends. We believed I was going to write an Oscar-Winning movie (I still have the original notebook to vouch for it.) Instead, I wrote a really terrible YA short novel (if it could even be called that) which had way too many personal anecdotes and inside jokes.

I even dream cast Elijah Wood, though that may have been for a certain muse's pleasure.

I have to credit my muse—Celeste—and our third at the time, Anna. They started as the original Alexa and Courtney (Of course without the murder.) and were who I saw every time I wrote (figuratively, given my aphantasia.)

And a special shout out to Collingwood. A town that inspired the setting and allowed me to feature some of my favourite places.

So many people go into the making of a book, at least in my experience. Especially with a book like this, given the number of eyes and suggestions that added to the story it ended up being.

I would be nowhere without my amazing publisher—Rising Action Publishing—and the two stunning women behind the company, Alex and Tina. The former who made me dig deep to find the perfect title (trust me, before, they were bad bad.) and the latter who gave me stunning copyedits and really pulled the characters from me and on to the page.

Or the many beta readers who looked at this before it was really ready for any eyes. Melissa Naatz, Charly Cox, Brooke Dorsch, Jen Craven, and Nicole Jones. A special shout out to the Sexy Train who always read my first drafts no matter how messy, Denise, Jess, and Kristen.

I'd be lost without my experts, my friends, Tash and Scott, who always answer my endless questions without a second thought and talk me through some of the most out-there scenes and ideas I have.

To my hard-working editors, Marthese and Jacinda, thank you.

And as always, a moment of appreciation for the stunning cover work by none other than the incomparable Miss Nat Mack.

To my community, online and in person, and the Toronto Area Women Authors. I am grateful for the endless support, amazing events, and stellar community we have formed.

To my best friends, my book club, and my family, I wouldn't be here without all of you rooting for me, reading my work, and believing I could actually get something (let alone four things!) published.

Mike, you've been by my side through a lot these last few years. I don't blame you for avoiding my words, given how scary my head can be, but I'm thankful you're always there when I need support or love, or hell, just an ear to complain to. And sorry not sorry for telling you about book plots you will probably never read. I know that happens a lot.

And finally, a shout out to all my amazing readers and the booksta-gram community. It has been so incredible to connect with you and continue to share my words. Meeting and interacting with readers will always be the best part of writing. We're all book nerds after all!

About the Author

Maggie Giles is a Canadian author who writes suspenseful women's fiction and thrillers. Her debut novel, *The Things We Lost,* was named a 2023 distinguished favourite in Women's Fiction by the Independent Press Awards. She is a member of the International Thriller Writers and currently works in Marketing. Maggie dove into writing a novel head first despite having aphantasia, a condition where one lacks a visual imagination. She lives in Ontario with her mastiff-mix, Jolene, and spends most of her days enjoying the outdoors, from swimming to hiking to skiing in the winter. *The Art of Murder* is her fourth novel, preceded by the thriller duology *Twisted* and *Wicked*.

Looking for more thrillers? Check out the next page!

And don't forget to follow us on our socials for cover reveals, giveaways, and announcements:

X: @RAPubCollective

Instagram: @risingactionpublishingco

TikTok: @risingactionpublishingco

Website: http://www.risingactionpublishingco.com

RISING ACTION

Recently fired and adrift, Charlotte Boyd agrees to oversee renovations on her parents' small-town summer home that holds a tragic past. After discovering an enthralling diary hidden amidst junk the previous owners left behind, Charlotte connects with the author—a troubled teen named Lark Peters who died by suicide at the house sixteen years ago.

When an unsettling incident forces Charlotte to seek refuge at the local pub, regulars, including the police, warn her of Lark's older brother, Darryl, who has become a recluse since Lark's death, and may know more than he's letting on. But Charlotte sees a side of Darryl others don't, being an outsider herself.

In a search to uncover the truth, Charlotte must question those closest to Lark and reconcile her own past trauma. Because if Lark was actually murdered, then whoever is responsible might be lurking in Charlotte's own backyard.

Releasing Aug 12, 2025.